# RED ROSE
# BLACK DAHLIAS



*Sisters are different flowers from the same garden*

MACY T. RIOSA

Red Roses and Black Dahlias



ISBN: 9798367941401

---

## TRIGGER WARNINGS

Please understand that while this book isn't a dark romance, it still deals with dark themes. These include murder, violence, mentions of sexual abuse on minors and mentions of suicide.
It's also destined to an 18+ public as there are graphic sexual scenes as well as praise kink and spankings (which both MCs find they enjoy very much).

One final thing: as you read, you may notice some inconsistencies or things that you believe don't make much sense. I assure you they do. Just trust the process, everything will make sense in the end.

# Dedication

*To my sisters, know that my love for you runs deeper than water.*

*And to all first born daughters who had to take on the role of a third parent. I see you.*

# 1

## SISTERS

### SOFIA

*"Sisters are different flowers from the same garden." Mama said quietly, making me shift my gaze from the little bundle carefully wrapped in pink covers, to her. She stood leaning against the door of her room, watching us with an emotion in her gaze I couldn't quite decipher. She smiled like only she could, full of grace and softness and warmth. My lips tilted up before I even realized it.*

*Her eyes then left mine to focus on the baby peacefully sleeping next to me on the bed. Rosa. My little sister. Mama had just come home from the hospital today, and I was so excited to meet the person who made me a big sister. Papa said being a big sister means I'll have responsibilities, and that I should always protect Rosa.*

*Mama said that once Rosa grows up, we'll have each other's back and she'll protect me too.*

*Seeing her now, so small and fragile, I couldn't fathom how she could ever protect me. Her limbs were so frail, her little fingers possessing surprisingly sharp nails — I knew because she had scratched me when I first tried to kiss her cheek this morning.*

*"Is that where we got our names from?" I tilted my head, speaking low because I didn't want to wake Rosita up. She had enough trouble falling asleep as it was and nearly pierced my eardrums earlier when papa was changing her nappy.*

*Mama didn't say anything, she just smiled and pushed off the threshold, entering the room and coming to sit in front of me. Her fresh scent of jasmine drifted to my nose and I was instantly appeased. She smelled like home. I was only ten at the time but the love I had for my mother was indescribable. It ran deeper than I could comprehend.*

*I would do anything for her, and I knew she would do anything for me. Mama lifted a tanned hand to my face and cupped my cheek while looking into my eyes.*

*"Sweet Dalia," she contemplated, her eyes moving across my face, "you've always been such a bright child. You and your sister are gonna be the brightest flowers this world has ever seen and I cannot wait to see you blossom, baby." She murmured, her eyes suddenly going misty.*

*I didn't understand what made her so emotional, but I didn't like seeing her cry, even if her mouth was still smiling, so I got up to my knees, wrapped my little arms around her neck and inhaled her familiar scent as she rubbed my back.*

*"Hermanas son flores diferentes del mismo jardín. Never forget that, mija." She whispered in my ear before kissing my temple.*

And as I watched both my mother and father being carted out of the house in body bags, those were the words that kept replaying in my head. *Different flowers from the same garden.*

Blue and red lights danced around us, police cars everywhere in our street and front lawn, the neighbors staring from their homes. Yellow tape was strapped to our front door as officers and people from the coroner's team ducked underneath it to go on with their examination.

I bit my lip to stop my chin from shaking so much, but it was no use. I knew this night would replay in my mind forever. What I had done, haunt me for life. But I didn't regret it. Not for one second.

Mama and papa would be proud of me, because I did what I was always supposed to do, I protected my little rose. Even if they were not here to see it anymore.

My eyes drifted from the front of the house and I looked down at myself, gulping at all the blood staining my clothes and my skin. Who would've thought this was how the night would end. Both parents in body bags, me at the back of an ambulance drenched in their blood, waiting for my little sister to get checked by the paramedics.

Of course, I knew she would be okay physically, it was the things she heard tonight and that were now inked into her mind forever, that worried me. Always so full of joy and innocence, and so pure— it broke my heart that my sister knew what happened earlier. It broke my heart that I couldn't protect her tonight of all nights, after doing it for almost ten years now.

As the ambulance carrying our parents' bodies pulled off the curb, another body bag was brought out of the house. I clenched my teeth, my heart beating fast as I watched them cart the man whose blood was on my hands into another ambulance.

Tonight, I had killed.

The realization hit me full force and for a minute I could barely breathe. Silent tears streamed down my face as a strange sense of peace fell upon me. The nightmare was over. After everything, we survived, even though we lost mama and papa.

I did it, I kept the little rose safe, just like they wanted. And I'll continue keeping her safe until I take my last breath.

I *was* my sister's keeper after all, and I was all she had left.

Someone clearing their throat startled me out of my thoughts, making me look up into the greenest eyes I had ever seen. Forest green eyes, reminding me of nature, pine trees and the scent of rain on a lazy day. Eyes I had gotten lost in countless times, usually as they looked down on me, admonishing and disapproving. Now those same eyes held pity and compassion, just like every person that looked at me tonight.

It made me sick to my stomach.

Detective Maddox Brooks was the bane of my existence. Ever since we came to live in Lakewood almost five years ago, and I started getting in trouble for minor instances, Maddox had been on my ass

See, if there's one thing to know about me, it's that I liked trouble. I liked the rush, I liked how alive I felt when doing something I shouldn't be doing; I liked the adrenaline that shot through my blood when I heard police sirens coming my way. It was the perfect form of escapism. At first it was just petty thefts and trespassing, then it graduated to underage drinking and vandalism. That's how they called it anyways. To me, it was art.

Each and every time I got arrested though, he was there. Detective Brooks had it in his mind that I was a sweet girl who simply needed discipline instead of a rambunctious kid in search of a rush. I thought deep down, I reminded him of his younger self. He was born and raised here in Lakewood, and in small towns, people loved to talk. I knew he was a single twenty-eight year old with no kids. He joined the forces at twenty-one and was promoted to detective five years ago, making him the youngest on his team at the time. His family was one of the most prominent in town, and from what I heard, they were nice people too. See, he's so proper, so nice, so *good.*

It made me want to punch him in the face.

His beautiful, *beautiful* face.

His lips were pinched together as he exhaled a long breath. "Miss Raymond." He nodded, and I said nothing, still staring at him, his eyes sucking me in. "I'm sorry for your loss."

I knew he was. I could see the truth in his eyes, right along with the pity. I knew it would happen, I knew others would look at us that way, but I didn't think *he* would too.

After all, he never had before. He's always given it to me straight, never cared who my father was, never cared about any of that. Some people might even have said his words towards me were harsh at times, but I knew it was because he wasn't too scared of small town mayor Jack Raymond's wrath to reprimand his eldest daughter. No, Maddox Brooks had no problem speaking his mind, and if anything, he was the only figure of authority I remotely respected since we moved in this hellish town.

"Spare me your pity, detective. I'm too tired for that." After one last look at him, my head turned towards the house.

His jaw clenched and just like that I knew he was still the detective Brooks I knew and tolerated. "I'm not here to interrogate you—"

"Well that's a first." I snapped as I stared in the distance.

“I think you’ve been through enough as it is, but don’t make me change my mind and take you to the station tonight. ” he asserted, his tone making me quiver before

I could help myself. Immediately, my eyes turned back to him. That’s just the kind of man he was; he exuded dominance, and he knew it.

“Do you have anywhere to go for the night? A friend’s house? Family?” He asked

A dark chuckle came out of me; “You know I don’t have friends and my only family is six feet under, detective. So unless you can bring people back from the dead, no, we don’t have anywhere to go tonight. But don’t worry, we’ll book a hotel.” I shrugged, furiously wiping at my tears.

Maddox went silent for a beat, just staring at me. He lifted his hand, like he was going to touch me, before he abandoned the idea and let it fall back to his side. But I could have sworn, at that moment, I could feel my cheek tingle, like his touch had truly been on it. I swallowed silently, my eyes boring into his.

He seemed so out of sorts, nothing like I’d ever seen him before, it showed how truly shaken up he was which got me thinking. Being a small town cop, it was probably the first time he was dealing with a triple homicide, and a really messy one at that.

Flashes of blood splattering on the walls flooded my brain and I really wanted to slam my head against something to make them go away. But I couldn’t, so I simply closed my eyes.

"I'll go back inside and make you and your sister a bag. Then I'll bring you two to the hotel near the station and I'll stay guard in front of your door so I know you're safe. Tomorrow we'll bring you in for questioning. Does that sound okay?"

His tone was incredibly softer, just like that time I trespassed on school property and graffitied the boys locker room three years ago. I'd drawn a man with a pig head, because of what the football team had done that week— created a *"girls I'd screw even if they were unconscious"* list. Of course the alarm had gone off and guess who came to check on what was going on?

That night was the only night he didn't take me into the station and instead turned a blind eye on what I had done. I guess he was just as disgusted with the list as I was. In his report he'd said the culprit had escaped before he came onto the scene— thank God the school didn't have cameras at the time. But in truth, he had brought me into a drive through, got us burgers and fries and we sat quietly in his car as I told him everything that happened.

I managed a small nod as I wrapped my arms around myself, appreciating his offer. "You don't need to stand guard though." My eyes drifted to the now closed ambulance with the last body bag inside. "It's not like he's coming back.". Flashbacks of the sound his ribs made as I stabbed my knife through his chest assaulted me. I closed my eyes and swallowed with difficulty, it was like my own saliva was chafing against the insides of my throat, like I was trying to swallow nails.

"He might not, but his accomplice still could." He said. A shudder went through me at the thought.

Maddox went to talk when suddenly the door to the ambulance behind us busted open and I turned in time to see my sister barreling towards me. My arms fell to the side, the blanket the paramedics had given me falling to the ground, and I crouched in front of her. Her little arms wrapped around my shoulders and she hid her face into my neck. I could feel the little sobs shaking her body, her grip around me like a vice. Tears brimmed my own eyes as I felt hers running against my skin.

"It's over, *Rosita.* The monsters are never coming back." I murmured, kissing her temple and rubbing her back like mama used to do so often.

I knew Maddox was staring at us during this very intimate moment, but somehow, it didn't feel like he was invading our privacy. More like a guarding presence, protecting us. That's exactly what Maddox was after all, more than a cop, more than a figure of authority, he was a protector. Maybe that was why I looked up to him in a way.

The blood on me had dried, so when my sister stepped back to take me in, little hands clutching my cheeks, she was clean, no blood had gotten on her. I was grateful for that. Her deep brown eyes scanned my face frantically, like she was trying to make sure I was okay.

"Do you promise?" She croaked, and hearing her normally sweet voice sound so rough did something to my heart.

"Yes baby. I take the monsters away. That's what I do, remember? Like those under your bed." I managed a small smile, still feeling Maddox's stare dig into my skin. I already knew what he was thinking, that I was technically lying to my sister because I had only killed one of the men who murdered the mayor and his wife. The other was still out there, free, and dangerous, probably waiting for the best moment to come and finish the work.

My little rose burrowed her face into my shoulder, her sobs slowly calming down while I kept on rubbing her back. My eyes drifted up to Maddox and he stared back, drowning me in a sea of green. I took in his messy dark blond hair, square jaw and plump lips. The way he held himself so straight, so tall, pushing his wide shoulders back, deliciously stretching his black dress shirt. For a second I forgot who we really were. He was just a friend who had come by as soon as he'd heard what happened, to offer me his help and support.

But then his badge reflected on a street light, grabbing my attention and I was reminded of our current situation, bringing me back to reality. I was a nineteen year old orphan, soon-to-be guardian to a nine year old, and he was the pain in the ass detective who was in charge of the case of my parents' gruesome murder.

I broke our staring contest and he looked away too.

"Come on girls, wait for me in the car so I can drive you to the hotel; I'll grab you some stuff from the house and we'll go." His voice came through, assertive but soft.

I nodded, still not looking at him, but caressing my sister's cheeks instead, reassuring her. I lifted her into my arms and started walking towards Maddox's car, which I knew too well because of all the times he had arrested me and driven me back home in it. Rosita clutched onto me, scared I would let go of her.

But I never would.

Ten minutes later, we were both huddled in the back seat of the black Audi and Maddox came back, handing me the big travel bag I kept under my bed, before shutting the door and taking his seat in front. He pulled off the street and we drove in silence. I glanced at the bag which was halfway open and could see a bunch of my underwear sitting on top of everything else, like he had decided to put them in at the last minute.

Knowing what I did about him, how self righteous he could be sometimes, he probably had. I felt my cheeks heat up at the thought of Detective Brooks rummaging through my underwear drawer, and against my better judgment, it was not because I was disgusted or disturbed.

When we finally made it to the hotel, he parked the car and came to take my sister who had fallen asleep during the ride. He told me to wear his jacket, because even though it was three in the morning and no one would be in the lobby, he didn't want the clerk to freak out at the sight of me all bloody.

The jacket smelled like him, all woodsy and spicy with a hint of sweetness and it was seriously intoxicating. He held my sister like she weighed nothing and then took the bag in his other hand. When I tried taking it from him, to relieve him of the weight, he glared at me and told me to walk.

Normal me would have rolled her eyes, or made a snarky comment. But nothing was normal about tonight and I was exhausted so I simply obeyed, walking alongside him to the lobby.

The clerk's eyes went wide when she saw me looking so disheveled, the blood on my face was still very much visible even though the jacket hid my body from the middle of my thighs up to my neck.

Maddox didn't let her reaction affect him and immediately started talking to her and she finally had the decency to stop staring at me.

I was suddenly too tired to listen to what they were saying and could barely think straight, but then the clerk finally turned to me and handed me the keys.

"Sofia and Valentina Raymond, room 36B."

# 2

# OBLIVION

## SOFIA

The suite was simple and clean, one queen size bed sitting in the middle, framed by two bedside tables, and a big window overlooking the town's park. Right next to the window was a plush armchair as two wooden doors faced the bed, one leading to the bathroom, the other to what was probably a small closet.

I heard the door click shut behind me as Maddox strode in, directly heading to the bed. He lifted the covers and laid Valentina delicately on the mattress before covering her. My sweet little rose slept peacefully, oblivious to the world of dangers that laid before us.

Maddox gently pushed a strand of hair that had fallen in front of her eyes aside, and gazed at her like she was the most precious and fragile thing he had ever seen. The softness in his gaze took me by surprise. When he turned back to me and saw me staring, he stared back for a beat before sighing and slouching down on the armchair.

His hands rubbed his face, elbows resting on his knees, his strong legs apart. He looked positively exhausted. I knew his job was not an easy one, but somehow tonight must have felt even harder.

"You should go and take a shower, Sofia," He nodded to the second door in front of the bed, "you can't—" he pursed his lips, "dry blood is harder to get off." He continued tiredly.

I didn't bother asking how he knew that. Too tired to argue with him, I just acquiesced and started rummaging through the bag he had packed for something comfortable to sleep in. When I finally found a pair of leggings and some t-shirt, I hightailed it to the bathroom.

As soon as I entered the white room, I was assaulted by the sight of me in the mirror.

I halted, my breath catching in my throat. I had known I probably looked terrifying, but I didn't expect it to be right out of a horror movie. My usually sleek black hair was all over the place, sticking to my forehead in a mix of blood and sweat, my elastic band tangled somewhere in the mess. This was going to hurt detangling, and I was too worn out to do it now so it would have to wait until tomorrow. I closed the door behind me before starting to get undressed, but I didn't lock it for some reason.

Shrugging off Maddox's jacket, I carefully laid it on the towel holder. So much blood had seeped through my beige satin pajamas, there was just no way it could be washed off, so I decided to just throw them in the trash. Once I stood naked in front of my reflection, I took some time to do something I hadn't done in a while; look at myself.

My upper lip was cut and slightly puffy, a bruise was starting to form on my forehead, and another cut marred my eyebrow.

The blood on my face matched the one staining my clothes, it was dry but still a little sticky somehow. It contrasted with the color of my skin. Blood red on light brown, I looked like a deadly painting.

Looking up, I caught my own eyes staring at me, hollow, void.

It scared me sometimes, how empty my eyes looked.

How dead they seemed.

So I didn't linger on them, and continued assessing the rest of me instead. Usually the sight of my body disgusted me, for various reasons I tried not to think about. I knew objectively speaking there was nothing wrong with it. My breasts were more on the smaller side, I had a really narrow and subtle waist, so much so that you could actually see my ribs whenever I inhaled deeply. I was petite but my thighs were strong, mostly because of all the running I did. I had gotten a lot of compliments about the way I looked as I grew up, be it for my body or my face.

Yet, I usually barely ever looked in the mirror because of all the things my body reminded me of.

Tonight, though, it was different. Tonight I looked at my reflection and the only word that came to my mind was *survivor*. I had survived.

I'd looked death in the eye and spat in its face.

Simply remembering the feel of my hand around the knife, the pungent scent of blood as it splattered on my face, the erratic beats of my heart against my ribcage, I knew that I still had a long way to go if I wanted to truly feel alive.

Turning away from the full length mirror I stepped into the shower, closing the glass door after me. As the water started dribbling on my skin, I could see it take a pink tint, sliding down my body before twirling on the tiled floor and disappear into the drain. My head fell backwards as I started rinsing my hair as best as I could given the state it was in. Having my arms up trying to detangle it hurt. Everything hurt.

The water was scorching hot, which was exactly how I liked it and I tried to relax, I really did, but every time I closed my eyes, the nightmare started again. So many images twirled and mixed inside my mind.

I heard screams, cries, saw my sister laying in my bed, shaking with fear. I saw my mama being dragged out from her room by the hair on her head, I saw all the disgusting things they did to her right before her throat was slit. I saw papa screaming at them to stop, unable to move, unable to do anything but stare as the love of his life suffered through the worst kind of torture you could inflict on someone.

Without even realizing it, I had started crying, and soon full sobs were rocking my body. I was shaking, my mind finally catching up to what had happened tonight.

*It's over, the monsters are gone.*

I tried reassuring myself but without much success.

Soon, my breaths were stuck in my throat and I was struggling for air. Losing my balance, I blindly grasped at the shower shelf, but instead of helping me stay on my feet, my soaped up hand slipped and I landed on my ass, shampoo and body wash bottles splattering around me. My hands were shaking and I just brought my knees back to my chest as I hid my face between them, sob after sob escaping me.

My mind was a whirlwind of sounds. Screams, moans of agony, cries. The squelchy sound of a knife sinking through flesh and bloody gurgling. It felt like my head was underwater and I couldn't even hear the rustling of the shower anymore. Nor did I hear the soft knocks on the bathroom door. I was too caught up in memories to pay attention when the door finally opened and Maddox came in, looking worried. The noise the bottles made when falling probably alerted him.

I looked up from my knees and saw his lips moving, but I couldn't for the life of me make out what he was saying. He opened the fogged up shower door and immediately cut the water off. Somehow his presence made me breathe a little easier, even though I was naked and should have felt mortified that he saw me like that. Yet, there was nothing leering or sexual in the way he was looking at me, he just looked worried and shocked.

I understood his shock, since he had never seen me cry in all the time I'd known him. Not even when he brought me home after the first time I was arrested at sixteen. My mother had slapped me in front of him and I was humiliated and hurt, but I kept the tears for when I was alone in bed.

I was good at faking, I had to, and I had managed to keep it together tonight, but now it felt like I was losing it, like I was losing years of pent up and repressed feelings. Like a dam had broken and I couldn't control them anymore.

"Fuck." I heard him mutter before he crouched in front of me without entering the shower. "Sofia can you hear me?" I just stared blankly at him, not answering.

I think a part of me wanted to scream that yes I was still there and I did hear him, while another was so tired of everything and just wanted it to end. I felt my eyes slowly droop close, when a hand— a strong, callused hand, gripped my jaw.

Immediately, they flew back open. "Good girl, keep your eyes open. Did you hit your head when you fell?" I slowly shook my head no. "Okay. Okay, great."

I wasn't even really crying anymore, the tears just took free reign over my body and streamed silently down my cheeks.

Maddox started to roll up his sleeves, and when he was done he grabbed the hair brush that was on the shelf and the shampoo bottle that had fallen, before looking back at me. "I'm going to touch you so I can turn you around and wash your hair, okay Sofia?" His deep green eyes bore into mine and again, I nodded silently.

After a beat, like he was trying to gather up the courage to do it, his hand grabbed my waist and he slowly turned me around until I was giving him my back. His touch was so warm and soft, like he was afraid of breaking me. My knees were still drawn up to my chest and crossed at the ankle as I stared at the tiled wall in front of me. My body was mostly clean from blood but I knew my hair was not. I knew I probably had little speckles of flesh in there as well and that made me want to retch.

Maddox didn't seem to mind. He wordlessly got the hair tie out of the coils, before proceeding part by part to detangle with the brush and his fingers. Having him brush out the tangles and then soap up and massage my scalp was oddly relaxing and peaceful.

Again, there was nothing sexual about the situation, only comfort. He was comforting me on what was one of the worst nights of my life. We were both silent as he rinsed out the shampoo, applied some conditioner and soon he was done with my hair. He cut off the water and brought me a big towel to wrap me in, without looking at my body.

Another smaller one went for my hair and before I could process what was happening, I was in his arms and he was strolling back into the bedroom. Maddox carefully deposited me under the covers next to Valentina, still only clad in a fluffy white towel.

It felt strange to have him tuck me in, but not in a bad way. It was nice to have someone take care of me when I was so used to being the one caring for others. Once the covers were back in place, Maddox wiped the tears that were left on my cheeks, and looked me over one last time before turning to move away. My hand shot up to grab his wrist before he was too far away, and his gaze went back to mine.

"Do you think we'll be okay, Maddox?"

It was the first time I ever called him by his first name, and I heard the little intake of breath as his gaze faltered a bit. I could tell he didn't know how to answer that, mostly because Maddox Brooks was not a liar. I don't even know what pushed me to ask him that.

Maybe I needed someone other than the voice inside my head to tell me the nightmare was over. Maybe I just needed reassurance.

After a minute or so, his voice broke the silence, with a determination I had never heard him muster before.

"You'll be more than okay, Sofia. I'll make damn sure of that."

# 3

# FAMILY

## SOFIA

My heart was in my throat, my stomach in knots as I stared out of our hotel room's window and onto the street. Flashes went off and I ducked away from view, letting the curtain fall back in place.

"Get away from the window, Sofia. These fucking people are rapacious. They've got no qualms about going after a wounded prey, just like they don't give a shit about respecting someone's fucking privacy." Maddox's angry voice startled me and made me turn around to face him.

His jaw was set as he gently helped Valentina put on her coat. She seemed wary of him when she first saw him this morning, but had quickly warmed up to the 6'2 gentle giant and now she even gave him shy little smiles. I gotta say, it warmed my heart to see her be so at ease with Maddox, and it reassured me too, because if Valentina liked him, it meant she saw something good in him, just like I did. After all we've been through, we're entitled to be distrustful of everyone.

Once Valentina was all buttoned up in her pink wool coat — Maddox had one of his colleagues bring us some more stuff from the house early this morning, he turned to me. His eyes roamed my body as he inspected my outfit, probably assessing whether it was appropriate for the season or not. Baggy gray joggers, a white cropped long-sleeved top and my black puffer jacket on top because the weather was still cool outside. To be honest, this was how I usually dressed so I didn't feel too out of place.

Apparently satisfied with the way I looked, Maddox put on his own jacket before nodding at the door.

The elevator ride to the lobby was tense, nobody spoke. Even Valentina seemed to catch on to what was going on. Her small hand gripped mine tighter as soon as the little ding announced we had reached our destination. Maddox led the way to the middle of the room, and again I could see the journalists waiting outside from the glass doors and windows. From upstairs I could only see a dozen, but now I saw that there were at least thirty. All of them scrambled to get closer to the doors, where three officers were trying to push them back.

Lakestone was a relatively small town, but since nothing really ever happened in our area, I wasn't surprised that other surrounding towns had sent reporters to cover the news, too.

Being the daughter of the mayor, this was not the first time I would be faced with journalists, but it didn't mean I ever got used to them. My steps faltered as we got closer to the doors, and the lump in my throat came back. Somehow noticing my unease, Maddox stopped too and looked back at me. My gaze was strained on the people outside, screaming my name and asking stuff I had no desire to talk about.

Valentina tugged on my hand, making me look at her. "It's okay. The monsters are gone, they can't hurt us."

My eyes instantly filled with tears at her words. Only nine and so wise already. I loved her so much.

I managed a smile and crouched down in front of her to hug her. She hugged me back fiercely before caressing my hair with a gentleness only her innocent soul was capable of. When I exhaled and got back on my feet, Maddox was there, looking at me with a strange expression on his face, right before he dived and took Valentina in his arms. My girl squealed in surprise but settled rapidly with her head on his shoulder and her arms around his neck.

"Are you ready?" He asked me.

"The day I let a bunch of gossip-starved vultures scare me hasn't come yet, Detective Brooks." I stood taller as I gazed into his eyes.

A small smile grazed his lips and he nodded once, "Good girl.". Despite myself, this made me shiver.

"Don't tell them anything, I'll deal with them."

I nodded and he turned back around and strode to the entry. I let out a long breath before following him. After one last look at me, Maddox pushed the doors open, and the first thing to assault me was the noise.

You could hear them a bit from the lobby, but their voices were muffled. Now, however, they resonated and made my head throb.

*Miss Raymond, what happened yesterday?*

*Did you see the murderers, Miss Raymond?*

*Are you being charged with murder, is it true you killed the man who broke into your house?`*

*What about the second robber, Miss Raymond, do you think he'll come back? Did you see his face?*

It was nearly too much, but I pushed through, looking at Valentina burrowing her face in Maddox's shoulder and covering her ears the whole time. Officers were pushing the journalists back, making room for us to go through, and I could already see the black SUV waiting for us next to the curb a couple meters away, but then my arm was snatched from behind and I nearly came crashing down. A microphone was put right under my nose as a man in his forties reeking of sweat and cigarettes screamed questions I could barely comprehend right in my face.

I tried to get out of his hold but he was stronger. My heart was beating erratically inside my rib cage and I could feel the panic rise in my throat. I wanted to scream, to slap his hand away, maybe even slap *him* across the face for daring to touch me at all, but I was frozen in place, my body would not move. It couldn't.

Suddenly, the hold the journalist had on me was gone, and I was drawn into strong arms. When I came back to my senses, I noticed the man who assaulted me was on the ground holding his now-bloody nose and, as I looked up, I saw Maddox was the reason why. He sent the reporter a death glare before lightly shaking the hand he used to punch him and gently taking my arm to help me walk towards the car.

Valentina was waiting for us inside the SUV with another officer I recognized as Detective Yakori, Maddox's colleague.

The woman looked angrily at Maddox when we finally got in and Valentina hurried to sit on my lap as my arms encircled her. I was breathing a little better now that I was away from all these vultures. As soon as the door was closed, detective Yakori lost it.

"What the hell Maddox!" She seethed "You hit one of these bastards in front of everyone! These people have fucking cameras, you're gonna make the headlines come tomorrow morning! Chief Piersons will be pissed!"

I swallowed and looked at Maddox who seemed unbothered by the things she mentioned. He clearly didn't regret what he just did even though there sure were gonna be consequences. I suddenly felt guilty because it would be my fault if he got in trouble with his boss. Or worse— if he got taken off the case.

My blood ran cold at the thought. Maddox was the only one I trusted enough to bring this case to its end.

"He knew better than to put his hands on her, Selena." Was his answer, and the look on his face didn't leave any room for argument. Detective Yakori— Selena, seemed to understand and didn't press the issue but she still glowered at Maddox. I had a feeling she would have ripped him a new one had we not been in the same car.

Her attention was pulled back to me and her eyes softened a bit before she nodded at me, "How are you?" She asked.

My jaw clenched and I stopped myself from snapping at her. I actually liked Yakori, she was one of the few women on the force and the only woman of color. For that reason alone, she had my utmost respect. She was Mexican, like me, and somehow, on the few occasions where I ended up in the back seat of her car after yet another petty crime, she would play music from back home and it would always warm my heart. She unknowingly gave me back a piece of myself I had lost over the years.

We didn't listen to it at home anymore and that was one of the things I missed the most from before I became the Mayor's daughter. Obviously, I liked it better when my dad was just that—my dad, and not this politician I barely knew.

"I'm as good as you'd expect me to be I guess." I answered, looking away. Valentina tightened her arms around my neck and I stroked her back.

Selena rubbed her eyes, probably realizing how dumb her question sounded. “Sorry, I’m not thinking straight, I barely slept.” Her gaze bore into mine in a silent apology and I simply nodded, accepting it wordlessly.

“What’s gonna happen now?” I asked as the ball of nerves in my stomach squeezed tighter and tighter. Maddox and Selena shared a look before he slowly turned to look at me.

“We’re gonna interrogate you, see what you can tell us about what happened exactly last night, and if you remember anything about the second man.” He explained.

My body tensed as I recalled the events of last night. I exhaled slowly, needing to get my shit back together. I could do this. For mama and papa. And then my little rose and I could start from zero elsewhere, away from this hell hole.

The ride to the station was quick, nothing surprising in Lakestone. It wasn’t tiny exactly, we had a primary, middle and high school, a grocery store and a public library. Add to that a bunch of restaurants ranging from fast foods to four stars, an arcade and a cinema and you had it.

Sure, it was better than most small towns, but I guess after living here for years, you quickly got bored. Of course, we were also famous for our lake which split the town in two, right in the middle. As soon as the weather warmed up a bit, teenagers would gather there, swimming and partying around a campfire. Once upon a time, I was one of them. But it felt like eons ago now, as if I’d aged years in the course of one night.

As we drove along the streets, people stared at the car. Old women gathered in front of the town's library, probably meeting for their weekly book club session, children were being ushered inside their houses by their mothers, people getting into their cars to leave for work, everybody stopped to gaze in our direction.

I got it, not a lot of things happened around here, but that didn't give them the right to act like we were fucking freaks.

At last, the SUV stopped in front of the station, and as I had feared, another horde of hungry journalists was waiting for us there.

I cussed under my breath as I braced myself to face them once again.

"I'm going first so I can push these fuckers back a bit."

Selena declared ducking out of the car, not waiting for an answer. Immediately, journalists were onto her, screaming questions and pushing their mics and cameras on her face, barely allowing her to move. There were even more people here than there had been at the hotel, because even townsfolk came to watch and probably get their daily dose of gossip.

Maddox grabbed Valentina from me, and she went without too much of a fuss, wrapping her arms around him and hiding her face in his neck, exactly like when we were leaving the hotel. That was her favorite position to feel safe, and I knew given the situation, she needed that sense of security. I was glad Maddox could provide that for her.

Looking back through the window, I saw some high school kids had gathered on the curb on the other side of the road, older men and women too. All were watching with attention, or discussing between themselves. Some were even recording. That pissed me off. I wanted to get the hell out of here, but I couldn't. For what felt like the thousandth time today, I closed my eyes and exhaled a long breath.

I could do this.

I would do this.

*I was a survivor, Goddammit.*

My eyes opened back and found Maddox's green ones. The look he sent me seemed to be saying "you good?" So I nodded.

"Let's do this," he said, opening the door.

Yeah. Let's do this.

***

## MADDOX

"This is giving me chills. And not the good kind." Adam, my work partner, whispered as we looked at the crime scene's pictures from last night. His hands were tensed as they gripped the pictures, his dark skin turning lighter on the knuckles.

I couldn't help but agree with him, this was by far one of the most gruesome murders I had ever seen. Enough to make a big guy like Adam queasy, and he was a 6'3 ex-navy SEAL whose muscles had muscles, for God's sake.

Blood on the walls, on the carpets, seeping through the wooden floors… It was a real massacre. The mayor's body was the one who took the brunt of it. He was stabbed twelve times, and left to bleed out on the living room floor while Marcella Raymond had her throat slit in the kitchen, where she probably tried to run to escape her killer.

Telling myself that Sofia and probably Valentina had seen this made my heart tighten up. That Sofia even had to look at her parent's bodies as she fought for her own life… I was livid.

Looking up into the interrogation room where she presently sat, fiddling with her fingers and looking down at her hands, the one-way mirror gave me free reign to stare without worrying about her catching me.

Her eyes were always the window to her soul, you could usually tell what she was thinking just by staring through them. So it scared the shit out of me that all I saw when I looked at them since last night was nothingness. Her eyes were void. The only times they filled with anything remotely close to emotions, were when she interacted with her sister or when she was angry. Other than that it was as if the old Sofia was dead.

"Poor girls…" Adam brought my attention back to him. He stood next to me, shaking his head while looking into the room where only Sofia sat. "So young and already been through so much."

Valentina was with the force's psychologist, Mindy Sheffield, who was having a hard time getting the youngest Raymond to speak to her, from what I heard. I found myself nodding absentmindedly.

As soon as we'd come in, they were both ushered to Chief Piersons' office for paperwork, before Mindy came to take Valentina with her. The little girl refused to go, she cried and gripped her older sister like her life depended on it. Sofia wasn't too keen on letting her go alone either. She's a naturally distrustful person, and has always been particularly protective of her younger sister. It made sense that after an experience as traumatic as the one they were faced with yesterday, they would be even more on the defensive.

After half an hour of trying to convince Valentina *and* Sofia to let the younger Raymond talk to Dr. Sheffield, they both finally relented. Valentina went with her while Sofia followed us to the interrogation room where she was now sitting, tapping her foot on the floor incessantly. I snatched my eyes from her and looked at Kenny. I nodded and he nodded back. It was time.

As soon as we entered the room, Sofia's eyes found mine. That was something I noticed early on, wherever we were, her eyes would always look for me first. I don't really know why that knowledge made my heart squeeze, but it did. I told myself it was because she deemed me trustworthy, someone she knew she'd always be safe with.

Over the years, Sofia Raymond had been one hell of a pain in my ass. She was what was commonly known as a brat: spoiled, but lonely. So to compensate and get her parents' attention, she would continuously commit petty crimes. At first it was stealing from the local grocery store— dumb shit like candies and chocolate, then it escalated to trespassing, underage drinking and vandalism—graffitis to be exact.

The Raymond family came here nearly five years ago and during all those years up until she turned eighteen, there hadn't been a week where she didn't have an altercation of some sorts with an officer of the law. She even used to spend the night at the station sometimes, when she'd beg me not to wake her parents up with a phone call, and just wait until morning to alert them.

Sometimes I'd indulge her, mostly because she truly looked terrified at the idea of disappointing her parents. Others I'd still call them because it wasn't me on the night shift and I refused to leave her in a cell with real criminals while I couldn't keep an eye on her.

When she turned eighteen and started to attend college a town over, though, she calmed down. She stopped acting out altogether. She still lived at home, and I'd still see her around town, but not as much. I didn't think the day I'd have her in the backseat of my car again would be under such circumstances.

"Can we please hurry? My sister has been with that woman for enough time now. I need to get to her, I promised I wouldn't leave her." She said, looking from me to Adam and back to me.

"Your sister is in more than capable hands, Miss Raymond." I saw her jaw clench, and somehow I liked that she still retained her spunk. I wasn't proud of it, but I had to admit that I enjoyed it when she talked back.

Sofia was a free spirit, she couldn't be detained or enclosed. She was made to speak her mind. And she was damn good at it too.

"I don't give a fuck about that, I want to see her!" She raised her voice and sat up. "You never said anything about her being alone, you know how terrified she is from last night, I need to be with her, Maddox." Her eyes bore into mine and it was my turn to clench my jaw.

In the few years I'd known her, she only called me by my name once— yesterday when we were in her hotel room, alone.

Now I could feel Adam's questioning gaze on me. If he started thinking Sofia and I were on a first name basis, it could be bad for me. He could tell Chief Piersons that I was too close to the victim and I would get taken off the case.

There's no way I was letting this happen.

"It's Detective Brooks, to you." My words didn't leave any room for argument, and I saw something falter in her eyes, but I held my ground. "We need your statement on what happened last night, Miss Raymond. You can't tell us everything with Valentina in the room, unless of course you want her to hear about the men who murdered her parents in cold blood and tried to do the same to her sister?" I lifted one of my eyebrows, eying her curiously.

She pinched her lips together, like she wanted to say something but then decided against it. Sofia shook her head, making her black hair bounce. I fisted my hands remembering how smooth it felt under my fingertips last night. Yet another line I had crossed when it came to Sofia Raymond, and somehow I couldn't seem to regret it. I liked to think we had grown into an amicable relationship over the years. After all, I was the one cop she seemed to tolerate and respect the most.

However after what happened yesterday, it felt like the lines had blurred, and I didn't know where I stood. I wanted to be there for her as a friend, but I also wanted to find the fucker who turned her life upside down and both those things didn't seem to be compatible.

Sofia sighed, looking dejected and worn out, before turning her light brown eyes back to us.

"Where should I begin?"

# 4

## IDENTITY

### MADDOX

Her eyes were fixated on the gray metal table, with her index finger constantly tapping onto the surface nervously. She was trying to breathe deeper but it didn't seem to work in relaxing her as her shoulders were still taut, and she was frowning.

In all the years that I'd known her, I had never seen her so on edge, not even the first time she was arrested.

It made me want to find the motherfucker who did that to her and fucking finish the job she started on his friend. The first time the thought crossed my mind, I was surprised.

Sure, I knew over the years I had developed a certain sense of protectiveness over her, but nothing as fierce as how I felt last night when I got the call about a murder at the mayor's house. I was in my car the second I hung up and broke all speed limits to get there on time. No matter how many times I tried to tell myself it would be okay, that neither of the Raymond girls had been hurt, I couldn't get the images of Sofia and Valentina lying in a pool of their own blood out of my mind. We didn't have any information on what had gone down when I got the call, so anything was possible.

When I finally got there and saw her shaking body gripping Valentina while an officer tried to calm them down, I nearly ran to hug the shit out of her. She was badly beaten, her arms were black and blue and her upper lip was split open. She was drenched in blood too, and for a second I thought it was hers and nearly lost it.

I had to stop myself because I knew how it would look to anyone else. I'd known her since she was sixteen, and even though I knew what I felt for her was nothing short of friendship, I still had eyes. And I knew Sofia Raymond was what most people would consider beautiful, gorgeous even. I wasn't an exception.

"You can take your time, Sofia, don't rush into it. I know how you must be feeling right now." Adam's voice was soft and understanding.

He probably knew better than me what Sofia was going through right now, considering what happened last year.

Sofia's eyes softened, knowing what he was referring to. "You're Abel's father, aren't you?" Her voice cracked and Adam's shoulders tensed.

He gave a curt nod, glancing away.

His youngest son's suicide still cut him deep.

"He was a great kid. I taught art classes at Lakestone Middle School two years ago, and he was the sweetest boy. Always brought me candies— *Sour Patch Kids*, because he knew I had a sweet tooth." She smiled sadly, and Adam joined her, his dark eyes looking into the distance, probably reminiscing sweet memories of his son.

Sofia was right, Abel was a great kid. When he was younger, he'd come to the station sometimes and quietly draw at his dad's desk while Adam worked. Kid was good at it too. His suicide came as such a shock to the town, everyone spoke about it for months, and even now, after a year, people would still look at Adam and his family with pity in their eyes.

We never found out what pushed him to do it, he seemed like a happy kid, loved drawing, football, and animes. But even the brightest and youngest souls can be plagued with the darkest thoughts.

Adam and his wife suffered from it, of course, but from what Adam told me, his eldest boy took it the hardest. He clammed up, started getting into fights a lot and then cut all contact with anyone as soon as he left for college. Adam and Eva went from losing one son, to losing both in less than a year.

My partner clearing his throat broke me out of my thoughts, and I decided to change the subject, lord knew he didn't like talking about it.

"Start from the beginning. You told Officer Reynolds it was around 11 P.M when you woke up from the noise." Sofia nodded softly, confirming my words. "Go on." I encouraged.

She took a deep breath, like she was trying not to suffocate, and then started talking.

"I came home late from work, because a friend from college wanted me to take a look at her paper after my shift." I knew she worked at her campus' local coffee shop. She didn't need to, her family was loaded, it was just another act of rebellion.

"Mom and dad were getting ready for bed, and Valentina was already asleep." She wouldn't meet my eyes, and even though that frustrated me, I let her speak at her own pace. "I think it was like nine when I got into the house. I re-heated some leftovers, wolfed them down because I couldn't wait to take a shower and sleep." She was biting her lips, so much she almost drew blood.

"At what time did you go to sleep?" Adam inquired.

"I remember it being 9:56 when my head hit the pillow and I last looked at the clock." Her eyes met his, but she still wouldn't meet mine.

Adam nodded absentmindedly, "Did you lock the doors before you went upstairs? Set up the alarm system? There was no sign of a break in."

That last statement made Sofia's lips tremble, and I swear she was keeping herself from breaking into sobs right in front of us.

"I thought I had." Her voice cracks, "But clearly I-I must have forgotten since they got in." Her hands came up and she violently wiped away her tears.

Adam looked at me, and it was clear he regretted even asking. I liked my job most days, but today was one of the hardest since I joined the force.

"Sofia, I didn't mean it like that. There are a lot of ways of breaking in without it *looking* like a break in nowadays. If you think you locked the doors then you probably did lock them, they just were better equipped." Adam had a real fatherly way about him, he knew what to say and when.

Just then, Sofia's eyes finally met mine, and I swear I could see all the pain she was feeling. It made me breathless.

She nodded quietly, "I do remember locking the doors, but I don't know about the alarm."

"Can you tell us more about what happened after?" I asked, "Take your time."

She frowned and bit her lip, fiddling with her fingers and looking away. "I woke up again around 11:15. I heard glass breaking downstairs and noises— like people fighting." She gulped, "I quickly got out of my room, and my mom was just getting out of Valentina's. She'd heard the noises and went to tell her to hide in the closet." Her fingers were playing with the ring she always wore on her middle finger.

"She told me dad had heard something coming from the ground floor a while ago and went to check, but didn't come back. She said she'd go see what was going on. I told her not to, begged her even," her nostrils flared and she pinched her lips to keep from crying, "But she said our phones weren't working— there was no signal, I think they had a jammer." Adam scribbled down everything she was saying, and I saw him underline the word jammer.

"Mom told me to go with Valentina and lock the door, but I didn't listen. I couldn't." She shook her head. "I did go inside her room because mom wouldn't budge otherwise, Valentina came to me, she was so fucking scared, her whole body was shaking." Sofia pursed her lips and breathed in. "I told her to stay in the closet and to not, under any circumstances, get out, unless I came to fetch her. She went inside, hid behind a box of her clothes we had planned to donate, and I immediately went back downstairs."

My eyes didn't leave her as she spoke. I could tell how much it pained her, of course, but there was something else there. Anger. Sofia was livid, and not even for herself, she was angry that Valentina had been subjected to it. Every time she mentioned the little girl, and how much that night impacted her, she got this glint in her eyes, furious, enraged. The love she felt for her sister remained unequaled. She would kill for her. She *had* killed for her.

"I was at the top of the stairs when I saw my mom run through the foyer, from the living room into the kitchen. Her pajamas were ripped and bloody and she looked frightened. I'll never forget her face that night." She looked down at her hands, letting her hair cover her face.

Something to know about Sofia is that she was one prideful girl. She'd never let anyone see her cry or act weak. Even last night, before her breakdown in the hotel bathroom, she held herself with pride and dignity. I knew her sister played a great part in why she was trying to keep up that façade.

"I was so scared I just stopped moving. My legs wouldn't work, I was already imagining the worse. Then I saw my dad." She whimpered. "He was crawling, trying to get to the kitchen too, but he could barely move. They s-stabbed him. Several times, he was sliding in his own blood, trying to get to the kitchen." Her hands came to her throat and she squeezed, "That's when I heard mom scream. I don't know what the other guy was doing to her, but dad could see from where he was and he started yelling at them to stop, he was getting so agitated, and moving his arms wildly. It was making him even weaker, he couldn't even crawl anymore.

Then someone I couldn't see grabbed his leg and pulled him back into the living room. Mom was still screaming, dad was too weak to fight anymore and he just left a trail of blood behind. That's when adrenaline kicked in I guess. I ran down the stairs as quietly as I could." My jaw clenched and she noticed, her eyes boring into mine.

"I know it was stupid, but I had to do it. My mom was screaming at the top of her lungs, I don't know what that man was doing to her. I-" she hiccuped, tears clogging her throat.

“Take your time, sweetheart.” Adam told her patiently.

I tried to reassure her too but somehow I was too horrified for anything to come out of my mouth at that moment. I knew she acted on instinct, I would probably have done the same given the situation, but Goddammit, she risked her life.

“The man had his back to me, so I took advantage of it. I grabbed the first thing I saw— the pan our maid Martha had left on the stove for when I came home from work.” She swallowed and started babbling, “I-I was too tired to clean it right away so I just put a bit of water in it and left it on the stove. I’d planned on washing it in the morning.” A small, sad smile graced her lips “Mama hates when I do that but I still do it every time I come home late.” As soon as she stopped talking, the smile was wiped off her face and she frowned, lips trembling. “Hated. She *hated* it when I did that.”

Silence stretched the room as Adam and I shared another look. A part of me hated that we had to sit here and make her remember what was most likely the worst night of her life.

Another part knew it was necessary if we ever wished to find the bastard that did this to her and make him pay.

“What happened then, Sofia?” Adam asked.

“I hit him.” She answered curtly.

“With the frying pan?” She nodded her head, eyes void like she was replaying the scene in her head.

"I hit him with all the strength I could muster. You see me, you know I'm not the strongest but damn if that fucker didn't hit the ground when I hit him." There was venom in her words and not an ounce of regret. "But it was too late, when he fell, mom fell to her knees too. She was clutching her throat. Oh God, there was so much blood."

She closed her eyes and her chest started heaving heavily. The tell-tale signs of a panic attack.

Without thinking my hand shot to grab hers and I squeezed.

"Breath, Sofia. Fucking breath." Her eyes opened, wide and glistening with tears, and she squeezed my hand back just as hard. Her nails were digging into my skin but I didn't give a fuck right then. She was holding onto me like I was her anchor.

Then she was a stuttering mess, crying and blabbering about how she tried to help her mom by applying pressure to her throat but it did nothing to keep the blood from spraying onto her face, hair and clothes. Her hands were bloody as she begged her mom to wake up, she wasn't thinking straight.

"I still remember how she looked at me when she took her last breath. Her eyes were so wide, she was so scared. Then all of a sudden she went limp, and wasn't struggling to breathe anymore." Sofia was quietly sobbing by the time she finished telling us about how she held her mother as she died painfully in her arms.

"I don't know how long I stayed there, holding her, clutching her to my chest and praying I would wake up from that nightmare. I wasn't even thinking about the second man, at that point I didn't even care. I don't think he was in the living room when everything went down, he probably was looking for whatever it was they came to take." She shook her head, and indeed there was a mess in her father's office, like they'd rummaged through his belongings.

"But then he came back. He saw his friend on the floor, in a pool of my mother's blood, and probably mistook it for his own. I thought the nightmare was over but it had just started. He charged at me, I tried to run but the floor was so slippery," her voice cracked knowing the reason why it was slippery. "He punched me in the face, I was already feeling queasy at the time but that only worsened it. I tried to get away from him as fast as I could but I tripped and gripped a kitchen drawer to keep myself from falling. I still did and the drawer came with me." She was staring into the distance, it was impossible to know what she was thinking.

"The drawer had knives in it. I swear I acted on impulse, I didn't think it through, I *couldn't* think it through, he had a knife, he had just killed my father, his partner killed my mother I-" she was breathless, in shock and clearly replaying last night's events in her head. "Valentina was alone upstairs, she was waiting for me, I'm all she has and-and…" she wiped her tears vehemently. "I took the knife, and I stabbed him before he could stab me. Right in the throat."

She looked like a warrior, the glint in her eyes was one of a survivor. She had done what many people would have cowered from, she fought back. I was mad she *had* to do it, but proud that she saved herself and her sister without thinking about it twice.

"It's okay, Sofia. It was self-defense, we know that. Any court of law would know that." Adam reassured her but she shook her head.

"I didn't stop there though, I pulled the knife out, and I remember his blood spraying me so vividly, it's almost like I can still taste it on my tongue." Her face was one of disgust. "He fell to the ground but I stabbed him again. And again, and again, and fucking again." She pursed her lips. "I just couldn't stop, I was so scared I hadn't killed him enough. That he was not truly dead and would wake up and take my life or worse— that he would hurt Valentina." Her hand was still in mine, and she was grabbing me so hard I swear she would draw blood. I didn't mind.

Adam was still taking notes, but I was incapable of moving, totally in awe of the woman in front of me. It was a really morbid fascination, I'll give you that, but her strength of mind just amazed me.

Still, something bothered me about this whole story. Why would two random men— one of which was presently being examined at the morgue, bother breaking into the mayor's house and not steal anything of value. And why the fuck did they kill Marcella and Jack Raymond so fucking harshly. Anyone that knew anything about the psychology of murder knew that knives meant personal— unless they're a last resource like for Sofia.

Jack Raymond was stabbed twelve times, in the torso at that, meaning whoever killed him looked at him while doing so. Sofia told the officers last night that both men wore ski masks, so it meant they didn't care for Jack to recognize them before dying.

But they wanted to be able to see the light leave his eyes.

"You did what you had to do to protect your own, Sofia." Adam's voice pulled me out of my reverie. "You don't have to feel guilty about that." It sounded a lot like he was speaking from experience.

She didn't answer, simply nodded and gave my hand one last squeeze before pulling away. I immediately missed her warmth. It got me wondering who was anchoring who.

"I think we have enough for today, you're obviously still in shock and we wouldn't want to add to that, Miss Raymond." Adam told her in an almost fatherly manner, before turning to me. "I'll go see if Mindy is done with Valentina, make sure she calms down before you join me out front. Journalists are still here and something tells me she wouldn't want them to see her like that." I nodded and he gazed at Sofia one last time before stepping out of the room.

She was drying her tears using her jacket's sleeve, her face was red and puffy and her eyes looked exactly how you'd expect someone who sobbed their heart out for the last hour or so to.

I wanted to take her pain away, to hug her and give her comfort, but I knew I couldn't. First, because it wouldn't be professional, and second because it might give her the wrong idea.

After a few minutes, she stood up, straightening her back and looked me dead in the eye. Her beautiful face showed no emotions.

"I'm ready."

***

Back at the hotel, Valentina and Sofia went straight to the elevator, ignoring the insistent stares and questioning looks. The little girl was clinging even harder onto her sister than she had been before the meeting with Mindy. The psychologist wanted to see her again, because she apparently didn't get much out of her today, but Sofia refused to schedule any further appointment when Valentina told her Mindy had made her cry.

“My sister doesn’t need to speak to a stranger, she has me for that. You’re not fucking up Valentina’s brain over a fucking case. I’m the one you go to if you need answers, she doesn’t know shit.” was what she told Mindy.

Right after she nearly dragged her by her hair for making Valentina cry.

When we arrived at the hotel, I took Valentina in my arms because Sofia seemed too weak to hold her. As we got out of the elevator and made our way to the girls’ hotel room, I immediately knew something was wrong. Because right in front of room 36B stood three people and I only knew one of them. Justin, the officer in charge of guarding the room in my absence.

The other two were standing in front of him, visibly arguing with the cop. An older blond woman that kind of reminded me of my mom with her perfectly styled hair and classy attire, and a tall, lanky red-headed man wearing a suit and holding a briefcase.

Next to me, I felt Sofia tense, and even Valentina, who was hanging from my neck with her face burrowed in it, seemed to know something was off.

Our halting in the middle of the hall apparently drew the three people in front to look at us, and the man and woman straightened, before walking in our direction.

“Detective Brooks, I tried to tell them to come back another day but they wouldn’t listen—“ Justin was cut off by the woman, who was now only a couple feet away from us and held her hand for me to shake.

“Detective Brooks, I’m Gwyneth Harvon and this is my colleague Harry Kensley. We work for Child Protection Services.”

# 5

# ABANDON

## SOFIA

It felt like dying.

My whole body just stopped working, my breath was stuck in my throat, my heart ceased to beat.

No.

*No, no, no, no, no*. I did *not* go through hell and back only to have some uptight bitch take Valentina away from me. Next to me, Maddox stopped moving too. He gripped Valentina tighter and cleared his throat.

"I was told you would get here tomorrow." My head snapped in his direction.

He knew they were coming and didn't tell me? Anger burst inside me, I was fuming.

Of course, I knew I'd be confronted to CPS at one point or another, but for God's sake, our parents weren't even buried yet.

"Yes, well, there was a change of plan and Mr. Kensley and I were available to come today." Her cold blue eyes then focused on me. "I gather you're Miss Raymond?" She didn't wait for my answer to continue, “I’m sorry for your loss.” But her condolences were cold and held no compassion whatsoever.

That woman was like a robot. Cold and pragmatic. Was this really the kind of person responsible for making sure children received the care and love they deserved? No wonder so many kids in the system lost it.

But that would never be my sister. I would make sure of that.

“And I assume this is Valentina.” Her snake eyes roamed my sister, who hid her face in Maddox’s neck, probably sensing that these weren’t nice people.

Harvon looked back at me, “Our car is waiting out front, if you could prepare a small bag for her, we would like to get going as soon as possible.”

Pure, unadulterated anger burned through my stomach as I took a step forward.

“Over my fucking dead body.” Maddox’s hand shot out and grabbed my wrist to keep me from doing something I’d regret. Assaulting a CPS agent surely wouldn’t be good if I wanted to get custody of Valentina.

Harvon didn’t seem affected at all by my statement.

“Unfortunately I don’t think you get to decide that, Miss Raymond. Your parents having passed and with no next of kin to take care of Valentina, she has to come with us so we can find the best home possible for her.”

So many emotions went through me at that moment, fear, anger, sadness. More than anything, I felt helpless. Valentina whimpered against Maddox's throat and my heart squeezed.

"*I*'m her next of kin, *I*'m her home. She just lost her fucking parents and now you're trying to take her away from me too?"

"You're only nineteen, a child yourself, really. How do you plan on taking care of her properly when you barely can take care of yourself? We only want what's best for Valentina—"

"Then you should leave her with me!" I cut her off.

I felt Maddox squeeze my wrist and pull me back a bit. I was a hot head, I knew that. It got me in trouble more times than I could count, but I usually could control myself enough when the situation demanded it.

At that moment, however, I felt like I was going to burst at the seams. My emotions were still raw from what happened last night and then recounting the events to Maddox and Adam had me ready to punch something. That something just so happened to be Gwyneth Harvon.

I wanted to scream that I could care for her, that I had, for years, but I knew I couldn't. I knew it would only antagonize me.

"I think we all should calm down." Harvon's coworker finally spoke up. He looked less like a robot than the blond, but he was still keeping a professional distance. "Miss Raymond, this is protocol, we have to take Valentina with us tonight. She is to remain with us until we find a suitable place for her. You can apply to be her guardian, but I got to tell you, the chances of the state granting you guardianship of a nine year old are slim." He stated with heartbreaking diplomacy.

His colleague scoffed. "Slim is a nice way to put it. Talk about nonexistent." The more she spoke, the more I felt like grabbing her by her bleached hair and shaking the fuck out of her.

"I don't wanna go." All of our eyes snapped to Valentina, who warily glanced at the strangers, her little arms still wound around Maddox's neck. "I wanna stay with Sofia. She chases the monsters away."

I felt like crying when she said that, my heart breaking at how fragile she seemed at that very moment.

"You can still see her, Valentina. Sofia will be able to visit you at your new home."

"Sofia *is* my home! And I'm hers! We didn't do anything wrong, why are you punishing us?" She broke down crying after that and my heart was in my throat. I was barely keeping it together.

Maddox immediately started rubbing circles on her back, like he'd seen me do often in the last twenty-four hours. He soothed her while she drenched his shirt with tears. We shared a look over her shoulder, and I could see he was affected by her reaction. I gulped and turned back to the agents.

"Please. Please don't separate us." My voice was incredibly softer than it was a second ago. I wasn't above begging if it meant I got to keep Valentina.

They both had the decency to look sorry, even Harvon, but eventually shook their heads nonetheless. "We're sorry Miss Raymond. This is protocol."

“Come on, surely you can give them another day.” Maddox said with urgency. “You weren’t even supposed to come until tomorrow.” He sounded as desperate as I felt.

“I don’t know what to tell you, Detective Brooks, we don’t make the rules. If it helps, we can have you accompany us to where Valentina will be placed for the night. Miss Raymond will not be able to come though, only law enforcement.”

I couldn’t breathe.

They were gonna take my *little rose*, my baby, and place her with strangers for Lord knew how long. Right then, I knew nothing I could do or say would change the game. It was over for me and that knowledge completely annihilated me.

Still, I wouldn’t go down without a fight. Adrenaline burst through my veins as I snatched Valentina away from Maddox and hugged her fiercely. “Please, please don’t do this. You have no right.” Tears brimmed my eyes and I could feel my sister sob quietly against me.

“Miss Raymond, we can require police involvement if you refuse to let us take her. Please don’t do that to her.” Kensley warned me.

I was ready to tell him where he could shove his warning when Maddox spoke up.

“Okay. We’ll leave Valentina to you for the night.” Both me and Valentina’s head snapped towards him, betrayal sipping through my pores. How fucking *could he*. “Just leave us ten minutes to gather her belongings and say goodbye in the privacy of their room. Then I’ll accompany you to make sure she’s in good hands. ”

My heart was beating erratically against my ribcage, I could feel silent, angry tears running down my cheeks at the injustice this was. How could they pretend they wanted what was best for her while separating her from her only living relative.

Surely, they could see how close we were. They had proof I would do anything to protect her, or was my taking a life not enough for them?

My whole body was shaking in anger and fear. It was a strange combination, really.

Harvon and Kensley agreed, and Maddox then put a hand on the small of my back as he led me to our room. Justin was still waiting out front and he gave us a sorry look, which I ignored.

Once inside, Maddox locked the door behind us while I took a seat on the bed, hugging Valentina even closer to my chest. She squeezed me just as hard and continued sobbing.

"Please don't let them take me, *Dada*. The monsters will come for me if you're not here." she cried and I joined her.

I just couldn't keep my tears from falling anymore. The last twenty four hours have been hell for us, but somehow it didn't even come close to what I was feeling right now.

Right now, it felt like I was being amputated a limb or like someone was carving my heart right out of my chest.

Like I was not whole anymore.

"I swear to you it's just for tonight, Valentina." Maddox was kneeling in front of us, rubbing her back and trying to reassure her.

"Tomorrow, first thing in the morning, I'll come and get you." He whispered and I could hear the sincerity in his voice.

He didn't want to let her go but he knew we didn't have a choice in the matter.

"I don't want to let her go, Maddox." My voice cracked, "Please don't make me let her go." To hell with pride and dignity, I would beg on my knees if it meant I didn't have to leave my baby with strangers.

Maddox looked at me with sad eyes and flared nostrils. "I have a plan, Sofia." His voice was softer than ever. "All you have to do is trust me and I promise tonight is the only night you and her will be separated." I gulped, hearing the sincerity in his voice.

I knew he would genuinely try to keep this promise, but I also knew it didn't only depend on him. What if despite his best efforts, CPS decided to place Valentina permanently? I'm not sure I could survive that.

"Do you trust me Sofia?" He asked gently, his hand finding my knee and squeezing lightly.

At that moment, I went against all of my instincts. Every single molecule in my body was screaming no, telling me to pretext something, grab my sister and flee to fucking Canada. Start from zero. But I did none of that.

Instead, I bore my eyes into his, and nodded, slightly unsure. *"Yes."*

***

The rest of the day was a blur. I think I blacked out after they wrenched a screaming and crying Valentina away from me. I remember yelling at them to be careful with her, I remember Maddox grabbing me, his hands on my waist to keep me from running after them, and then nothing. Darkness swallowed me as I passed out from exhaustion.

When I woke up it was dark outside and the silence inside the room was deafening. My eyes felt puffy, my throat raw. I had no doubt I looked as bad as I felt. Dried tears stained my cheeks, and my lips felt sore from how much I'd bitten them in the last twenty four hours, the cut from yesterday probably reopened.

I groaned as I sat up, my head was fucking throbbing with a killer headache and it felt like I'd been rolled over by a four wheeler.

"There's Tylenol and water on the bedside table" I yelped, startled by the deep voice coming from the corner of the room. I nearly broke my neck turning towards it.

Maddox was sitting on the armchair, legs spread, tie undone and shirt sleeves rolled up to his elbows. He looked positively handsome, even with exhaustion marking his face. My eyes were drawn to the veins on his forearms, bulging out as he squeezed his hands together. His elbows rested on his knees as he leaned down slightly, looking at me.

"How are you feeling?" He asked, getting up and walking to my side of the bed. My eyes didn't leave him as he prowled in my direction.

"Like shit." Was my hoarse answer.

I tucked a strand of hair behind my ear and brought my knees to my chest, feeling the sheets against my chin. I was still in my outside clothes, which gave me the ick because mama always said you should never lay on your clean bed with dirty clothes.

Damn, I missed her so much.

Maddox sat on the side of the bed and grabbed the Tylenol. He popped two and handed them to me with the bottle of water. I gulped them down immediately, never meeting his eyes but feeling them dig holes on the side of my head.

"Is she okay?" My voice was almost shy, and I hated how weak it made me seem.

"She's in good hands. I liked the family they placed her in and the woman guaranteed me we could come and get her first thing in the morning." He reassured me. "Her husband also took my number and has been texting me updates on her every now and then. She cried for a good hour after I left but eventually calmed down enough to get something to eat. Aisha— the mother, made something called *maqlooba*. It's a middle eastern dish apparently and Valentina seemed to like it." He tapped something on his phone before showing me the screen.

My sister was sitting at a dinner table, delicately feeding herself spoonfuls of what looked like rice. She had a bit of sauce on the corner of her mouth and looked up sadly at the camera. I could feel myself tearing up again.

"She also seemed to get along fine with their daughter, Sameera." He swiped and another picture of Valentina playing dolls with a brown haired little girl popped up. "They only live a town over, so even when we get her back tomorrow, she'll be able to go on playdates with her if she wants." I nodded absentmindedly, tears blurring my vision.

"She's sleeping now, but from what Nurdeen– the foster father, told me, she hasn't cried again since I left and even seemed to take a liking to Aisha. Said she reminded her of, I quote, *her mama*." I froze, my breath lodged in my throat, and Maddox visibly noticed. "It's normal for her to make such a comparison, Sofia, she just lost her mom, it doesn't mean she's trying to replace her. It's an instinctual reaction." I forced myself to swallow and nod, knowing he wouldn't get it.

"How long have you been sitting there?" I asked in an attempt to change the subject.

"A little less than two hours." I frowned as he placed the bottle back on the nightstand.

"You watched me sleep for that long? That's kinda creepy." I tried to alleviate the tension, and he broke into a small, tired smile.

"I had a lot to think about. It's actually a miracle I could think at all given how loud you snore." His small smile turned into a smirk and I gasped before hitting his shoulder.

"I do *not* snore!"

"Oh but you do. It's cute though."

Whatever I was gonna say got stuck in my throat and I could feel my cheek redden. I was grateful that the only source of light came from the window, that way he couldn't notice the effect his words had on me.

"I'm gonna adopt her." I blurted. "Come tomorrow I'm getting in all the work necessary to officially adopt her, become her guardian, whatever it's fucking called, but I'm not letting anyone take her away from me again."

It was Maddox's turn to tense up, breaking the playful atmosphere that had taken over the room and replacing it with a strained one. He got up and started pacing in front of the bed.

"You can't do that Sofia. You won't have access to your trust fund until you're 21 and you can't raise a child on a barista salary." His words weren't harsh, his tone was actually soft, yet the blow they delivered hurt all the same because I knew that was how a court of law would reason too.

"Watch me." I said through gritted teeth, getting to my feet in front of him. He still towered over me but not nearly as much as he did when I was sitting. "I'll take two jobs if need be, or, fuck it, even three!"

"Oh yeah? And what about college? Where will you find the time to study and attend your classes while you work three fucking jobs, Sofia?" He spat, clearly getting angry with me.

I was used to it, anger was the main emotion Maddox Brooks felt whenever I was near him. I had years of practice when it came to dealing with an angry Maddox.

"I'll fucking drop out then! Raising Valentina is more important than any level of education!" That was probably the last thing I should have said while knowing he was already angry to begin with, because the thought of me dropping out of college? It *enraged* him.

Maddox really got in my face after that. He didn't yell, no, he did worse. His jaw tense, he stopped centimeters away from my face and with an eery stillness he spat:

“Like fucking hell you will.”

My chest was erratically moving up and down by then, I was torn between wanting to apologize, or wanting to claw his eyes out for thinking he could tell me what to do. In the end, I didn’t cower away from him, I even moved closer just to show him he wasn’t intimidating me.

“You don’t know how far I’d go for that little girl. She’s the only thing I have left of my parents, she’s my only family. What I did that night will seem like child’s play compared to what I’d do to anyone trying to keep us apart.”

Venom was laced with my words, and I expected him to completely go off after I said that.

Yet, against all odds, I saw his eyes flash with what could only be described as arousal.

It disappeared as soon as I saw it, because Maddox was at least as good as me when it came to hiding his emotions, but I knew what arousal looked like, and I knew for whatever reason, having me stand my ground and talk back to him had turned him on. Maybe it should have weirded me out by it, but it didn't. Quite the contrary.

His breathing turned erratic and he looked through my eyes like he had a direct view on my soul. For what felt like hours but only were mere minutes, no one moved. We were standing so close our breaths mingled, and our chests almost touched with each exhale. I felt warmth spread all the way down my body, the situation oddly erotic. Seeing him so furious over something having to do with my well being? I couldn't quite put words on how that made me feel.

"You won't apply for guardianship, Sofia. Because I will. I'll ask for custody of Valentina."

# 6

# DESPERATE

## MADDOX

"W—what did you just say?" Sofia pulled back, looking as shocked as I felt.

I didn't plan on telling her now. Hell, I was still unsure about the whole custody thing, but when I saw her so angry, so desperate to have her sister back safely with her, I couldn't stop the words from flying out of my mouth.

I'd been thinking about it since the moment those CPS workers introduced themselves to us, because I knew there was no way any judge was giving Sofia custody of her own sister. Not only because of her age and financial situation, but also because of the traumatic events she had just been through.

She had killed a man.

Sure it was selfdefense, but these things left their marks. And no court of law would deem her able to raise a child right right after such an experience.

While she was sleeping, I made some phone calls to make sure that Valentina could come back to us tomorrow, and one of those phone calls had been with my mother. Angeline Brooks was a retired judge but she never shied away from helping people in need.

I told her everything about the situation and she agreed that no one would grant Sofia custody. That's when I asked if *I* would be. Her silence on the other end was deafening, until eventually she said

*"Well, yes, I believe so. You have a stable job, you're respected in the community and both your father and I are well known in town. Plus, you know you have an amazing attorney if need be. The real question is whether or not you could handle raising a nine year old, Maddox."*

The answer to that was *absolutely fucking not*. But I would if it kept the Raymond sisters from being set apart. Plus I had no doubt Sofia would insist on micro managing everything so it wasn't like I would truly be the one raising the kid.

I didn't know why I cared so much about these girls, I could just do my best to have Valentina put in a good foster home, but I didn't want that for them.

The Raymond sisters had been through enough loss as it was. I didn't want them to be separated on top of that. Not when they only had each other left.

"Listen," I sighed, sitting down on the bed and rubbing my face frustratedly, "I talked to my mom about it, she thinks I have a better chance of getting custody than you. I have a stable job, I own my apartment and my family is well known and liked in Lakestone. Judge Michealson has known me since I was a child, he used to golf with my father." She started pacing restlessly in front of me. "This is our best bet at getting her back, Sofia."

"Fuck. When did my life become so complicated." I heard her mumble in her breath. She was massaging her temples, not knowing what to do. “How would that even work? Can you do that knowing there’s a case we’re involved in going on?”

Her eyes roamed my face as she came to stand in front of me. Since I was sitting and she was so fucking short, my head was at the same level as the bottom of her breasts. And let’s just say after the things she said earlier, I was having a hard time trying no to look.

*What I did yesterday will seem like child’s play compared to what I’d do to anyone trying to keep us apart.* What the fuck was wrong with me for this sentence to turn me on so much?

Clearing my throat, I answered her.

“No, I don’t think it will be a problem. We had a meeting with our Captain this morning, and considering you and I have known each other for a while and you always seemed more comfortable with me than you did with the other officers, he thought I’d be a great asset to the team. I don’t think he’ll be enchanted by the idea of me filing for custody but I don't believe it would put my spot on the squad in jeopardy either.”

She went silent for a while, just staring at me, trying to decipher what were my thoughts on it exactly.

“And how would it work? Valentina would move in with you and you’d let me visit her everyday for however long I’d like?”

She seemed so small right then, her tone unsure, like she wasn’t a fan of the idea, but was willing to go with it if she got to stay close to her sister.

“Actually,” I cleared my throat, my heart beating fast, “I was more thinking along the lines of you *two* moving in with me.” I felt like a fourteen year old asking his crush to the school dance.

Why the fuck was I so nervous, it’s not like I was asking her to *move in* with me, I was asking her to move in with me, for the sake of her sister.

I finally gathered the courage to look up and gauge her reaction. Her eyes were wide, dark eyebrows nearly reaching her hairline, an expression of shock plastered on her face.

“You—“ she gulped, “You’re asking me to move in with you?”

“And Valentina. I'm asking you and Valentina to move in with me.”

More awkward silence stretched the room and I was praying for the floor to open up and swallow me whole. The tips of my ears felt hot, I knew I must’ve been blushing and I thanked God for the room being dark. The few times I’d blushed in front of Sofia Raymond in the past, she’d given me hell for it.

“Maddox… are you sure about that?” Her eyes wouldn’t meet mine, she was frowning and sounded as unsure as I felt.

“Listen, it’ll only be for a few months, until we find another solution for Valentina and finally close this case. The second man is still on the run somewhere. I’m not risking you or Valentina getting hurt. It’s a two birds, one stone situation.” Still sensing her hesitation, I added, “I live right outside of town and my apartment is big enough that we wouldn’t even have to bump into each other if we didn’t want to. You and Valentina would each have your own room and bathroom too.”

Why did it sound like I was asking her to do me a favor by moving in with me when it was supposedly the other way around? Why was I trying so hard to convince her?

"I hate this." She muttered, folding her arms, looking beat.

"Hate what?"

My voice was almost a whisper, I always found myself in awe whenever she let her guards down. It was so fucking rare with her.

"I hate how much like charity this feels. I hate that I have no fucking control over the situation. I hate that this is happening to us." She seemed so dejected, so tired.

Her spark was dying. It made me positively livid to see her like this.

"Hey," Getting to my feet, I made my way to her and against my better judgment, cupped her cheek.

As soon as our skins touched, she shuddered and my heart missed a beat. She looked up and her eyes bore into mine. For a minute I didn't even remember what I wanted to say in the first place. The scent of flower and sugar was fogging up my mind.

Knowing Sofia trusted me enough to be vulnerable in front of me just enhanced that growing feeling in my chest.

"You're not a charity case. I know we don't always get along, but you're a good person, Sofia. Sure, you used to drive me out of my mind sometimes, and I'll always be the police officer that kept you from spreading your art on Lakestone's citizens *private* properties," She chuckled sadly and a small smile pulled at the corner of my lips.

"But I like to think we're friends. And that's what friends do, they help each other." Gold orbs shone with tears as they lingered on me.

Her hand came up on top of mine and she leaned her head into it, like a cat seeking comfort. After the last couple of days, it wasn't surprising.

"Thank you."

Her tongue came out to wet her lips, and she never looked as beautiful as she did in that moment, with the moonlight bathing her skin, her golden eyes shining like a million stars, hair cascading around her face like a halo of darkness. Sofia Raymond was a work of art

***

## SOFIA

When I woke up again the next morning, I felt much better. Like some weight had been lifted off my chest, and in a way, I guess it had. Knowing Maddox was on my side and was willing to help any way he could reassured me a lot. It felt strange knowing I was not alone in this anymore, that I could delegate a bit and not constantly worry about Valentina or our current situation alone.

It was nice knowing someone had my back.

A knock resonated on my door just as I came out of the bathroom and I said "Come in!" Without really thinking about it, assuming it was Maddox.

I was dressed in a white bathrobe embroidered with the hotel's logo, rubbing my hair dry with a matching towel since my hairdryer was at the house. I knew sooner or later I'd have to go back there and gather the rest of my stuff.

But Lord knew I was never coming back to that house of horrors after that.

The door opened and Maddox came in with a steaming cup of coffee and a brown bag that smelled like heaven.

"Good morning." He set both items on the nightstand and nodded at me.

I felt my cheeks heat up, remembering last night's events. When he touched me like I was the most delicate flower on earth. I remembered the warmth of his fingers against my skin, his delicious scent invading my nostrils. I remembered the heat emanating from his body and seeping into mine. I never considered myself to be starving for proximity I was but yesterday had me questioning myself.

I tightened the belt on my robe and cleared my throat.

"Morning."

"How did you sleep?" His eyes roamed my face, like he was trying to answer his own question by assessing me.

"Pretty good actually," I shrugged, "What about you? Did you manage to get some sleep at all?"

He left a bit after the whole "we're friends" moment, when I told him I accepted his offer and would move in with him if court granted him custody of Valentina.

I still couldn't believe he was willing to go as far as sharing his space with us to help me and my sister stay together. I knew Maddox Brooks was a good guy, he's got that whole hero, *I-come-from-a-rich-*

*family-who-loves-to-help-others* kinda vibe going on, but I didn't actually think he valued me that much.

"Yeah. I stayed in the room next to yours actually, got a good three hours of sleep in." He pointed to the brown bag and styrofoam cup on the nightstand, "got you some coffee with a salted caramel and chocolate muffin. Better eat something before we get going. I think we're in for a long day."

I didn't even wait for him to finish and went straight for the bag. Salted caramel and chocolate muffins were my favorite and I had no idea how he knew that but I didn't really care at the moment, too busy enjoying the delicious food.

"Do you have news on Valentina?" I sat on the bed while stuffing my face, one leg folded under my butt, the other still touching the floor.

"Yeah, Nurdeen said she woke up at four this morning and was in front of the door waiting for us as soon as she was dressed." A sad smile graced his lips and my heart seized in my chest.

It was six in the morning right now, I thought I was being dramatic when I told him I would be at their door at seven o'clock sharp but clearly my sister outdid me in that area.

Shit I missed her so much already.

"Just lemme gulp this down to wake me up, get dressed and we can go." I shifted, making myself more comfortable so I could eat and sip my coffee at the same time. "I can't wait to see her, she's never slept over at anyone's house before, but I'm glad she found a friend there and that she seemed to like the family—"

“Sofia.”

I kept talking, knowing he was probably just gonna tell me to slow down and not eat as I spoke.

“We also need to get more stuff from the house but I don’t want Valentina to go back there. There are just too many bad memories associated with that house, so maybe you could stay here with her while I go? I’ll take an officer with me of course, maybe Adam or Selena—“

“Sofia” he cleared his throat and I just licked my finger where a bit of gooey caramel had run down.

“Damn, this muffin is good, is that from Krista’s bakery? I never —“

“For fuck’s sake, Sofia, your robe!” He exploded, and I finally looked up from my muffin to him.

Pink cheeks, pink ears, hell even the tip of his nose was pink and he was staring at me, nostrils flared. Damn he was cute when he blushed. Don’t ask me why but there was just something about a man who blushed that made him instantly more attractive in my eyes.

“What?” A frown etched its way to my face, and I simply tilted my head to the side, not understanding where he was getting.

Then he nodded to my lap and I looked down at myself. Oh fuck. *Oh fuck, fuck, fuck.*

I did *not* just flash him my pussy.

I did *not.*

Shame and uneasiness wrecked my stomach and for a second I wished to disappear.

I immediately closed my legs, jumping up, giving him my back and refastening my robe as tight as I could. I even did a double knot since the hollow between my breasts was also showing.

The muffin I was eating fell on the floor in my haste to cover up but I still swallowed the last bite that was in my mouth with difficulty. It was either that or choke on it and I'd had enough embarrassment for the day. The delicious treat now tasted like cardboard, its sweetness drowned by the force of my humiliation.

"I-I didn't look, I swear. As soon as I noticed I tried to tell you but — yeah, uh, okay. I'll wait for you outside."

He scratched the back of his neck, a boyish look on his reddening face.

I appreciated that he had the decency to act like a gentleman and seemed even more uncomfortable than I felt. I had no doubt anyone else would have looked their fair share before even mentioning anything to me, watching me make an even bigger fool out of myself.

I couldn't look at him as he left the room and he wouldn't meet my gaze either.

*Oh my God I flashed the cop investigating my parents' murder and who I was supposed to be living with soon.*

I think at this point there's no denying to myself that I was attracted to him. Maddox was so *obviously* gorgeous. Tall, strong, he had mesmerizing eyes… and to top it off he was nice. *Actually* nice.

From experience, I knew I should be more careful and not jump to the conclusion that because he was liked by everyone in town it meant he was a good person. Yet, there was just something, a voice at the back of my mind, that was screaming at me to let go of my wariness and just trust him.

He stood by me and washed blood out of my hair, he was willing to disrupt his whole life to give me and my sister the chance to stay together, and even before that, he might have been a bit of an ass whenever we came across each other, but not once did he make me feel less than.

Hell, he'd always say I had a great potential. He was the only officer on the force who never referred to my art as vandalism, telling me instead that I was talented and should put this talent to good use.

Now that I thought about it, Maddox was probably one of the only constants in my life. Had been for the last five years. And I felt fucking safe with him.

So yes, I was attracted to Maddox Brooks but I would not be doing anything about it, because I valued his presence and his person too much to sabotage it. He was too good for me, and I knew one way or another, I'd end up fucking everything up.

Maddox didn't deserve to be tainted by someone like me.

# 7

# ICEBREAKER

## SOFIA

When I came out of my room, Maddox was nowhere to be found. Justin, the cop from yesterday, the one who was arguing with the CPS people, was there though. He was leaning against the wall opposite my bedroom's door.

When he noticed me, he straightened up and cleared his throat. "Miss Raymond, good morning."

I gave him a small smile.

"Hey, Justin. Have you seen M— Detective Brooks?" I scanned the hallway absentmindedly.

"Yes, he said he'd wait for you in the lobby. He received a phone call and had to go downstairs."

My shoulders slumped a bit, and I tried to convince myself he really had an important thing to take care of down in the lobby, that it was not some dumb excuse to escape me.

Oh my God, what if he decided to rescind his offer? My stomach dropped at the thought, I really hoped I didn't fuck this up for Valentina.

I thanked Justin and made my way to the lobby with haste, ready to apologize profusely until he told me it was fine and that he still would ask for custody. The ding from the elevator broke me away from my thoughts and I immediately spotted Maddox near the hotel's door.

He was staring through them as if looking for someone while holding his phone to his ear. It looked like he was directing someone through the phone. Journalists were still out front, fighting to get in, but between police officers and the hotel's security guys it was quite impossible. I didn't wait any longer and just made my way to him.

When he saw me, he mumbled something to his interlocutor before hanging up, which if I was being totally honest, kind of irritated me for some reason.

"Hey." He said, avoiding my eyes.

"Please don't do that." I hated how pleading I sounded right then, "Don't act all weird with me. Not now. Let's just forget this thing fucking happened. Please."

He sighed in relief and nodded "Fuck, I'm sorry. It was no big deal anyways, I'm being weird for no reason."

"Right? It's not like mine was the first pussy you've ever seen, anyways."

It tried making light of the situation but this was so obviously the last thing to say because the second the words left my mouth, Maddox was choking. On fucking air.

His ears were starting to get red again.

My eyes widened and I cursed before giving light taps to his back with the palm of my hand.

"Oh shit, I'm so sorry, I was trying to turn it into a joke. Please don't die on me." He seemed to gather himself quickly and coughed one last time before straightening up.

"No more talking about it." He gave me a pointed look, his voice the epitome of authority.

For some reason it made me blush and clench my thighs. I nodded wordlessly.

Just then a voice came from behind me as a small mass of blond hair and pink fur jumped on Maddox.

"Maddie!" The woman squealed.

She was wearing a cozy looking pink fur coat, pink killer heels and her blond hair had a pink bow in it. She was like the live version of Charlotte, from *The Princess and the Frog*, Valentina's favorite *Disney* movie.

I'd never seen her before, but from the way she hugged Maddox and seemed so familiar with him, a small part of me instantly disliked her.

"Callie." Maddox smiled down at her as soon as she pulled away from him.

Her lipstick stained his cheek— pink, you guessed it, and again, the urge to wipe his cheek assaulted me out of nowhere. Maybe it was because of everything that went down lately. Maybe I felt weirdly possessive of him because I'd just spent the last few days with him and that somehow brought us closer— or at least I thought it had.

One of his hands remained around her back as she smiled, showing off her straight white teeth. Her outfit looked fancy, her hair was styled impeccably, her face was beautiful and fuck even her voice was nice. I wasn't close enough to tell but I could swear she smelled like candy cane or sugar plum or something sweet like that. She radiated feminine energy.

I looked homeless in comparison with my cargo pants and black, long-sleeved, cropped top. My long hair was in a loose braid and I probably had bags under my eyes from the sleepless nights I'd been accumulating.

Barbie— or Callie as Maddox called her, finally noticed me and turned around, offering me a smile which, unfortunately, didn't look fake.

"Hi! You must be Sofia?" She offered me her hand, "I'm Calliope, but you can call me Callie!" I smiled back as best as I could despite the jealousy remaining in my heart and shook her hand. "I'm so sorry for your loss." her smile slipped and she genuinely looked like she was sad for me.

Actually, she looked like she was three seconds away from bursting into tears.

I cleared my throat and nodded, suddenly uncomfortable.

Maddox noticed it and took over, "Callie is here to help us get Valentina back." I frowned, not really understanding how this little woman was supposed to help us woo the judge so he'd grant Maddox Valentina's custody.

Seeing my confused face, Callie laughed light heartedly, “I know I might not look like it but I’m an attorney. I specialize in children and family law. Maddie called me yesterday saying you both might need my help, so here I am. I spoke to the prosecutor and convinced them to let Valentina stay with you until she could get properly evaluated and placed into a permanent home.” My hand went up to my chest and I clutched the fabric of my top in it. “Now all that’s left to do is get Maddie here the proper license to become a foster parent which could take some time.”

Her calling him Maddie was getting on my nerves. And that thought kind of made me feel guilty because she was being so fucking nice to me.

“How long are we talking?” I asked, my voice hoarse.

“Two to three months is what’s most common in our state but given the circumstances and the fact that Maddox wouldn’t be taking on more kids, only Valentina, it could go way faster. Let’s hope it does.” I nodded, swallowing the lump that had begun to form in my throat.

Hope.

Hope was all we’ve always had. Hope brought us out of this horrible situation we were in.

So let’s hope.

***

My stomach was in knots as Maddox parked his car in front of the two stories suburban house where my sister had spent the last night. Callie was in her own car which, I could hear, parked right behind us.

I gulped as I took in my surroundings, seeing how green and well kept the front lawn was, how white the fence seemed. I was suddenly doubting myself. This was the kind of house Valentina could be living in. This was the kind of life she could be given.

I had no idea when or if I could ever afford such a lifestyle for her. The numbers on my bank account had three figures on a good day, I had school and barely managed to balance my job as a barista with it. Maddox said he'll help but I refused to let him pay for Valentina's expenses. He's already offering us shelter which is more than anyone has ever done.

Maddox clearing his throat brought me out of my thoughts, and I turned to him, only to see he was already watching me. "Are you okay?"

I bit my lip, diving into his eyes, "What if this is a mistake, Maddox?" He frowned and killed the engine, leaning towards me.

"What are you talking about?"

"What if what's best for her is being with a normal family? What if I can never give her a future like this." I motioned to the house, gulping.

Maddox was silent for a moment, observing me, then he hesitantly took my hand in his. Tingles worked their way under my skin and my heart nearly stopped.

"Those are your nerves talking and you know it. You already know I'll do everything in my power to help you give her the life you both deserve. A beautiful house doesn't mean a perfect life, or a perfect family." I swallowed, suddenly uneasy. I probably knew that better than anyone. “What Valentina truly needs is her family, and like you said yourself, you're it. You’re her home.”

Tears started blurring my vision as I processed his words. His hand gave mine a squeeze, the last bit of comfort I needed to pull myself back together. He was right, I was letting my doubts and insecurities get in the way of my duty. No more.

I was getting my sister back and giving her the life she fucking deserved.

His thumb wiped at the single tear that had gotten out of me, right underneath my eye, and he gave me a small smile which I answered in kind. Electricity sizzled between us, the tingles I had been feeling earlier grew even more noticeable as he held my gaze.

His eyes were so fucking beautiful.

Just as I was about to open my mouth and tell him how grateful I was for everything he was doing for us, a loud knock on my window startled us and made me turn around.

Callie stood there, smiling so hard her cheeks must’ve been hurting. Then she motioned to the house.

“Let’s get our girl!” She didn’t wait for us and started strutting down the path leading to the house.

The way she walked was both graceful and funny, she seemed right out of a Disney movie. I swear she even stopped when a squirrel darted in front of her, hurrying towards the bushes. She crouched down and started talking to the small creature.

"She's… interesting." I noted, leaning my head to the side. Next to me, Maddox chuckled lightly.

"Yeah, she is. We met in college. Everyone underestimated her because of the pink clothes and angel face, but I've seen her shred grown men to pieces in court. She's our best asset to get Valentina back." Well, there went my hopes of her being his sister or cousin.

I had to bite my lip to stop myself from asking who she was to him, if they ever dated or God forbid, had sex.

I really, *really* didn't want to imagine Maddox having sex with another girl.

I meant any girl. Me included. After everything that happened this morning it was probably wise to just *not* imagine him in any sexual situation whatsoever.

At my lack of response Maddox decided to clear his throat.

"Come on, little one, let's go." He tapped the wheel and was out of the car right after.

I took a deep breath and followed him. Callie was still crouched in front of the bush, cooing at the squirrel which still didn't seem keen on getting out of hiding. When she saw us arrive, she got up and dusted her knees for invisible dirt before grinning at us.

We made our way to the door and she gave me one last look before knocking. Almost immediately the door opened and a tall man with dark brown skin, black hair and matching dark eyes smiled down at us. He had a trimmed beard and wore a white button down with black slacks. In his hand he held a briefcase and his phone, clearly heading to work.

"Oh, hi." He extended his hand towards Maddox. "You must be Detective Brooks, Miss Raymonds and Mrs Hayward." We all nodded. "I'm Nurdeen, my wife is inside waiting for you, I wanted to be there for the meeting but an emergency came up at work." He didn't offer me or Callie his hand like he did with Maddox but he did give us a genuine smile and incline of his head instead. "Please come in."

He moved over, letting us in. Callie was the first to step inside the house, and I followed suit while Maddox closed the door behind us. As soon as I was in, the scent of jasmine assaulted my nostrils and I got hit by a wave of nostalgia. Mama's favorite flower. She used jasmine scented products and perfumes. A part of me relaxed at the familiar scent and I knew Valentina must've felt at ease too, which made this whole situation slightly better.

Small footsteps were heard coming from the living room before a mass of black hair ran towards us and hurled itself at me.

"Dada!"

I crouched and caught Valentina with ease, her small arms encircling my neck as my own squeezed her tight. I needed to make sure it was really her, that she was really here and that I wasn't just dreaming. My nose got its fill of her sweet scent, a mix of roses and honey, and I could feel her silent tears run along my neck. Small tendrils rocked her slight frame as she soundlessly cried on my shoulder. I rubbed her back, trying to get my own tears in check.

"You came. You really came." She sniffled, playing with my hair.

"Of course I did, my little rose. It's you and me against the world, remember? You and me against the monsters." I held her tight, afraid somebody would come in and take her away from me again.

"I love you so much." she sobbed, pulling away and holding my cheeks.

She looked at me like I was the most important thing in the world to her. She was just that to me.

"I love you too, mami." I whispered as I wiped her tears.

Another set of footsteps echoed from the living room before a woman that looked to be in her late twenties to early thirties, with brown skin and dark green eyes came into view. She was wearing a pair of jeans with a white sweater and a purple headscarf that hid the entirety of her hair. The woman, who I supposed was Aisha— the foster mother Maddox spoke about yesterday, greeted us with a dazzling smile.

"Hello, you must be Sofia." her eyes were fixated on me but I didn't answer, words evading me.

I understood why Valentina said she reminded her of mama. If her hair underneath the headscarf was shiny, jet black and wavy, she could've been Mama's twin. The resemblance was uncanny and made me stare. I forced myself to swallow the lump forming in my throat in order to answer her greeting.

"Hi. Yes, it's me. Thank you so much for looking after Valentina." I got back on my feet and offered her a small smile.

“No thanks needed, really. Valentina was adorable and Sameera loved having her over.” That would be the little girl who played dolls with my sister yesterday in the picture Maddox showed me.

Valentina tugged on my pants “Sameera is Aisha’s daughter, she’s nine like me and she loves dolls too! She didn’t think they were dumb.” My heart warmed seeing her so happy.

She told me girls at the private school mom and dad enrolled her in didn’t want to play with dolls anymore because they said they were for babies. They all had cell phones already and spent recess scrolling through social media.

“Well, Sameera is welcome anytime if she wants to come over and play dolls with you.” I caressed her smooth hair and sent a grateful look to Aisha. She smiled back at me and nodded as if to say thank you.

I couldn't help but stare as Callie started talking with her. Smooth facial features, full lips, an ethnic nose, thick black eyebrows, she looked so much like mama. Feeling a pair of eyes on me, my gaze drifted over to Maddox who was looking at me with a strange expression. I immediately straightened up and dropped my eyes, bringing Valentina closer to me.

Nurdeen left for work and Aisha told us to come sit in the living room while we waited for the social workers to get here. She asked if we wanted something to drink and brought us tea over.

“This is called *chai*!” Valentina exclaimed, snuggling between me and Maddox on the couch. “It means tea in Arabian!”

A small smile graced my lips, she seemed so proud to be teaching us something she, herself, must've learned only yesterday.

"Arabic, love. Arabian is an adjective, the correct term to refer to the language is Arabic." Aisha smiled down at her and corrected her ever so patiently.

"Oh. Right, sorry." Valentina offered her a sheepish smile and leaned her head on Maddox's shoulder.

The atmosphere was really light, we spoke mainly of Valentina and all the things she had learned about Middle Eastern culture since yesterday.

My sister told me the headscarf Aisha was wearing was called a *hijab*, that they ate something called *maqlooba* yesterday for dinner, and that they had chai almost right after— which she found weird because mom and dad wouldn't let us have tea after dinner. Or anything sweet for that matter.

For a second it was as if we were just having tea at a family friend's house, catching up and telling stories. Aisha was a fashion designer and her husband was an engineer. They both immigrated here from Palestine right after they got married. Sameera was their only daughter so far but they were trying for another one. She didn't say it explicitly but I got the feeling they were having trouble getting pregnant and that was the reason they became a foster family.

Even though I still wasn't happy about my sister being taken away from me and spending the night with strangers, I was glad she was put into their care. They seemed like good people, and we needed good people in our lives. Especially Valentina, she needed friends, and Sameera was a good start for that.

As I looked at my sister, I noticed her drooping eyes— Aisha had informed us she didn't fall back asleep after waking up at four this morning. She simply sat quietly in the living room waiting for us.

It was funny because Valentina was never an early riser, she'd sleep for as long as possible then wake up and just get ready quickly. Her head rested on Maddox's shoulder, and his fingers played with the ends of her long hair. For a second there, I was jealous. They looked cozy as fuck and I knew from experience that having Maddox' fingers in your hair was soothing and relaxing.

At first, I refused to admit it but seeing Valentina and Maddox' relationship evolve and become this easy, comfortable one was heartwarming.

There were very few people I trusted in this world— two of which were dead, but the more we went on with Maddox at our side, the more I trusted him.

And that only meant it would hurt more in the end.

# 8

# DISSOCIATION

## SOFIA

My fingers tapped my thighs lightly as I recalled yesterday's events.

Once Harvon and Kensley arrived, the joyful, friendly and warm conversation drastically cooled down. They grilled Maddox every chance they got, asking him questions about how he planned on taking care of a nine year old without having any prior experience with children, they kept reminding him of his young age and demanding job — the fact that he could work weird hours definitely didn't play in our favor.

Thankfully, Callie argued back and found a reasonable answer to every one of their queries. If that's how she presented the case to the judge, I had no doubt they would grant Maddox custody in less time than first anticipated. I hoped they did.

Still, Harvon and her colleague wrote down every answer. Then they spoke to Valentina, who I was proud to say, didn't stutter when she said she felt safe with Maddox. She even argued with them that since he was a cop, there was no way any *monster* could ever get to us again. My heart hurt for her little soul, but I was happy she was not retracting into her shell.

Then, the question I was dreading most was asked.

*"And where do you plan on living while you get stable enough to ask for custody, Miss Raymond?"*

My throat was so tight I could barely speak. I knew the answer to that was going to raise even more questions, that it probably was gonna play against us at some point. Thankfully, Callie intervened, making all eyes drift to her.

"Miss Raymond will be staying with my client in the meantime as we, along with the station's psychologist, Miss Sheffield, believe that separating both sisters after an event as traumatizing as the one they'd been through would be a huge mistake."

Mrs Harvon scoffed, her sharp eyes going back and forth between me and Maddox, "Surely you're not serious, are you? That is absolutely inappropriate."

"In what regard? Both my client and Miss Raymond are above the age of adulthood, they have known each other for years and get along just fine. Mr Brooks is like an older brother figure to Miss Raymond." I wanted to scoff at that.

*An older brother figure.* Sure if we lived in freaking *Alabama*, given the way my body reacted to him.

"Not to mention, they have been spending quite a lot of time together lately and Mr Brooks is one of the officers in charge of the investigation, thus he'll be aware of the advancement of it and all the more able to assure both the Raymond girls' protection. Plus, living with them while they can possibly remember important details regarding the murders is also playing in their favor." Callie stayed calm and cordial, even granting Harvon and her acolyte a small smile in the end.

A smile which I was sure was genuine too because that woman was too kind to fake anything. Harvon looked like she was looking for more arguments when Kensley suddenly started speaking.

"That's just not right. She's a young woman and he's a young man, there's bound to be some—" Callie cut off his sputtering by holding a perfectly manicured hand up.

"I'll stop you right there Mr Kensley, before you go and say something highly inappropriate in front of a nine year old child. If you don't believe yourself capable of reigning in your hormones in front of a beautiful woman, I advise you work on it outside of your job hours and don't project your own insecurities onto others. That being said, if you hint at something like that again in front of my clients or behind their backs, I will not only sue your for defamation but also for sexual harassment. Keep your personal thoughts to yourself."

My own mouth hung open as I looked at her. Damn. Maddox was right, she was good.

I chanced a look at him and he looked right back at me, a smug smile hanging onto his pink, plump lips. His eyes screamed "I told you so" but the tips of his ears were burning red, probably from what Kensley was implying.

The latter looked positively livid, like he'd either faint or shit himself in front of everyone. Possibly both. That served as a good reminder to never piss Callie off because even though she looked regal with her all pink attire, she was a real killer at her job.

I was suddenly nervous, feeling like a fraud, because this conversation stirred something quite ugly in me. Callie had so much faith in us living together without crossing lines, but I couldn't say the same about myself. I had no idea how this was going to turn out, no idea whether or not I would be able to resist the pull I felt towards Maddox and that scared the shit out of me.

“Are you okay?” Maddox’ voice brought me back to the present.

My head snapped towards him so fast I thought I gave myself whiplash. He was watching me, a worried expression etched on his beautiful face. I nearly sighed aloud at how perfect he looked with his hair tousled and his lips wet.

“Yeah,” I squeaked before clearing my throat and trying to compose myself, “Just lost in my thoughts, you know? I have a lot on my mind.”

“Tell me about it.” His eyes went back on the road as we cruised through the streets of Lakestone.

Valentina was asleep in the backseat of his car, I was riding shotgun and Selena and Adam, his two colleagues, rode in a car behind us. Callie had texted us saying she had a meeting with the DA later in the afternoon so he could give her a temporary decision before we went to court in two weeks.

My eyes caught sight of a familiar oak tree and I shuddered as I recalled where we were going. I had no idea if I was ready to set foot in that house again, too many bad memories were attached to it. Not knowing how my mind would react to being there again was scary.

“Stop thinking too hard about it.” Again, his voice startled me. “It’s just a house, nothing in it can hurt you anymore.”

Our eyes collided before his warm and calloused hand engulfed my much smaller one. On a spur, I turned it around and spread my fingers so that they could entangle with his. I heard his small intake of breath, before he squeezed my hand, still staring into my eyes like he could see right through the depths of my soul.

His hand never left mine as we parked outside of the three stories house that never truly felt like a home. Chills went through me as I stared at it. From the outside, it looked so perfect that years from now, when Valentina and I would be far away from here, nobody would have a clue about the crimes that were committed inside it.

Right then, images of red splattered everywhere assaulted my brain. I could hear blood curdling screams and feel the tears mixing with the blood on my cheeks. Much like that first night in the hotel room, I could feel myself starting to spiral out of control. My breaths were coming out ragged, a deafening sound resonated inside my throbbing head, the nasty voice inside my brain was screaming at me to let go of whatever remained of my sanity.

But I didn't. I didn't let go, I didn't spiral, because the hand holding mine was somewhat anchoring me into the real world and making sure I would not be sucked into my own brain. It reminded me I wasn't alone, that my sister was counting on me, and that, maybe, my life mattered to one other person aside from her, now.

"Breath, Sofia." I nodded absentmindedly, his hand never leaving mine, as we sat in silence for a few minutes. Maddox never spoke during that time, like he knew that I needed time to work up the courage to go back where the most terrifying night of my life took place.

Too bad he couldn't pass on that information to his colleagues.

I was startled out of my thoughts when a hard knock resonated on his window, both our heads turned in that direction as Selena stood there, gazing at our joined hands. I heard Maddox curse under his breath before he let go of me like I was burning him. My heart felt pinched right then but I understood why he did it, I understood how him holding my hand might have looked… suspicious, to outsiders.

Maddox cleared his throat and avoided my eyes. He avoided my eyes when I was dying to find his.

He opened his door and Selena took a step backward, letting him out. I could feel her questioning gaze on the side of my head as I stared at the big oak tree in front of me. I gulped, counted to five and finally went out myself. Adam was just closing his car door, walking to Selena's side, oblivious to everything.

"Valentina is asleep, keep an eye on her while Sofia and I get their things."

Maddox's tone was calm and composed, like he'd been thinking of what to say, thinking of how to maintain an act of professionalism in front of his colleagues.

"Why don't I go with Sofia?" I froze at Selena's voice.

I didn't want to go in there with Selena. I didn't feel like going with anyone other than the pain in my ass cop standing in front of me who looked like he'd break his jaw from the force with which he was grinding his teeth.

"I'll only go in there with Maddox." I sounded way more confident than I felt.

I didn't want to get him in trouble but he was the only cop I trusted. Fuck that, he was the only person I trusted right now. Selena looked like she was going to speak, then thought better of it, and halfheartedly nodded, kissing her teeth and making her discontentment known. I couldn't bring myself to care.

"Don't be too long. We'll keep watch of sleeping beauty over there." Adam nodded to the backseat of Maddox's car where my sister was still in deep slumber.

There was something in his eyes as he looked at her. Sadness, longing, nostalgia, his somewhat familiar green eyes were drowning in those. I didn't feel totally comfortable leaving her with virtual strangers, but I knew Adam wouldn't let anything happen to her.

"Come on." With one last look at a suspicious Selena, I followed behind Maddox as he opened the front door and ducked under the yellow crime scene tape.

My breath caught in my throat as soon as we were standing in the foyer. So many memories clouded my head at the moment. Some good, most bad, but none making me want to stay here longer than needed.

"Let's start with Valentina's room. Just take some clothes and some things you know she loves or will bring her comfort. The rest of your stuff will be delivered to my place once the DA approves of you moving in while we wait for trial." I nodded at his instructions and led him upstairs.

We were supposed to have the DA's temporary decision regarding our situation by the end of today. Callie told us not to worry, that she was working her magic and to trust her. We didn't have any other option so I went with it, but as the hours passed with no news from her, I started to lose hope.

Maddox climbed silently behind me, and with each step I took, I could feel my heart beat faster and faster inside my chest. Like it was seconds away from coming out of it. Once we reached the top of the stairs, I stopped. I knew I needed to be brave, but it proved more and more difficult. My eyes closed, I pictured Valentina's face, her mischievous smiles and innocent eyes. I had to do this. For her.

A strong hand came to rest on my waist and my breath hitched, eyes flying open. A hard warmth emanated from my back, where the only things between me and Maddox were our clothes. In the almost five years we've known each other, this is the closest we've ever stood. My breaths were still coming out ragged but for a totally different reason. A reason that scared me as much as it excited me.

I was *turned on*.

Dios mio. What kind of woman was I for feeling this way when he was only trying to help and reassure me? Guilt weighted in the pit of my stomach. How could I feel something even akin to excitement while in that house?

"You got this." He whispered encouragingly, his breath fanning my ear. "It's just a house. Nothing in it can harm you anymore." Maddox drew circles on the exposed skin where my top had ridden up. It was soothing, it was intimate and felt familiar even though it was the first time he touched me this way. Like he was always meant to do it "Say it."

I gulped at the authority in his voice. I'd always had trouble respecting figures of authority in my life, Maddox being maybe the only exception, but something in me yearned to obey him whenever he used that tone.

"It's just a house. Nothing in it can harm me anymore." I whispered back.

"Good girl." If I thought I'd been turned on earlier, it was nothing compared to what these two words did to me.

I had given up denying how attracted I was to Maddox a long time ago, at least to myself, but at that moment I was actually scared he'd see right through me.

My fight or flight response kicked in and I all but ran to Valentina's room.

***

"Ready to go?" Maddox' voice startled me as I knelt next to my bed, ready to retrieve the reason why I agreed to come here in the first place. Reaching a hand to my erratic heart, I nodded slightly.

"Just a minute." Gripping the bedding, I held it up and bent over to get the small box hidden under my bed.

Once I had my hands on it, I sat on my haunches and stared at it for a beat. Flowers were engraved into the wood: roses, dahlias and jasmine. It was old, had probably seen better days and a thick layer of dust had settled right on top, but it didn't change a thing in what it meant for me.

That was mama's old jewelry box, she'd given it to me when I was nine, and since then it had become my treasure trunk. It was full of memories, of trinkets, and pictures from my childhood.

This box contained my identity.

All safely locked away, for my eyes only.

"What's that?" his voice was way closer than it was when he arrived.

"Nothing. It's stupid." I did my best to hide the box with my body, I didn't want him to see it, I didn't want him to think it was childish.

"Nothing that brings such a big smile to your face could ever be stupid." I hadn't even noticed I'd been smiling while looking at it, and his saying that got my heart warm. "Is it a treasure box?" He knelt next to me, a small smile grazing his lips.

I could feel myself grinning at the fact that he guessed what was in there. "It is. Mama made it herself, she gave it to me when I was little. It used to be hers."

"Woah, your mom made this?" He looked truly impressed as he took in the intricate designs, the flowers swirling around each other, petals and leaves on the corners. He let his fingers follow the engravings. "I had no idea Marcella Raymond was an artist."

My smile dimmed at that, and I worked hard not to let it fall completely. "Yeah, well, there are a lot of things nobody knew about her. She wasn't just the mayor's wife."

Suddenly angry but not wanting to take it out on Maddox because it wasn't his fault, I took the box and stood up. Walking to where my bag was laying on my bed, I stuffed it in there and zipped it close, ready to get the fuck away from here.

"I'm sorry if I offended you. That was never my intention, Sofia."

"It's okay, you did not offend me. I— it's hard talking about her, about them." I couldn't meet his eyes, focusing on wrapping up instead.

"I understand. I'll be there if you ever need to, though." At that I looked up, our eyes locking, but words wouldn't come out so I only nodded.

We made our way downstairs, me holding a small bag as he carried my and Valentina's suitcases. As we arrived in the foyer, I couldn't help but stop and stare at the small pictures that were arranged on the small dresser right in front of the door. It was the first thing you saw when you entered the house and had several picture frames laying on top.

Some of mom and dad together, some with all of us as a family, even a couple of only me and Valentina. In all of them we looked happy, smiling for the camera. Mom had insisted we had family pictures to hang in our house and dad had agreed because it looked good on paper too, especially during campaigns, he hated pictures otherwise.

"You should probably take some of that too. For Valentina, I'm sure she'd like to see them."

"No." I looked away from the frames and into Maddox's eyes. "I don't want her to see pictures of them yet, she's not ready." He frowned so I sighed and explained, "Valentina has anxiety, Maddox, she's just coming around to the idea of them being gone forever, I know seeing their pictures will just trigger her. Hell, it's this close to sending *me* into a crying fit. I'd rather just speak of them for now, and work our way up as we go." I bit my lip, looking away.

I could see understanding dawning in on him and he nodded. "I get it. You're probably right."

Relief spread through my chest when he didn't press the issue and as we made our way out, I hoped against hope this was the last time I had to set foot in there.

***

The day went on fast. After we got our things from the house and went shopping for some first necessity items we lacked at the hotel, it was already late afternoon so we ditched Selena and Adam and decided to get something to eat, just the three of us. It felt oddly good to share a meal with Maddox and my sister. Not awkward at all, quite the opposite, much like we all belonged together. Like a family. Valentina kept on talking about her new friend Sameera, about her favorite cartoons, and how she couldn't wait to get back to the hotel and take a bath with the new fluorescent bath bomb we'd bought at the store.

Or maybe I should say, the bath bomb *Maddox* bought for her, as he categorically refused to let me pay. In all honesty, my ego was bruised by his refusal, but I kept my mouth shut because I knew I was limited when it came to money and I truly wanted Valentina to have whatever she needed. Of course, a bath bomb was not essential, but it was the comfort I knew it would bring her that made me accept Maddox paying for our stuff. She didn't stop there of course, she bought a new shampoo, conditioner, shower gel and everything rose scented because she, I quote, *''could not take the hotel stuff anymore''*. Maddox also got her all types of cute hair ties and clips because they were, I quote again, *"too cute not to buy and she would look amazing with those."*

It was dark by the time we came back to the hotel. We found Justin standing guard in front of our door, as always, only today he looked a bit distraught. As soon as he saw us, he jumped and came to us.

"Detective Brooks, I need to talk to you, there was a problem earlier with the journalists." He gulped and Maddox looked at me, gesturing to our room with a small sign of his head.

"Go ahead, I'll be right with you." I hesitated, wanting to hear what Justin had to say, but ended up listening to Maddox because I didn't want whatever the officer had to say to freak Valentina out.

Grabbing my sleeping little sister from Maddox's arms, I stepped into our room. It was dark and the only source of light came from the bright moon shining through the window. I decided not to turn any light on and just laid Valentina down on the bed.

As I worked on taking off her shoes, an eerie feeling overcame me, I felt like I was being watched. My blood ran cold and I looked around, but everything seemed in order. Just like we'd left it earlier today.

Once her shoes were on the floor, and her coat was at the foot of the bed, I sighed, putting my earlier feelings on the fact that I was stressed since we still hadn't heard back from Callie. Maybe a bath would help me relax too.

I got up, walked to the bathroom and closed the door after me. Not wanting the lights to be too bright, I put them on dim and faced the mirror, my hands clutching the hem of my shirt.

That's when I froze, eyes wide, heart in my throat, because, guess what? I realized I was not alone in the room.

A man stood behind me with a black hood on, hiding his face.

I shrieked at the top of my lungs before fear could make me speechless.

It seemed like monsters never truly died after all.

# 9

# IDEAL

## MADDOX

"We did our best to keep them out but some came in as guests and actually paid for a room so we couldn't—" an ear shattering scream echoed in the halls, effectively cutting off whatever Justin had to say.

My whole body seemed to freeze as soon as I realized it came straight from the girls room. Before I could even comprehend what was happening, I was there, busting the door open with no second thought, gun aimed straight in front of me and ready to shoot at whoever was hurting them.

On the bed, startled awake, eyes wide and lips trembling in fear sat Valentina. She clearly was woken up by the scream, which meant it came from Sofia. I found it a little hard to breathe as I looked the room over but she was nowhere in sight. My heart was torn between taking Valentina in my arms to reassure her and finding her sister.

Glass shattering in the bathroom drew my attention there. Behind me, I could hear Justin and other officers entering. I didn't wait for any of them to spot me and just ran straight to the bathroom, pushing the door open and stopping at the sight that greeted me.

In all of my twenty-eight years of living, never once had I experienced true, soul crushing, blood curdling fear. I had a pretty good childhood, a great family, friends, I was never bullied or in any type of real danger, so I had no reason to be afraid of anything, really.

Yet as I pushed the bathroom door open that night, and saw a hooded man holding Sofia to his chest with a hand on her mouth while she was fighting to get out of his hold, I was terrified.

I was terrified because I didn't know if he was armed, I didn't know who he was, I didn't know if in the five minutes the girls were alone in their room he had had time to hurt them in any way. That scared the shit out of me.

When she saw me, Sofia's eyes widened and something akin to relief shone in them, but it was really short lived and fright soon came to replace it again.

As soon as her assailant saw me gun in hand, he lifted both hands in the air. My heart started beating a little faster, thinking he was gonna pull a weapon out of his sleeve, but he was actually just putting his hands in the air as a way to signal he was not a danger to us. Then one hand gripped his hoodie and he pulled it over his head, showing us his face.

That's when I realized he was speaking. His lips were moving but I couldn't hear anything over the deafening sound blaring in my head. I was aware of movement behind me as two officers came into the room and aimed their guns at him.

As soon as she realized he was not holding her anymore, Sofia all but ran to me, encircling my waist with her arms and burrowing her head against my chest. My left arm came down, hugging her even closer to my body, while the other one was still holding my gun up, pointing at the son of a bitch who was responsible for this whole mess. I could breathe a little easier, fear giving way to white hot anger.

"Who the fuck are you?" I surprised myself with how much venom was in my voice.

"I'm sorry, I'm sorry! Don't shoot! I just wanted to talk to her!" This pathetic excuse for a man was still holding both hands in the air, looking even more frightened than Sofia did two seconds ago.

"Answer the fucking question if you don't want my bullet in your motherfucking throat!"

Voice trembling, he fell to his knees, "My name is Andrew Harrison, I work for The Lakestone Tribute! My ID is in my back pocket!" My nostrils flared as soon as I heard his words.

Fucking journalists. Justin was telling me all about their latest scheme right before we heard Sofia screaming.

A couple of them tried to sneak into the hotel, they were escorted out and caused some ruckus. Apparently three others had taken advantage of the security staff being busy and came in undetected to get a room. I would bet good money this fucker was one of them.

I nodded at Justin and the latter put his gun away and went to search for his ID. He did find it in his back pocket and shook his head, letting me know what he was saying was true.

Slowly, I pulled my gun down but feeling Sofia's trembling body against mine made me want to shoot him for traumatizing her more than she already was.

"What the fuck are you doing here, Andrew? Don't you understand the meaning of trespassing? Of fucking privacy?" Nothing made me more angry than someone not respecting others' boundaries.

"N-no, none of that! I just wanted to ask Miss Raymond some questions." He had the decency to look ashamed.

"By breaking into her room and startling her in the bathroom? By putting your fucking hands on her without her consent and trying to smother her screams?" I swear to God I was gonna lose it.

"It's your fault! You wouldn't even let us near them! We're just trying to do our jobs! She started screaming before I could even talk!"

"*Hijo de puta*!" Sofia's weight on my side disappeared as she launched herself at him, hands fisted and ready to pound his mouth.

That startled me. She was screaming and scratching Harrison's face, Justin moved just in time, before she could do real damage to the journalist, grabbing her by the waist and hauling her away from him. For some reason, I didn't like his hands on her, so I stepped in, leading her closer to the door, but she wouldn't stop wriggling, trying to get out of my grasp.

Sofia kept insulting Harrison in Spanish, her hands flying everywhere, eyes red with tears, her voice hoarse from screaming. I'd never seen her so mad before, but I knew her anger probably emanated from fear.

That son of a bitch must have scared the shit out of her, reminding her of a night I was sure she would much rather forget.

"Me cago en la puta madre, cabrón! ¡Vete al diablo!"

Instead of staying put or even trying to flee, Harrison grabbed his camera, which was hanging around his neck. I could see it now that Sofia wasn't in front of him anymore. He started taking pictures of her as she continued yelling, probably thinking about the piece of shit article he'd be able to write with that.

"Son of a bitch."

I pushed Sofia behind me and took hold of the camera, smashing it on the floor. It took superhuman strength to keep myself from knocking the fucker out. When I punched that journalist a few days ago for daring to touch Sofia, Chief Piersons almost ripped me a new one. Adding a second name to that list would probably get me off the case and I couldn't risk that.

Harrison didn't take well to his toy being destroyed, and started complaining and threatening to sue me. That man was ridiculously too sure of himself and clearly didn't know anything about law if he thought me destroying his camera would encompass him trespassing and assaulting a victim, who by the way, was under police protection.

"Get him to the station, I don't want to see his face anymore." Justin and Ian, the second officer who came in earlier, obeyed without question, handcuffing the scumbag and taking him out of my sight.

Sofia calmed down a little, she wasn't yelling anymore, but her breathing still wasn't back to normal if her heaving chest was any clue.

Once I heard the door close after the officers, I took her head between my hands, making her look up at me. I couldn't help assessing her, scared she'd been hurt in a way I hadn't noticed before.

"Are you okay?" She gave a small nod and sniffled quietly. Her hands gripped my wrists as she held on tight.

"I- I thought he was back." Her eyes wouldn't meet mine, they were still wide and staring into nothingness, like she was replaying memories from that night. "I thought he came back for Val-" she stopped and looked at me, panicked, "Valentina!" She dodged me and sprinted out of the bathroom.

I followed her, and felt myself starting to panic when I noticed the little girl was not on the bed where I left her. Sofia's eyes were taking in the room, looking everywhere for her sister. Finally, she spotted her in the farthest corner from the door, on the floor with her knees brought closer to her chest and her little hands hiding her face, in a perfect fetal position. She ran to her.

"Fuck" I cursed and walked closer while still giving them space.

I didn't know how Valentina would react to me, I was tall and broad-shouldered, I had no idea if seeing a big man would trigger her or not right now. I had no idea what was going through her head but what I did know was that it would break my heart if she was suddenly afraid of me.

"Rosita, look at me." Sofia was kneeling in front of the little girl, trying to pry her hands away from her face to no avail.

Valentina's little body was shaking like crazy, she was silently crying and trying to block out the world surrounding her. I felt so useless at that moment, knowing there was nothing I could do to erase the last half hour from her mind.

"Porfa, mi amor, mírame." I didn't speak Spanish other than for a few words, and prior to today I'd never heard Sofia use the language either.

It was common knowledge that Marcella Raymond was from Mexico, but she didn't have even the slightest accent, and I'd never heard her speak Spanish before. So hearing Sofia speak so fluently and effortlessly, I found myself at loss for words. I thought I knew her fairly well, but it seemed like she'd never cease to surprise me.

Valentina finally looked up and after a second or two of staring at her like she was trying to get out of her own head, she launched herself at Sofia. I felt like I could breathe a little easier knowing Sofia finally got to her sister, knowing Valentina was not spiraling back into unwanted memories anymore.

The little girl started speaking fast, still in Spanish, words mixed with sobs and all the while, Sofia patiently nodded and wiped the tears off her cheeks. When she was done, they both hugged tight and I suddenly felt like I was invading a really private moment between sisters. I was ready to get up and go when Valentina's gaze suddenly fell on me.

She didn't say anything and simply reached a hand out to me, surprising me. I didn't wait long before grasping it in my much bigger one, she pulled me to them until I was kneeling and hooked her right arm around my neck while still hugging her sister with her left one. I could feel her calm breath on the side of my cheek and it brought inexplicable peace to my soul. Sofia's head fell on my shoulder and as her free hand found mine I squeezed it.

Having them both in my arms, where I could protect them and give them the affection they deserved but so obviously lacked, it felt right.

It felt like home.

That's what made me say 'fuck it.'. They were not staying in this hotel another night.

"Take your stuff, girls, you're moving in with me tonight." Both sisters looked up at me after that, surprise shining in their similar eyes.

The DA's decision be damned, I was done waiting.

***

I turned around as soon as I locked the door to my condo. Justin and Ian were still standing guard outside because I didn't trust that some journalist wouldn't try something again.

Sofia was holding her sister's hand while they both took in their surroundings. I found myself doing the same, trying to see through their eyes.

The foyer gave into a big open space where you could see the open kitchen and living room, and obviously the huge bay windows with a view on the lake. I could see Valentina eying the huge TV my cousin Mateo had insisted I buy when I moved in— all because *watching football on that thing would be fucking awesome*, as he said. I could tell from the look on her face that she was already thinking about which *Disney* movie she'd like to watch on it first. She was seriously obsessed with those.

"Your house is really big." Valentina's little voice pulled me out of my thoughts and I smiled.

It wasn't bigger than their two stories in the suburbs but it was a great condo. My parents owned the building so as soon as I finished college and came back to Lakestone, this beauty was waiting for me. It had four bedrooms, one of which I had converted into an office and three baths, lots of closet space and a huge kitchen which I never used because 1) I couldn't cook and 2) I never had time to.

"Thanks, Pretty Girl." I grinned at her and she grinned back, loving the nickname. "Come on, I'll show you to your rooms."

Grabbing the suitcases we'd taken from their house earlier today, I walked through the corridor leading to the two guest rooms. Entering the first one, I deposited the suitcases next to the closet, and turned around, looking at them.

"Here you go, that's Valentina's room, mine and Sofia's are the doors right in front of you, in case you ever need to find us during the night." The little girl nodded at my instructions but a frown still marred her baby face. "I think it's better if you two sleep together tonight. Again, I'll be in the room right in front of yours if you need anything, okay?" Valentina looked instantly relieved but she kept biting her lip like something was bothering her.

"Thank you Maddox. I can never thank you enough for what you're doing for us." Sofia's eyes shone with sincerity as she looked at me.

My throat felt tight, seeing her so vulnerable did something to my heart, I had to say.

"You don't have to thank me, Sofia. I'd do anything to help you guys."

Silence filled the room as we stared at each other, communicating without words. I was beginning to think I'd do *anything* for these girls. They grew on me more and more every day, their bond with each other slowly shifting to make space for me. Being with them almost felt like spending time with family.

Clearing my throat because I realized I was still staring at her while lost in thoughts, I scratched my neck and gestured to the door next to the closet.

"You can shower in there, there should be towels under the sink cabinet, I'll go and make you something warm to drink before you sleep, okay?" They both nodded and Valentina then cocked her head to the side.

"Do you have hot chocolate, Mads?" I smiled at the nickname she insisted on giving me earlier today.

She said since I called her Pretty Girl she had to have a nickname for me too. I'd suggested Maddie, since it's what my friends from college called me, but she said no because she'd heard Callie use it and she wanted something that was *only hers*. So Mads it was.

"For pretty girls like you? Of course I do." I bopped her nose and she beamed at me.

I could swear I saw a hint of a blush on her cheeks. She was too cute for her own good. I was more and more fond of that little girl everyday, my attachment to her growing almost as quick as my attraction for her sister.

It took me about thirty minutes to change into my pajamas and make the hot chocolates. I put whipped cream and all the toppings I could find in my cupboards on it—marshmallow, sprinkles and caramel. I made two glasses and brought them to the girls' room. Valentina was already showered and in her pajamas, waiting under the covers and she squealed when she saw me entering with the two cups. Just as she was taking her drink from my hand, Sofia came out of the adjoining bathroom, and our eyes collided.

I swear I almost spilled the beverage on the white bedding because all she was wearing was a white oversized tank top with some satin shorts. Her long black hair was damp, falling around her shoulders, leading to her breasts, which were obviously free of a bra. I gulped.

"It's hot." My eyes widened in embarrassment, "I-I mean you're hot— no! The drink, I made you hot chocolate, *that's* what's hot. Oh God." I looked down and all but thrusted the drink in Sofia's face.

My eyes found Valentina who was giggling at my predicament, whipped cream all over her upper lip, giving her a cute little mustache. I found myself smiling despite the fact I could feel my ears getting hot. They always gave the fact that I was fucking blushing away.

When I felt warm fingers wrapping around mine, taking the cup from me, I looked up. Due to the fact that Sofia was pretty small, I was at eye level with her tits from where I was sitting on the bed. I struggled not to stare and looked into her pretty eyes instead.

She seemed amused and mouthed a 'thank you' as she silently took the cup from my hands. I could feel myself getting hot and prayed to God I would not be sporting a hard on before I could get to my room. I did not need them to think they'd just moved in with a pervert.

Valentina moved around, making room for her sister and the latter just slipped beneath the covers next to her before taking a sip of her drink and moaning in delight.

"*Mhh*, I had no idea how much I needed some sugary comfort right now. Thank you for this." I simply nodded, not trusting my voice at the moment.

I all but jumped up, ready to get the fuck away from the temptress in front of me.

"I'll leave you to it, then. Just put the cups on the nightstand when you're done, I'll clean everything in the morning. Good night." I gave them a small smile before starting towards the door. I was almost out when Valentina's small voice stopped me.

"Wait, Mads!" I turned around and saw both mine and Sofia's attention were on the little girl.

Valentina suddenly looked shy, she bit her lips just like she did earlier, trying to gather the courage to speak.

"What's up, pretty girl?" I frowned, sharing a worried look with Sofia.

"I—" She put her almost empty cup on the nightstand and started fiddling with her hands. "Would you… would you sleep with us please? Just tonight."

"Valentina!" Sofia reprimanded her while I just stood there, stunned. I didn't know what to say to that. "That's inappropriate, *Tina*, you can't ask Maddox things like that."

Seeing Valentina being chastised pinched my heart, but at the same time, I agreed with Sofia. Getting as close as I felt to them was dangerous enough, if anyone found out about how much they've come to mean to me, I'd be fucked and probably taken off the case. Sleeping in the same bed was crossing a line.

"But Mads protects us, Dada! He said he'd chase the monsters away too." Valentina was still distressed from what happened earlier, I knew it would take time for her to forget or feel comfortable at night again.

"*I* chase the monsters away, Valentina, *me*. I told you that already, I'll always protect you against the monsters." I could see Sofia was getting emotional speaking of that, like she was reminiscing.

"But who will protect *you* from them!" Everything went silent after Valentina's outburst.

Sofia's eyes were wide and shining with unshed tears while her mouth parted but no words came out. It was rare for her to wear her emotions out on her sleeve like that, but I think she was taken absolutely off guard with what her sister just said.

Pain was etched on her face, her eyes haunted by the events of the past, of that night where everything changed for both of them. I didn't know what was going on exactly, the two seemed to be having a silent conversation, but they both seemed on the verge of crying so I decided to intervene.

"Okay. I'll sleep with you." Sofia's head whipped in my direction, surprised, while Valentina's face was etched with relief. "Just for tonight, just for you to see that there will be no more monsters here."

Her lower lip was trembling a little, clearly trying to keep herself from crying and she nodded wordlessly.

I could see Sofia was not fond of the idea, just like me, but she didn't say anything else and just put her cup on the nightstand. I cleared my throat and turned off the light, the only source of light now coming from the large bay window. Valentina shuffled until she could glue herself to Sofia's right, leaving the latter in the middle of the bed.

I cleared my throat, suddenly realizing what I had just agreed to do. I was going to spend the night next to Sofia Raymond. The girl who seemed to be trusting me more than anyone else in her life right now. The girl I saw at her most vulnerable state, and still couldn't get out of my head.

My heart beat harder, I swear we could all hear it. Gulping loudly, I got under the cover, the farthest I could be from her while still remaining on the bed. It would be okay if we weren't touching. Sofia laid just as rigidly on the bed next to her sister, her arms were stiffly along her body, and was staring at the ceiling. As I was trying to do the same, while still trying to control my breathing, a little head suddenly popped up from beside Sofia.

"Hey, what's wrong?" Valentina was only nine, so obviously she didn't understand what was the big deal, yet she still noticed something was off from how rigid her sister and I both held ourselves. "Why aren't we cuddling?" It was so innocently asked, I almost chuckled.

See, that's what I liked most about kids. Valentina's soul was so pure that she didn't see anything wrong with us all sleeping together. To her, it was just a big sleepover with the people she cared for.

"Tina!"

I could tell it was not usual for Sofia to reprimand her sister because Valentina's eyes widened in surprise and filled with tears almost instantly at her tone. It was a hard night for both sisters, with everything that happened in the hotel, then them suddenly moving in—without the DA's support at that, since we still hadn't heard back from Callie. I got it, Sofia was on edge, Valentina needed comfort, their emotions were all over the place. I truly got it. So I tried to ease it, make it better.

As silence stretched the room I slowly edged closer to Sofia, until my pajama clad thigh bumped her naked one. I could hear her small intake of breath, and when I rested my hand on her hip, turning her slightly so I could spoon her, she looked at me with wide, questioning eyes.

"What are you doing?" She sounded out of breath, just as much as I felt.

My gaze strayed to Valentina for a second, she looked at me with hopeful eyes which only made me more sure of my decision. I was a grown ass man, I could control my body. It was only inappropriate if we made it that way. Plus, we were both fully dressed, Sofia laid between her sister and I, and with how tired we all were from this day of hell, I'd say Valentina would be out in a matter of minutes, which is when I'll go to my own bed for the night.

"Cuddling." I breathed.

She looked like she wanted to say something but then took a look at the watery smile her sister was giving us and decided against it. It took us some time, finding a position where we were all comfortable and where Sofia and I were not pressed too tight against each other but we eventually did.

I was spooning her, doing my best to keep my dick from pressing into her ass, my hand on her waist, while Valentina used her sister's breasts as pillows. Small fingers wrapping around mine on Sofia's waist made me open my eyes, and they came in contact with Valentina.

The little girl was smiling up at me, eyes droopy with sleep. "Good night, Mads. Night night, Dada."

Something inside my chest felt tight, like my whole life truly made sense for the first time at that moment right then.

"Good night baby." Sofia's whisper could barely be heard, so I followed through with a "Good night, pretty girl."

"I love you guys." Was the last thing Valentina murmured before succumbing to the call of sleep.

I never felt more at peace than I did at that moment. It was like I was born to take care of those girls, like it was destiny.

# 10

# TEMPTATION

## SOFIA

You know that moment right before you wake up? When you're still not fully out of the realm of dreams yet not into the real world either? Yeah, that moment. That moment was always when I felt more at peace.

I could pretend my parents were still here, could pretend mama and I were making *enchiladas* in the kitchen while papa and Valentina were laughing in the living room. I could pretend Maddox would come by and eat dinner with us, talking soccer with papa and complimenting mama's cooking. I could pretend I was majoring in art history like I'd always wanted and not fucking political science like dad wanted me to. I could pretend I had someone other than my sister to count on, to care for, and to love.

What I loved most about that moment between fantasy and reality, was that anything could happen, my past mixed with both my future and my dreams, giving me something I could never have but yearned for so deeply I could feel it in my soul.

Slowly coming to my senses, I felt something soft brush my stomach underneath my shirt. It felt good and warm, like a heating pad made of velvet. A low moan came out of me before I could do anything about it. My body was so relaxed, for the first time in forever. It was so warm under the thick covers as rays of sunshine seeped through the window and crashed directly on my face. Burrowing my head in the pillow beneath me, the scent of cedar wood assaulted my nostrils and I inhaled it like an addict.

That scent. It was familiar.

Just as I was trying to recall where I knew it from, the covers moved, a groan coming from behind me. I froze, dread pitting in my stomach, not daring to open my eyes as I could feel the panic seep into me for a second.

Then I remembered.

Last night, Valentina demanding we cuddle all together in one bed, Maddox and I agreeing to please her then Valentina falling asleep and us talking until the early hours of the morning, before succumbing to sleep ourselves. He was supposed to go, he was supposed to get back to his own bed. I guess he didn't.

I remembered his hands on my skin as he gripped my waist, his thumb drawing circles onto my hip, illicit goosebumps betraying the arousal gathering in the low of my stomach. I remembered his voice, hoarse from sleepiness, as he told me all about his childhood, about his parents and his sister and his cute niece.

He told me about his best friend Derek and all the troubles they put themselves into when they were younger, often resulting in the cops showing up. I called him out on that and he simply chuckled and squeezed my side a bit tighter than he had been up until that point. I think exhaustion made him reckless because he touched me more last night than he did in the whole time that I'd known him.

And I loved it, reveled in it, even. I was starved for his attention and I couldn't get enough of it.

It was a part of Maddox I had never seen before, that sleepy, reckless, almost boyish version of him. It was a part of Maddox I could see myself growing to love.

But I knew it wouldn't last, I was certain once morning came he would have been long gone, avoiding me as much as he could for the next few days because he would have seen our late night conversation as inappropriate.

Yet he didn't go. *God*, he didn't. He was still here, right behind me.

Maddox groaned again and that thing, that warmth on my stomach, I suddenly knew what it was.

His hand. Maddox Brooks' big hand was under my shirt, caressing my stomach and slowly making its way to my breasts.

My breath caught in my throat and I slowly opened my eyes, only to see that the spot where my sister had slept all night had been vacated. I would have freaked out if I couldn't hear the low hum of the TV coming from the living room. Of course she would have figured out how to work the television first.

A small gasp left me as his hand finally reached my breast and squeezed. I was frozen in place, waiting for the panic to hit, topple me over and grip me at the neck but nothing came. Nothing came because I knew it was Maddox, and I knew he would never hurt me. His steady breathing, his chest moving up and down against my back, told me he was sleeping, not even aware of what he was doing to me. I tried not to let that thought stir disappointment, in vain.

Then his fingers pinched my nipple and my eyes widened. Against my will, I whimpered, my body got even warmer if possible and I didn't know what to do.

I didn't know what to do because I was turned on. And that hit me way harder than I thought.

I mean, sure, I was attracted to him, that much I could not deny to myself, but the fact that I would let him touch me so intimately? That was new to me.

I was not a virgin, but my experience with sex was not good. Sex hurt, both mentally and physically and was more humiliating than anything to me.

Yet here I was, practically writhing as a sleeping Maddox pinched my nipples and massaged my breasts. I told myself that I should wake him up before it was too late, before he became aware of the warmth sipping between my legs, but then I heard it. A small intake of breath and a whispered curse.

"Fuck."

I should have noticed earlier that his breathing was not as steady, that he was waking up. But I didn't. I was too preoccupied by how he was making me feel, too preoccupied by his fingers strumming my nipple and my pussy begging me to bring my hand to it so I could finally find relief. It was too much.

Too much, too much, *too much.*

So I didn't even notice him waking up. I didn't even notice his erratic breathing or his hips pressing against my ass. The feeling of his hardening cock though, that I noticed.

I don't know how anyone wouldn't, it was really hard… to miss.

"Oh fuck." His hand froze on my breast, like he was just coming to his senses. We both remained frozen, not knowing what to do.

Or perhaps we did know what we had to do, but didn't want to do it. Perhaps he too knew that the best thing to do right then would have been to take his hand out of my shirt, apologize and get out of bed.

Perhaps I knew I should apologize too because I woke up first and felt what he was doing to me. Perhaps we both should get out of here and away from each other before things went any further, to the point where we wouldn't be able to blame sleep for our actions.

Perhaps.

But I was feeling so ravenous, so greedy that morning. For once in my life desire was flooding my stomach, my whole body was prickling with need. For him. For Maddox.

Tentatively, I undulated my hips, my ass grinding against his erection. We both let out a gasp simultaneously, the sensation even better than what I anticipated.

"What are you doing, Sofia?" I gulped, suddenly shy.

All I wanted was relief, for the ache between my thighs to finally relent. All I wanted was to feel him, hard and hot and out of breath. Once. Just once before we had to go back to the reality of our lives. I clearly wasn't thinking straight, my mind foggy with lust.

I knew it would come back to bite me in the ass. I knew if we did that there would be no going back to pretending there was no attraction between us— because I knew Maddox was attracted to me, now. Probably not in the way *I* was attracted to him, but at least physically.

I knew if we did this, it would make it so awkward to live together. Yet I didn't care, my mind was too hazy with desire.

"I need it, Maddox. Please." My voice came out so breathy, almost sultry. I heard him groan.

"We can't. Fuck, we can't."

But his hips ground onto me, his erection digging into my ass. I squeezed my thighs together, the force of his body rocking against mine added to my thighs rubbing together produced the most delicate brush against my clit. It was delicious.

Slowly, my hand found his under my shirt and I squeezed my breast over his hand.

"Shit, Sofia." He growled and suddenly, his hips moved faster against my ass. I squeezed harder, moving back with each thrust, while he played so delicately with my nipple. "You've got the nicest little tits. And those nipples, oh God…"

And I preened at the compliment, purring in delight as the movement of his hips coupled with his expert fingers made more wetness ooze out of me. I didn't recognize myself, didn't recognize him either— we were feral, desperate to come.

The dam which contained all those forbidden feelings, those forbidden thoughts I'd had for him all these years finally bursting open.

"Please." I moaned. "Please, make me come, Maddox. Please, just this once, to take the edge off."

I was aware of how desperate I sounded, like a bitch in heat. I knew how degrading it was for me to beg him to do these things to me. To make me come.

*God, I wanted him to make me come.*

But I didn't care. At that moment, I didn't care if I looked like a slut asking for it. For the first time in my life I didn't even think about it because I was too busy *feeling*.

"Please, Maddox, it's okay if it's through our clothes, right? It's okay."

I didn't know what to say to make him touch me anymore. I was willing to tell him just about anything so he'd make me come.

"Only through our clothes."

"Y-yes." My hips had a mind of their own and moved faster, inciting him to do the same.

"Fuck, Sofia." His free hand gripped my waist as he hovered slightly over me, thrusting against me.

I could feel the ridges of his hard cock through the flannel of his pants and the light fabric of my shorts. I never wore panties to bed because I thought they were uncomfortable and at that moment, I was thankful I didn't. I could feel everything and it was so good. He was not only grinding against me, he was fucking me through our clothes. And I loved every second of it.

But of course, greedy little thing that I was, I needed more.

More, more, more.

Nothing was enough when it came to him.

Moaning and thrashing my head against the pillow while he growled and pounded his hips against mine, seeking his release as much as needing mine. My hand left his on my breast and instead took hold of the one he gripped my waist with. Slowly, I brought it where I needed it most.

When he felt my heat through my pajama shorts, the rhythm his hips had taken got messed up, he visibly wasn't expecting me to do that.

"Sofia… We said through our clothes only."

"Yes. Yes. Through our clothes." I whimpered as he cupped my pussy with his big, veiny hand.

Technically my shorts separated it from my pussy, but the fabric was thin and it was slightly oversized so the shorts gaped around the crotch area. When I closed my eyes I could pretend we were skin to skin.

"I just need to… I just want to rub against it. It's so hard." Eyes drooping from need, I threw my head back.

It felt so good, having his hips working against my ass, the sensation of his erection against me, sending me grinding against his hand. When his thumb moved and pressed right on my clit through my shorts, I nearly lost it, my nails digging into his hand.

"Oh my God, yes. Yes, yes, yes!"

I squeezed my eyes shut, teeth digging into my lower lip to keep me from making more noise.

I knew it wasn't attractive, but the sensations he was eliciting in me made it impossible to be silent.

"Fuck, baby. I can feel you drenched through your shorts." I nodded absentmindedly, ready to apologize but he had just called me baby and that made me so out of breath.

I'd never gotten that before— sweet words during sex, or even out of it. Pet names were a myth to me.

"You're so fucking wet, Sofia. I need you to come, I won't last much longer."

Desperation was evident in his voice, and I ground harder against his hard, warm palm. We were both restless and desperate, like all the tension from those last few days had accumulated to finally break us. It was exhilarating and stiffening at the same time.

Then he did it.

Maddox pinched my clit through my shorts, *hard*, and I exploded.

The pleasure was so raw, so high, so unlike anything I'd ever felt before— even on the rare occasions when I touched myself, I had to bite the pillow to keep from screaming. The delicious pounding of his hips against my ass, the rubbing of his palm, all of that coupled with the sting on my clit, made me see stars.

Maddox followed closely. He groaned against my hair, his thrusts relenting until stopping completely. All we could hear in the room was our erratic breathings entangling, becoming one. His hand was still cupping my quivering pussy, my shorts must've been soaked through with the force of my orgasm. His softening cock was still wedged against my ass and at that moment— time just stopped.

But as the mist of desire started to disappear, it slowly dawned on me what we had just done.

We crossed a line, opened Pandora's box.

And there was no coming back from it.

***

## MADDOX

What the fuck happened?

What the actual fuck did we do?

My breaths were still coming out irregularly, chest moving up and down, and I could feel Sofia's doing the same against me.

My hands. Oh God. My hands were still on her.

One on her delicious little tits, pinching a more than lickable nipple between my index and thumb and the second… fuck. My second hand was right between her legs, pressed tight against her drenched cunt and sandwiched between her soft thighs. Her sleep shorts were made of a material so thin I swear I could feel her clit twitch against my palm.

I needed to get the fuck away from her because if I didn't? I was going to fuck her through the mattress. Fuck her until she couldn't stand or walk straight and that was definitely not on the list of things I should be doing.

Oh my *God* what did I do?

I swore to myself it wouldn't be a challenge living under the same room as Sofia. I gave my word to Callie and my mom for goodness sake.

And here I was, on their very first night at the apartment, having a sleepover with her in the same bed, cuddling her, spooning her from behind, letting her rub herself to orgasm on my fucking hand!

Guilt assaulted my stomach and forced me to wrench myself away from the little minx next to me. I literally jumped out of the bed and then almost ran to the bathroom door. I couldn't put enough space between us.

Mom and Callie aside, I couldn't believe I did this to *her*.

To Sofia.

The girl had just lost her parents, she survived an attempted murder and killed a man in self-defense. All within the same night. She was under so much pressure to make sure her sister was not taken away from her, she had to deal with fucking journalists breaking into her bedroom and CPS people breathing down her neck. And here I was basically molesting her in my sleep. Coming in my fucking pants from the force of my orgasm.

Fucking dammit, that was the best orgasm of my life.

I wanted her so much.

The first time I saw something in Sofia Raymond was three weeks before her eighteenth birthday.

The last time I arrested her.

It was nothing sexual or even physical, really. I just felt that pull to her, the urge to get to know her and to discover what was hiding behind a seemingly troubled girl. The need to help her had lingered ever since I first met her, but that night, it intensified ten folds.

She had been graffitiing an old building in the south side of town, and I'd gotten a call from the old lady living in the apartments right in front of it.

Honestly, it bummed me out to arrest her before she'd finished because what she had been painting was beautiful. It was a myriad of three different flowers of which I only recognized jasmine and roses. The last one was unfamiliar though, I wasn't sure I'd seen any flowers of that kind before, but it was just as beautiful.

So I waited in my car, on the side of the road until she was done. And then I took her to the station.

I felt so captivated with her that night. So drawn to that tiny girl with a big attitude who made several of my officers cry, that I realized I was attracted to something in Sofia Raymond. And it wasn't even physical, that would've been too easy. She was wearing one of her signature cargo, sneakers, with a cropped top, letting some skin at the top of her stomach show.

She was attractive, sure, only a liar would say otherwise, though I had never really looked at her before this whole debacle started. Now I saw how she had naturally smooth and long black hair, golden skin and eyes so lively just looking into them was like taking a breath of fresh air.

She had perky tits that were more on the smaller side but fuck if I didn't love that and her waist was small and narrow. She had the ass of a volleyball player, considering she'd played in high school.

Yet even with all that, it wasn't her body that made me realize there was something to see in Sofia Raymond.

It was her soul that had captured me and wouldn't let me go. She was a walking, talking contradiction, doing everything in her power to get her parents' attention but at the same time avoiding being home as much as she could. She could be so fucking rude and make me want to bang my head against a wall, yet at the same time I saw how gentle and lovely she was with her sister. She didn't respect authority but didn't indulge in bullying either. In fact, she hated bullies.

I arrested her once when she got in a fight with Andrew Barrymoore, the town's resident troublemaker, after he tagged a homophobic slur on the locker of another student. I don't even think she was friends with the victim, she just hated bullies.

See, Sofia Raymond was one thing I hadn't seen in another human being a long, long time: fair. And that was what drew me to her the most.

That painting she had been making that day, she seemed so passionate while working on it. She moved so gracefully as she worked on the mural, it looked like she was dancing. It just broke something in me, made me see her in another light. And just like right now, I almost drowned in guilt.

Feeling my hasty movements, the object of my thoughts turned around, hair whirling through the air as she looked at me with wide golden eyes. She looked so vulnerable at that moment, it sliced my heart in half.

I wanted to hurl, my stomach tightening. She trusted me, enough to sleep in the same bed as me to appease her sister, and here I was taking advantage of her weakened state. She was younger than me, thus more naive, and I was older and should've known better than to give in to my desires.

The urge to bang my head against a wall returned, stronger than ever.

"Maddox." She got up on her knees, started crawling off the bed and towards me. I couldn't have that.

"No. Please, just don't. Not now."

She stopped, eyebrows furrowing at my tone. I felt like such a fucking ass putting distance between us right after sharing something so intimate, but I had to. I fucking had to. For her, for Valentina, for the case. I owed it to her.

"I'm sorry, I never should've done that. It won't happen again."

I didn't let her answer and just dived into the bathroom adjacent to the room. Once inside and with the door locked, I leaned against it, releasing the breath I didn't know I was holding. I took some time to get my breathing in order and once it was, rubbed my mouth, a habit I took on when I was still a nervous and frustrated teen.

Only as my finger brushed against my lips, the sweet flavor of Sofia rested upon them. Heart beating so fast I was afraid she would hear it from the other side of the door, I slowly licked the stickiness off my lips. I couldn't help but groan, wishing I had taken a taste directly from the source.

I could see it already, Sofia lying down, her legs on either side of my face, smothering me with her thighs while I just dived in her pussy, licking and sucking at that taut little clit, her wetness running down her skin and down my face, creating a puddle on my sheets.

Fuck, what I would give to have that happen.

But it couldn't, of course, so I had to settle for pitifully licking my hand clean. There wasn't much of her on it, because most of her sweetness remained on her shorts, but it was still enough to keep me from running back to the bedroom and make her ride my face.

Mad at myself, I took my cum-stained clothes off and looked under the sink where I kept a pair of pajama bottoms for when Derek came to visit. That was his designated room whenever he came back to Lakestone.

Jumping in the shower, I resisted the urge to fist my half-hard cock, gritting my teeth and washing my cum off of my stomach. I hadn't come in my pants in ages, must've been around fourteen the last time that happened.

Angrily rubbing at my stomach, my dick was still weeping and begging for me to give it some kind of release— never mind that I came ten minutes ago, the minute my lips made contact with the remnants of Sofia's wetness on my hand, it was hard again.

As I was almost giving up and ready to fist it, the sound of shattering glass made me open my eyes wide.

I immediately shut off the shower and jumped out. Not bothering with a towel and straight up putting on my pants, I sprinted out of the bathroom. Sofia was nowhere to be found and I could hear her running down the hallway towards the living space, where the noise came from.

My erection was long forgotten, nothing made a hard-on go down like fear.

Valentina had been alone in the living room.

I ran in the direction of the noise, scared out of my life that something had happened to her.

When I finally reached the room, I saw Sofia crouched down in front of a crying Valentina and my heart froze.

"It's okay, Vale, it was an accident. Maddox will understand, baby." Sofia's soothing voice did nothing to calm the little girl down and she shook her head.

I was next to them in no time and got on my knees so I was more or less on eye level with Valentina.

"What wrong pretty girl? Are you okay?" My eyes asserted her body, looking for clues that maybe she had hurt herself somewhere, but luckily, no blood, no scratches and no bruises visible.

As she finally looked at me, her chubby cheeks red and wet with tears, her lips trembling with silent sobs, she shook her head.

"I- I'm so sorry, Mads." That was all she said before bursting into tears and jumping on me, wrapping her small arms around my neck and burrowing her head in my neck.

Over her shoulders, I looked at Sofia, putting aside the unease still unsettling my stomach at the memories of what had occurred earlier. She nodded at the kitchen, her gaze evading my own.

I looked and sure enough, there was the glass I had heard shatter.

Actually, I was surprised that my kitchen was still standing. There was food, flour, — what I thought was orange juice? Everywhere.

On the floor, a platter with two now-broken plates and what looked like scrambled eggs on them, some bread that hadn't been toasted laid not too far, and a mug filled with what looked like chocolate goo.

"Valentina wanted to surprise us with breakfast in bed," My gaze went back to Sofia, but hers was fixated on her little sister, who squeezed me a bit harder, as if to apologize. "But she lost her balance while trying to take the platter to us and— yeah."

Not being able to look at her any more than I already had, I returned to Valentina who was watching me with dread in her eyes and again, trembling lips.

"I-I'm so sorry. Dada says I'm not allowed to use the stove, so I baked everything in the microwave, it was too high though so I used a stool, then I wanted to do the same to get the platter from the island b-but I tripped a-a-and—"

Her little body was shaking from the force of her sobs. She looked so fucking afraid and vulnerable at that moment, it broke me.

"I-I didn't mean to break your plates, I'm so sorry! I know I deserve to be punished, I'm sorry."

I felt Sofia tense next to me, probably because she realized that since I was applying to be her legal guardian, discipline would also be on my list of responsibilities.

She didn't need to worry though, I had no intention of punishing Valentina, not now, over some fucking plates and glasses, and certainly not ever.

I caressed Valentina's hair away from her face, offering her a reassuring smile, "Hey, pretty girl, it's okay. I don't care about any of that stuff. You could break all my dishes and I still wouldn't be mad at you. I know it was an accident, please stop crying."

She didn't say anything and just hugged me tight for what felt like hours. I didn't move, just hugged her back and rubbed her back like I'd seen Sofia do it often to reassure her.

"I just wanted to thank you for helping us. And for protecting us from the monsters last night." She sniffled against my neck and it took all my strength not to burst into tears right then.

I, a twenty-eight year old man, was totally and utterly wrapped around that little girl's finger. I knew at that moment I would do everything to protect her. She had wormed her way into my heart in such a small amount of time, it was insane.

Valentina and I, we got each other somehow, her pain spoke to me, and I wanted nothing more than to erase it.

Knowing she had planned on thanking me for helping them after they were left alone in the world with no one to protect them? It broke my heart. Because a child should never have to thank anyone for protecting them. They were pure, unadulterated innocence and shouldn't have to suffer at the hands of corrupted adults.

Valentina Raymond was only nine, but her eyes were so much older.

"You never have to thank me for helping you, Valentina. I never want you to feel like you staying here relies on doing or—" I cleared my throat, my words clearly bearing a double meaning, one her sister would understand, "giving something in return. I want you here, and I will help you. Always."

I heard Sofia sniffle from beside me but I couldn't bear to look at her, knowing I'd want to take her in my arms and appease her if I saw her crying. I couldn't. I had to put distance between us.

"Thank you Mads." Valentina's whisper warmed my heart, and I swooped her in my arms before getting to my feet, making her squeal.

"How about we go out to eat breakfast huh? My dad used to take me to that diner right outside of town where they serve the best pancakes." I offered a small smile to the youngest Raymond sister and she responded in kind, nodding her head and clapping her hands.

Her excitement was dampened by the reality of the chaos surrounding us.

"But what about the mess?"

"We'll clean up faster and better once our bellies are full, don't you agree?" I smirked, pulling a strand of hair away from her face.

She grinned back and nodded, “I do. Pancakes always put me in a better mood to clean.” Mine and Sofia’s chuckles resonated around us.

“It’s a date, then. Let’s get pancakes.”

# 11

## REGRET

### MADDOX

It doesn't make any fucking sense." I threw the papers on the table, sighing and bringing a hand up to rub my face.

Adam sat in front of me, looking as dejected as I felt. This case was driving us nuts. There were no clue regarding the second guy, no fingerprints, no footprints, no hair, fucking *nothing*. It had been a week since the girls had moved in with me and we didn't have any fucking progress on the case.

"It's the perfect crime. Whoever that second guy was he planned every fucking detail." My partner sighed and slumped on his seat.

I hated the words perfect and crime being in the same sentence, but even I had to admit it was. The killer definitely thought it through. I gulped and looked at the time, the girls were probably asleep by now.

While we were out eating breakfast on their first day home, Callie called me saying the DA had given the green light regarding the girls moving in temporarily. Since their meeting had lasted well through the evening the day after she didn't want to bother us that late. So it was settled, the girls were officially living with me for the time being. Child Protection Services would be coming to check on us on random days to see if Valentina felt at ease in this new environment while we waited for the permanent settlement of her case.

"It's late, maybe we should head home." My attention was brought back to Adam who had taken off his glasses to rub the sleep off his eyes. I sighed again, knowing he was right.

Still, the feeling that something was escaping us kept nagging at me.

"You will go nowhere with a fried brain, Maddox, get home with the girls. Tomorrow is an important day, Lord knows they'll need you."

Tomorrow was Jack and Marcella Raymond's funeral. Jack's assistant actually took care of everything since Sofia wasn't in the right headspace to do anything. They barely even mentioned their parents except from some old memories here and there. When they did that, a huge smile usually took place on their faces, and Valentina's eyes sparkled with emotions as she watched her sister speak of them.

Yet Sofia didn't even want her to attend the ceremony, she said she didn't want the little girl to witness their parents being put in the ground. Plus, the paparazzis would be here to see her baby sister in a vulnerable state and that was just another reason why she didn't want Valentina to attend.

When I mentioned that attending their parents' funeral would give Valentina the closure she would need growing up, she eventually came around. Sofia was not an easy person to barter with, but she would do anything for her sister, so she eventually saw the sense in my words.

Things were tense between us ever since that morning after they first moved in. Sometimes I could still feel the warmth and weight of her body against mine at night, then I'd wake up, realize I was alone and spend the rest of the night just tossing and turning until exhaustion. I haven't had a good night's sleep since that first one with her.

The knowledge that she was so close to me yet so far away, that I couldn't touch her, that she probably hated me for the way I used and discarded her right away. All of that was eating at me.

I couldn't do anything about it though, so I avoided her, as much as I could. In fact, the only times she and I spoke were when Valentina was in the room, and our curt conversations all revolved around her. I couldn't risk being alone with her again and being unable to control myself.

Now that I'd had a taste of her, though, I wanted more, so much more. It physically hurt staying away.

"You're right. I'll go, just please let's start back from the beginning one last time, maybe we missed something."

Adam stared at me for some time before sighing and falling back down on his desk, grabbing the Raymond file.

"Okay, one last time then I'm fucking going home, you hear me? My wife is waiting for me." I nodded, used to his grumpy behavior by now. "The alarms and cameras were cut off around midnight and no alert was given to the security company. It's like they just ceased working. The intruders came through the back door which Sofia could have sworn she had locked after her but there's no sign of infraction. We went through the list of all the employees who had direct access to the house, but the list is short and all of them had rock hard alibis. The housekeeper, Gloria, was out of town for the weekend with her two sons and the maid, Emily was at a college party—"

"Are we sure about that? Could several people attest that she was there?" I cut him off as he read the files. He gazed up at me and gave me a bored look.

"It's the age of social media, Maddox. Several pictures of her were taken and posted on Instagram, look," he handed me a few printed screenshots of an instagram feed and indeed, the seemingly shy little maid seemed to be having the time of her life.

"Damn, she drank all that pint of beer?" The thing was the size of her head.

"Yup, impressive, huh? But non-consequential to our case." I nodded, the exhaustion of the day catching up on me.

"And those are the only two staff members with keys to the house. No fingerprints or footprints for that matter were found on the property, but the house was ransacked. Especially Mayor Raymond's office; they rummaged through it like they were looking for something specific."

"Has his assistant been through it yet? Does he know if something is missing and what it is?"

"He did go through it, but nothing was missing to his knowledge, which means they either didn't find what they came for or they did but it was something personal which the assistant couldn't have known about."

"Fuck, this is so fucking complicated." My hands tucked at my hair.

"It is. Especially since the first culprit doesn't have anything to do with the mayor. I don't even think they ever crossed paths."

I grabbed the file with our first man's infos on it and opened it.

"Harold Crawford, twenty nine, grew up in foster care in Ravenbridge, lived in a small trailer park whenever he was out of jail

— he was convicted and incarcerated for car theft, housebreaking and sexual assault, served several years in prison."

"He was a known sex offender, there were several more complaints against him even after he came out of prison, but somehow that motherfucker didn't go back to jail for it."

"How the fuck does the Ravenbridge police work? Letting a man like that wander their streets." I was disgusted just looking at his file. Knowing Sofia had came face to face with that fucker made my skin crawl.

"Yup." Adam nodded pensively. "List of suspect is short and mainly composed of men we knew he fucked with in the past and who have been known accomplices of his; Ben Karrock, Jay Titcher and Hal Malcoms." He threw the file against the desk and laid back against his chair. "Jay moved to Maryland two years ago, we're still working to get in touch with him, Hal has been in jail since last year for assault on a police officer and all that's left is Ben, which we haven't been able to locate yet but the boys at IT are working hard."

"It just doesn't make sense for it to be one of them." I couldn't take my eyes off of Harold's file. "These guys are clowns, they're petty criminals at best and this was clearly not the work of some inbred fucker." Adam frowned, sitting up straighter.

"What are you thinking?"

"I think we have been looking at it the wrong way this whole time." I pressed my finger onto the table, driving my point home. "We've taken this case assuming Harold was the lead man, thus looking into some of his old acolytes, but what if he wasn't?" I let the file fall down on the desk and got up, eyes narrowing at the board.

"What if Harold was meant to be the scapegoat this whole time? What if he was supposed to be the easy man to find— since his fingerprints and DNA were fucking everywhere, while the second one got away? What if we were not even supposed to know there was a second guy?"

I rearranged the murder board where Harold's photo had been at the center. I put it aside instead and drew a question mark in its place before circling it a bit more forcefully than necessary. I knew I had Adam's attention then. He got up, looking over the files with a new, vigorous look on his face.

"Only Sofia messed up his plan when she saw him and fought him off." It's like something clicked in his head right then. "She saw there were two guys, and she killed Harold, so he couldn't take the fall. Fuck, that would explain so much! Harold had nothing to do with Lakestone or Mayor Raymond, so if the real man behind all of this just used him as a scapegoat to take the blame away from him, that would mean—"

"That would mean the other killer was someone closer to Jack Raymond than we imagined."

***

It was ten minutes shy of one in the morning when I finally got home. Entering the dark, soundless apartment and locking the door after me, my keys clinked as I let them fall on the table next to me.

Yawning, I rubbed my eye with the heel of my hand before walking to the kitchen.

Everything was dark so I assumed the girls were already fast asleep, and I was grateful somehow. As much as I loved having them over, loved how they filled the house with laughter and warmth, even after everything they've been through, right then I just felt like a failure. And I needed to be alone.

Even after the small revelation at the office earlier, this case still seemed so far from being resolved, and although I never let my cases — as hard as they could get, weigh on my mental state, this one felt personal. This one felt fucking personal because I had two girls counting on me to protect them and bring justice to their parents' names.

And even though Adam seemed really optimistic about this new point of view we decided to work with, I couldn't help but think it wasn't enough. I couldn't help but think we were missing something.

The light turning on in the corridor leading to the bedrooms got me out of my thoughts and I straightened up from where I was slouching against the kitchen island.

Sofia appeared before me, frowning and looking shaken up. Immediately, worry took control of me and I matched her frown, walking to her.

"What's wrong?"

She gulped, her hands coming up to her bare arms and rubbing her skin. My eyes spied her movements, my own hands itching to touch her and make sure she was okay.

Sofia looked so small right then, so vulnerable. As always since that morning, she evaded my gaze and bit her lip before speaking.

"Nothing. Just a bad dream is all." It obviously wasn't nothing if it shook her up so much.

"Wanna talk about it?" For the first time, she looked up and my breath got caught in my throat.

I don't think I'll ever get used to Sofia Raymond looking at me with those doe eyes. She's the only person who can annihilate me and completely subjugate me with one look.

"I lied." She confessed and I tensed.

Her eyes in mine and she must've sensed my confusion because she pursed her lips, her arms squeezing her body tighter. She was wearing pajamas again, but these covered way more than the ones she had on the day we… the day we crossed that line.

"I lied to Valentina, Maddox." She gulped, her eyes brimming with tears. Whatever it was she dreamed about, it must have freaked her out. "I told her I killed them— told her I killed the monsters, that I chased them away." It took all of me not to take her in my arms and squeeze her tight until she stopped shaking. "But I haven't, have I? I lied. Because monsters are everywhere, and they will never stop existing." She closed her eyes and a single, lone tear rolled down her cheek to the corner of her lips. "Even we are the monsters of someone else's story."

If asked about it, I'll say the fatigue made me do it, but in reality, it was that irresistible need to protect and comfort Sofia that pushed me to cup her jaw and bring her closer to me. Her eyes flashed open as soon as my skin touched hers and she sent me a questioning look.

This was the first time I touched her since the morning they moved in.

I let my forehead bump into hers as I held her and she seemed to take comfort in our proximity. Good, because it was the most I could give her without crossing a line again.

"You're not a liar, Sofia. You're the goddamn best sister I've ever met, all you ever do, you do with Valentina in mind. You didn't lie to her, you reassured her the only way you knew and we'll catch that second motherfucker, you have my word. I will not let him make you a liar."

She stared at me for so long, eyes wavering and lips trembling. It's like she wanted to tell me something but wouldn't dare.

Then her gaze fell to my lips and her head moved up, just the slightest bit. I tensed, knowing what she meant to do, her mouth was only a breath away from mine.

It took all I had to put my hands on her shoulders and pushed her away as softly as I could. I heard her breath catch in her throat. As soft as my movements were, I knew they still hurt her feelings. My own heart screamed at me for putting distance between us, but I couldn't hear it over my brain maintaining this was best for both of us. And Valentina.

"I- I'm sorry." She took another step back, looking down at her bare feet, while pursing her lips.

"It's okay, I— you know we can't do that." I wanted nothing more than to take her in my arms.

"I don't know what came over me, I didn't mean to— I know you don't want me like that."

I could've denied it, reassured her and told her that she represented everything I ever desired and more, but where would that get us? More frustrated because we both wanted each other but couldn't do anything about it? Giving up on resisting and crossing a line once again?

We couldn't have that.

So I said nothing, and let her believe that I wasn't into her even though I wanted her so much it burned.

She gulped at my silence, nodding to herself and ready to turn around and get back to bed. For some reason, I wasn't ready to part ways yet so I blurted the first thing I could think of.

"There is some news on your parents' case." She froze, her head snapping towards me.

"Did you—" she cleared her throat, "Did you arrest someone?" Her eyes shone with interest and she unconsciously leaned towards me.

I shook my head, "Not yet. We just started to look at it with another eye."

"What does that mean?"

"It means that Harold, the guy you killed, might have been just a decoy." She frowned, looking down again. "We think the real mastermind behind your parents' murder was close to your dad, maybe someone he worked with or owed money to." I looked at her intently, trying to catch her gaze and see if that reminded her of someone.

She shook her head. "Dad didn't like owing anyone, but it is possible it was someone who owed *him* money." She looked up suddenly, "His office. Did you find his debt book?"

It was my turn to frown and shake my head, “I don’t have his assistant’s report in head but I don’t remember a debt book being on the list.” Something in her eyes wavered at the mention of her father’s assistant.

“Conan made that report?”

“Yeah.” I nodded, and she seemed to be wanting to add something but then thought against it at the last minute. “Why? What do you know about him?”

She shrugged, “Nothing, he’s just… he’s weird. Always gave me the creeps.”

“We’ll go check your father’s office again tomorrow, look for that debt book, alright?” She nodded absentmindedly, “After the… service, we’ll leave Valentina to Selena and go check it out.”

“Okay. Okay.” I took a step towards her, wanting to rub her arm and tell her everything would be okay, but she moved back. I let my hand fall along my body and looked down, my jaw clenching.

I couldn’t push her away when she wanted to kiss me and then try to comfort her. It didn’t work like that. The message was clear.

I cleared my throat, fingers drumming nervously against my thigh.

“Let’s get to bed, okay?. Tomorrow is a long day.” She stared into nothingness, deep in thoughts.

“Yes, you’re right.” When her eyes met mine she pursed her lips and managed to give me a small, sad, smile. “Good night, Maddox.”

# 12

## GLOOM

### SOFIA

The day was gloomy, gray, and it looked like it was going to rain any moment now.

It was the perfect day for a funeral.

The world slowed down around me, I was dreading the moment we'd get to the cemetery, where the whole town was probably waiting for us. The looks of pity on their faces, the false condolences, shoulder rubs and back patting.

A shit show of hypocrisy was what it was. It made me sick to my stomach.

Where were these people when we needed them most? When Valentina and I were alone against the world? Where were they when we had to endure the loss of our parents, of being uprooted away from everything we've ever known? When we cried ourselves to sleep each fucking night?

They weren't there. They never saw through our smiles. Ultimately, the only person that's always been there for me, was Valentina, she was the only reason I was attending at all, because Maddox convinced me that it would bring her closure, and he was right, more than he had known, actually.

"Dada?"

My attention was taken away from my reflection on the mirror and to my sister. She was standing against the bathroom's door frame, looking at me with teary eyes.

I immediately went to her, squatting so I was at eye level with her. My hands caressed her hair away from her face and she looked down. "What's wrong, *Rosita*?"

She sniffled and her arms shot up as she hugged me tight. I squeezed my own arms around her, and inhaled her scent. She smelled like home.

"I don't want to go." She whispered against my neck and I closed my eyes. I knew this would happen, I knew I couldn't protect her from it, but it still hurt like hell hearing her say that.

Even though I initially wasn't too keen on her attending the funerals, I knew in all objectivity that she needed to go. She needed the closure it would give her, whether now or when she was older. She needed to see the caskets go into the ground to understand that mom and dad would not be coming back.

As hard as it would be at her young age.

"But we have to." I whispered back, pulling away slightly so I could look at her face. "We have to, baby. Don't forget we're doing this for mama and papa, not anyone else."

"But they're not here anymore."

My heart tightened. Sometimes it felt like it would never get easier, living without them.

"They're always here, Valentina. They're watching over us, and they're in our hearts too. I know it's hard, but you're so strong, baby. You're so strong and they would be so proud of you." I could feel the tears burning my eyes but wouldn't let them fall.

"La muerte no existe, la gente sólo muere cuando la olvidan."
*Death doesn't exist, people only die when we forget them.*

A small smile grazed her lips as she recognized the words mama so often spoke when we were younger. She leaned into my hand holding her cheek and nodded.

"This is the last thing we have to do. The last effort, then everything will go back to normal, I promise you, baby." I kissed her forehead and hugged her tight.

We agreed with Maddox that Valentina should get back to school next week. I was also going back to class since I couldn't afford to miss more, academically speaking.

That child psychologist from the police department actually was the one to advise it, said that we should bring back as much stability and normalcy in her life as we could. She also said she was afraid Valentina would develop separation anxiety if we waited too long and I half heartedly agreed with that. Except for that night she was placed in foster care, we had spent every waking moment together since the night of the murders, and that couldn't be healthy in the long term.

I was dreading the separation though, possibly even more than Valentina. She seemed content enough to be going back to school. Not to see her friends— she didn't have much of those, but because she genuinely loved learning. She went to a private school in Lakestone where she was first of her class. All of her teachers loved her, and she loved them too, my girl had tons of love to give.

The problem came mainly from her classmates. Children were cruel little creatures, that's a known fact, but Valentina didn't have a mean bone in her body. Plus, she actually acted her age, making her seem childish at times to a generation that was born knowing how to work an iPad before they could walk. That made her an easy target for bullies. I couldn't even recall how many times she snuggled to me at night, crying about mean things other students said to her.

I wanted to do something about it, call the school, talk to the parents, but she refused. She said it would only cause more drama and that their taunts wouldn't hurt her as she'd grow up. It killed me to agree with her, but she was right, we couldn't afford to cause drama and bring the spotlight onto ourselves.

That didn't keep me from vandalizing their parents' houses or their cars though.

"Do you promise? Do you promise this is the last push before we finally get a normal life?"

Her little voice resonated in the empty bathroom. I nodded against her neck, biting my lip and doing my best to keep the tears from falling.

"Yes, Rosita. I promise."

***

**MADDOX**

She was magnificent.

Sofia possessed the kind of beauty that made it impossible to look away and, unfortunately, I was not the only one who seemed to think so.

All eyes were focused on her as she walked down the aisle, her red soles shoes matching the deep red she painted her lips with. Those were the only two touches of color to her all black outfit. Her dress was conservative enough, it had long sleeves and came down to her ankles but clung to her body in a way that highlighted how fit she was. I could positively say that was the first time I'd even seen her wear a dress, and what a waste that was because she was rocking it.

A silk black scarf was wrapped around her head, and her smooth black hair could be seen from underneath, cascading down her back. She wore black totally opaque sunglasses and I couldn't help but think it was because she didn't want anyone seeing her tears.

She walked confidently, holding her sister's hand while people— nearly the whole town was here, looked in awe. I could hear them whispers, see them look her up and down, probably judging if her outfit was appropriate or not.

Appropriate.

That was one word they loved in Lakestone.

I heard a lot of things about Sofia over the years. The way she dressed, the way she spoke and the things she did— often resulting in her arrest, were deemed *in*appropriate. She spoke her mind and didn't care for pleasantries. She only said things she meant and didn't try to suck up to anybody which was not really what Lakewood inhabitants liked.

Sometimes it felt like it was all people recognized in her. Like her knack for illegal paintings and her sailor mouth were the only things that defined her. They didn't see how courageous she was, how loyal, how creative, they didn't recognize her empathy and her fire.

Because that's what Sofia was. Fire.

Magnificent and hypnotic to watch, but once you got too close you got burned.

That's probably why she was constantly alone.

Sure, she had some friends here and there, but they were not true friends, friends you'd call at the end of a rough day so you could feel slightly better. Friends you could count on and who gave back the same energy as you.

When she was still in high school, I could tell she wanted that. She wanted to fit in, to make friends. But somehow, she always ended up being screwed over. One time a group of girls convinced her to steal a bottle of vodka at the local grocery store because they intended to go to a frat party a town over.

Sofia got caught, the other three fled and she was the only one who was arrested that night. Her so-called friends still went to that party, and from what I knew, Sofia never spoke to them again. She never told my colleagues their names either, although I had a pretty good guess who they were.

She had a really peculiar sense of loyalty. It was all or nothing with her, she gave everything to the ones she loved without waiting for anything in return except loyalty.

These people here didn't deserve her. They didn't deserve to see her, to talk to her, to pity her and give her fake ass condolences, they certainly fucking didn't deserve to see her cry.

Some part of me agreed with her not wanting to attend and stay with Valentina at home, namely that was also the part that yearned to spoil her rotten and give her all the attention and affection she so obviously lacked. The rational part of me though, knew she had to assist. She had to see her parents' graves, see they were now resting in peace, for her own closure, her own peace of mind.

Not only that but not seeing her in attendance would make people talk, and I wouldn't be responsible for what I did to anyone shit-talking her. Lord knew she got enough of that.

My eyes were stuck on her back and Sofia looked tense, more than I'd ever seen her. Her hand clutched Valentina's, and the little girl squeezed hers just as hard. They were giving each other the strength needed to get through this day, and I had to admit, it was beautiful.

I'd never witnessed a love like theirs. It was friendship, it was devotion, it was pure and unadulterated sisterhood.

Beautiful.

Coming to a stop at the top of the aisle, Sofia turned around towards the first row of benches before stopping again, this time looking startled. I followed her gaze and saw *him*, sitting on the pew specifically reserved for the family.

Conan Michaels, Jack Raymond's assistant, sat there, looking forward and not sparing Sofia a single look, like he had every goddamn right.

I noticed how Sofia seemed to tense up even more, and how her hold on Valentina seemed to shake. Her chest heaved, but it was so controlled and discreet that nobody who wasn't looking would notice.

But I did.

I noticed everything about Sofia Raymond.

And at that moment, I knew Conan's presence made her uncomfortable.

She decided not to show it and to ignore him the same way he was decidedly ignoring her. She helped Valentina sit down at the very end of the bench and sat right next to her, leaving two seats between her and the assistant.

Frowning at her antics and writing a mental note to do a background check on Conan, I took my seat in the row behind them while Adam sat next to me.

I chanced a look at him, to see if he witnessed the same thing I did but he seemed too preoccupied by his own demons to notice other's.

The last time my colleague had attended a funeral was last year, when he had to bury his own son. Unwanted memories were probably bubbling inside his head; he had that distant look in his eyes that he'd get sometimes, when he thought we weren't paying attention.

The thing was, we were. We saw how haunted Adam still was from the death of Abel and the unanswered questions that echoed to it.

People started to settle down around us and eventually, the church became silent. You could feel all the eyes being strained on the two caskets on the stage, next to the priest. For obvious reasons, the lids were closed. I knew it must've drawn even more questions from the guests, given that the details of Jack and Marcela's deaths were still undisclosed. People didn't know how gruesome their murders were, Chief Pierson had decided to tell the media it was just a burglary gone wrong, and to be honest, only a few details pointed to the opposite.

One of these few details being my gut feeling, and Lord knew we could not build a case with that only.

Conan was the one to organize everything—maybe that's why he felt so entitled to sitting in the front like he was fucking family, and I had to say it looked decent for now.

I could also see he heeded Sofia's only request that there wouldn't be any picture of their parents, for Valentina's sake. She was scared to death that seeing them would trigger a panic attack from her younger sister, just like she had explained to me the day we went back to their house.

"Dear friends and family, we gather here today to say goodbye to two beloved members of our community…" Father Gareth started and everyone listened attentively.

Valentina's head fell against Sofia's arm, and I could imagine the little girl's eyes brimming with tears and closing of their own accord. Neither sister had shed a tear coming here, and that worried me. The way they didn't talk about their parents' death, the way they totally shut down their emotions whenever it was mentioned, that couldn't be healthy.

I heard Sofia sob into her pillow last night after our little conversation, and it had gutted me not to do anything about it. I yearned to open her door and take her in my arms, make her feel better any way I could.

I wanted to touch her, feel her, *taste* her, but my brain was stronger than my desires. Thank God for that, really.

The last thing we needed was to complicate things by starting a physical relationship. Not only that but I was pretty sure I could never have just a physical relationship with Sofia. She was the only woman I'd ever wanted to own in every sense of the word.

I wanted everything: her body, her heart and her soul.

Not only that, but I kind of wanted to give her mine, too.

"He could be here." Adam whispered next to me, taking me out of my thoughts.

I looked over at him and noticed his narrowed eyes drawn to the front of the church where Father Gareth was still going on and on about the mayor's good deeds for the town.

"You think?"

"Of course. We established he was probably close to Raymond. Do you think he'd miss an opportunity to see him being put in the ground?" That made sense and I gulped.

If the fucker who took everything from my girls was here, I would damn well find out who it was.

My gaze zeroed on the man sitting straight in the pew in front of me. I could only see his back and occasionally, he would turn his head discreetly towards Sofia. His little eyes would sweep her from head to toe before returning to the front of the church.

I frowned. Sofia was obviously uncomfortable by his presence alone. Yesterday, when I'd mentioned him, she had the same reaction. And she obviously didn't trust him because she wanted to get back to her house and check for that debt book herself, even after Conan said it wasn't there.

He made a pretty good suspect, when you thought about it. He was close enough to Jack Raymond to have an issue with him, even though most people we interviewed at the city council attested they had a good relationship. Lord knew appearances could be deceiving.

Raymond was in a position of superiority regarding Conan, so everything could have happened. He might not have liked how he was treated, might have wanted a raise his boss declined, the possibilities were endless.

Faster than I could comprehend, the service was being moved from the church to the cemetery right behind it. As people walked quietly towards the two empty graves, I fell in step next to Sofia. I wanted to hold her hand, hug her or even just put my arm on her shoulders, but I knew how people would react to that sort of public demonstration of affection.

Before we knew it, the caskets were lowered into the ground and covered in dirt. I heard Sofia gulp next to me, as Valentina buried her face in the skirt of her dress. The eldest Raymond daughter played with her little sister's hair, caressing it and soothing her while maintaining a stoic stature. Her lips were pinched together and I couldn't see her eyes but I could have bet they were red from crying.

Valentina had shed a few of her own as she watched her parents being buried. It was as heartbreaking as it was reassuring, to see her have a reaction, see her express feelings she had repressed up until then.

As the ceremony came to an end, people went and threw petals of flowers on the freshly covered graves before making their way back to their cars to attend the reception that was supposed to take place in a posh restaurant downtown.

Adam had left my side to go wait in his car with Selena. They filtered away until the only ones standing there were us.

Sofia's bottom lip was caught between her teeth as she stared at the tombstones.

*Jack Raymond, beloved husband, father and mayor.*
*Marcela Raymond, beloved wife and mother.*

It was simple, loving but straight to the point. Conan had probably ordered them, since he took care of everything else.

Sensing she might need to be alone for a few minutes, because Sofia was bashful when it came to her feelings, I squatted down in front of Valentina and presented my hand to her, asking her quietly to come with me.

My brave girl agreed and put her hand in mine. She ended up hugging my neck so I lifted her into my arms.

I could hear her sniffle a bit and hide her face in my neck. I gulped. I couldn't stand to see her like that. To see *them*, like that.

"We'll wait for you in the car. Find me if you need anything, okay?" I tried to make my voice as soft as possible so she wouldn't feel startled.

Sofia slowly nodded and I nodded back, once, clutching Valentina firmly in my arms and making my way back to my car.

In the warmth of the vehicle, Valentina sat quietly in the backseat, resting her head on the window and sighed wistfully. I had a direct view on Sofia's back, and I couldn't help but watch her surroundings.

The cemetery was crawling with cops, every exit was being guarded, but it wasn't enough for me. I needed to make sure for myself that she was safe, that no one would harm her while she said goodbye to her parents.

My phone ringing cut me out of my thoughts and I answered without checking who it was.

"Detective Brooks speaking."

"Woah, what a nice way to say hi to your sister, you petulant child." Against myself, a small smile came to stretch my lips.

"Hey, Andrea. Sorry, I'm in a bit of a delicate situation right now."

"Yeah, mom explained. How are you doing?"

The concern in her voice was evident. Growing up, and even though she was only three years older than me, Drea had some trouble realizing she was my sister and not my mom.

She's always been super overprotective of me, she always concerned herself with my safety and my wellbeing. Even after she got married and had her child, my niece, Adrianna, she kept on calling me every other day to check on me, see if I ate well, slept well, or didn't forget to put on SPF.

"I'm good, Drea. Honestly. I'm not the one people should be concerned about." My eyes found Valentina's now-sleeping form in the rearview mirror.

"Yeah, I heard. It sucks what these poor babies have to go through."

I hummed, knowing that, unlike the hundred or so people who were there today at the church, lamenting over the two orphans Jack and Marcela Raymond had left behind, my sister was genuinely concerned about them.

"It does. But they're so strong, Drea. I've never seen two girls who have lost everything as suddenly as they did cope as well as they do."

I checked on Sofia again, only to see she had walked closer to the grave and that her shoulders were shaking. Crying. I gulped, closing my eyes and totally missing my sister's answer.

"Sorry, what?"

"I said I would love to meet them someday. Why don't you bring them around to the house sometime? Adrianna would love a little mate to play with." Eyes still strained on Sofia's shaking figure I rubbed my forehead.

"Yeah. Sure. Listen, I gotta go, okay? We're still at the funeral, it's — it's a mess."

"Of course. Sorry, I just wanted to check on you and see how you were getting used to life with two strangers. I hope to see you on Sunday. Bye, Maddox."

"Bye, Drea."

Sundays were family days at our house. We all gathered there for dinner before spending the evening reminiscing about our childhood. Sometimes our cousins joined us, sometimes it was just our parents and Drea's little family. No matter how many people attended, it was still my favorite part of the week.

I loved those evenings, even though I haven't gotten to enjoy them in a while. I'd been busy with the case, and then the girls moved in, it was hectic. But a part of me thought maybe I could bring them to the next get together. I thought they might like it, given how much family meant to them.

Locking my phone, I looked back up to Sofia, whose back was still shaking due to the force of her sobs. Her slender shoulders moved up and down as she leaned over, until finally she fell to her knees.

My first instinct was to jump out of the car and go to her. But Valentina was sleeping in the back and I knew Sofia would freak out if she knew I'd left her alone even one second. I had to swallow down my every instinct and remain seated while watching the object of my desires being wrecked by her sorrow.

It was like watching someone rip my own heart out.

Eventually, she calmed down, but remained on her knees, haunched over between the two graves.

I was so focused on her that I didn't even notice the woman approaching from behind.

A frown marred my face as I couldn't recognize her. She wasn't in church, nor was she there when the caskets were lowered into the graves. I had never seen her around town either.

Much like Sofia, I could only see her from the back, long curly black hair fell down her back. She wore a long black bodycon dress with black platform boots, hidden by a black leather coat which pockets her hands were stuffed in. She had on a hat— you guessed it, black too.

She stopped in front of Sofia, facing Marcela Raymond's grave and giving her back to the late woman's daughter. I could see the latter's head rise to take her in. I think they started talking, but I couldn't be too sure because I couldn't see their faces or hear them from a distance.

Who was that?

Marcella didn't have any family that I knew of and all her friends were en route for the reception at the moment. Sofia seemed wary, her shoulders were tense and she had straightened up as soon as the strange woman had come into view..

They spoke for a long time, until finally, the woman turned her head to the side, looking down at Sofia.

She had a smirk on her blood red lips as she muttered words I wish like hell I could hear. Black sunglasses hid her eyes making her face practically impossible to see. After that, she nodded once at the girl on the ground and started walking in the direction she came from, disappearing in the trees.

I immediately grabbed my phone to dial Adam and ask him to get a lead on the stranger when his name appeared on my screen.

I swore and immediately answered, "I was just going to call you. I need someone following—"

"Maddox, we have a problem." His voice was stern but I could hear the panicked undertone after years of working with him. Ice coursed in my veins as I waited for the other shoe to drop.

"The Raymond house. It's burning."

# 13

# MEMORIES

## SOFIA

The smell of burning wood and rotten memories tickled my nose. As I stood on the sidewalk, quietly watching the house I spent a great part of my life in go up in flames, all I felt was…numb.

So many things happened in this house. Good and bad things alike, of course, but right then, the bad seemed incredibly more suffocating. Flashes of blood kept appearing in my mind, tears, screams. I could almost taste them.

I couldn't say I felt sad about this house burning. If anything, relief was more akin to what I was feeling at the moment. It was like by burning it somehow took all the bad memories with it. Like it was giving us a new chance at life.

Kind of like a phoenix, we would rise from those ashes.

A few feet away from me, Maddox was talking to one of his colleagues, trying to understand what happened and if anyone had seen anything.

This was a huge setback for the case and I could feel Maddox' frustrations during the car ride. Valentina was still sleeping in the backseat of his car, thank God. She hadn't slept much last night, she had a nightmare right after I did, only hers seemed to be much worse. Maybe it was because of her age, maybe it was something else. All I knew was she started sobbing in her sleep and then it was hell to wake her up. It was like she was back to that night, vulnerable and without anyone to protect her. I'll never forgive myself for not staying with her then.

"I'm sorry, Sofia." Startled from my own thoughts, I looked up into forest green eyes.

A lot of things made Maddox desirable. He had an amazing body, a sweet personality and a naturally assertive persona. But to me, the most addicting thing about him were his eyes. They truly were the window to his pure, beautiful, soul.

I gulped, looking away, not wanting him to think I was a creep for staring for so long.

"It's okay. We took everything we needed the other day, the rest doesn't matter."

"Yeah, but it doesn't make it okay. This is your and Valentina's home." I bit my lip to keep from replying and he continued. "This just fucked up our case, big time. Now there's no way of knowing if that debt book was—" He stopped and frowned, like something suddenly clicked in his mind.

"Sofia, what do you know about Conan?" My heart missed a beat and I looked back at him.

"Why? Do you think he could have been linked to this?"

"Everything is possible, we're working every angle here."

I sighed. "I never liked him. He— he makes me uncomfortable and I'd rather not be alone with him if I can help it." I was surprised I was able to talk about it so truthfully.

This was just another example of how much I trusted Maddox, words just naturally came out of my mouth whenever I was with him. It was also an example of why I didn't trust myself with him. Not controlling what I said in his presence was not something I could afford to do.

"Did he ever do something to you?" My heart squeezed at having to lie, but I knew it was inevitable.

That was part of the one thing I could never tell him, or anyone else. The one secret only Conan and I were aware of now, the one piece of information I swore I would take to my grave.

"No." I shook my head and bit my lip, evading his gaze. "Just a feeling." Maddox looked at me for the longest time without saying anything before nodding silently. He grabbed my arm gently and ushered me towards the car.

"Come on. There's nothing to save here, let's go home."

***

It's insane how quickly children get used to new environments. It had been two weeks since the disastrous funeral and our house burning down, both me and Valentina had gone back to school. She said people in her class were not being mean to her anymore, and thank God for that because now nothing was keeping me from fighting those little shits on her behalf. No election season, no bookclub ladies to impress on mom's behalf, nothing. For the first time in forever, my life was blissfully empty of social expectations.

Today was Saturday, I was home alone with Valentina, she was playing with her new dolls Andrea—Maddox' sister, gifted her when she came to visit us on Wednesday. I was chilling and binging TV while stuffing my face full of *Corn Nuts*, something I hadn't been able to do in a long, long time.

Maddox was working. He promised he'd be home for dinner so that we could all eat together, but I knew things were strenuous at work. Ever since the fire took place, Chief Pierson had been breathing down their necks to rule the case as a burglary gone wrong. A part of me was pissed, because my testimony proved that it wasn't, and making it a cold case would just mean they were disregarding me and what I had endured during this night of hell.

Another part of me was just tired though. I just wanted everything to fall back in place, I just wanted to put what was one of the worst nights of my life behind us and finally live.

Life had been surprisingly good lately. Living with Maddox was like having a family again. The domesticity of it was giving us the stability we've so painfully obviously lacked growing up. I'd never seen Valentina so happy. She actually made a friend in Maddox's niece on Wednesday and kept on talking about how she would love to go on a play date with Adrianna and Sameerah. It was adorable.

Andrea was amazing. She gave me her number when she visited and we've kept in touch via texts. She was older than me but somehow I didn't really feel the age difference. She shared little stories about Maddox as a kid, sent me selfies of her throughout her day and even invited me over to their parents' house on Sunday.

I felt really touched by that. She was trying to make us feel like we were part of the family and I was super grateful. I didn't know if I was ready to attend one of their Sunday dinners yet, but the thought was here.

Her warmth helped me cope a little better with the fact that Maddox was actively avoiding me. Ever since the day of the funeral, we had little to no conversations that didn't revolve around Valentina. He'd come home to have dinner with us, play with my sister and always took care of cleaning up afterwards, especially when I was the one to make dinner, but even when I didn't. He smiled at me and even asked how my days went but other than that, it was like we were strangers living under the same roof. Which, I guess was kind of the truth from an outside eye.

The thing was, what we've shared felt more intimate to me. I had opened up to him in ways I never had to anyone before. I let him see me at my worst, cried in front of him, I trusted him with my sister, for God's sake. And now, he was pulling away and it was killing me.

The doorbell ringing pulled me out of my thoughts. I frowned, checking the time on my phone. It was just a little after two in the afternoon. Maddox had his key, he wouldn't ring the doorbell. He also wouldn't be home this early.

His family, other than his sister, never really dropped by, especially if he wasn't home, and his sister worked today. I knew because she had sent me a selfie this morning saying "what a beautiful day to catch babies". She worked as an OBGYN, so that made sense.

Valentina stopped playing with her dolls as soon as she heard the bell and looked at me with anguished eyes. I got up from the sofa, smiling reassuringly at her, even when my own heart was beating fast. I didn't know who was behind that door, and I hated that fact.

My hand shook a little as I grabbed the knob, but I pushed myself to unlock the door and pull it open.

I wasn't ready for who was behind it.

A redhead with a gorgeous red dress, highlighting every curve of her gorgeous body stood on the other side of the door, holding a big plate that smelled positively delicious in her hands. She had a big white smile that immediately vanished when she saw me, replaced by a confused frown.

"Oh. Who are you?" She asked, looking me up and down. I felt underdressed even though I shouldn't have. If anything, she was the one overdressed. Who wore stilettos to deliver food?

"Excuse me? I live here."

"Oh. Oh! You're the poor little orphan girl Maddox took in!" My eyebrows nearly touched my hairline at her words.

I couldn't believe she'd just said that. A part of me wanted to punch her in the face for belittling me like that, while another one just wanted to burst out laughing.

I exhaled and did neither. "I'm neither poor nor little. You are?"

"I'm Giorgianna, the neighbor from down the hall. Well, I came to see Maddox. I know he rarely has time to cook so I made him lasagna." She smirked, assessing me again, "My nonna's recipe, he loves it." She smirked, shrugging like it was no big deal.

Right. For a second I wondered if the lasagna was the only thing from that girl Maddox loved to eat but then I refrained. Those thoughts were better being nipped in the bud. It wouldn't bring me anything to know if the two of them ever… frolicked. It was none of my business, plus Maddox already made it clear he wasn't into me like that.

Yet I just couldn't stand the thought of Maddox eating anything from that woman.

"Right. Well he's not here right now and even if he were, there's no need for you to cook for him anymore. I'm here."

"Serve it tonight at dinner. He loves Italian." She pushed the plate towards me, an asinine smile lighting her gorgeous face. Ugh, couldn't his neighbor be eighty and wrinkly and in love with her cats or something?

"It's too bad, I think he said he was in the mood to eat something Mexican tonight." My smile matched hers.

After years of attending galas and charity balls under the Raymond name I pretty much mastered the art of faking it. Her smile didn't falter, if anything, she looked like she found me funny. Again, she pushed her plate at me, forcing me to take it, which I eventually did.

"It's okay. He can have Mexican tonight, he'll come back to Italian food eventually. It's always been his favorite." With one last wink and a smirk, she turned around and walked back down the hall like she was on a runway.

Of course his neighbor had to look like she belonged in Vogue while I spent my days in pajamas watching cartoons with a nine year old.

Sometimes I wished that could be me. I wished I could be in phase with my feminine side and dress like her from time to time. But I think I still had a long way to go when it came to that. Just another thing I'd have to work on. Gritting my teeth because I hated that she had had the last word, I closed the door and locked it before turning around and marching to the kitchen.

As I stepped on its lever, the trash can opened and I let the lasagna fall into it, plate and everything. It was truly sacrilegious because it smelled amazing, but I didn't trust that bitch. What if she put something in it? I remembered mama telling us not to eat food from strangers because we never knew what they put in it, after all.

I was only trying to avoid us getting drugged or poisoned.

Pulling my feet off the lever, I dusted my hands with a satisfied smirk on my lips. "Oops."

Maybe Giorgianna and Maddox had something going on and, as much as it gutted me, I couldn't do anything about it. But at least I could make sure he wouldn't eat her stupid lasagna tonight.

I turned around, satisfied with myself but then stopped abruptly. My eyes made contact with my sister's, who stood there with her hand on her hip, shaking her little head in mock disappointment. The look of boredom on her face told me she had seen everything.

I gave her a sheepish smile and shrugged. "Wanna make tostada tonight?"

***

**MADDOX**

Everything was a mess.

Chief Pierson had been on my ass since the funeral, said people were starting to wonder what exactly happened to the mayor and his wife. The press said it was most likely a case of burglary gone wrong, they were not aware of the second man and think that Harold Crawford was alone that night.

Adam and I thought it would have been a good idea to just call for witnesses, see if we could get any intel on our second guy, but Pierson said releasing the fact that there *was* a second guy, out on the loose, to the media would be a bad idea. That it would only freak out the population more. I had to agree with him on that, even though it definitely set us back in the case.

The house burning was the last nail in the coffin. Any clues the killer might have left behind went up in ashes along with the rest of the house. Sofia and Valentina didn't seem upset about it. When I asked her, she said the memories of her parents would never fade, that they would never cease to exist in their hearts.

We still had no clue who set it on fire though, because, yes, it *was* a criminal fire. The insurance guys guaranteed it: nothing was faulty inside the house, so whoever did it, did it to erase something. This somehow didn't dismiss my theory about Conan, even though he was at the restaurant when everything happened as several witnesses could attest. He could have paid someone to do it.

I just couldn't help but think something was wrong with him. Especially since that conversation with Sofia where she lied to me. For the first time since I'd met her, she fucking lied to me.

See, Sofia Raymond had a tell. When she wasn't telling the truth, she'd bite her lip and look away. She didn't even realize she did it, but over the course of her staying with me, I had.

That's mostly why I'd been staying away from her lately. I just didn't understand why she'd feel the need to lie to me to protect that little shit.

I'd done my research on him and nothing seemed out of the ordinary: man was twenty-seven, high school and college valedictorian, he started working at the mayor's office as an intern and then was offered a permanent place as an assistant, which he accepted because that was one step closer to making it into politics, which was his end goal.

I stalked his facebook and instagram pages and homeboy was obsessed with Mayor Raymond. He considered him a father figure and a "real example for any man out there who thrived to make a good life for himself and those he cared about". A total suck up. He was a mama's boy, still lived at home with her and his father left when he was a child, which could explain his weird and a bit over-the-top fondness of Jack Raymond. He seemed to be well liked at work and in town in general but I honestly couldn't help but wonder what would anyone find him.

I guess he was good looking, if you liked preppy boys with so much hair gel it made it look greasy, who probably had a collection of Star Wars dolls— sorry, *figurines*, displayed proudly in their room.

No shade to any Star Wars lovers, of course.

Anyways, on paper that man was a model citizen, but my gut was screaming there was something fishy about him.

"You're still here?" I looked up from my desk, where the file containing the Raymond case was open, to see Selena standing against the doorframe.

I leaned back against my chair and rubbed my eyes. It was only five but the sleepless nights I'd been pulling lately were starting to catch up on me. I couldn't wait to get home and see my girls.

The thought gave me pause. I didn't know when exactly I had started thinking about them as mine but I had. They were both mine and I would do anything in my power to help them get through life and its hardships.

“Yeah, I should probably wrap up for the day. The girls must be waiting.” I started pulling the file back together. “What’s up?” She looked like she wanted to say something but didn’t know how.

“You talked to Adam lately?”

I frowned, “Yeah, I mean it’s hard not to. We share a case, we work together on the daily. Why?”

Selena rubbed her arm, shaking her head. “He just seems out of it. I think this case brought back bad memories for him.”

“I know what you mean. I’ll talk to him and see if he wants to check out for a bit. A break would do him good.” She nodded and went to add something when a uniformed officer came barging into my office, looking out of breath.

“Detective Brooks! There’s an emergency at the park, I thought you should know it. It involves both Raymond sisters.”

Son of a bitch.

# 14

# BATTLE

## SOFIA

I knew it was a bad idea.

It was past four in the afternoon when we finished prepping the tostada, and Valentina all but begged me to go out. Other than for school and the occasional pancake run on Sunday mornings with Maddox, we haven't gone out into the real world without a police escort since the night of the murders.

I knew Valentina was getting restless, she loved the outdoors. Before everything happened, we had a huge backyard, and she'd spend hours there when she was home and I was in class. She loved making up stories about elves and fairies in the woods behind the house, loved chasing butterflies and ladybugs.

And now when she wasn't at school, she was at home with me, watching movies or playing with dolls. She liked it and never really complained but I could tell she was getting restless.

That's mostly why I agreed to take her to the park, because I knew my sister, her feelings were mine and I could sense she needed to go out.

Everything was fine at first, we both dressed warmly because the weather was getting chilly in Lakestone. We said hi to Osman, the doorman, on our way out of the building and started walking down the street to the park I had located when we first moved in with Maddox.

Valentina was humming and skipping on the way there, her hand firmly clutched in mine. Occasionally, she would look up at me and just smile, warming my heart and filling me with happiness.

It was crazy how such a small being could have such a huge impact on my life. I suffered when she did, was happy when she was, my emotions were so intricately woven with hers that sometimes it felt like we were one person. It may sound insane for those who didn't believe in it, but Valentina was my true soulmate, she was and always would be my favorite person in the world, the one I would do anything for.

I'd been taking care of her since she was a child. Hell, *I* was a child myself. So much in fact that the lines between sisterhood and motherhood blurred. I would love to have a family one day, even though I didn't really think it could be in the cards for me, but Valentina would always remain the first person I'd felt like a mother to.

As we arrived at the park, the playground was full of boisterous kids screaming and running around. I noticed a mom squad sitting not far from them, all in velvet tracksuits and puffy jackets holding coffee mugs. I gulped.

Whoever said kids were mean clearly had never met Lakestone's mom squads. They were judgmental, frustrated little shits. Mean girls who peaked in high school and never got out of that phase.

Valentina and I stopped in front of the gates, just taking in our surroundings.

"You know I love you, right mama?" She whipped her face towards me and nodded, still holding my hand.

“I love you too. You’re my favorite person in the whole wide world. And not just because you’re my sister.” I smiled and squatted down to come face to face with her.

“You’re my favorite person too.” I caressed her cold cheeks, because winter was coming sooner than anticipated this year.

“Is it okay if Maddox is my second favorite person?” She asked sheepishly, like she thought I would reprimand her. “I know it’s only temporary, until we can leave and start elsewhere, but…” she shrugged, not knowing how to finish her sentence and I felt my heart squeezing.

It broke me to see how losing the people she cared for one after the other made her scared of getting attached again.

Part of it was my fault, I had to admit. For the longest time, it was just the two of us. We took care of each other, we looked out for each other. When we lost mama and papa, I told her one day we would go out in the world and make a great life for ourselves but that in the meantime, we couldn’t trust anyone else.

Then Maddox came into the picture and somehow wrecked this idea I had. Before I could see anything coming, we were living with him, having dinner together, cooking together, watching movies and going out for pancakes. I knew what kind of beer he drank, what his favorite brand of fabric softener was and even got jealous of his damn neighbor.

It was scary as shit but at the same time, I hadn’t had such stability in my life in a long time and it made me realize how much I craved it. I wondered if maybe it was the same for Valentina. It hurt just thinking about it, but maybe I hadn't been enough. Maybe there were some things I couldn't give her that Maddox could.

"Of course it's okay, mami. You have such a big heart." I put my hand over it, on her puffy jacket. "There's place for more than one person. There's nothing wrong with forming bonds with people other than me, baby."

She didn't say anything, her trembling lips and watery eyes kept her from speaking. Instead, she jumped on me, nearly making me fall over. Her little arms wrapped around my neck and her face burrowed against it.

I gulped, swallowing my tears down and hugged her tight.

"You're the most important person in my life and I hope you know I'll do anything for you." I managed to whisper even when my throat felt tight with emotions.

"I know. You always have. You take the monsters away."

That nicked my heart and had me on the verge of crying but I held on. My beautiful, brave girl. My little rose.

We stayed that way for a few minutes, I think mainly because neither of us wanted to let go of the other. Then, eventually, we pulled away and started walking into the park. She wanted to go to the playground first, so that's where we headed.

Valentina gave me one last smile before running towards the slides as I sat down on a bench near it. Next to me, the raging mom squad whispered to themselves, tossing me the occasional side look.

I ignored them.

They didn't deserve me to even acknowledge their poor, miserable existence. They wanted to talk about me? Let them. The whole town was, anyway.

Ever since word got out about me killing that man, townsfolk seemed to be… almost scared of me. Never mind that the newspaper specified that it had been self-defense, never mind that I was never even charged.

Apparently, in their self righteous, narrow little minds, since I'd been capable of taking a life once, I could do it a second time.

To be completely honest, I don't think they would have reacted that way had it been anyone else. People in Lakestone already hated me, and for various reasons.

I was too loud, too opinionated, too wild, and disrespectful in their eyes.

What was funny is that the only thing I did to gain that reputation was stand up for myself. I never took any of their shit, whether it was adults trying to undermine me at galas or dinner parties or kids my age trying to bully me for not feeling the need to belong with them.

Also, there was the fact that I was arrested for painting on some of their properties. But in my defense, all those white facades looked bland. They needed color.

Looking at my angel, I smiled when I saw she was playing with a little boy her age. They smiled and giggled to themselves, chasing each other. It felt like forever since I heard her laugh so freely and I missed that sound.

But like every good thing in my life, it didn't last.

Suddenly the little boy who was being chased by my sister tripped on his own two feet and fell to the ground. Everything happened so fast, one minute the kids were playing, the next the boy was wailing and his mother was running to him, yelling at my sister.

I got up and rushed towards them, ready to pacify her and tell her to back the fuck off Valentina.

"What did you do to him? Can't you be more careful!" Her beady eyes narrowed as she pointed a perfectly manicured finger towards my sister.

The look of fright in Valentina's eyes was all it took to put me in a rage. She didn't react well to being yelled at, it triggered her.

"Who the hell do you think you're talking to?" Startled, she turned around and looked appalled to see me approach.

"Your spawn tripped my little boy!"

"Your little boy is a dumbass who thought looking behind him while running was a smart idea and *tripped*." She audibly gasped.

The other mothers started to surround us, looking as shocked and upset as the fake blond in front of me.

"How dare you! You shouldn't even be here! Criminals like you belong in jail, not in playgrounds! You're a danger to our community!"

I could feel my nostrils flaring, anger simmering in my blood. I wasn't a criminal. I was a goddamn survivor and posh little bitches like her could never understand me or what I'd been through.

"Shut up! " All eyes turned towards a clearly upset Valentina who in turn was glaring at the woman with pure hatred in her eyes. "Don't ever say that again! You don't know her!" Angry tears ran down her eyes and her chest was erratically moving up and down.

I think I hadn't realized until that moment just how much this situation was affecting her. Of course, I knew the trauma of that night would always remain, I knew she was probably sad and disoriented and upset about everything that happened.

What I never took into consideration was that my nice, polite, loving little sister might have been *angry*, all this time.

I never even realized how what I did that night might affect her and the way people would perceive her.

"How dare you." That came from another mom and brought me out of my thoughts. "Is that how you plan on raising her? To be disrespectful and rude, like you?" She looked at me, disgust seeping into her features.

"We've really tried with you!" Another bleached blond jumped in. "We've tried, for Marcella's sake, because she was an astounding member of our community, but no more. You never tried to fit in, always wearing your *ghetto* clothes and spray painting our streets like a vulgar delinquent!"

"We will not let you raise this girl to be like you." My heartbeat was out of control, so many of them spoke at the same time, Valentina was crying, these awful women were spitting the nastiest things at me.

My world was spinning. I was overwhelmed. I was sad. I was fucking livid.

"Prepare to hear from CPS soon, Miss Raymond." The first mom snipped, eyes narrowed at me.

These people never liked me, they never *tried*, like they'd just claimed. They only wanted me to conform and as soon as I didn't, deemed me an outcast. They had participated in making my life hell over the last few years, and now they were openly threatening me with taking away the most important thing in my life? The one person I would die and kill for?

That's all it took for me to snap.

***

**MADDOX**

Furious didn't even begin to describe how I was feeling as I stepped out of my car.

Adam exited next and tried calling my name but I was already ten feet ahead of him, marching in the direction of the playground.

A small crowd composed of two police officers, several onlookers and a horde of women in hideous tracksuits gathered on one side of it, while a police car was parked on the other. The women were all trying to talk at the same time and the uniformed officers standing in front of them looked completely in over their heads. They didn't know where to look, who to listen to. That made me even more fucking angry.

One of the women turned her head towards me and did a double take before gasping.

"Detective! Finally someone competent around here!" She all but ran to me, or should I say power-walked? She looked like a goose and it honestly was ridiculous.

"What the fuck is happening here and where the hell are the Raymond sisters?" I side-stepped her, not sparing her a glance and looked at Remy, one of the two officers present. My tone was much more brusque than I had intended and he straightened, eyes wide.

"S-she— huh, Sofia is the car and Valentina is on the bench right here, sir— fuck." He pointed to where Valentina was, or was supposed to be because the bench was fucking empty. I could see the exact moment Remy understood he'd fucked up. He totally blanched and even had the smart idea of taking a step back, away from me.

Red contorted my vision. I was angry a few minutes ago but now it was more than that. I was feral at the incompetence of the men in front of me. I took a threatening step towards Remy, when a strong hand came clasping my arm from next to me.

"Maddox, calm down."

"Calm down? How can I fucking calm down, Adam, when these two idiots preferred listening to a bunch of women yapping God knows what than to keep watch of a nine year old girl prone to daydreaming and living in her own world!"

"S-she was here, sir, I swear! We have the other one cuffed in the car and—"

"Cuffed!"

Somehow the idea that these men put their hands on Sofia and manhandled her to the point of putting her in handcuffs enraged me even more. I took another step towards them, ready to rip their heads off, but again, Adam stopped me.

"I want to know exactly what the fuck happened and I want to hear it now." I was grateful Adam was lucid enough for the both of us and acted like a goddamn cop, because Lord knew I was in no condition to.

"She assaulted me!" My eyes were brought back to one of the women, and they widened.

She had been slightly hidden by the others due to the fact that she was sitting down on a bench while her friends, I assumed, were standing.

She sported a huge, inflated eye that would no doubt blacken by tomorrow, and cuts everywhere on her face. Blood was seeping from her busted lip and eyebrow. Her hair and clothes looked disheveled and she had a mixture of blood and grass on her pink tracksuit.

Fuck.

*Fuck, fuck, fuck, fuck, fuck*!

What did Sofia do?

"We were trying to help her! Give her advice on how to raise the little one, and she blew up on us! Tackled me to the ground and started marteling my face like a freaking punching bag!"

The blond started crying, or at least I thought she was, I couldn't really tell with the way her face was so fucking rearranged.

I closed my eyes and gulped, rubbing the heels of my hands against them. I could feel the headache coming from a mile away. Why would she do that? How could she be so fucking careless.

We were so fucking close from having permanent custody of Valentina, my case file had been forwarded to the social services in charge of approving demands of fostering, the DA and chief of police were on our side, it was all in the work, but she just put everything in jeopardy and for what? Not being fucking able to control her *goddamn* temper?

"Sofia denied it, sir. She said she *had* thrown the first punch but that the other women ganged up on her then. She's in pretty bad shape but nothing like this one."

"I can't believe you didn't call 911! This is so unprofessional, be ready to hear from us!"

"You should have called them yourself, then, lady. Your friend was healthy enough to cuss us five ways to Sunday, I think she'll be fine to sit in one of your cars while you bring her to the hospital so she can get some ice on that eye and stitches." The other cop, Jody, looked about done with them.

My head was ringing, I could feel panic start to seep through my pores.

Valentina.

Valentina was the number one priority right now, I had to find her.

"I want one of you at every entrance, no one gets in or out of this park before we've found Valentina. Call in for reinforcement, I want these woods fucking combed through before night falls!"

The officers in front of me nodded and immediately dispatched to heed my orders. Adam took off towards one side of the woods and I went in the opposite direction.

"Valentina! Valentina, come on, pretty girl come over here!"

The thought that she was somewhere in here, alone, scared out of her mind and probably crying made me want to punch something.

"Valentina! Come out, please!" I was so desperate and not above begging. I walked for five, ten, fifteen minutes, but nothing.

Dead leaves crunched under my feet as I got further into the woods. All the trees looked alike and I started to wonder if I wasn't just going in circles. I usually liked the outdoors but right then, the greenery was nauseating and the foliage might as well have been wrapped around my neck and strangling me. I couldn't comprehend for the life of me, what brought us here right now, how could everything have gone to shit so fucking easily.

This morning we were having breakfast all together, Valentina's smile warming my soul as she and Sofia laughingly told me about how hectic breakfast used to be at their house.

And now one of them was handcuffed in a cop car while the other was God only knew where, probably having a panic attack.

My phone started ringing and I brought it to my ears without checking the caller, thinking maybe it was Adam telling me they had found Valentina. It wasn't.

"Maddox, what's wrong? I got your message. I just pulled up at the park!" Drea was clearly panicking.

"Something happened, I— fuck. Listen, I'll need to bail Sofia out of jail, so I need you to take care of Valentina for the night, please?"

My eyes were looking everywhere as I spoke, searching for clues of where the little girl who came to mean so much to me in the span of a month, could be hiding.

"Of course! Anything to help! Where is she?" My hand gripped the top of my head, where I let my blond hair grow longer.

"That's another fucking problem, we don't know. Drea I'm panicking, I— what if something happened to her? What am I—"

"Mads?"

The little voice coming from behind me made me pause and I don't think I ever spun around so fast in my entire life. At first I really thought I was hallucinating. At that point, I'd been walking for thirty minutes and daylight was starting to disappear. Perhaps the day's exhaustion coupled with the fear of not finding Valentina made me delusional.

Eyes searching where it came from, I called again,

"Pretty Girl? Where are you? Please come here."

Rustling came from behind the bushes and I could hear the sound of leaves crunching under her little feet. In the background, my sister's voice was calling my name on the other side of the phone, but I didn't pay it any attention.

All I cared about was the wave of fucking relief I felt slam into me as soon as I saw Valentina's black hair and askew beanie emerge from behind the bushes where I supposed she had been hiding this whole time. I ended the call.

"Valentina, oh my God."

I all but ran to her and picked her off the ground. I didn't even realize how tight I was squeezing her, I just needed to feel she was there and that it wasn't my imagination playing tricks on me.

"I-I'm so sorry. I was scared, everyone was yelling. They're taking Sofia to jail, it's not fair!" She started sobbing against my shoulder even as her arms circled my neck and she hugged me.

"Shhh, don't cry, pretty girl." I rubbed circles on her back, inhaling her sweet scent of roses and honey.

"She did what she had to do! They deserved it! They hurt us! Please don't take her away, she did it to protect me." She went on crying and I frowned.

"Valentina, what did those women do?"

She was silent for a moment then sniffed and pulled slightly away so she could look me in the eyes. Hers were full of tears and it enraged me. I never wanted to see her cry again.

"They—they said really mean things to Sofia. And me. They called me a spawn and said they didn't want me to be like Sofia and that they would call CPS." Watery eyes and trembling lips stared back at me as I could feel my anger flaring.

Those bitches. Those *fucking* bitches.

"Nobody is taking you away from us, pretty girl, I promise you."

"I just want a family." She whispered tiredly, and I could've sworn my eyes watered at that.

There was so much pain in those five words, so much longing, it felt like someone had plunged their hand directly into my chest and was squeezing my heart until it might explode.

"And you'll have one." I swallowed the lump in my throat. "But you need to be strong, okay? And you need to trust me." She looked down, dejected.

"Sofia says we can't trust anyone."

"I'm not anyone, am I?" Caressing the hair away from her face, she looked back at me. "I care about you and Sofia, Valentina. Very freaking much. And I need you to trust me, okay?" She waited a beat before she quietly nodded.

Almost shyly, she laid her head on my shoulder.

"I will need to take care of Sofia tonight, so you'll sleep at Andrea's house, alright? Remember Andrea? My sister? Adrianna's mother." She nodded and I continued. "They're family too. You'll have the best sleepover, watch all those Disney movies you love and eat popcorn until your tummy is full." I tickled her and she giggled tiredly. That brought a small smile to my face. "And in the meantime I'll be taking care of everything. Believe me, Sofia isn't going anywhere."

She frowned and pinched her lips together. "Pinky promise?" Valentina put her pinky finger in the air and looked at me expectantly.

"Pinky promise." I laced mine with it and kissed her forehead. She hugged me a bit tighter, like she didn't want to risk me getting away.

I wasn't going anywhere.

***

## SOFIA

Over the years and the numerous arrests I'd gone through, I encountered various versions of Maddox.

I'd seen him angry and screaming, worried, disappointed, wary, even amused sometimes. But all these times, he communicated his emotions through words.

The version of Maddox I had in front of me right now, however, was not speaking. In fact, he had barely spoken a word to me since he came back from those woods with Valentina clutched in his arms.

The relief I'd felt when I saw him was tremendous. Being alone, handcuffed and locked inside that car as I watched those officers pacify the blond gang and not care about my sister discreetly running away, I never felt so helpless.

Do you know that feeling of powerlessness when you know a disaster is coming, you're watching it arrive, but you can't prevent it?

I'd screamed my throat raw in that car. Nobody heard me.

I yelled at them that a nine year old little girl had just disappeared inside the woods even as night would soon come, but no one heard me. That just reinforced my idea that Valentina and I were made to be alone. That nobody could care for her as much as I did.

But then Maddox came into the picture and I could see from the car window how angry he got as soon as he saw Valentina was missing. It took him less than a minute, but by then she'd been gone for almost twenty.

When he went inside the woods, I found it easier to breathe. Worry still twisted my gut, of course, but less than before, because somewhat, deep inside, I just knew I could count on Maddox to bring my baby back.

And what a weird, unusual feeling. To be able to rely on someone.

After he found her and came back, he left her with his sister and came to check up on me. I was expecting him to scream and tell me how stupid I was, how I just put our whole plan in danger, but he didn't.

He silently unclasped the handcuffs from my wrists and said "don't move" in a freezing cold tone. I didn't. I stayed in the car, watching from a distance as Andrea clasped Valentina's hand in hers and they started to walk towards her car. My sister tried to look back over her shoulder at me, but then she turned around and started walking, head down and sulking.

My heart was in my throat at the idea of her being away from me and with virtual strangers, but I knew it was all my fault. I fucked up, big time, and now I risked not being able to have custody at all.

I was brought back to the station and interrogated. They also tended to the cuts on my face. My ribs were killing me after one of those bitches kicked me so I would get off her friend, but they assured me it wasn't broken.

I don't really know what happened at the station, I was in a daze, just going through the motions. All I knew was that it was their word against mine, and they didn't have a past of petty crimes and high school slugfests like I did.

Guilt and dread mixed in my stomach as I thought of what would happen now. Would they take Valentina away from me? Not grant Maddox custody?

The man in question locked the door after entering the apartment and tossed his keys on the side table.

I stood in the middle of the living room, not daring to move. I knew this was on me. I knew I risked it all because I let my temper get the best of me.

“I—“

“Shut up.” Were his words as soon as I tried to apologize. I winced.

Maddox looked positively wrung out. He leaned back against the door, eyes closed and hands rubbing his face in frustration. He'd been up since five this morning and it was past one in the morning right now.

“Do you have any idea of the repercussions this could have on our case? On me being granted Valentina’s custody and you living here?” His voice was quiet, he was not yelling, yet I think I would have preferred it if he were.

“I’m sorry, I didn’t think.” I almost didn’t recognize this guilty, pathetic voice as mine.

“You clearly didn’t. You acted like a stupid brat is what you did! These women are snakes, and Goddammit, you know it Sofia!” Finally the screams were here and it almost made me miss his freezing cold tone from earlier. “They could write you off as being violent and irresponsible and take her away from us forever! I thought you were a smart girl but I was obviously wrong.”

His hands came to clutch his hair and he yanked at it as he paced the living room.

"T-they said all kinds of nasty things and I—"

"So fucking what! Let them fucking talk, dammit! This whole town *lives* to gossip, you know it better than anyone!"

"They said they were gonna call CPS! I couldn't let them try to take her away from me!" I yelled back, my calm suddenly breaking.

"No, so you decided to do it yourself! Because guess what? That woman you assaulted, Candi Stein? She filed a complaint!" Of course she did, I had no doubt about that.

Tears filled my eyes as the reality of the situation downed on me.

"They hit me too, they all ganged up on me, there has to be something we can do about it!"

"Even if they did, without proof it's your word against theirs! I can't believe you were so careless!" His words hit me in the face so hard he might as well have slapped me.

"How can you say that when all I do is care! Care, care, *care*! I never stop fucking caring! She's my whole world and I'd do anything for her! Why the fuck do *you* care so much?!" His head snapped back towards me as soon as the words left my mouth and he rushed in my direction, crowding me against the wall.

"Because you're mine, goddammit! Both of you are mine! We're supposed to be in this together but you let your temper get the best of you and didn't think of us! You and Valentina are mine and I'll be damned if something happens to you."

I stopped breathing.

I think Maddox did too. I think his confession might have surprised him as much as me. For the longest time, neither of us spoke, we just stared at each other in shock, chests heaving up and down, breaths intertwining.

"Yours?" I whispered.

"Mine." He took a step closer to me.

"Yours."

I don't know who made the first move, I think we both did to be honest, simultaneously. One second we were breathing fast, his chest pressing against mine, and the next I had my hands entangled in his hair while his were on my waist and our mouths fused together.

# 15

# DESIRE

## SOFIA

It was phenomenal.

No other word could describe the feeling of Maddox's soft, velvety, full lips against my own.

His tongue licked the seam of my lips and I immediately parted them, ready to taste him. God, I wanted to taste him, I needed it. I moaned against his mouth and he reacted by bringing my body even closer. Pressed against him, nothing else around us mattered. This was years of attraction, at least on my part, finally blowing up and exploding into a whirlwind of desire and lust.

I could hear his heart hit against his ribcage, ricocheting against my chest in a hard, fast, violent rhythm. It was delicious. I moaned again, not able to stop myself from doing so. I knew it wasn't considered attractive, but I couldn't help it when his hands were all over me like that.

I'd never felt this kind of attraction, of desire, before in my life. It was like a dam had broken and I found myself battling my own reason. I knew we should probably stop, I didn't want to go back to that awkwardness we went through after we shared a bed that very first night. Yet I couldn't help but want to continue in this madness, I wanted Maddox every way I could get him.

"I'm still fucking pissed at you." He mumbled against my lips right before he started peppering kisses all over my jaw and neck. "But fuck baby you taste so good." His lips were back on mine, licking, sucking, kissing, I never felt so turned on in my life.

"I'm sorry, Maddox. I'm so sorry." I pulled away slightly to look him in the eye. My fingers were grasping his hair, nails slightly scraping against his scalp but if the growl he let out was any indication, he seemed to like it.

"Yeah? Are you really, though?"

"More than anything. I don't want us to be separated. All three of us."

Reaching on my tip-toes, I nuzzled my face against his neck, seeking his warmth and comfort. He was so tall and it was comforting, I felt so safe in his arms. It felt so right to finally admit it, finally say out loud what I'd been thinking for weeks.

"Say we belong together." His hand came up to my hair and he wrapped it around his fist, groaning against my lips. "Say we're a family."

I whimpered at having my hair pulled, marveling at the fact that I seemed to fucking love it. I had no idea a pinch of pain could be so pleasurable. It never was in the past. I could feel myself getting wet, not only at the proximity between our bodies or the fact that I could still taste him on my lips, but at his words, too. Him saying we belonged together, that we were a fucking family. I wanted to never stop kissing him.

"We belong together. We're a family." I nuzzled his jaw before reaching up, almost shyly, and licking the path from his jaw to his neck.

"Don't ever pull something like that again, Sofia. I don't want to lose you."

Tears sprung in my eyes, begging to fall. "I'm so sorry, please forgive me. I feel so bad, Maddox." I sniffled, moisture running from my eyes and down my cheeks.

Guilt was eating at me from the inside. If they took Valentina away from us because of me, I'll never forgive myself.

Just not having been able to say goodbye to her earlier as she left with Andrea made me feel alone and worthless, like I had failed her. And I guess I did. I just hoped she could forgive me.

Maddox' hand grip on my hair got softer when he saw my tears and he started caressing it instead, pushing it away from my face. I moved my hands to his jacket, holding onto it firmly like I was scared he'd let go of me.

"You do, baby?"

The rumble of his voice, low and grainy, made warmth travel from my stomach to my pussy. I nodded quietly, keeping my watery eyes on his. He looked deep in thought, his hand that wasn't in my hair was drawing circles on my hip, where my top had ridden up.

"Do you trust me, Sofia?"

My breath hitched, not expecting him to ask me that question. It was tricky, because I never really gave anyone my trust before. This was the biggest thing I could ever offer somebody and he knew it. He knew I was wary of everything surrounding me and that my number one priority was and would always be Valentina. He knew any attempts at trusting people in my past had ended in a disaster.

Yet this was Maddox. He proved on more than one occasion that he was trustworthy, that he was loyal and would do anything to help us. Valentina loved him and my feelings for him grew stronger everyday.

When I thought the world was ending, he was the only person that stood up for me. He had literally gone out of his way to make sure Valentina and I wouldn't be separated, he took on the responsibility of getting custody of a nine year old he didn't even know. He protected us from danger, went feral when he thought Valentina was gone and even the way he was reacting now proved how much he cared.

So I decided he was worthy. Of us, of our trust.

"Yes. I trust you. More than I ever trusted anyone." He kissed my lips like he would my soul. So quietly and delicately, it felt like silk against my lips. I would have thought I had dreamed it if not for his grip on my waist and hair.

"Go to my room and take your clothes off." My breath hitched at his command.

Although I was crazy for him, although I wanted him with every inch of my soul, a small part of me dreaded his words. As I said, sex wasn't pleasurable for me in the past, and I wasn't sure I was ready for that. He must have sensed my anguish because he cupped my cheek and made me look him in the eyes.

"Hey, we're not having sex." Despite myself, my shoulders slumped in relief. Actually, it was paradoxical how relieved and disappointed this news made me feel. "Go wait for me, I think you'll need what I have in store for you." I gulped and nodded quietly.

Then I got on my tip-toes and pressed my lips to his, just because I could. It felt amazing, kissing him because I felt like it, not worrying about making things awkward or about him pulling away.

As I moved back, his eyes slowly opened back and they stared back at me in undeniable hunger. "Go. Hurry up before I change my mind and bend you over the couch so I can eat your sweet little pussy from behind." I squealed at the visual this created in my head and hurried away in the direction of his bedroom.

Entering it felt strange, I hadn't set foot in there since the first day when Maddox gave us a tour of the apartment. His room smelled like him, woodsy and musky, completely addictive.

A full-length mirror stood right in front of his bed and my cheeks warmed up at the idea that we would be able to see ourselves pleasuring each other. And damn, I was dying to pleasure him.

Every time I closed my eyes for the last two weeks, all I saw was him behind me in my bed, his calloused hand between my legs as I ground into it, using him to get off. That morning had been haunting me. I would have given anything to relive it, and now I finally was. I didn't waste any more time getting naked, and once my clothes were strewn across the floor, I stood staring at my naked body.

I often got compliments about it, slender waists and slightly fuller hips were definitely considered attractive in this day and age, yet I just couldn't make myself appreciate my physique. For years I actually hated it. I hated what it reminded me of and the comments I had gotten because of it.

Now, though, knowing Maddox liked it, I couldn't help but think maybe it wasn't so bad.

My musings were cut short as I heard the door to bedroom snap closed, making me look up. Maddox was leaning against it, eyes roaming my naked form like he wanted to eat me alive.

I could feel my breath hitch in my throat. God, yes. I wanted him to do just that.

"Get on the bed, Sofia. On your knees, shoulders on the mattress and ass in the air." I frowned, his voice was a tone colder than it had been earlier, it didn't leave any room for argument.

It sent a thrill down my spine and I could have sworn I felt wetness seep from between my legs. My clit was throbbing like never before, the excitement of not knowing what he had in store for me made me almost giddy.

I took my position, exactly the way he wanted me, and waited quietly. I had never been so quiet and obedient around him. I just felt so guilty, like I had no room to argue or talk whatsoever. What I had done today was stupid and bordered on bratty. I didn't know what Maddox had in mind, but I knew whatever it was would bring me out of my head and expiate those toxic feelings and thoughts from my body. I knew whatever he wanted to do to me would make me feel better in the end.

Cheek on the mattress, ass up in the air, I had to fight my mind not to be reminded of bad memories. Maddox wasn't *him*, Maddox *cared* about me, he would not demean me or degrade me. Maddox. wasn't. *him*.

I repeated the words non-stop, lost in thought until a hard slap landed on my left ass cheek, wrenching a surprised scream out of me.

"W-what are you doing?" I gasped.

"Taking your guilt away, Sofia. Don't you think you deserve a punishment after how you acted?" I winced at the choice of words but kept my mouth shut.

This man was taking my every fear and giving them a whole new meaning. My breath hitched inside my throat when he slapped my ass again, on the same spot he landed the first blow.

I whimpered and wiggled around, trying to get up. He put pressure on the top of my back, making sure I wouldn't. I felt so confused, part of me hated what he was doing, while the other longed for it. I didn't want to feel the guilt anymore, I wanted to be free of it. I knew if I endured the punishment I would feel like I deserved to put everything that happened today behind me and thus would be able to focus better on fixing my mistakes.

I stopped fighting and Maddox noticed. His hand on the top of my back moved to my hair, he wrapped a fist in it and tugged lightly.

"Good girl. You're gonna count with me, okay baby? Fifteen spankings for today." I gulped, not knowing what to make of my emotions.

Like the few times he called me good girl, my pussy dampened, so much in fact that I was afraid I would make a mess out of his sheet. "I want you to count." He didn't wait and spanked my ass again, making me yelp.

"O-one!" I bit my lips to keep myself from moaning.

Why was this starting to get pleasurable? The knowledge Maddox was helping rid me of those bad thoughts that were plaguing my brain somehow turned me on. Those nasty thoughts who screamed I was an irresponsible brat, that I would lose Valentina forever, that she would end up hating me, they seemed further and further away with each swat.

They evaporated as Maddox kept on driving the palm of his hand against my ass cheeks, again and again. My skin felt so fucking warm, it hurt so fucking much I though it might start to peel off. But it wasn't possible, I knew it deep down, Maddox would never inflict such pain to my body.

Nothing mattered but the feel of his hand on me, the sound of his groans as he took in my small figure laying face down and hips tilted up on his bed. I was on clear display and I knew he could see every inch of my body, including my damp heat.

"Thirteen!" I yelled, tears flowing down my cheeks.

I wouldn't be able to explain why crying felt so good right then, like with each tear, it was one of my sins that was being drained away from me. It was cathartic, it made me feel good about myself and my body, and from the way Maddox praised me after each slap, he seemed really proud of me. I loved that fact. It made me feel accomplished somehow.

“Fourteen!” Sobs after sobs were wrenched out of me by the force of his hand.

“You’re doing so well, baby. Give me one more.” There was such a difference between the force of his blows and the softness of his voice. It made my head spin in paradoxical delight.

The last spanking was by far the worst, maybe because my skin was already tender, or maybe because Maddox put a lot more strength into it, either way, it hurt like a motherfucker.

“Fifteen!” I sobbed, as tremors rocked my whole body.

The tears just wouldn’t stop, I was crying like a baby, letting every little thing I had kept to myself for so long, finally out. The whole thing was so freeing, so liberating that I just didn’t want it to end. I didn’t want to stop feeling the satisfaction of having gone through with it. Telling myself that I’d done it, I’d taken my punishment felt so good I just wanted it to last forever.

“You’re the most delicious thing I’ve ever seen. And you took your punishment like such a good girl, baby.” Soft lips pressed against my burning skin and I swear I could feel my face warming up at the intimate contact. “You deserve a reward.”

Maddox rubbed my ass delicately, making the spots he had slapped ache ever so deliciously. The tremors shaking my body were getting lighter and lighter, and my ears perked up as soon as he started talking of a reward.

“Spread your legs and let me make you feel good.” I did as told without even thinking about it.

This simple act gave me pause, because who the hell was I? Since when did I do what I was told so quickly and quietly, no questions asked? When was the last time I had trust someone as much as I do Maddox? I had just let that man spank my bare bottom and now I was spreading my legs for him, opening myself up to his heated gaze.

My internal musings didn't last long however, because before I could overthink it further, a warm, wet tongue made contact with my thigh. The whole time Maddox was reddening my ass, I could feel wetness gathering and soaking my core. It started dripping down the inside of my thighs when I spread them wide.

It was new to me, being this vulnerable, this open in front of someone and not feeling like I might throw up or lose consciousness. Yet, as soon as Maddox started touching me, licking up a drop of cum that had been running down my thigh, nothing mattered anymore.

I started moaning but then chose otherwise and bit my lip instead. I didn't want him to stop because I made too much noise. I breathed heavily, trying to get my core closer to his mouth but he was only giving me the tip of his tongue. It was driving me insane.

"P-please…"

My own voice was strange to me. It sounded so needy, so high pitched, almost like a purr. I had a hard time believing it was really mine.

"What do you want, baby?" His words resounded against the most intimate part of me and I whimpered in delight. I tried muting it again, but this time, Maddox noticed. "Don't do that. Don't muffle those sounds, I want to hear them, I want to hear you."

My eyes widened in surprise at his confession. "Y-you do?"

"Fuck yes, baby. The sounds you make got me so fucking hard."

Granted, I didn't have much experience with men, but the little I did have was nothing like this. It never felt good, never felt right, like what we were doing right now. I was in a position that had me wide open for his eyes, that should probably have made me feel uncomfortable, yet I couldn't bring myself to feel either. Mostly because I knew I wasn't on display for just anyone's eyes. I was on display for Maddox, and that changed everything.

"I-I want you. I want to feel it." I managed to get the words out even though it felt like my face was on fire.

I had never done something like that, never spoken up about sex to my partner, saying what I wanted or what I liked. I never got the opportunity.

"Feel what, Sofia?" I whimpered in frustration and desire; he knew what I wanted. He just wanted me to spell it for his own pleasure.

"I want your tongue, please lick me, Maddox!" Words made their way out of my mouth before I could keep them from doing so.

My chest was heaving up and down against the mattress and I kept on wiggling my ass to get his mouth to finally touch my core. So far, he had stirred clear of it and chose to make me crazy instead by licking and sucking all around it.

"Fuck, I can't refuse you anything. You're so fucking hot right now." I was about to start begging when finally, *finally*, he put his mouth exactly where I wanted it.

Pure, unadulterated delight was what I felt the moment Maddox basically buried his face against my pussy.

I moaned, glad he didn't want me to keep my sounds to myself. My hands fisted the sheet underneath us and I ground myself back against his face. His tongue was bringing me more pleasure than my fingers ever could, hell even more pleasure than grinding against his hand had brought me that other day.

"Oh my god, Maddox!" Fueled by my screams of pleasure, he just kept going.

Two of his fingers formed a V and he encased my lips with them, rubbing up and down as his tongue went in and out of my slit, licking up and down before going inside again. It was so skilled, so delightful, I never wanted it to end.

Grabbing my ass with his other hand, he spread me even wider, his tongue finding my throbbing little clit at the front. He groaned and I could feel the vibrations, nearly sending me over the edge.

"You taste so good, Sofia. That day you finished against my hand, your scent was all over my fingers. I sucked on them just to have the slightest taste of you. I could eat you for hours." As soon as the words were out, he went back to work.

I couldn't take it anymore, I was moving against his mouth, my hands flying everywhere, desperate to come. When his middle finger started tracing my soaked slit and then dipped inside of me, I thought I would die from pleasure.

"Maddox! Oh yes, yes, yes. Please, don't stop!" And he didn't, his finger plunged in and out of me with no reprieve, so thick, so hard, so… "Fuck, that's so good." I groaned, my eyes closing to their own accord.

"Yeah? You're gonna come for me, baby? Drench my face in cum and then let me clean you up all over again?" The dirty, filthy things that came out of his mouth just fuelled me and pushed me even closer to the edge. I swear I could come from his dirty talking alone.

He thrusted his finger in and out of me relentlessly, the wet slapping sounds the palm of his hand made as it slapped against my wet skin just made the whole scene seem even filthier and I loved it. I never would have thought I would but it just made me more turned on.

"Fuck, you're soaked baby." He mumbled against my pussy, his lips grazing my most sensitive skin with each word. "Your cunt is soaking my face. Come for me."

His licks went faster, his finger ramming inside me, his whole palm slapping against my cunt with each thrust and I never felt so cared for in my life. I was so, so, so close—

He bit my clit and it sent me into overdrive, finally pushing me over the edge as the most intense orgasm of my life made me shudder and arch my back. I screamed to the top of my lungs, nearly getting on my knees on the bed as he kept licking the juices flowing out of me, gripping my hips to keep me in place.

The feel of his wet tongue against the more-than-sensitive area made me spasm. I opened my eyes only to feel tears running down my face. He made me cry. I couldn't believe it.

I had cried after sex before, but it was for entirely different reasons.

With Maddox, the pleasure was just so intense, so ground-breaking, that I couldn't keep the tears from flowing as I experienced it. I was still breathing hard, half from the aftershock of my orgasm, half from the fact that this was my first ever orgasm that's been given by someone other than myself.

I felt like I had entered a whole other dimension, like I was just floating around and enjoying the sensations going through me. Strong hands grabbed my waist and rolled me around on my back, caressing and rubbing my arms and shoulders. Then I was hoisted onto his lap, my legs wrapping against his jeans clad waist.

"That's it, sweetheart. Come back to me." He rubbed my butt and pepper my neck and collarbone with kisses.

I whimpered when I saw my cum drenching his mouth and chin. I wouldn't know how to explain the deep satisfaction I experienced at seeing a part of myself etched on him like that. Like he was mine. I reached up for him and he grabbed my hand, leaning over me and casting his lips upon mine. His kiss was demanding, rewarding, I could taste myself on his lips, and I didn't even mind. Actually, I love it.

He groaned, his body growing taut as I ground my sensitive heat against his growing erection. His jeans rubbing against me were the most delicious type of torture. I moaned at the friction his jeans created against my still throbbing clit. One of his hands went down between our bodies as he cupped it, pulling his lips away from mine.

I bit my lips as I looked up at him.

"This is mine. I tried staying away. I really did, but I want you too much." The determination in his gaze made the breath catch in my throat as one of my hands went to his face to cup his jaw.

"I've wanted you too, for so long." I breathed. Getting the words out of my chest felt so good. It was my turn to sneak my hand between our bodies and grip his very big, very obvious erection. "Is this mine, too?"

I never even knew I could be possessive over a man, but my altercation with Giorgianna earlier and my nerve wracking need to know his body was mine proved the contrary.

His head went down and he kissed me again, lighter this time, before pulling away again to catch my eyes. "Of course it is, baby. I only have eyes for you."

My heart missed a beat.

***

Two hours later, we found ourselves laying next to each other on his bed, freshly showered and sharing body heat. My head on his chest, his fingers playing with my hair while mine drew abstract patterns on his skin. It felt so natural just being here with him.

"This can't get out. At least not until we get custody of Valentina, okay?" I found myself nodding, knowing exactly where he was getting at. The fact that he was willing to go behind everyone's back for me meant a lot. "Fuck, I can't believe we did that." His lips pressed against mine and I reveled in the proximity.

I let out a small laugh, "Me neither. I thought you hated me." He frowned and shook his head.

"You made me crazy sometimes, but I could never hate you, Sofia."

Maddox accented his words with a soft kiss on my lips and for a while that's all we did, we exchanged soft kisses, just because we could. I would lick his lips because I couldn't get enough of his taste, and he would lick my tongue back just to be playful.

The dam had finally broken and we were getting to experience feelings we have had to put away for the longest time.

"This feels unreal." I whispered. "Like we're living in a bubble right now but tomorrow everything will come back and burst it." I kissed his neck, burrowing my face against him and inhaling his scent.

"Let's take things one day at a time, yeah?" After a beat, I nodded.

He was right. I wanted tonight to remain this perfect memory, I didn't want to tarnish it with worries and what ifs.

"Tomorrow we'll deal with the repercussions, but you have to know something." I frowned and he continued, "I made a promise to a precious little girl that I intend to keep, so you're not going anywhere."

Emotions clogged my throat as I sneaked my arms around him, hugging him tight as he squeezed me to his chest.

"There's nowhere I'd rather be."

He kissed my head and said nothing while we just sat there, reveling in each other's company. Eventually Maddox fell asleep though, leaving me alone with my thoughts again. I was trying to come up with a plan for tomorrow, to fix what I had broken, but I kept coming back to the same conclusion. The only solution to our problem.

Gulping and closing my eyes, I reached for my phone, keeping an eye on the man next to me who was still sleeping peacefully.

I swiped it open and got into my text app, searching for the name of the only person I knew could make it all better.

**Sofia:**

`I fucked up. I need your help.`

# 16

## MYSTERY

### SOFIA

Rays of sun streaming through the window woke me up, my eyebrows scrunching. As I started stirring, trying to find the will to finally open my eyes, a groan sounded from behind me. I tensed for a second, right before remembering the events of last night.

Maddox spanking me, then eating me, then cleaning me, then eating me again in the shower. Us falling asleep in each other's arms. Memories just swirled inside my brain.

One of his big hands was splayed on my stomach, which made me realize I was naked and if the thick erection digging into my back was any indication, so was he.

Last night felt like a dream.

When I fell asleep, I was half-convinced I would wake up to find out that I had hallucinated everything that happened. Or that I hadn't but Maddox would be gone and acting like nothing ever happened.

You can imagine my surprise when none of that happened and instead of waking up alone, I had a big arm wrapped possessively around my middle and a big, hot and hard cock pressing into me from behind. A small smile splayed on my lips and I pressed back against him, marveling at the feel of his body surrounding mine.

“Good morning.” He whispered from behind me, hot breath caressing my neck.

A thought just went through my head right then. I loved his voice in the morning and it was the first thing I wanted to hear whenever I woke up from then on.

The possibility of having him for an undetermined period of time was mouth-watering, definitely something I would love. He gave another purpose to my life. Where everything revolved around surviving before him, now it was more than that. Now I didn’t only want a good life for Valentina, I wanted one for me too, and it didn’t seem unreachable or even incompatible.

His hand that was on my stomach made its way to my breast and he cupped it before pinching my nipple. I moaned and arched my back. My breasts had never seemed like a particularly erogenous zone to me, but with Maddox, let’s just say I was pretty sure he could be pinching my small toe and it would make me wet.

“Good morning…” I moaned back, grinding against him, hoping he would see just how much I wanted him to make me feel good.

“So greedy.” He bit my earlobe, seeing clearly in my game. “First thing in the morning and you’re already rubbing against me like a cat in heat. Dirty kitten.” I whimpered, eyes closing and head thrown back in pleasure, hitting his chest.

“I’m not greedy.” It was pointless trying to defend myself when I was so shamelessly rubbing my ass against his erection. What was it with this man and making me horny?

Was it the years I had to watch him from afar, afraid he'd see through me and know how badly I wanted him? Or was it the fact that I could finally own up to wanting him, that I could finally play on my feelings without being afraid of the consequences? To an extent, of course, since no one could know about us just yet.

"It's okay to be greedy. It's okay to put yourself first sometimes." Maddox kissed my neck and I moaned, my eyes rolling back inside my head. "Spread your legs and ride my hand, baby."

I didn't even hesitate. He had made me come three times yesterday, which was three times more than anyone I'd ever been with, but somehow, I just wanted more each and every time.

So I spread my legs and let his hand wander between them. He found my clit and rubbed two fingers against it, using the fact that I was already wet and only getting wetter to lubricate it.

"I just love how responsive you are and how excited you get." I closed my eyes, focusing on the sound of his voice and the feel of his finger as he slowly entered me with it. His middle finger was thrusting in and out of me as his thumb was rubbing my clit and it was simply incredible.

"It feels so good." I couldn't help but groan, burrowing my head against his pillow as I moved my hips against his hand.

"Yeah? Tell me how it feels."

My breath hitched, I hesitated, not used to even speaking during sex. I gulped.

"Your f-fingers feel so good against my pussy, Maddox. It's like I can never get enough of you. I want to taste you."

I don't even know where that came from. I had little experience in oral sex, matter of fact, yesterday was the first time I ever received it. While we were showering, I had felt like it was only natural to return the favor, especially since Maddox hadn't come all night. It made me a bit uneasy but I still got on my knees in front of him, telling myself that this was Maddox and it would never be anything like my previous experiences.

But he saw right through me.

He took hold of my arms and held me up, telling me right then was all about me and that he could see I was not comfortable with going further yet. He had kissed my forehead saying he was already really proud of me for taking my spankings and accepting my reward. He said I was a good girl and every time these words were out of his mouth, I could feel my heart soar a little higher.

On the outside, I just frowned and rolled my eyes but internally, I beamed at being called a good girl.

I had no idea before Maddox started calling me that, of just how much it could mean to me. Of how much I would like it and how much I would crave it.

Yet, him telling me he didn't want me to suck his dick, paradoxically made me want to do it. It was like a switch was turned on in my brain. He didn't want me to do something I was uncomfortable with and, unconsciously, it made me instantly comfortable with it. He just kept on proving to me that I could trust him and that was the biggest turn on.

"Tell me more." He let out a groan against my skin and I felt his hips buck against me. "What would you do to me?"

"I'd get on my knees for you." I breathed, one of my hands reaching back to bury itself in his blond hair. "I never thought I'd like giving anyone so much power over me, but I'd get on my fucking knees for you, Maddox."

"Fuck, baby."

Hearing him growl just spurred me on and soon I was describing very vivid images of all the things I could see us doing to each other.

"I'd rub you, wrap my hand around your cock and squeeze, see how tight you like to be gripped." Maddox added another digit and had two fingers going in and out of my pussy as I resumed speaking. His breath hitched in his throat and he bit my neck, making me moan. "I would use my other hand to thrust two fingers into my—my—" I gulped, trying to find the courage to say the word.

"Your cunt, baby?"

He buried his two fingers inside me to the hilt and stayed there, scissoring them and hitting all the right spots. I screamed because the sensation was just too good to stay quiet.

"That same cunt I have *my* fingers buried in right now? And you're taking them so beautifully even though you're so fucking tight, baby. Say it. Say the word."

"I'd thrust two of my fingers inside my *cunt*!" I yelped as his thumb pressed hard against my clit. "I would use my wetness and get it all over your cock so my hand could glide more easily—oh my God!" His hand whose fingers weren't inside me snaked around my neck and gripped it.

"Go on, baby." He squeezed my neck and I loved it.

"I'd get my cum all over your cock and— and then I'd take you into my mouth."

"Yeah? You want me in your mouth?"

"Fuck, yes. Yes, I want you everywhere. You're the only one I feel safe with." My confession seemed to give him pause. "I want to wrap my lips around you so bad, I wanna taste you like you tasted me and give you as much pleasure." I closed my eyes and let my head fall back against his chest.

"I could give you my tongue while you gave me yours, baby." His fingers went back to thrusting in and out of me, making me crazy. "Fuck, I'd love to feast on this pussy while your pretty mouth is choking on my cock." Between his words, his fingers ramming inside me and his hand squeezing my neck, I didn't even notice the orgasm that hit me like a tsunami.

"Maddox!"

My eyes widened as so many fucking emotions and sensations assaulted me at once. The climax wrecked me as my whole body started trembling in his hold. He didn't let up though, and continued fucking me with his fingers, his palm making an obscene sound every time it slapped against my wet slit as he drove his digits home.

"Give me another one!"

"I-I can't!" The first one wasn't even over yet!

"Yes you can, baby." Squelching sounds rang out in the room, so fucking dirty and filthy and—and— "Drench my hand in your cum."

He simultaneously pinched my clit and bit my neck, hard, probably leaving a mark, but I didn't even care. Because before that first orgasm was even done wreaking havoc on my body, another one assaulted me, this time so intense I felt liquid gush out of me. My eyes widened, thinking I had been so incapable of handling all this pleasure that I had just peed myself.

"Holy shit, Sofia!" I heard Maddox exclaim in what sounded a lot like wonder and ecstasy. Then without warning, his hips bucked against my ass and he tensed, his fingers still deep inside me, my clit still being pulled between his thumb and index.

An animal-like groan was wrenched out of him as he, too, reached that pinnacle of pleasure. He fisted my neck so hard as he came that my oxygen was completely cut off. I didn't mind, I was blissfully coming down from a high that had nearly made me pass out, breathing was not in my list of immediate worries.

Maddox finally let go of my neck and cursed as he tried making his breathing go back to normal. No one spoke for the longest time as we both just caught our breaths.

Every time this man touched me was better than the last. I don't know what it was exactly, maybe the fact that he was my first sexual partner I had deep feelings for and felt safe with or maybe it was just his naturally dominating persona. Either way I knew I would never encounter such chemistry again.

“I can’t believe you squirted.” We were both lying on our backs, staring at the ceiling, breathing loudly and I felt myself flush at his comment.

“I’m so sorry. It never happened to me before, I’ll try to be more careful, I promise.” I hated how vulnerable I sounded at the moment, but I knew Maddox was probably put off with me after what happened. He probably thought I was disgusting.

“What the fuck, Sofia?” I winced and closed my eyes. Just when I finally got intimate with the man of my dreams, I had to go and fuck it all up. “That was fucking hot, baby.” Calloused fingers gripped my chin and tilted my head up. My eyes opened in surprise as I stared at his handsome face. He looked like he just woke up —which I guess was true, with his tousled hair and hazy eyes.

“What? You don’t think that’s gross?”

He frowned, “Fuck no. That’s a huge boost to my ego, next time I’ll try making you squirt with my tongue.” My eyes must have been wide as saucers with shock because he started laughing.

Maddox moved his body to lay on top of me but he actually crawled down the bed a bit so that his head would lay on my ribs. His arms wrapped tightly around my waist and he kissed my naked skin as he looked up at me.

“I could never find anything you do disgusting, Sofia, especially not during sex. You’re like my every wet dreams come true.” Another kiss to my stomach and my hands came to entangle in his hair.

“I can’t even begin to tell you how many times I wanted you to kiss me or touch me in any way those times you arrested me.” My revelation seemed to surprise him, and I had to admit it even surprised me. I hadn't planned on admitting it to him.

"I haven't arrested you since a few weeks before your eighteenth birthday. You were attracted to me back then?"

"Since I was sixteen." I shamefully admitted.

Maddox was the first guy to ever hold my attention. There were some cute boys at school, but none of them fascinated me the way the pain in the ass cop did.

He didn't say anything and just kissed my stomach. I knew he wasn't attracted to me that early on. To be honest, I had never even felt any confusing vibes coming from him before this whole debacle started. He was always professional and sometimes even brotherly whenever we met in the past.

For the longest time we just laid there, cuddling. Maddox peppered kisses all over my abdomen and I played with his hair, scratching his scalp. I was so content, so fulfilled and happy.

These were the last moments of peace we'd have before the wreckage I had made of our lives came back to bite us.

***

We decided not to shower together because we both knew we wouldn't be able to keep our hands off of each other. Maddox went in first, while I stayed on the bed talking to Valentina on Andrea's phone.

She cried a little which made me feel like shit, but then she surprised me by saying everything would be okay. My nine year old sister was the one trying to reassure me. I didn't exactly know how I felt about that.

She said Maddox promised her we wouldn't be separated and that he was just like me, he always kept his promises.

I had forced myself to swallow the knot forming in my throat and told her we would be over to get her back from Andrea's in a couple of hours. I knew she was in good hands, and she had grown to love Adrianna and Andrea, so she didn't mind.

Maddox got out of the bathroom to find me still sitting on his bed, looking in the distance. He had smacked a quick kiss on my lips before getting dressed and telling me he'd make us some breakfast before we had to go.

As hot water dripped along my body, I closed my eyes and let my head fall back. I had checked my phone at least ten times since waking up, and there still weren't any texts from *him*. A chill went down my body at the thought that maybe he was through with helping me. He was my only friend, my secret weapon, and if he'd given up on me, then I was well and truly fucked.

The only thing left for me to do was find Candi Stein and beg her for forgiveness, in hope that she might withdraw her complaint. My ego would be badly bruised, but if that was the only way to get this incident off the record and make sure CPS wouldn't hear of it, then so be it.

As I cut the water off and dried myself off, my mind drifted back to last night and this morning. I felt myself smiling. Maddox was incredible.

Not only did I feel safe with him, but that safety also made me feel like I was strong enough to vocalize my needs and wants. For the first time in my life, I felt like I could live my sexuality the way I wanted. I wouldn't be shamed or hurt or degraded for it.

It was the first time I actually wanted to have sex, and in my mind, it was like Maddox was the one to take my virginity. What happened before him didn't count, and it was time I started to acknowledge that.

Dressed and ready to face the day, I grabbed my phone off the counter and walked out of the bathroom. Again, I checked if he had answered my text from last night but nothing. He read it almost as soon as I sent it, but didn't bother answering.

I sighed and put it in the pocket of my sweatpants before walking to the kitchen from where the sweet scent of pancakes emanated.

Maddox's back was to me as he flipped them, dressed similarly to me in gray sweatpants and a black long-sleeved top that highlighted his well muscled back. I bit my lip before finally gathering the courage to join him and wrap my arms around his middle, my forehead pressing against the his back.

He relaxed almost instantly and we just stayed that way, him silently cooking as I watched from behind. It was so new to me, this proximity. I never had a boyfriend, never even flirted with anyone before Maddox. I didn't know how I felt about labels, didn't know if I could really consider him my boyfriend— the title sounded almost childish compared to what I truly felt for him and everything we were facing together. All I knew was he was mine, and that was enough for now.

"Mind telling me why there's a whole plate of lasagna in the trash? Untouched?" His voice sounded amused but my eyes widened. Shit. I should have thrown the whole bag away but I forgot.

"One of your groupies brought it over yesterday."

I could feel myself frown at the simple mention of Giorgianna. Maddox just chuckled.

"Giorgianna, I suppose you mean?" I growled back, making him laugh again. "Yup, definitely her."

"Did you and her ever…?" I couldn't even bring myself to finish that sentence, the simple thought of Maddox and her making me sick to my stomach.

"No. She moved in three months ago and I helped her bring in some boxes and furniture a couple times, but that's it."

"She wants you though."

"Maybe. But I don't want her. I never did and even less now. I found out I had a thing for black haired girls with big attitudes and even bigger hearts." I couldn't help but smile stupidly at that. Was this what having a crush on someone felt like?

What I felt for Maddox sure seemed like a whole lot more than a crush.

I was gonna answer him when the doorbell rang, making us tense. I frowned and looked at him as he turned around.

"Watch the pan." He wiped his hands on a rag before walking in the direction of the door.

My eyes followed him until they couldn't anymore. I didn't wait any longer to turn off the pan and jog to join Maddox at the door. I couldn't hide my surprise when I saw who stood in the hall outside the apartment.

Looking even more disheveled than yesterday, with bags under her red-rimmed eyes, even more prominent where the shiner I was responsible for was. Candi Stein looked like she hadn't slept a wink last night. She wore a ratty old t-shirt and sweatpants with a gray worn out cardigan on top and had her arms wrapped around herself.

I joined Maddox who was leaning against the door, looking just as surprised as I felt. "Can we help you?"

Her eyes drifted to me and she looked positively wrung out. What the fuck happened to her?

"I came here to apologize." Her voice was small and almost shy.

Yesterday, I hated that woman with all my heart, but right now I couldn't help but pity her, for some reason. I didn't know what had happened in the less than twenty-four hours since I last saw her, but she seemed positively shaken. I gulped and my eyes met Maddox's who looked just as shocked as I did.

"What I did yesterday was bad, I provoked you even though you… you're probably already going through a lot at the moment. I wanted to tell you I had withdrawn my complaint and had all charges against you dropped. They shouldn't even contact CPS, I made sure of it. I don't want to add any more drama to your or Valentina's lives and I hope you—" She cleared her throat, looking down. "I hope you can find it in you to forgive me." It seemed to hurt her to say that, but nevertheless I didn't care. I would take her half-assed apology in a heartbeat if it meant putting everything that happened behind us.

I nodded, silently accepting her excuses. "I— thank you." I didn't know what else to say. She shook her head and looked down again, evading my eyes.

Maddox looked at me, suspicious, before returning his gaze to Candi's face.

"Can I ask why this change of heart?"

She gulped, never meeting our eyes. "I just— let's say I got reminded we all made mistakes. But they shouldn't impact our families." Finally, she looked up at me and pinched her lips. "I'll get going. Thank you for listening to me."

Without waiting for us to acknowledge what she just said, she started down the hall and disappeared behind the stairway's doors.

Silently, Maddox closed the door and we stared at each other, mouths ajar and eyes wide.

"What—"

"—the fuck." I finished.

"This was… unexpected." He rubbed his face the way he did whenever he got nervous. "Did— did she just solve all of our problems?" I was speechless.

"I— yeah? I think so?"

"I need to call Adam and see if what she said is true. I'll be right back." He kissed my forehead and went for his phone that was charging in his room.

I stood in the hallway, staring at the door, still stunned when my phone vibrated in my pocket. I took it out without really thinking about it but stopped when I saw the text on the screen.

**AK**

You're welcome.

# 17

## SURPRISES

### MADDOX

"Mads, no! It says one *teaspoon*, you put one *tablespoon*!" Valentina squeaked, perched on a stool as we both did our best to make this cake at least edible.

"Shit, are you sure?" She nodded her cute little head, her pigtails swaying back and forth.

She was just so cute, I hoped she'd never grow up. Pulling up the recipe book she ran to get as soon as I told her we would be baking a cake together today, she showed me the open page.

"Look, right here." She put a finger on the recipe, her pink nails— nails *I* had painted pink the night before because she had asked me to, mocking me. "*Una cucharadita,* it means one *tea*spoon!" This book belonged to their mom, or as Valentina had said, to their *mama*. And it was all written in Spanish for some reason.

Valentina insisted we use it to make Sofia's birthday cake. The latter was still soundly asleep— in her own bed, although she did spend a great part of the night in mine in an early celebration of her twentieth birthday.

"How would I know? You're the one translating this for me!" I flung my arms out in the air while the little shit glared at me like it was my fault. “I took French in high school, okay? *Je ne connais pas l’espagnol*!”

“I think it’s time you learn Spanish, *gran bobo*!” She pulled her tongue at me, shaking her head like I was stupid. Which, by the way she said it, I was pretty sure was what she just called me.

I chuckled, and put the spoon back on the counter before grabbing her by the waist. She squealed and bursted out laughing as soon as I started tickling her. Her laugh was music to my ears. I didn’t know how or when but this little girl had wormed her way into my heart and decided it was her home now.

It had been close to a month since that whole debacle at the park, and we had fallen into a perfect routine. On some mornings, when I started work later than Sofia, I drove Valentina to school, then Sofia usually came to retrieve her at the end of the school day.

Sometimes she and I met at lunch to eat together, out of town, since we didn’t want people to speculate. We did our best to eat dinner all together every night, although there were some times we couldn’t, when Sofia had to study or work a later shift at the cafe, or when I stayed in late at the station to work on their parents’ case.

Chief Pierson insisted we take on other cases since we refused to label theirs as a robbery gone wrong. He was getting more and more adamant on us moving on. Especially since nothing related to the case happened after the fire that took away everything that remained of the Raymond household.

Still, I worked on it whenever I could, and Adam helped me too. We interviewed Harold’s old accomplices from other felonies he had committed, even tracked down the last remaining members of his family and searched his trailer over in Ravenbridge, but nothing so far.

We did a more thorough background check on Conan too, but on paper nothing was wrong with the guy. After the funeral though, I had heard he had gotten up the ranks and joined the city council after one spot was made vacant by the now honorary mayor they had elected. We had convoked him a week ago to interrogate him, which he apparently didn't take kindly. He didn't like being treated like a criminal in a case revolving around the man he had admired for a good chunk of his life. His words, not mine.

Sometimes I thought to myself, that maybe it *had* just been a robbery gone wrong, that the second man had long left the city, or even the state.

Then I remembered the two girls who made my heartbeats steadier and my evenings warmer, and I knew I just couldn't stop there.

They deserved the truth, they deserved to have their parents avenged.

Sofia had been… incredible in the last month. We still haven't had sex, but we did plenty of other things with and to each other. Nearly every night, when Valentina fell asleep— in her own room, by the way, we would lay together, kiss, touch, caress, anything we felt like at the moment.

I was twenty eight and hadn't had a real relationship before, at least not since college where my longest relationship had taken place. It lasted four months, then we graduated and both went our different ways. No hard feelings. Other than that, I'd lasted maybe a month or two with other women I dated, but none of them made me feel even a third of what Sofia made me feel, let alone fall in love with them.

Just laying next to Sofia while watching a movie was enough. I didn't even need to be touching her because her simple presence was soothing to my soul.

The more time went by, the harder it became to deny my feelings for her. And I knew I didn't have to anymore, but I didn't want to scare her off. We'd agreed to take things slowly, make the best out of the small moments we got to ourselves. I didn't want to scare her off by telling her my feelings for her were growing so fast and so big that I was convinced I was already halfway in love with her.

Plus, I had never been really good at expressing my feelings. My love language, like my sister would say, were acts of service. Whether it was buying her favorite snacks so she could eat them while we were having our weekly movie night, or spending the whole weekend painting Valentina's room pink after she requested it because she thought the white walls were too bland.

I loved seeing their faces light up whenever I did those small things for them. It warmed my heart more than any words ever could.

"What is going on here?" Both me and Valentina turned our head towards the hallway leading to our rooms, where Sofia stood, rubbing the sleep off her eyes. I stopped tickling the little girl in my arms and instead held her up with one arm. She put her hand on my head, steadying herself.

"*Noooo*!" She screamed as soon as she saw her sister eyeing us suspiciously. "You can't be here, go back, go back, Dada!"

"Yeah, *Dada*, go back!" I liked the cute nickname Valentina gave her sister.

I never really bothered asking what it meant, figuring it was probably a Spanish endearment she had shortened. "We're working on something right now and you can't be here. Right, pretty girl?" I looked at her and she nodded solemnly.

"Right."

Sofia looked amused as she looked at her sister and me, clearly ganging up on her.

"O-kay. You're not being weird at all. I'm going back to sleep, call me when you finish the cake." She turned around and looked at us above her shoulder and through her lashes. She was so fucking hot.

"Will do!" Valentina answered cheerfully and I looked at her, eyes wide.

She understood her mistake and gasped, putting both of her hands on her mouth. My little drama queen.

"Aha! I knew it. I can see Mama's old book on the counter from here." Dammit, she was good.

"You're no fun!" Valentina frowned, crossing her arms on her chest.

"Hey, it's fine. She doesn't know what recipe we're making, we can still surprise her." I tried to pacify her.

"The only cake recipe in this book is a *tres leches* cake." Sofia smirked at us.

"You don't have to look so smug!" She just laughed at me and shook her head. Sofia slowly made her way to us and kissed her sister on the forehead. That seemed to soothe Valentina's ego a little bit.

Then the birthday girl surprised me and got on her tip-toes, laying a sweet kiss right on top of my lips. I stared, shocked at her boldness, especially when Valentina was right next to us and clearly saw everything if her agape mouth and stunned eyes were any indication.

"Huh… you two just kissed." Heads spinning in her direction, both me and Sofia stared at the little girl I held tightly in my arms.

Her eyes were blurry with tears as she took us in. I frowned, bringing my head closer to hers, worried about the tears but she blinked them all away.

"We did." Sofia answered quietly and calmly. "Does that freak you out?" I could see she wanted to know how Valentina felt about what she just saw and about us being together.

We hadn't really discussed telling her about us just yet, but we hid it from her in fear she would babble to my sister during her weekly play dates with my niece, or God forbid, to Callie whenever she came around to check on us and give us news on our case. The final decision should be falling next week. It looked positive, but who knew what could happen until then. CPS workers had come over several times in the last month, to check the house, to interview us and Valentina, to see how she felt about living here with us.

So because of all of that, we just figured it would be easier not to tell Valentina.

"I don't know. I mean, I do think it's gross because boys have cooties and you shouldn't kiss them—" I cut her off.

"It's absolutely true, boys have cooties and you shouldn't kiss them until you're at least thirty. Possibly older."

She gave me a dead-pan look and rolled her eyes before going back to her point. It's crazy how much she reminded me of Sofia when she did that. It's like the more she stayed here with us, the more she blossomed and the more confident she got.

She spoke her mind, even got angry sometimes, which was something she never did before. I suspected she had been too shy to do so and repressed those emotions in fear. Sofia told me Valentina put a lot of pressure on being the perfect little girl, silent and obedient. She thought if she wasn't, I would get fed up with them and leave them.

I'd had to have a conversation with Valentina, where I told her this was never happening. I wouldn't leave them and wouldn't get fed up either. Ever since, she started opening up a little each day. It felt good to see her blossom and be comfortable enough in her space to be herself, to act like any nine year old would.

"—but, I think I don't mind." She looked at us and gave us a small smile.

"You can't tell anyone, baby, okay?" Sofia explained softly, "At least not yet."

Valentina nodded solemnly, "You know I'm good at keeping secrets, Dada." Her sister offered a small smile and nodded. "Just don't kiss in front of me again because that is *gross*." She made a face again, but a small smile played on her lips.

"Gross, huh?" I started tickling her again, and she laughed out loud, trying to wiggle out of my grip.

"Hear that, Mads, she thinks this is gross." Sofia mocked her sister before pecking my lips again and again while Valentina made 'ew' sounds, still giggling. I couldn't help the smile splitting my face.

"You're so weird!" She complained while trying to get us to pull away from each other. The sound of laughter echoed in the kitchen as we chased each other around, mock-attacking Valentina with kisses all over her little face.

The cake was soon forgotten but I think the best gift we could have gotten Sofia was us playing around and having fun.

***

**SOFIA**

Getting the grocery bag out of the trunk of my car, I started walking towards the apartment building.

After ordering breakfast this morning, since the cake was nowhere near being done, I had to get to work for a quick shift at the café. Maddox wasn't working today and it was teacher's work day at Valentina's school so she got to stay home with him and have fun.

This morning felt like a relief. I knew how much Valentina loved Maddox, and to know she approved of him not only as a guardian but also as being mine, it meant everything.

They said they would use their day together to finish my birthday cake so that we could celebrate tonight, just the three of us. I went to get some things I knew they liked to eat so that I could cook us a great meal to go with the cake. It might sound crazy but I actually missed them, even though it's only been four hours. They truly were my favorite people.

Saying hi to the doorman, Osman, I made my way to the elevator, balancing my phone and purse in one hand, and the paper bag of groceries in the other. I couldn't keep myself from smiling foolishly. I wanted to see how their cake turned out, I wanted to know if they had fun baking together. It felt like forever since I'd been this excited to come home.

It was almost like having a family again.

When the elevator's doors finally opened though, my smile was quickly wiped off my face. Standing a couple feet away from me, was the one person I never wanted to be alone with again. Hell, the one person I never wanted to *see* again.

A shudder went down my spine as I felt my face close down. Conan leaned against a wall in the hallway leading to the apartment, and my blood froze.

Hearing the elevator ding, his head spun towards me and he glared. Deciding he would never try anything with Maddox a couple doors down the hall, I ignored him and walked to my destination.

He decided otherwise though. His hand gripped my forearm tightly as he brought me closer to him. Nausea hit me in the face as I recalled the last time this piece of shit had his hands on me.

"What the fuck do you think you're doing?" I hissed, glaring with all my might.

My arm squeezed the grocery bag like a lifeline, my whole body was tight and trembled slightly.

"I could ask you the same thing." His breath smelled like whiskey and that only made me want to throw up even more. "Why the fuck is your little boyfriend all up in my business?!" Conan was not as tall as Maddox, but he hovered well over my 5'2 frame.

I frowned, not understanding where he was getting. Maddox kept me updated on the case from time to time, but he never said anything about Conan being a suspect.

"You better not open your whore mouth, and if I find out you had anything to do with—"

"Is everything okay over there?" A voice interrupted him before he could finish his sentence and I had never felt so happy to see Giorgianna in my life.

Conan instantly let go of me and put on his friendly face, the one he used to get people's trust. The one people in Lakestone knew him as. He put a step between us and looked over at Giorgianna, waving and smiling like nothing was wrong.

"Everything is fine, we were just having a little chat."

"I wasn't talking to you." She snapped, making me look up. Her eyes were concerned as she stared at me. "You okay, girl?" I blinked before nodding silently, trying to put as much distance between Conan and I.

"Yeah. Conan was just leaving actually." Her gaze turned to him as we both stared expectantly.

His eyes had darkened at being snapped at but now they were getting twitchy. He looked positively insane. Conan put on an even faker smile and nodded his head once before walking in the direction of the elevator.

As soon as the doors closed after him and he was out of sight, I let out a relieved sigh and I noticed Giorgianna's shoulders slump too.

"I'll tell Osman not to let that creep in again, okay?" Her voice was surprisingly soft, nothing like the bitchy tone she'd used with me before.

I nodded and she pursed her lips. "I had to deal with abusive exes in the past, too. I won't tell Maddox but I think you should." I didn't bother correcting her and saying Conan was as far from an abusive ex as he could and simply nodded again.

With one last look at me, she turned around and the clicks of her high heels resonated in the hall as she made her way to the elevator.

"Thank you, Giorgianna. I owe you one." She turned her head slightly in my direction and gave me a small smile.

***

The smell of a freshly baked cake assaulted my nostrils as soon as I entered the apartment and it brought the smile right back on my face. I had to wait ten minutes in front of the door just to catch my breath and let my heartbeat go back to normal. Ultimately, though, I decided not to let my impromptu meeting with Conan waste my day, he wasn't worth it.

I'd have to send AK a message to see if there was anything he could find on him that would get him off my back. In the meantime, though, I had other things to focus on. Like spending my twentieth birthday surrounded by my two favorite people.

"Honey, I'm home." I sang jokingly and heard Maddox chuckle from the kitchen. I joined him as soon as I had taken off my shoes and put my keys on the side table.

He was finishing up cleaning the kitchen, which, I could imagine, had been a mess with him and Valentina trying to bake with no prior experience. Putting the bag on the counter, I made my way to Maddox and pecked his lips.

He wasn't satisfied with that though and instead deepened the kiss, his tongue coming out to play with mine. I let out a moan, my hands traveling to his hair as I pulled his head even closer to mine.

I would never get tired of kissing Maddox Brooks.

"How was your day?" I asked as soon as we pulled away to breathe. His hands were on my hips, drawing circles.

"Good. We finished the cake, it's in the fridge. Valentina got a bit cranky towards the end, kept on saying her stomach hurt." I frowned, worry twisting my gut. "At first I thought she was faking to get out of cleaning duty with me, but I could see she really was hurting so I put her in bed with a hot tea and some Disney movie on her iPad. That was an hour ago so I think she fell asleep." I nodded as he pressed a kiss to my hair.

"I'll take a shower and check on her." Getting on the tip of my toes, I pecked his lips again and gave him a small smile before making my way to the bathroom.

I stopped by Valentina's room on the way there and sure enough, she was sleeping peacefully underneath the pink and white covers, her back to me. My gaze wandered around her room, taking in the stuffed animals Maddox got her, the pink walls he had spent a whole weekend painting on his own and all the dolls and toys strewn across the floor.

She had a little desk where she loved to draw and several of her drawings were actually pinned just above it. My eyes stayed on one painting representing the three of us, Maddox and I holding hands, and Valentina in the middle holding what looked like a cat. Gosh, I hoped she wouldn't ask Maddox for a cat one of these days, God knew he was incapable of saying no to her.

The little minx even insisted on having a dressing table with a big mirror so she could paint her nails and put on face cream before going to bed and sunscreen in the morning. Maddox had swung by the store and found one for her after work one day, he brought it home and put it together so that when Valentina came back from school that day, everything was in place.

When I told him he didn't have to, that he spoiled her, spoiled *us* if I was being honest, he simply said we deserved it. That he wanted us to feel at home in this apartment because he wasn't letting go of us anytime soon. It should have freaked me out, him saying that meant all my plans for the future were falling apart, but it didn't.

I loved that. I loved how much he cared for us. I loved the connection he and Valentina had, how close they had gotten to each other. My sister was everything to me, and to know she meant so much for Maddox too, it just reassured me in my choice of taking things a step further between us.

The more time I spent with him, in bed or out of it, the more I could feel myself falling for him. It wasn't just an attraction anymore. It was an addiction, pure and simple addiction.

When I finished showering and getting dressed in a pair of satin pajamas, I went back to my baby's room, to see she hadn't moved. I could hear the TV playing in the living room, which was probably where Maddox was.

Sitting on the edge of her bed, I caressed her hair delicately. A frown hit my face when I felt her burning skin, though. Valentina stirred, her eyebrows pulling together as she looked up drowsily at me.

"It hurts, Dada." She moaned, clearly in pain. She was burning up with a fever and I could feel the panic seep into my pores.

I swore and called for Maddox. This wasn't the first time I'd had to take care of a sick Valentina, but somehow this felt different and I knew having Maddox close by would help me.

He came in as I was touching Valentina's forehead again, "She's burning up." I sounded as panicked as I felt.

"Shit, I'll call Andrea, okay?" I nodded absentmindedly and he went out to retrieve his phone.

"It hurts, Dada. My tummy hurts." silent tears streamed down her cheeks and my heart started beating a little faster.

"It's okay, mami, can you get up a little? I'll get you something to drink and a cold towel to put on your head." I tried helping her sit up but a gut-wrenching moan fell out of her lips and more tears ensued. Frowning, I decided to take the covers off of her to try and massage her stomach.

But as soon as I did, I regretted it.

Blood.

There was so much blood on the white sheets, on her pink pajama pants, *everywhere*.

I was instantly brought back to *that* night, where blood had been everywhere too and I felt my whole body lock up in shock. I couldn't breathe anymore as I bore my eyes into Valentina's panicked ones. A whirlwind of bad memories assaulted my brain, one after the other. Screams and cries and *blood, blood, blood.*

So much fucking blood.

It was like going back in time, Valentina crying against me as I did my best to hold my own tears in, when all I wanted to do was scream all my rage and anger away.

My vision became blurry, I took several steps back and bumped into her dressing table, knocking over a row of nail polishes. I could barely hear Valentina's cries or Maddox's panicked voice as he came back into the room and took in the scene before him.

I couldn't focus on anything and soon enough black took over my vision as I fell into nothingness.

# 18

## FRIGHT

### MADDOX

I thought my heart might have stopped.

Too much information hitting home at once, the blood on the sheets, the tears on Valentina's cheeks, her cries for help, Sofia's wide eyes taking in the scene in shock, her not responding to the sounds of our voices.

Then she collapsed and I thought I might have followed suit if it wasn't for that flash of adrenaline shooting up my brain. It made me move forward, just in time so she didn't hit her head on the hardwood floor while falling.

I gathered her small body in my arms, my own limbs trembling.

Valentina was freaking out, there were no other words. She brought her knees to her chest, pushing her face between them and muttering "I'm sorry" repeatedly. Clearly, I had underestimated this whole situation. I had underestimated how hard it would be to live with those two and help them through their trauma. I had no idea what was going on, just that I was way in over my head.

In the end I did what I always did whenever I felt lost: call my sister.

It helped that she was a gynecologist and that I was pretty sure Valentina had gotten her first period. I had no idea it could come this early, I thought we still had some time before we even crossed that bridge, but clearly not.

When Andrea finally came, fifteen minutes after I called her in a panic, Sofia was still passed out on my bed and Valentina was on hers, covered up to her neck, looking completely frozen in shock.

I had tried to reassure her, rub her back like I knew she liked, but she started crying any time I went near her. I knew both Raymond sisters were extremely bashful, which was probably why Valentina wouldn't let me close. She was embarrassed. I tried telling her it was natural, that it was something every young girl went through at some point, but that only made her cry some more.

I was overwhelmed.

Which is why my shoulders literally slumped in relief as soon as my sister entered my apartment, in a rush.

I was in the living room, sitting down trying to gain my breathing back. One of my hands was grasping the ends of my hair as I forced myself to inhale and exhale slowly.

"Where is she?" I was so lost in thoughts that I didn't even notice Andrea using her key to get in. She didn't bother locking the door behind her, just rushed to me with a big plastic bag full of, I guessed, period supplies.

"S-she's in her bedroom, she refuses to leave her bed, I tried to get her to take a shower or at least change but she starts sobbing as soon as I get one foot inside the door." I never felt as powerless as I did at that moment. I had gotten so close to that little girl, she came to mean so much to me in a relatively short time, and seeing her like that made me physically ill.

"Where's Sofia?"

"She passed out. Fuck, she saw all that blood and she looked so scared, I think it made her think of the night her parents were killed. The sight of blood must be a trigger she was unaware of." I let my head fall back between my shoulders, "Shit, this is all so fucked up."

"Go see that Sofia is okay, I'll check Valentina and make sure everything is alright. I'm pretty sure it's just her period coming in early, it's rare but there are some instances that make it possible to get your period at nine." I just nodded, not really knowing what to say to that and watched as Andrea disappeared in the hallway.

I stared into the distance, trying to gather my wits. Finally, I exhaled a long breath and got up, ready to check on Sofia. Deep down, I was totally freaking out, but I tried not to let it show. I had to be strong and put together, for Valentina but also for Sofia. We couldn't both be panicking, someone had to anchor the other.

She was still sleeping when I arrived in my room, but it looked like she was having a nightmare. Her eyebrows were furrowed and she shook her head relentlessly, muttering in Spanish under her breath.

Fuck, I really needed to start learning the language.

Sitting down on the side of the bed, I caressed her face as slowly and softly as I could. She looked so anguished, so vulnerable right then. Knowing there was nothing I could do about it felt like being ripped apart.

I kept on replaying how well the day had started, how well everything was going before two hours ago. It seemed to be a recurring thing with us, every time things were good, something came up and seemed to wreck that fragile peace we'd built.

Earlier, when I tried to enter the room and take her in my arms, Valentina seemed so fucking scared and lost, it truly broke my heart. As if her little shoulders hadn't held more than enough weight already.

Sofia tensed in her sleep, right before she shot up straight, gasping and startling me. Her eyes were wide and red with tears I hadn't even noticed until then. She was breathing erratically, chest moving up and down as she took in her surroundings.

"Rosita!" She exclaimed, still in a daze.

When she saw she was in my room, which, quite frankly, had become *our* room through the last month, since she spent almost all her nights here, her breathing eased a little bit.

"V-Valentina! Where is she?" Her eyes were frantic as she gripped my forearm, looking at me with crazy eyes.

For a minute I wondered if she even recognized me. I had never seen her so frazzled. It was insane, but even the night of the murders she somehow seemed more collected than she did now.

"Sofia, calm down okay? You passed out, you need to breathe."

"Don't fucking tell me what to do!" She hissed and for a second I was the one who didn't recognize her. She was feral, not herself. "Where the fuck is Valentina, Maddox? Tell me now or I swear to God —"

"Calm the fuck down!" I grasped her arms when she tried to get up and pushed her into the mattress.

The minx kept on trying to free herself, she scratched my wrists, screamed at me, but I wouldn't budge.

"You don't understand! Let me get to my sister!" I had never seen her so mad, she was freaking out. "Let me go! She needs me!" I didn't let her go. I couldn't. She wasn't thinking straight and I wouldn't let her scare Valentina more than she already was.

Eventually though, her screams and glares turned into sobs and tears, as she stopped struggling and slumped down on the mattress. Her cries shook her body and I felt tears gathering in my own eyes. The energy in the room was tense and thick, we were both on edge.

Grabbing her, I brought her closer to my chest and she wrapped her arms around my neck tiredly as she sat on my lap. I started rubbing her back and rocking her softly so she would calm down. Sofia kept on crying, and somehow I didn't think it was just for what happened earlier.

I thought seeing all the blood triggered her and all the tears she had kept locked up tightly inside finally found their way out. I had to do something about it. I couldn't stand here and watch my woman destroy herself because she kept everything bottled up.

She was shaking on my lap as she muttered incomprehensible words under her breaths. I heard "sorry" and "blood", but other than that I wasn't even sure it was English she was speaking right then.

Sofia had a habit of switching to Spanish whenever she was feeling strongly, whether it was anger, anxiety, joy, fear or, like right now, shock.

Throughout all of this, I said nothing, busy trying to understand and put words on my own emotions. I simply rubbed her back, letting her bury her face in my neck and inhale my scent, thinking maybe it would reassure her, ground her.

One of my hands rubbed her thighs as the other played with her smooth hair. Eventually, she calmed down, only sniffling from time to time.

“She’s okay, baby. Andrea is with her, she said it was probably only her period coming in early. Nothing bad.”

“H-her period? But she’s nine.” She pulled away slightly to look at me. Wet, red rimmed eyes met my own, the tip of her nose taking on a rosy shade too. I kissed it, unable to resist.

“I know, but apparently it can happen sometimes.” She sniffled, looking relieved and dejected at the same time. “It’s okay. I’m sure Andie will know what to tell her. Plus, Valentina is smart, she’ll understand.” Sofia didn’t answer, she just let her head fall back against my chest as she sat sideways on my lap.

She laid still for a few minutes and I didn't say anything as I simply appreciated the fact that I got to hold her.

“I’m sorry I yelled at you, Maddox.”

I almost missed her whispered apology because her voice sounded so low and weak. I couldn’t hold her accountable for that since I clearly saw how affected she was from the whole situation, she wasn't herself.

“You’re good, baby. Thank you for apologizing, though.”

She turned lightly and pressed her lips onto mine. I kissed her back, because I couldn't honestly imagine a day where Sofia Raymond would kiss me and I wouldn't kiss her back.

Unless I was dead, and even then I would probably do everything possible to come back from the other side and taste her lips one last time.

The door to Valentina's room, the one right in front of mine, opened, pulling us out of our kiss. We turned our heads towards it only to see my sister staring at us with stunned eyes.

Shit.

The rational part of me knew I should probably push Sofia off of me, that Andrea was certainly suspicious of seeing us so close, that she had all but witnessed us kissing. But the part of me that was falling for the hotheaded, protective brunette didn't want to let go. Not when Sofia needed my closeness, not when she was so weak and vulnerable.

"I-uh…" Andrea looked at loss for words, especially when we didn't do anything to move away from each other, seemingly unbothered by the fact that she had caught us kissing.

The truth was, I knew my sister. She might disapprove at first, but she'd come around eventually. She might try and lecture me, but at the end of the day, she'd see there was nothing wrong in my and Sofia's relationship. Yes, there might be a slight conflict of interest now that we were involved since I was still in charge of her parents' case, but if anything, it would only push me harder to find out who killed them.

My sister eventually cleared her throat and looked away, "Valentina is doing much better, I gave her a pull-on diaper because I thought dealing with pads or tampons might be a little difficult at her age, especially if the flow intensifies. She showered and put on new clothes. I stripped her sheets and wanted to put them in the hamper but she—uh…" Andrea rubbed her face, wincing. "She insisted we throw them in the trash, she wouldn't budge. I figured she was embarrassed so I just went with it."

I nodded, not giving a shit about those sheets, I'd buy her a thousand more if she wanted.

"So that was her period? Coming in early?" Sofia's voice was hoarse from crying so much.

My sister nodded.

"But then… Why the fever?"

Andrea shrugged, "Some women get fevers during their cycles, it's nothing bad, as long as it doesn't happen every time. It might just mean Valentina will have really bad cramps and it could even be a very early sign of endometriosis, but there's no way to tell for now. We'll have to keep an eye on her. Actually, Valentina's period might stay for a few days and then disappear for years before she gets them again. It's not uncommon for some young girls to bleed for the first time when they're really young and then get their real periods at age twelve or older."

Something was bothering her though, I could tell from the way her eyes kept on staring at Sofia, and I don't think it was only because of our close proximity.

"Maddox, Valentina actually asked if you could come in and see her. Sofia, may I talk to you for a second?"

I felt Sofia tense against me, but she nodded nonetheless. Looking at me with anguished eyes, she got up on wobbly feet and sat back down on the bed next to me. Not caring anymore what my sister saw or not, I pressed a light kiss to her lips before getting up and joining Valentina's room, leaving them alone.

When I entered, I saw her sitting on the now bare bed, her back to me. There wasn't any blood stain on the white mattress so I assumed Andrea had turned it around so that Valentina wouldn't get reminded of it until we got it replaced or cleaned.

Closing the door behind me, I approached carefully, not wanting to make her cry again.

"Hey, pretty girl. You okay?"

I heard her sniffle but she said nothing. Walking until I was facing her, I got on my knees in front of her, not daring to touch her.

She looked at me with watery eyes and I didn't know what to do, so I helplessly stared back. Eventually, her lips wobbled and without warning she launched herself at me and started sobbing on my shoulder.

Fuck, these girls had cried way too fucking many tears these last few months.

"I'm so sorry! I'm so sorry Mads!" I frowned and hugged her back, squeezing her tight against my chest.

"There's nothing for you to be sorry about, sweets. It happens, it just does. I'm not upset. I could never be upset with you." I rubbed her back.

"I don't want you to think I'm afraid of you. Not when you're the best thing that's ever happened to us." Wet tears drenched my shirt as she cried quietly.

Fuck. What is it with these girls and making me speechless? I don't think I'd ever felt as much love and affection as I have these last few months. They just give a new purpose to my life, one that begins and ends with protecting them and making sure they get everything they want from life.

"I'll never think you're afraid of me, Valentina. You're a young girl and you have the right to want your privacy. I know why you didn't want me to come in and I understand. This is your home too and this room in particular is yours, you get to decide who comes in or out, okay?" I felt her weak nod against my chest after a beat. "Are you okay?"

A second passed, then two, then five, before she finally answered.

"Yeah. I will be." I said nothing and kissed her head. I just held her for the longest time, she sniffled sometimes and gripped my shirt tighter but other than that, neither of us made a sound.

Somehow it hit me then, Valentina was the closest thing I ever had to a daughter. What I felt for her, the fierce way I wanted to protect her, the raw fear I had felt when I thought she was lost in the woods and then earlier today when I saw all that blood on her, it was more than brotherly protectiveness. I wanted children later in life, but somehow, I had a feeling Valentina would always feel like my first child.

We may not be linked by blood, but Sofia, Valentina and I, we were becoming a family.

***

By the time Andrea and Sofia came into Valentina's room, the little girl was sleeping in my arms as I sat on the floor, my back against her bed. She was curled up on my lap, her head resting on my chest as she snored quietly.

Sofia immediately knelt in front of us, her hand caressing Valentina's smooth black hair. Her eyes were still red, and she looked so exhausted it pained me.

"Rosita..." eyes still fixated on her, she bent over to kiss her forehead.

I looked up at my sister who was watching the scene warily. She seemed distraught, but I didn't really pay attention to it at the moment, figuring she was probably still trying to wrap her head around me and Sofia being together.

Eventually, Drea cleared her throat, "I'll leave you to it. There's everything you might need in the bag on the dresser. Heating pad, Tylenol, more diapers, everything. I—uh, I'll see myself out. Call me if you need anything."

She looked like she wanted to say something else but then decided against it and fled the room before me or Sofia even had time to thank her.

We heard the front door close and lock and Sofia then crawled next to me, sitting down and resting her head on my shoulders. Her close proximity somehow recharged me, gave me strength and hope about the future. Sofia's hand gripped mine as she laced our fingers together, needing the closeness as much as I did.

We stayed that way for a while, not talking, just reveling in each other's presence. Valentina was still fast asleep on my lap, and I had a feeling Sofia would join her soon. Today was so intense, I knew they both needed sleep, even though it was only a little after four in the afternoon.

"Sofia?"

"Hmm?" She sounded drowsy.

"Come on, baby, get up. Get on the bed, okay?" Sofia nodded sleepily as I got on my feet, holding tight onto the little girl in my arms, and helped her get up too.

Valentina stirred in my hold but eventually just wrapped her arms around my neck, half asleep, as I held her with one arm and gripped Sofia's hand with the other.

I guided them to my room and pulled the duvet off before slowly depositing Valentina in the middle of the bed. Once she seemed comfortable I pulled Sofia to me and kissed her forehead before pushing her down on the bed so she could lay with her sister.

She gripped my shirt, looking up at me with tired hooded eyes. I grabbed her hand softly and bent down to kiss it, "Get some sleep, baby. I'm not going anywhere."

Having me whisper those words seemed to reassure her and her grip on me loosened as she closed her eyes, turning around in bed and engulfing her sister in a hug.

I watched them sleep for a while, a sense of peace falling upon me, as always when I was in their presence.

We still had a long way to go, a lot of stuff to go through, but I truly believe that as long as we were together, we'd be able to encompass them.

***

It was nearly eight at night when they woke up. I was finishing setting up the living room when I heard the light pitter-patter of their bare feet on the floor. Sure enough, I turned around and there they stood, both rubbing the sleep off their eyes. Both in their pajamas, their long, straight black hair a similar mess.

"What are you doing?" Sofia asked me, just like she did this morning when she caught me and Valentina baking her cake.

I straightened up from the floor where I was just about done fluffing out the pillows so they could rest against the sofa. The whole thing wasn't as perfect as I had imagined it, but my attempt at a fort was still pretty successful.

Cozy fleece blankets and pillows were strewn all over the rug beneath the sofa, creating a little nook. I had some Christmas lights left from last year in a closet, which I lit and hung around the living room so that I could dim the overall light and create a warm decor. The coffee table was covered in snacks and the girls' favorite sodas. With everything that happened, I didn't have time to get any birthday decor, so I made do with what I had at home.

The girls were taking in their surroundings and I got on my feet, gesturing to my little creation by widening my arms.

"It's not much, but… I thought we shouldn't let the incident from earlier keep us from celebrating your twentieth."

I rubbed my head, suddenly self-conscious. What if she thought I was trying to sweep it under the rug and downplay it? I wasn't, I just wanted to give them something else to think of.

"If you don't want to and just want to get back to sleep, it's fine, we can—" Sofia cut me off.

"I haven't celebrated my birthday since I was twelve years old. This is… this is wonderful. Thank you so much, Maddox." Her voice was a whisper, emotion clearly audible in it as she continued to take in her surroundings.

Valentina was smiling at me and she's the one who got Sofia out of her thoughts as she pulled on her hand and started walking to me. I had showered and changed into my pajamas while they were asleep, so I sat down as they joined me, Sofia curled up on my right, an arm wrapped around my middle as mine was on her shoulders, while Valentina was resting against my left side, holding my hand in her much smaller one, using my chest as a pillow.

We turned on the TV as we munched on chips and cookies. Valentina chose the movie and obviously, she put on one of her favorite Disney movies, the Princess and the Frog. We watched it in sweet, sweet harmony, laughing whenever Ray the dragonfly did something funny. Valentina graced us with some comments here and there which made me chuckle too because she just knew the lines by heart given how many times she watched it.

When it ended, Valentina and I went to grab the cake we made earlier from the fridge. We placed it there hoping the cream wouldn't melt and as I opened the fridge door I was glad to see everything was still in place. It didn't look as good as the ones I had looked up on the internet, but at least we tried.

I grabbed the cake as Valentina started singing *Las Mañanitas* with all her heart. She'd tried to teach me earlier but my Spanish accent was so bad I was actually ashamed of trying.

Next year, though, I promised myself I'd have learned enough to sing it to her. Next year and all the ones after, because these girls were never leaving my side.

We put twenty candles on the cake and Sofia blew them out looking happy as ever. Tears shone in her eyes as she sat in the midst of a dozen pillows, surrounded by people who truly cared about her.

People who loved her

.

# 19

## BETRAYAL

### MADDOX

Absolutely not." Was exactly the answer I knew I'd get from Sofia when I decided to talk to her earlier today.

Three days after Valentina scared the shit out of us, everything seemed to have gone back to normal.

Well, with one exception.

Callie came knocking on our door yesterday morning, with a huge smile on her face, brandishing a piece of paper, but my brain was too tired to process what it was.

Sofia didn't have that problem though, because she instantly knew what it was, rushing to Callie and grabbing the paper from her.

The official decision regarding me becoming a foster parent was in, and it was amazing news. Because the judge and DA both agreed to grant me custody of Valentina. I remember Sofia leaping into my arms in joy, Valentina clapping her hands together in victory, hugging our legs. I remember feeling so damn happy I thought my heart would explode out of my chest.

It was official. I had legal custody of that incredible little girl, and with her came the most amazing woman I'd ever met.

I was in an amazing place.

That's why I was scared to speak to Sofia. I knew what I had to tell her would just be ground for a fight so I procrastinated for as long as I could.

But hearing her cry in her sleep, not even aware she was doing it, seeing how careful and protective she became around Valentina, even more so than usual, I just had to do something.

"Sofia, you have to listen to me, after everything that happened it's evident you have to—"

"I will not see a shrink, Maddox,. Don't you fucking dare suggest it again." I clamped my mouth shut at the cutting tone she suddenly used.

See, if there was one thing you had to know about Sofia Raymond it's that she was the most infuriating, hard-headed, foul-mouthed and hotheaded little minx I'd ever met. She made me fucking crazy, especially when she wouldn't even let me speak and explain myself.

She joined me at the station for lunch and we were currently in my office, just finishing up our shrimp tacos.

When I first said the dreadful words, *"Sofia, have you ever thought of going to a therapist after what happened with your parents?"* she stopped right in her tracks, put her half-eaten tacos down and simply said 'no'. Then she went back to eat as if nothing happened.

Then I made the bad decision to mention Mindy, the police psychologist she'd already dealt with, and she started getting mad and shutting down, not leaving room for any discussion.

"There's no shame in having to talk to someone, Sofia. Actually, I also wanted to talk to you about getting Valentina therapy." That's when all hell broke loose.

Her food forgotten, Sofia got up and started pacing my small office.

"My sister already has someone to talk to, Maddox, *me*! We don't need a shrink to tell us what to think and how to feel! Valentina wouldn't be comfortable talking to a stranger and neither would I, end of discussion." She tried grabbing her things and hightailing it out of my office but I was quick to grab her wrist.

"No, it's not the end of the fucking discussion since it still has to start yet! You didn't even let me finish, this is not a conversation, you have to hear what I have to say before storming off like my opinion didn't fucking matter!"

"Because it doesn't!" She hissed, pulling herself out of my grasp, "It doesn't matter what you think and what you want because it's still my decision!"

"You barely ever speak about your parents, about that night! You think I don't know you have nightmares every time you fall asleep? You fucking cry in your sleep, Sofia! And the way you reacted the day Valentina had her accident says it all, goddammit. You're traumatized and you don't even care enough to help yourself or your sister!"

Fire blazed in her eyes and I could see my words truly her feelings. I regretted them instantly.

"How fucking dare you." Her words were so cold. "How fucking dare you, Maddox."

I gulped, a hand passing through my hair.

"Listen, I understand how hard it can be to admit you need help and actually seek it. But, baby, put yourself in my shoes. I wake up in the middle of the night only to see my girl crying right next to me, not even aware that she *is* crying. I want to help you, that's all I've ever wanted— to give you and Valentina all you need and want, but I– … there are some things I can't do on my own. I want you to get better and in order to do that, we'll have to get you to talk to someone."

I took a step towards her, wanting to take her in my arms but she stood away from me.

"You want to give me what I want? What I need? Let us fucking deal with it how we please. I refuse to talk to anyone and Valentina won't either. Especially not to that bitch working here. That's the end of this fucking delusional conversation. Drop it, Maddox."

I could see she was stuck inside her own head, and quite frankly, it was starting to piss me off.

She didn't want help? Fine, but I was not disregarding Valentina's needs because Sofia was being careless with hers.

"Fine. You don't want to talk to someone? Don't. Stay stuck in your head and continue to cry in your sleep as much as you fucking want. Freak out anytime you see blood, I don't care. But I won't let Valentina go through the same thing because you were too proud to accept that someone could help you process your parents' deaths. I refuse to see her grow up with questions and traumas plaguing her little heart."

Sofia froze, her eyes meeting mine and throwing daggers at me. She knew what I was about to say.

"What are you trying to say?"

"I have custody of Valentina, Sofia. *I*'m her guardian and what *I* say goes. I will take her to talk to Mindy, whether you like it or not. Once you finally get out of your own head, you'll understand this is for the best."

She physically recoiled at my words but I didn't budge. I stood straight and stared at her waiting for her answer.

Truth be told, I was bluffing. I would never do that, disregard her decision and just act on my own. That's not how I wanted us to work, that's not how I wanted our family to function.

I just wanted her to see how serious I was about this. Looking back at what I said, I realized how stupid it was, though. She wasn't up for debate, wouldn't try to see my point of view and just wouldn't budge from her positions. So I did what I thought was best.

I instantly regretted it when I saw her eyes watering. Her nostrils flared and I could tell she was physically stopping herself from crying. She took one step towards me, looking up into my eyes. I just wanted to grab her waist and bury her face into my chest, tell her I wasn't serious and I would never do that to her. But my body just wouldn't work.

Glaring up at me, the top of her head barely coming to the top of my chest, she pointed one perfectly manicured finger at me. When she started speaking, I could feel my heart compressing inside my chest. She wasn't yelling, she wasn't insulting me, like she usually would in such instances. Yet her following words cut ten times deeper than they would have had she just been her regular angry self.

"If you do that, Maddox, if you go behind my back after I specifically said I didn't agree with what you were saying, I will *never* forgive you. And trust me when I say I'll find a way to get my sister and get the hell away from you. You'll never see us again."

Not even waiting for my response, she turned her back on me, grabbed her stuff and stormed out of my office, leaving the door open after her. A couple uniformed officers peered inside, wondering what was going on but I didn't pay them any attention. Instead I closed my eyes and let myself fall back into my seat, dejected.

***

Hours later, as I was getting deeper and deeper into the Raymond case, spiraling out of control with ideas that compared to conspiracy theories given how far fetched they got, someone knocked on my door.

"Come in."

I looked up and slumped back on my seat, rubbing my stinging eyes. I expected Adam or maybe Selena to come in, but to my surprise, it was someone else totally. Someone I didn't even know.

Longish straight black hair brushed back, tanned skin and green eyes stared back at me. The guy must've been no older than nineteen, but he already had more tattoos than most of the grown men I knew. He wore a long sleeve white shirt but I could see them peeking on his neck and hands.

"Hello, detective Brooks?" He looked unsure, like he was gauging whether or not he could trust me just from the way I looked.

I frowned, wondering what this kid was doing in my office and who even sent him.

"Yeah, and you are?"

"My name is Aiden Walker, sir. I'm from Ravenbridge and I came to report a disappearance." He stood a little straighter, trying to show how serious he was, but his words only confused me.

"I'm sorry kid, you're in Lakestone here. You'll have to report this to the Ravenbridge police."

"I tried. They're not taking me seriously." He entered and closed the door to my office behind him before I even allowed him. I frowned, not sure if I liked his gut or wanted to send him back on his ass for it.

"My neighbor, Oscar, was supposed to come home from his football practice at four, but it's six and he's not home or answering his phone." I sighed and rubbed my face.

I got why he was worried, I really did. If this had happened with Valentina, I would be worried too. But there was nothing pointing towards the fact that this could be a kidnapping or something serious. Two hours were nothing to a kid, he probably went out with some friends and forgot to check his phone.

"We have to wait forty-eight hours before opening a kidnapping case, it's protocol."

"Not when three kids have already been missing in the same fucking neighborhood." Now that got my attention. I straightened up in my seat and put my elbows on my desk.

"Sit and talk, I don't have much time, gotta pick up my girl from dance class in an hour." Calling Valentina my girl felt more natural than saying 'my ward'. Plus I didn't have time to explain our complicated relationship.

"I'm from north of the Bridge," Aiden started, and I instantly understood why the Ravenbridge police didn't do shit about him.

See, that town, which was situated right next to Lakestone, was divided by a bridge, creating two *very* distinct parts. North Bridge was not really well reputed, it was where most of the city's crimes emanated from, where the poverty rates were higher and where kids typically got in trouble. South Bridge on the other hand, was the complete opposite. The richest elites lived there, houses which looked more like mansions, country clubs, everything you thought of when the words 'fancy' and 'posh' came to mind.

I, myself, came from a pretty wealthy family but thank God our parents never raised us to be spoiled brats. They always made sure we knew how lucky and privileged we were. From the few altercations I'd had with them, I can't really say the same about Ravenbridge elites. I'd always thought it was insane to have such drastically different sides within the same town. A Northy family could make a year what a Southy made in a day, and nobody said anything about it, acting like it was a normal occurrence.

Aiden took the seat Sofia had vacated earlier, which made me look at my phone to see if she answered the dozen phone calls and messages I left her. She didn't.

"Oscar Vasquez, my thirteen year old neighbor, went to his football practice directly after school but when I went to get him at four, he wasn't there. I thought maybe he'd hitched a ride with a teammate's mom or something, but he's not answering his phone. I usually have his location but even that has been turned off. I— listen, I normally wouldn't be bothering you but I truly have a bad feeling about all of this. He's the closest thing I have to a brother." he let out a breath and continued.

"I went to the station over in Ravenbridge, the pigs fucking laughed in my face, said I was behaving like an old lady who lost her grandson at the fair. They said I shouldn't worry about it and that he was probably out causing trouble again." The kid seemed truly distraught and for a second he reminded me of Sofia, the way she cared for Valentina was really similar.

"Tell me about the other missing kids."

"All from North Bridge. When the first one disappeared, Katarina Avelok, we didn't think much of it. She's run away before, nothing new. Her dad is an alcoholic and cares more about his next fill than he does about her. But then Stevie Martins never came home after school one day and her mom went to the police but they said there was nothing they could do for now. She had to wait forty eight hours."

"Who's the third one?"

"Ravi Muhammad. Great kid, head of his class, everyone likes him. His parents went to the police and that's actually when they decided to take it seriously. Both his parents showed up and refused to leave the precinct before they spoke to the chief of police. They threatened to go to the press and tell them how badly the police treated us as soon as they knew we came from North Bridge." Aiden gulped and looked down.

I agreed with the kid on that part. Ravenbridge police department was run by a bunch of bigots who all came from money and privileged backgrounds. Even the few that didn't often ended up turning their backs on their Northy roots and looking down on them. I knew because that's what happened to one of my friends from the academy. As soon as we got our badges, he started speaking ill of the North, saying it was packed with a bunch of useless little shits who would never amount to anything.

Suffice to say, we weren't friends anymore.

What Aiden was telling me right then though, it sounded like a lot. I didn't have any open cases at the moment, except for that goddamn puzzle that was the Raymonds murder.

"This does sound suspicious. Where are Oscar's parents? Have you tried talking to them?"

"I went next door to their house as soon as I saw he wasn't in football practice anymore. His mom was passed out on the couch. She —uh, she works weird hours, so she mostly sleeps all day and works all night."

He looked slightly embarrassed and that made me guess Oscar's mom was probably a stripper. That was one of the main sources of income in North Bridge, *Tatum's Gentlemen Lounge*.

Having been there a few times for work, I could say there was nothing gentlemanly about the place. But there wasn't any need to be embarrassed as I wasn't one to judge. She had to put food on the table, and I got how hard it could be for what I presumed was a single mother, since Aiden didn't say anything about Oscar's dad.

The kid was looking at me like I was his last resort, completely desperate. I don't know for sure what made me decide to help him, maybe it was the fact that his eyes held the same emotion while he spoke of Oscar as Sofia's had when she spoke of Valentina. Maybe it was the fact that I couldn't fucking stand injustices and that Ravenbridge was full of them.

It could have been the frustration I felt at myself for not being able to solve the Raymond's case. Maybe I thought that by helping this guy I could be useful to someone and redeem myself for failing my girls.

I don't know what made me decide for sure, but I still found myself wanting to help him.

"Okay, listen, kiddo, I can't really help you since this falls under Ravens jurisdiction," his shoulders slumped, "but I don't have any cases going on at the moment so I will leave you my number, okay? Start by going to Oscar's coach and see if he even attended practice today. I'll help as much as I can but it will be off the record, you hear me? No one can know." Looking instantly relieved, he nodded his head insistently.

"Of course, yeah, I won't tell a soul." He got up and held his hand to me. I shook it and gave him my card where I scribbled my personal phone number at the back.

"Thank you so much, Detective. He was right when he said I wouldn't be disappointed in you." That made me pause.
"Who said that?" I frowned.

Aiden shrugged, "Just a… friend. You helped him a while ago and he never forgot what you did. Told me you were a good one and that I could trust you. I'm glad I listened."

He gave me a small smile and was out of the room before I could question him further. I didn't mind though, because the moment he was out, Adam came in with a file in his hands. Ever question I had regarding this mysterious friend went out the window the moment the following words got out of my partner's mouth.

"I got good news. It's about the Raymond case."

His smirk told me I would like what was in that file. Fucking finally.

***

**SOFIA**

"Girl, I mean he's not wrong."

So, remember when I said I didn't have any friends? I kind of lied. Once a week I helped tutor students from my old school, Lakestone Academy. I especially helped those in their pre-college program. The whole thing consisted of a year, post-high school and pre-college, that aimed at preparing students so they could attend an Ivy League once they finished it.

The tutoring program actually favored kids with scholarships, which was Sammie's case. They usually weren't able to afford tutors, like most of the other rich pricks did, so the Academy asked their best alumni to tutor them. I'd been helping her for a year, and we kind of struck a friendship. We never hung out other than that one session per week, but somehow she was easy to confide in.

Her black curls fell over her open book as we sat quietly in the back of Lakestone Academy's library. It was around four thirty so most of the school was empty, but since the library didn't close until seven, we usually took advantage of that.

She looked at me sheepishly, like she was trying to tell me tactfully that she was not on my side. Tact wasn't one of Sammie's forte, though.

"I mean… You did go through some pretty traumatic shit. It would make sense to talk to someone." She shrugged and went back scribbling on her notebook.

Sammie was smart as hell, and I knew she'd get into some elite college. I mostly tutored her to bring her some more perspective and methodology, which was what seemed to be lacking in her work. She was on the run to be valedictorian too– a second time, since she'd been it her senior year, too. The parents body didn't seem too pleased about that. They didn't think a scholarship student, especially one who wasn't even from Lakestone should represent their promo.

Sammie was also black and that certainly didn't sit well in the narrow little minds of the Lakestone elite. Lord knew, one of the reasons we had to practically erase our heritage was because Jack Raymond feared he wouldn't get the support from the elite if they knew his daughters spoke better Spanish than English.

"What do you mean he's *not wrong*? He threatened to overrule me and bring my sister to a therapist against my will. That's the one reason I was reticent about this whole custody thing in the first place, him not taking my parenting decisions into consideration. Because, legally, he's not obligated. Hell, he could tell me to get my shit and be out of his apartment by morning and there's nothing I would be able to do about it. I can't believe I was so stupid as to give someone that much power over me." I looked away, angrily doodling on my notes.

"Yeah, what he did wasn't really savory but he did that because your stubborn ass was totally closed to discussion." She shook her head like it was obvious. "I mean, damn girl, you killed someone! There's bound to be something you want to get off your chest."

Oh if only she knew. There were so many things I wanted to get off my chest, but that was the main reason I refused to see a therapist. I was scared that if I started talking I just wouldn't stop, and I couldn't afford to spill all of my secrets to a stranger. Or anyone, really.

"Would you not yell that, please?" I hushed her when I saw a couple heads turning our way. "It was self defense! This town hates me enough without you reminding them that I killed someone."

"Right, sorry." She smiled sheepishly. "Still, I think maybe Cop Guy is right. If not you, then at least Valentina. Maybe she wants to talk to someone, you know?" I couldn't explain to her why exactly I didn't trust strangers with her, so I just shrugged and looked away, dejectedly.

"Whatever. I'm sure Valentina wouldn't want to, anyways."

"Ask her and let her decide. You love your sister, Sofia, anyone who sees you two can tell, so come on. Put your feelings aside and just think of what's best for her. She's growing up, she's starting to know what's good for her." I gulped, knowing she was right. I wouldn't admit it to Maddox yet though, because I was still mad and I wanted to let him simmer a bit longer.

I was totally ignoring him, his texts and calls going straight to voicemail. That would teach him to give me ultimatums.

Sammie's phone vibrated on the table and she looked down at it. "Oh, looks like my brother is here to pick me up!"

She started putting her stuff back in her bag and got up. I followed closely and we walked out of the library together. Once we were outside, I guessed her brother was in the only car with the headlights on in the parking lot. It was an old black Camaro. Papa would have said she was beautiful. He loved cars.

Thinking of him always brought a wave of sadness through me. I missed him.

"Look, just give it a chance." Sammie pulled me out of my thoughts and I turned towards her. "You know my mama got a foster home, right? Well a lot of the kids actually come from really fucking broken families and shitty backgrounds. They basically all have therapists, nothing to be ashamed of if you ask me. I've seen the progress they made just talking to someone. You really should give it more thought." She shrugged.

I smiled, grateful for her insight. "Thank you, babe. For listening to my rant." She smirked and was about to answer when her brother honked.

She groaned and turned around. "One fucking second, Aiden! I'm coming!" Rolling her eyes she turned back to me. "Can you believe he's actually my *little* brother? Well, only by a few months, but still. Little shit works at a garage and built this baby back from scratch over the summer. Now he got a ride and I still don't." She shook her head as I watched, amused. "Anyways, I better go. Take care." She smacked a kiss on my cheek and started walking to the car as I watched, my gaze lost in the distance.

I sighed and started back towards my own car. Maybe Sammie was right.

***

I was home and getting started on dinner when the front door opened and slammed close. I startled, nearly dropping the bowl of pasta I had just cooked. Angry little steps resounded in the apartment as I saw Valentina pass right in front of me without sparing me a glance. Her little face was drawn in a frown, eyebrows pulled down on her forehead and lips pinched together. She continued until disappearing in the hallway and I heard the door of her bedroom slam shut too.

Right at that moment, the front door opened again and a confused looking Maddox stepped in.

"What the hell was that?" Since when did my sweet little sister slam doors? Stomp to her room and not even glance at me or say hello?

Maybe it was the hormones? She told me her period had stopped the day after she bled the first time, exactly like Andrea had predicted.

"I don't know, she's been pissy since I picked her up from dance class earlier. She didn't say a word during the whole ride." When I looked at him, really looked at him, Maddox seemed positively tired.

I knew he pulled almost all nighters working on our case, that he promised himself he would bring our parents justice. I didn't know what to say to that, though. All that mattered to me was that we were safe and together. As far as I was concerned, I had avenged our parents. I'd probably spend the rest of my life thinking of that night, but it was worth it. The last thing I wanted was for Maddox to work himself raw and spiral over a case that seemed unsolvable. Even if I was still pissed at him.

"Well, looks like you have a knack for pissing off Raymond women." I muttered as I wiped my hands and stalked to Sofia's room.

I could feel his exasperated gaze on me, but I ignored it, too preoccupied by what was going on with my sister.

When I reached the door, I knocked quietly. I could feel Maddox's body at my back and it took all of me not to lean back against him and let him wrap his arms around me.

A muffled "Leave me alone!" resonated from the other side which told me Valentina probably had her head against a pillow.

I turned the knob and indeed, there she was, lying on her bed, her face pressed against a pink pillow, still in her school uniform. I didn't know if she was crying exactly, but she sounded upset.

"What's up, Pretty Girl, talk to us." Maddox walked past me and kneeled on the side of her bed. I followed suit and sat next to her, my knee grazing Maddox's forearm.

"No!"

"You know you can tell us anything, *Rosita.* We won't be angry. Did something happen at school?" Dread filled my stomach at the mere idea that someone had hurt her.

She didn't say anything, just screamed in her pillow. My mouth opened slightly and I saw Maddow have a similar reaction. I don't think I'd ever seen my sister this angry, except maybe that day at the park. It was seriously starting to worry me.

"I don't wanna go with Jensen the Janitor!" Somehow, that only made me more confused.

"Uh… I think you need to elaborate, baby." She sniffled and finally straightened up, sitting down in front of Maddox and I. She wasn't crying but her eyes were red-rimmed and wet.

"The daddy-daughter dance. I don't wanna go with Jensen the janitor. He's nice and all, but I don't wanna go with him, okay?"

Maddox frowned, "Of course not, sweets. I mean, to be honest, even if you *wanted* to, I'm not sure we should or would let you go with a stranger anywhere."

Looking dejected, Valentina glared at her hands. "It's the first year my grade is allowed to go. And the kids in my class said since I didn't have a daddy anymore, I would go with Jensen. They said since he's Mexican like me we could pretend he was my daddy. He's not even Mexican, he's Puerto Rican!"

Anger coursed through my veins. I hated this fucking town. The people were awful, the kids were awful, fucking dammit this school was so fucking expensive and still the staff let things like that go unnoticed? Unpunished?

Maddox's hand came to clasp Valentina's and he looked fondly at her.

"You're not going anywhere with Jensen, okay? And if you don't want to go to that dance, no one is forcing you. We could stay here and watch a movie or even go out and spend the night out of the city." She looked like she wanted to say something but didn't dare, pursing her lips instead.

And I instantly knew.

I knew she wanted to ask Maddox to be her date to the dance but her pride and fear of rejection were keeping her from doing so. I understood where she was coming from, it might be weird for him to take on the role of a dad, even for a night.

She just shrugged and took her hand out of Maddox's. I saw the anguish on her face and couldn't do anything about it.

"Now that you know what's wrong, can you please leave me alone so I can cry in peace?" She sprawled back on the bed, her face against the pillow. Both me and Maddox shared an anguished look, putting aside our differences for a second.

I saw him gulp before his gaze went back to my sister. He got on his feet and grabbed her waist, lifting her up in the air.

"Nope, sorry, there will be no wallowing alone under this roof. We're going to get pizza and then we'll try out the new arcade that opened in town."

Maddox effortlessly threw Valentina over his shoulder and held her like a sack of potatoes. She wiggled a bit in her blue school uniform, trying to set herself free from him, but even she had to know it was a lost cause.

"Let me wallow! I want to wallow!"

"Nope, sorry. No wallowing in this house."

"Mads, I want to wallow!"

A smile split my face because the scene was honestly comical, but then Maddox caught me and I remembered I was supposed to be angry at him so I wiped the smile right off my lips.

Still, he seemed to find it amusing and smirked at me. Beautiful bastard.

"Nope. You're gonna change into some comfy clothes and we'll go out tonight, just the three of us."

He straightened her up so she could look at us and she did. She seemed like she wanted to go but also like going would be admitting defeat. Eventually, she rolled her eyes— the little minx was looking like me a little more everyday, and shrugged.

She tried to play it cool but I could see she was excited to go. She was the one who actually talked our ears off about the new arcade in town. A bunch of kids from her school hung out there on the weekends and they made it sound so cool Valentina was really excited about trying it.

"Fine. I guess I can wallow when we get back from the arcade."

Like hell she would.

# 20

## WATER

### MADDOX

Valentina fell asleep in the car during the drive back home and neither Sofia nor I had the heart to wake her up once in the parking garage. The night had been great, even though there definitely were tensions between Sofia and I, and not the good kind that usually ended up with my head buried between her thighs.

No, we barely spoke all night and the times we did, Sofia's tone was cold and aloof. She only smiled and laughed with Valentina and even though she did her best not to let it show in front of the little girl, I knew she was smart enough to pick up on things. When Sofia had gone to the bathroom at some point, the younger Raymond sister looked expectantly at me and asked 'what did you do?' in an accusatory tone.

Of course I played dumb and evaded the question, distracting her with an endless roll of tickets that eventually got her a huge teddy bear which now sat on the backseat next to her sleeping form. She named him Gilbert.

"We need to talk." I breathed out, cutting the engine off and turning towards the one woman who could drive me crazy without even trying.

"Oh, do we? What, you wanna remind me again of how I was dumb enough to trust you?" Her words stung but I knew I deserved them.

"I never should have said what I said, okay? I'm sorry. It was dumb and I would have never done it anyways. I just— you wouldn't listen to anything I said. I knew I had to do something to get your attention."

"Congrats, you did get my attention, but you lost my trust in the process." She unbuckled and got out of the vehicle.

It hurt to hear her say that, it really did. But again, I deserved it. Following after her, I closed my door and opened Valentina's to get her out. The princess was still fast asleep, mumbling about Gilbert in her dreams. That brought a smile to my face but it went down as soon as my eyes met Sofia's. She looked at me with a mixture of yearning, disappointment and wariness.

I hated it. If I could turn back time and punch myself in the face to keep me from uttering that useless threat, I would have.

I knew in the end I was right, Valentina did need to see someone. But the means I'd used to get my point across were far from right.

I held Valentina in my arms as Sofia grabbed the huge bear which was almost her size and locked my car. We walked to the apartment in silence and once inside, I deposited our girl in her bed. Sofia put Gilbert in a corner and started rummaging through Valentina's closet for a set of pajamas. I stood in the middle of the pink room awkwardly as she blatantly ignored me. Once she had the clothes in hands she made her way to the bed before looking expectantly at me.

"I got it from here, you can go to your room." I hated the way she dismissed me. I hated the way she called it *my* room when it was supposed to be *our* room, even more.

"I'll wait for you to come to bed so we can talk."

"Don't hold your breath." I tried to catch her gaze but she wouldn't look at me and started to take Valentina's shoes off instead.

I cleared my throat, but seeing no reaction from her I simply walked back to my room, shoulders slumped.

I spent two hours sitting in bed, waiting for her to join me.

She never did.

***

"What's up with your face?" Turning around from the coffee machine in the common room of the station, my gaze found Selena's.

"What do you mean?"

"You look awful." Yeah, well I felt it too.

"Jeez, thanks a lot." A hand came up to rub my face as I waited for this fucking coffee to be ready. "I didn't sleep much yesterday."

"Yeah, it shows." I leveled her up with a glare before grabbing my mug and sitting on the sofa.

"Adam here yet? We got some shit to do today." Reminding myself of where we were going today was the only thing giving me a modicum of joy.

We finally were making progress in the case. Adam went to several locksmiths in the area to see if they knew of any copies having been made of the Raymond's house key. Guess what? A certain individual had made one exactly two weeks before the murders took place.

And that person was none other than Conan fucking Michaels.

***

“Fuck I forgot how weird this place was.”

Adam seemed positively uncomfortable among people scrambling around the city hall. They all looked like clones, dressed in black and white and walking with almost military-like stature. We looked like two sore thumbs sticking out dressed in jeans and long-sleeved shirts. Way too casual compared to them.

“Tell me about it.” I muttered, as a tall blond wearing a pencil skirt and high heels walked our way with a big bright smile on her face.

“Hello, detectives. How may I help you?”

“We’re here to see Conan Michaels.”

“Is he expecting you?”

“No, we’re on an investigation. It’s an urgent matter.”

She looked uneasy and gave us a fake smile. “Well I’m sorry, Mr. Michaels is really busy today but I may be able to squeeze you in sometime this week.”

“I don’t give a shit if he’s in a meeting with the fucking president right now, either you let us see him in the privacy of his own office or we’re putting him in handcuffs and bringing him in for questioning. Your choice.” Adam was quickly losing his legendary patience and quite frankly so was I.

"Now that you mention it, I do think it would make an amazing headline." I snapped my finger, casting a falsely impressed look at my partner.

"Right? I can already imagine it: '*Former assistant of the mayor becomes prime suspect in lead investigation.*'"

"*From politics to prison: a tale of treason and—*"

The blond cleared her throat and interrupted me before I even finished, looking like she was three seconds away from an aneurysm.

"Okay, okay! I'll take you to his office right now. It's his lunch break, I'm sure he'll have a couple of minutes to spare." I didn't bother telling her it would take much longer than a couple of minutes and just followed her through the hallways.

The town hall was an old mansion heavily inspired by greek architecture, with heavy white pillars, marble floors and portraits hanging on the walls. A big white marble statue of a half naked man sat in the center of the room, and everything was fucking immaculate. It gave the whole place an eerie vibe that just instantly made me uneasy.

We finally stopped in front of a door with a gold plate written "Conan Michaels" on it. I shared a look with Adam that told me the older man thought the same as me: Conan sure seemed to have settled well into his new position as a member of the city council.

He was the youngest there, but from what I heard, his peers really liked him. He even seemed to have found himself a new mentor in Lex Dunavan. He was a creepy old dude who was pushing ninety and honestly had no business deciding the future of so many people when he looked three seconds away from death.

Blondie knocked and Conan's voice resonated through the door. My jaw set just hearing him. I still hadn't forgotten how Sofia lied to me to protect him the day of the fire. I had a feeling these two had history but I didn't know how to look into it or prove it. I didn't want to ask Sofia directly because she clearly wasn't feeling up to talk about it and pushing her wouldn't be a good idea.

As soon as his secretary opened the door and Conan saw us, he looked pissed. Closing down his laptop, he straightened up in his chair.

"Mr Michaels, Detective Brooks and Detective A—"

"I'll take it from here, Barbra, you can go back to your desk." Barbra clamped her mouth shut and nodded, hightailing it out of there as fast as she could. All the while, Conan's eyes stayed glued on us.

Well, actually, it's *me* this cunt was glaring at.

Not waiting for an invite and wanting to piss him off further, I stalked around his office, looking at the books on his shelves and the pictures on his walls.

There were several of him and the mayor, but my eyes were drawn to one picture in particular. One where he stood with the Raymond family, grinning and looking like he fucking belonged there.

My eyes traced Sofia's figure, she was clearly younger there. Maybe sixteen or seventeen. She seemed really tense and wasn't smiling at the camera. Her eyes looked… dead.

"How can I help you, gentlemen?" He gritted his teeth and somehow, knowing we were getting on his nerves pleased me.

“You can begin by telling us why the hell you had a key to Jack Raymond’s house made two weeks before he was killed.”

Forcing my gaze off of that picture, I turned around and stared him down. Adam, who had closed the door after the secretary left, walked to Conan’s desk and tossed the file at him. It contained all the information we were able to get from the locksmith. And there were a lot.

Conan frowned, looking genuinely surprised as he opened the file. His eyes widened when took in what was inside.

“I never got Jack’s key copied. I don’t know where all this information comes from, but I swear I had nothing to do with it.”

“Oh, really? Then please explain how come the call to the locksmith was made from your address *and* phone number, why your car was filmed on CCTV on the street of his shop the day you came to pay for his services and why it’s your card number on his files.” Adam sat down on one of the two chairs in front of his desk and I joined him, sprawling my legs in front of me.

Conan chuckled like he couldn’t believe what was happening. “You can’t be serious, right? You can’t seriously think I would have harmed Jack in any way. He was the father I never had!” He was clearly outraged, like the mere idea of him being a suspect was more than farfetched.

“We don’t care about your sob story, we want to know why you made a fucking copy of his home key.” I griped, feeling my control slip away.

Why the fuck would Sofia protect this guy? What wasn't she telling me? Did they have a past of some sorts?

"I never fucking ordered it, detective." His tone matched mine and Adam, ever the peace-holder, felt the need to intervene before it escalated.

"Mr. Michaels, your name and signature were on the receipt, the locksmith recognized you from a picture we showed him and we checked the dates and times with the days you were working. Everything proves you did make that copy and all we're asking is *why*."

Conan took a deep breath to seemingly calm himself and was about to speak when suddenly the door opened. We all turned towards the intruder, only to see a short blond girl with bangs and glasses entering quietly.

She was wearing a simple short black skirt and long-sleeved white shirt—like fucking everyone here, with black flats. Only thing is she accessorized her outfit with a pair of satiny white gloves and a cute white bow holding a part of her hair to the side. On top of the outfit, the girl had a real baby face and couldn't have been a day older than seventeen. Even that was pushing it, actually.

She stopped dead in her tracks when she saw us, looking down shyly.

"Oh I-I'm sorry, Mr. Michaels. I didn't know you had company. Your secretary told me to bring you some water like you requested earlier." Her voice was sweet and soft, it almost sounded vulnerable. Somehow, this whole situation sent a shiver of something down my spine but I couldn't quite say what or why.

Conan's face totally changed, it contorted back to that friendly, smiling, almost charming face he knew how to use so well.

"Oh please, don't apologize. Bring it here, thank you—?"

"Jane." She supplied with a shy smile, pushing her glasses up on her nose.

"Right. Jane. I don't even remember asking for water, I have so much work I forget about my most basic needs sometimes."

He chuckled in an attempt to be endearing and gave her a once over as she walked towards his desk. She put the bottle down and smiled again before turning around and walking to the door.

My hand just itched as I watched Conan eye her ass like the fucking creep I knew he was. Again, that girl looked like a fucking *child.* I knew it might have seemed hypocritical of me given the nature of my relationship with Sofia who was eight years younger than me, but nothing happened with her until she was almost twenty. And even then I struggled at first.

Plus, Sofia didn't a baby face and she didn't dress childishly either.

And God knew I never leered at her the way that fucker had at that poor girl.

Adam mirrored my disgusted expression and when the door clicked shut after Jane, Conan finally brought his gaze back to us. He smirked and my fist was just dying to kiss his fucking smug face.

"Sorry about that. We get a lot of interns, especially seniors in high school looking for good recommendations for college." He shrugged,

"I can't learn all their names by heart." He opened the bottle and took a long swig of water.

Neither Adam or I spoke because quite frankly I was still reeling from seeing him leer so obviously on a minor in front of two cops. Did that guy think he was invincible?

"As I said, I never ordered that key." He finished drinking and put the half-empty bottle down. "I don't know how you found this evidence but it's obviously forged, someone must be trying to frame me." He was suddenly serious.

"Mr. Michaels, with all my due respect, I don't believe that for a second."

"Looks like life has been looking up for you, huh?" I said suddenly, interrupting Adam. "New job, higher rank, better pay, your own office. Seems like Jack Raymond's death was a blessing in disguise after all."

His face shuttered and he tensed up, "I would give all of this back in a heartbeat if it meant having him and Marcella back and healthy."

"Right. I believe that."

"Look, I don't know what your problem is with me, exactly but—" He stopped suddenly, and cleared his throat. "But—" he tried continuing his point but started coughing instead.

For several seconds, he did just that. Coughed and couldn't seem to stop, it just wouldn't let go of him. That made me frown, my gut was screaming that something was wrong..

And something was fucking wrong, alright. Adam looked at me warily as Conan just kept on choking on air.

I got up, went behind his desk and started tapping his back lightly.

Adam too burst into action too and grabbed the bottle of water, opening it up and putting it against his mouth. Conan tried to drink but it was like his throat had closed up and all the water dripped down on his desk, drenching the papers laying on top of it.

“Fuck! Call 911!” I screamed and Adam ran out of the room to get help, holding his phone in hand. The bottle fell on the desk, forgotten as it soaked the surface, slowly emptying itself.

Conan started suffocating then, his coughing turning into wheezing, his arms flying around in panic. His eyes were nearly bulging out of their sockets and I had no idea what to do. I figured if something was blocking his windpipe, I could get it out by using the Heimlich method, but as soon as I started helping him up, something happened. Something bad.

Conan started crying.

Only his tears were not clear. They were blood red.

Thick red liquid started oozing out of his ears too and at first I couldn’t believe what I was seeing. Blood seeped from his ears, his eyes, his nose, and eventually, he started coughing it out of his mouth too.

“Fuck!” I jumped away, shock coursing through my veins as I stared in stunned stupor.

When it started to wear off, adrenaline settled in and I tried to pull him up but he couldn’t fucking move. His air supply was completely blocked. He slumped face first on his desk, blood dripping on it from every orifice on his face. His body kept on convulsing, like it was fighting whatever substance was making him that way.

I tried helping him, applying pressure on his chest, his ears, anything, but I didn't even know what was causing the bleeding. He just kept on thrashing about while losing what seemed like gallons upon gallons of blood. I watched powerlessly as life slowly and painfully left his body.

My own was in locked shock, after years on the force, this was the first time I witnessed anything like that. Heart beating fast and bloody hands trembling, I grabbed my phone to call for reinforcements when an ear-splitting scream resounded in the room. I looked up and sure enough, a shaking Barbra was at the door, staring at Conan's body which ceased moving a few seconds ago. His blood was pooling underneath him and the whole room was silent enough that you could hear it dripping onto the floor.

"Step back! Get back to your desk, nobody is leaving the premises until further order!" She nodded, clearly panicking as she ran back to her desk.

Approaching Conan, I pushed two fingers against his bloody neck and closed my eyes in defeat when I couldn't feel his pulse.

Fuck, fuck, *fuck*. What happened?

We were finally making progress and then our main suspect dropped fucking dead!

I could feel myself starting to freak out when my gaze caught sight of the water bottle still sitting on the desk in a pool of hemoglobins. My eyes widened in sudden understanding.

The water.

Conan was doing fucking great before he drank that water *Jane* brought him.

My eyes widened and I ran out of the room, yelling for Barbra. I found her in the main hall, on the floor with half a dozen other employees, hugging their knees and silently freaking out. Adam was at the door, on the phone, probably with the precinct, his gun in hand. He was making sure nobody got out of here or came in.

I swiped the hall for the small glasses-wearing blond but somehow couldn't find her anywhere. *Fuck, fuck, fuck.*

"Barbra! Where the fuck is Jane?" The blond looked up at me with wide eyes shaking her head.

"W-who?"

"Jane, the blond intern you sent to bring Michaels some water!" I was frantic, there was no time to spare.

"I-I don't know what you're talking about!" Barbra bursted into tears and Adam sent me a look of anguish and confusion from the other side of the room.

"There's no intern called Jane working here, officer." Another, calmer, voice called from my left and I turned around. A middle aged man sat against the front desk and he looked as confused and panicked as I felt. "The only interns we have at the moment are Robbie and Bill."

Dread piled into my stomach and I cast another look at my partner.

*I don't even remember asking for water.*

He hadn't remembered asking for it, not because he was too busy, but because he *hadn't*.

There was no Jane.

That girl came into Conan's office, gave him a poisoned water bottle and was probably out of here before he even started drinking. That's what the gloves were for, she was not leaving any clue behind, they were not fucking fashion accessories.

"Check the back entrance!" Adam yelled.

But it was too late. By the time I arrived in the small alley the back entrance led to, all that was left was a blond wig and a pair of smashed glasses in one of the trash cans.

Someone had just murdered Conan Michaels right in front of us and we had no idea who it was.

# 21

# FIGHT

**SOFIA**

He didn't call.

Maddox didn't come home for dinner and he didn't even call or text to tell me.

Actually, I hadn't heard from him all day. No text to ignore, no call to let go straight to voicemail, *nothing*. I couldn't even be obvious in my ignoring him and letting him simmer.

I would be lying if I said it wasn't worrying me. I would also be lying if I said it didn't piss me off.

He should be begging me for forgiveness, getting on his hands and knees to grovel. That's the main reason why I spent all day yesterday blowing him off and why I hadn't slept next to him last night.

Speaking of last night, I barely got any shut-eye. After dressing Valentina in her pajamas, I put her under the covers and headed directly to my old room, the one I used to sleep in before Maddox and I even got together. I originally loved that room, it was cute and cozy, and it felt like me.

I had gotten home from class one day a week or two after we moved in and found all kinds of candles, throw pillows and fleece blankets sitting on the bed, waiting for me to use as decor. Maddox had gotten them for me because he thought the room didn't match me . He was right, it was all white and had no color whatsoever because I didn't feel comfortable enough to truly make it mine.

That gesture was one of many that had me feeling way more at ease in this apartment. I had added a couple of vases in which I put fake flowers because, unlike my mama, I didn't have a green thumb worth a dime. I put pictures of Valentina and I, even one we had taken with Maddox, the three of us at the diner on the day we first moved in. My wooden box stood proudly on the dresser and my painting supplies were all collected in a corner of the room in organized chaos.

I loved that room and I used to love to sleep in it.

But last night, my usually comfy mattress might as well have been granite, the soft covers felt prickly and thorny and my pillow felt so hard against my head I thought I'd have a stiff neck waking up today.

I slept like shit. All because I had gotten used to falling asleep in Maddox's arms, feeling safe and cared for.

I guess that's just another thing that made me pissy about today. Added to the fact that he didn't call all day, he didn't show up for dinner and didn't call to warn us like he usually would, and that Valentina had gone to bed without getting to ask him the question she had spent all evening preparing for.

My baby wanted to ask Maddox to be her prince to the Daddy-Daughter dance her school organized. The theme was fairytales, so obviously Valentina was out of her head with excitement.

The fact that she immediately thought of Maddox made me feel good and worried at the same time. Good because I reveled at seeing their relationship unfold, seeing how Valentina was finally letting herself trust someone that wasn't me. I loved how protective Maddox was of her, how he treated her like she was his as much as mine.

That's part of why I couldn't keep on reproaching him our fight forever. Sure, he hurt me when he suggested he would go over my head to bring Valentina help, but in truth, I could admit I wasn't the most reasonable person to argue with at that time. I was caught off guard, and when he suggested Mindy from the police department, I lost it.

That's why I was ready to make him sweat a bit today, then forgive him and spend the night letting him please me and apologize to me in all the right ways. Ways that involved, but were not limited to, his tongue between my legs.

But of course he had to go MIA on me all day. Now *I* had to act like I was still mad and maybe even sleep in my own bed again to make a point. That little fucker was fucking up all my plans.

Valentina had gone to bed nearly an hour ago and I was finishing cleaning up around the apartment when I heard the familiar sound of keys being turned into the locks.

Fucking finally.

Trying to act like I didn't care, I continued to wipe the counter as he entered and tossed his keys on the table. Still not looking up, waiting for him to fall to his knees and start apologizing to me, saying his phone got stolen or his thumbs got broken or fuck, even that he was kidnapped by aliens who wanted to destroy our country!

Anything would've done it to be honest. I really wanted us to make up already even if a part of me was still itching for a fight, for some reason. I guess I wanted to get my frustrations out.

But when a minute passed and nothing happened, I finally did look up.

Maddox was slumped against the front door, eyes closed, head thrown back against it, looking like he was trying to find the strength to even finish this day.

Oh he would need it, indeed.

My eyes narrowed, "Your shoes." I said, because he knew I hated it when people left their shoes on inside the house.

Maybe it was because I was raised by a clean freak, maybe it was a cultural thing, I didn't really care for the reason, I mostly just found it disgusting.

He didn't even seem to hear me, he just stayed in the same position and didn't move.

What the fuck? Was he seriously giving me the silent treatment? If anything, *I* should be the one doing that, for fuck's sake. He was not robbing me of my grovel.

"I—"

"Not now, Sofia." My eyebrows were nearly up to my headline after he said that.

Not now? Not *now*? Oh he was in for a surprise if he thought a shit ton of orgasms and cute little attentions would make me docile all of a sudden.

"Oh, so he does have a voice, huh? How fascinating. Didn't hear it all day, even when me and my sister were sitting down, waiting for you to join us for dinner. She kept on asking me where you were and I didn't even know what to say!" I tossed the towel on the counter, exasperated with him.

"Sofia, I said *not now*." He growled, finally looking at me, only to glare. Somehow that made me even more mad.

"No? Then when, pendejo*?* Tell me! I'm waiting. When you disappear again for a whole day without giving us news that you're even alive? When you threaten to disregard my will again? When, Maddox, when is the right time?"

I was aware of how irrationally angry I sounded at that moment, and how I was pushing for a fight, but again, I just needed the confrontation. I really wanted all animosity between us to be purged out.

"Conan is fucking dead! He was the only lead we had on your parents' case and now he's fucking gone!" He blew up, breathing erratically, clearly frustrated and angry and going through a whole bunch of other emotions that would make me feel uncomfortable to be around him had he been anyone but Maddox.

Then his words actually registered and I took a step back, in shock. Eyes wide, I brought my hand to my mouth.

"That's where I was all day, why I couldn't come home and didn't even have a second to talk." He explained more calmly, rubbing a hand over his face. "Everything was a mess, I didn't have time to myself I– fuck." A hand went through his head in frustration.

I didn't say anything, and simply sat on the nearest barstool, still processing all this information, looking at the floor.

"I— how?" Was the only thing I could muster.

"Poison. The coroner said it was too early to say what exactly but he highly suspected it was venom. A… mix of venoms found in different tropical snakes which don't even live in this continent, let alone in our town."

I looked up immediately. My ears were ringing.

"Snakes? How would he get bitten by a snake?"

"He didn't. Someone gave him a poisoned bottle of water, right in front of us. She evaporated before we could do anything."

"Wait, *she*?"

He nodded, dejected. "She. She had such a babyface and— fuck, I can't believe I thought she looked innocent."

I bit my lips, not saying anything about how Conan wasn't all white either. It didn't matter, anyways. He was dead.

Dead.

Conan was fucking dead, and my secret with him.

I didn't know how to feel about that, other than being confused.

"He was our only true suspect in the case, especially since we found evidence of him having a spare key to your house." I didn't say anything and he continued. "Now everything is going to fucking shit and Chief Piersons wants us to rule the case as a robbery gone wrong."

Maddox took off his shoes and walked to the sofa where he let himself slump down to put his elbows on his knees, looking exhausted.

"He doesn't believe Conan's murder had anything to do with my parents' case?"

He shook his head. "No, because he didn't believe *Conan* could have anything to do with your parents' murder in the first place. There's also the fact that we saw his murderer, or his murderer's accomplice or whoever she was, clear as day and that she didn't look anything like the second guy you described from that night." He closed his eyes again, falling back against the sofa and groaning. "This is a fucking mess I don't even know where to look anymore! Piersons gave us a week before putting it in the cold case section. I— I feel so fucking useless."

Maddox actively avoided my gaze then he suddenly got up and started pacing around the living room. I got up too, and joined him there. I had never seen him so worked up before, and although a small part of me was still mad at him, I couldn't stand watching him beat himself up.

Damn, was this what falling in love felt like?

Caring more about someone else's feelings than we do our own and being willing to prioritize theirs above our own? The mere idea wasn't strange to me. What truly was strange, however, was that I never felt that way for someone other than my sister.

Maddox truly had wormed his way straight through my heart and now shared the space with Valentina and all the people I loved that were taken away from me.

How… bizarre.

"I failed you, Sofia!" His outburst brought me back to reality. He looked through the windows, one hand braced against it as the other laid along his side. His words confused me.

"What are you talking about?"

He turned around, and for the first time since he came in I could truly see the exhaustion, the sheer fatigue and frustration and anger in his gaze. All directed towards himself.

"I failed you and Valentina and it makes me feel so fucking weak. I made a promise to myself that I would help you get anything you might need. That I would do everything I could so that you'd feel cared for and appreciated and— and I couldn't even do my fucking job and find the person who took everything from you in the first place." I'd never seen Maddox so dejected, so disappointed in himself.

"How dare you say that." Were the words that left my lips as I stared at him, dumbfounded. "How dare you say that you think you didn't do all that and more?"

I put both hands on his chest and pushed him slightly. I wanted to comfort him in a sweeter way, but I knew he'd take any overly kind gestures as pity.

"Piersons gave me a *week* to solve a murder I haven't been able to solve in months, Sofia! It's over, I didn't stay true to my promise, I didn't give you and your sister closure. I didn't avenge you."

"So what! You gave us a roof over our heads, food in our stomachs, you buy everything around the house and refuse to take my money for anything! Hell, you said I should quit my job so I could focus more on school, Maddox!"

"These are material things, they won't give you closure!"

"Yeah? How about all the love you keep on showering my sister with? How about the fact that the mere mention of your name brings a smile to her face? How about the fact that you hug me in your arms every time I have a nightmare and let me cry my eyes out against your chest, sometimes for hours? You tried every fucking thing under the sun to close this case, to bring us closure, and don't you dare think we don't know that. That counts more than any results you might have had from this case."

I pushed him again and again until his back hit the window. He looked down on me with a scorching gaze. Fuck, there wasn't a time I didn't want this man.

"And so what if you didn't find out who that second man was, huh? Who cares? I killed the first man. He's done for, the second one won't be coming back for us. I'm not even sure he came for our parents the first time, maybe Piersons is right and it *was* a robbery gone wrong." His eyes left mine and he just looked down, defeated. I bit my lips, looking away, before letting my head fall against his chest.

Both of us were breathing harshly. I could feel the erratic beat of his heart against my cheek, it was comforting. Everything about being in Maddox's arms was comforting. Sometimes I just wanted to bury myself in his chest so I could rest against his heart and hear it beat to a steady rhythm.

"Please let it go. The last thing I want is to see the man I'm falling in love with spiral out of control. We lost our parents, don't let us lose you too." Hands gripping his shirt, head against his chest, I just closed my eyes and let myself be soothed by the sound of his beating heart.

His fingers came up to my hair and started playing with it briefly before he hugged me tight to his chest. No more words were spoken, just the sounds of our breaths mixing and creating one single symphony.

Heaven was in his arms.

But I still had to give him hell for the things he said yesterday.

Because yes, that nagging feeling, that urge for confrontation didn't leave me. It was still there, more silent than before, but still damn too annoying for me to ignore.

Pushing myself off of him, I exhaled and looked up. I had to force myself to say the following words, not because I liked unnecessary drama, but because I couldn't let it go without a fight.

Some part of me just wanted to get in bed with Maddox, let him do whatever he wanted to me, but another just couldn't let that happen without a confrontation, it was *aching* for it.

"Go to sleep" I tapped his chest, "I'm gonna finish cleaning up and head to bed too." I nodded to myself and pursed my lips.

Just when I was going to turn around and get back to the kitchen, his hand shot out and grabbed my wrist, pulling me against him.

"You're joining me in bed tonight." He demanded and I frowned.

"No, I'm not. I'm still mad, in case you'd forgotten what you did yesterday."

"You can be mad at me in bed."

I narrowed my eyes at him, "No, I can't. You're gonna take a shower and get some damn sleep— Lord knows you need it, and I'm going to do the very same thing, but in my own bed." My own fucking uncomfortable and cold bed.

I pulled my wrist free of him and stood my ground even though inside, I was fighting all of my instincts.

"You're cute, baby. Acting like you have a choice and all." He smirked but I could see a dark spark in his eyes. He looked like he was through with this sham of a fight.

Pushing himself off the window, he walked towards me slowly, almost like a predator seeking his prey. Somehow I loved it.

When he came close enough, his hand grasped my throat in a soft grip and made me look up at him. My heart of hearts was beating so fast at that moment, a mix of excitement, wonder, surprise, and something else I couldn't quite decipher.

"I don't give a shit if you're mad at me, Sofia. I am never spending another night away from you. Matter of fact, I'm never even going to bed while one of us is angry at the other. Life is too fucking short, and

I'll be damned if the last thing we said to each other were curse words or dumb threats we didn't even mean."

I didn't know what to answer. The restlessness I was feeling was still here, still aching, and I didn't know what to do with it. It yearned for a fight, it yearned to let out some of the tension that had been accumulating for the last few weeks. It just didn't know how.

So I just glared at him as my brain kept on roaming for something to throw his way but to no avail.

He seemed to notice my brain going a hundred miles per hour and bent down so that his head was at the same level as mine. He whispered against my lips and it took all I had not to give in and slam my lips against his.

"Don't make me put you over my knee, baby." My mouth fell agape and all of a sudden, everything made sense.

The ache somehow eased as the words left his mouth and I swear I could have moaned out loud at how tempting it sounded.

*That* was what I needed. The rush, the adrenaline, the fucking catharsis it gave me the first time I experienced it.

I was yearning for another spanking.

The realization hit me full force and I really didn't want it to be true at first. How fucking humiliating was that? I had spent the biggest part of my adult life avoiding being at anyone's mercy, yet here I was, willing to be under Maddox's?

It didn't make sense.

Seeing my reaction and sensing my hesitation, the cop I had found myself living with narrowed his eyes. He took another step towards me, putting us chest to chest and his hand around my neck squeezed delicately.

"That's what you want, isn't it?" He narrowed his eyes and I lowered mine in shame.

I couldn't tell him. I knew he wouldn't judge me for wanting to explore my sexuality, if anything, he seemed to revel in that, but still. My insecurities were rooted too deep in me to simply disappear after a month of amazing sex.

At my lack of response, Maddox simply stated, "You're aching for another spanking."

I was mortified but at the same time I wanted it so much my body was actually starting to shake slightly. I wanted Maddox to just sweep me off my feet and carry me to his bedroom or hell, just sit down on the couch and take me over his knee.

Anything to make the voices in my head stop being so fucking loud.

"I can't say no to you." Maddox placed a piece of my hair away from my face and behind my ear and I squeezed my thighs in anticipation. "But before I give you what you want, kneel and open that pretty little mouth of yours."

I could feel my eyes widening, my heart beating faster and faster. It was crazy how much I craved this proximity to him, how much I wanted to please him when an hour before I was so mad I could have strangled him.

I was undeniably attracted to Maddox, sure, but what I was feeling at that moment actually went way beyond attraction. It was a desire to please him, to have him to myself, to be consumed by him and to consume all his waking moments. That's why it made me mad when I thought he was ignoring me. That's why it hurt me when he said he could just dismiss my opinion and overrule me.

It was actually impossible to resist him, especially not when I knew he would give me what I wanted in the end.

His grip on my throat went lax and I wordlessly got on my knees in front of him. My eyes were still on him when I started unzipping his pants. I lowered them along with his black boxer briefs and his hard cock sprung out, hitting his stomach. I gulped. The sight he served above me only made more moisture seep between my legs.

Maddox looked down at me like a king while I was on my knees just waiting to serve him and willing to make his every desire a reality.

This whole situation, knowing he was in a position of domination over me, made me wet.

Knowing that I could be in a vulnerable state with him without actually *feeling* vulnerable made me wetter..

Because deep down, I just knew he would never hurt me. And that was the biggest turn on.

One of his hands came to cup the top of my head as he brought me closer to his cock. I licked my lips before slowly gliding my tongue up the length of his shaft. His taste hitting my tongue made me moan in delight. I loved everything about that man.

"Fuck baby, stop playing around."

He almost sounded desperate to finally have my mouth on him. In the month since we started getting physical, I had only gone down on him once. Not because I didn't want to, but because he never actually let me. He could spend hours licking and sucking on my clit, but when I wanted to return the favor, he'd say we wouldn't have time, or that him going down on me was just as pleasing to him as it was to me.

So the fact that he actually had asked for it meant a lot to me, and I was about to savor it as much as I could.

I opened my mouth and took the head between my lips, sucking and bobbing my head so that as I went down I took as much of him as I could. Maddox was big, both in length and girth, so giving him head was not the easier fit, but I was determined to make him feel good.

As I sucked on his dick, he kept on making noises that made me want to go faster. He moaned, his grip on my head sliding to grip a chunk of my hair instead. I tried my best and went even deeper, feeling him hit the back of my throat and making me gag a little bit. Spit was dripping from the seams of my lips, tears were gathering in my eyes, but I didn't relent. I loved that I was doing this to him.

"Yeah, baby, you're doing so good. Taking my cock like a good girl."

I came up for air and the slurping sounds echoing in the room were obscene and dirty and somehow only made me slicker between my legs. I loved the praise, God, I loved it. I could hear Maddox calling me a good girl every day for the rest of my life and wouldn't tire of it.

Pushing myself off his cock, I let it sit against my bottom lip for a beat as I looked up at him through my lashes. "Do you like it? My tongue running up and down your cock?"

The vibration of my voice against his shaft seemed to have an effect on him. He looked like he could have come from my words alone.

"You have no idea what you do to me, baby."

Grabbing his hand, I intertwined my fingers with his through my hair. He pulled me closer and I took him back inside my mouth, making him groan aloud. I sucked harder, bobbed my head faster, he twitched inside my throat and my first thought was that it tickled.

Tears were rolling down my cheeks but I wasn't crying. I was feeling so proud of myself for bringing that strong man down to his knees.

"Yeah, Sofia, just like that. Fuck baby, I'm gonna come."

His grip on my hair tightened to the point it probably would have hurt had I not been so focused on making him feel good. He tried pulling his hips away, giving me an out, in case I didn't want to swallow, but I wanted him to come in my mouth. I wanted to swallow his cum and see the satisfaction in his gaze as I did. I wanted to make him proud and maybe even earn one of his praises.

Fuck, I wanted it so bad.

So I swallowed and I actually enjoyed the taste of his cum hitting the back of my tongue while he groaned and let his head fall back. When he pulled his dick out of me, some of his seed I couldn't swallow mixed with my own saliva dripped down my chin, probably staining the black t-shirt I had on, but I didn't care. His legs actually shook as he emptied himself inside my more-than-willing mouth, and I took everything he had to give.

I probably looked a sight, kneeling on the floor, eyes lost in his sea of green, as I waited for his next words. My hands were holding his jeans-clad legs, and I was trying my best to get my breath back to normal.

His hand came down from where it was gripping my hair and cupped my cheek instead. He caressed my skin tenderly with his thumb as we stared into each other's eyes.

"That was so good, baby. You know how to take me so well."

I swear I moaned at his words. Who did I even become when this man was around? How could he turn me into a mewling, purring mess by simply existing and being himself?

Did I have the same effect on him? Could I render him speechless the way he did me?

"You earned your spankings baby." My thighs pressed together after hearing his words. Yes, yes, yes. Please.

I could have begged.

Ever since earlier when I actually got to put words on what was eating at me for the last few days, I wanted to be back over his knee so bad.

"Get up and bend over the arm of the couch." He ordered and I couldn't have been off the floor fast enough.

Once I was in position, I waited with bated breaths on what he would do next. I heard him refasten his pants and then walk quietly towards me. I bit my lip, willing my heart to beat slower.

When his fingers gripped my sweatpants and he slowly dragged them down over my thighs, I whimpered. With them off my butt, I was left only clad in a black lace thong, one I had put on with my original plan of letting him grovel in mind. He hummed his approval as big veiny hands started massaging my ass cheeks.

"I love your ass. Every time I see it I just wanna take a bite."

Do it, that devious, shameless hussy stuck inside me screamed. Bite me, lick me, slap me, do whatever you want with me.

"And I love those panties, did you put them on for me, baby?" He goaded as one of his fingers ventured between my cheeks and down further between my lips.

When a beat passed and no answer was mustered from my part, he slapped my ass, hard, making me yelp in surprise.

I had to bite my lips and remind myself to not be noisy because the last thing either of us wanted was my nine year old sister waking up and stumbling upon this.

"I asked you a question, Sofia. Did you wear this for me?" I nodded hurriedly.

"Yes. Yes, all for you."

"Why?"

"What?" I frowned. What did he mean, *why*?

"You were mad at me when I came in earlier, so why did you wear this for me in the first place?" My teeth came down to bite my lip, ashamed to even admit my stupid plan out loud.

I was bad at apologizing, okay? So that plan had been my way of admitting I might have overreacted yesterday by still maintaining the upper hand and not seeming like the one who was most to blame.

But then my stupid hormones had to come out as soon as Maddox mentioned the word spanking. Speaking of which, another slap befell my sore ass. He was going harder than that first time, but I loved it all the same if not more. It was exhilarating.

"Answer the goddamn question, Sofia, or help me God you won't be able to sit down tomorrow." He followed his threat by three swift and hard slaps all on the same spot.

I had to bite my fist to keep from screaming.

"Because! I wanted to make you want me! I wanted to let you simmer and beg for forgiveness so I wouldn't have to address the fact that I was wrong too!"

I felt like a child being chastised, but God did it feel good to get it off my chest. The whole experience was liberating, getting spanked was the healthiest way I'd found so far to deal with my emotions and feelings of guilt.

Maddox stopped for a few seconds, probably letting my words sink in. For a beat, none of us spoke and all that could be heard was the sound of our breaths.

"So you weren't really mad at me?"

"I was at first, then I had a conversation with a friend yesterday afternoon and I—"

"Yesterday! You let me toss and turn all night, spend the shittiest night of my life and then worry all day at how you were gonna react that I couldn't contact you, even though you weren't even truly mad at me anymore?" He hissed angrily and slapped my (probably) red ass, making me yelp.

"I was still angry! Mostly at myself though because I could see the truth in your words but you dismissing my opinion hurt…" Maddox stopped moving again, his hand rubbing my warm skin.

Then, out of nowhere, he ripped my thong and I gasped. "Maddox! That was my prettiest pair!"

I didn't care much for lingerie before coming to live with him, but a week ago when I went to get some shopping done for Valentina (that girl was growing so fast and going through clothes like Kleenex), I happened to see this thong and matching bra set in a small lingerie store.

I felt out of place there, dressed in my signature cargo and long-sleeve cropped top with just a little bit of my midriff showing. I wore a sleeveless puffy jacket and some sneakers because I loved to be comfortable when going to class, especially when I had a shift at the café afterwards.

The salesladies were so well dressed and feminine in comparison, I wished I could be like that. So in an attempt to make myself feel more feminine, I bought the ensemble. It had been sitting in my drawer all this time, waiting for the right occasion to be worn.

Only now it was ruined.

"I'll buy you more. I definitely want to see your ass in lingerie more often." His fingers that had been rubbing against said ass moved to between my cheeks and I gasped. Nobody ever touched me there before, and I wasn't sure I would like to start now, even though I had loved everything I'd done with Maddox so far.

Thankfully I didn't have to overthink it more because his digits traveled further down until two of them nudged my slick entrance.

"But don't change the subject, baby." He entered me with two fingers at once and I could feel my pussy stretch to accommodate them. I moaned, my arms were no longer able to hold me up and I collapsed, my cheek hitting the sofa.

I was bent over the armrest, trembling and whimpering as Maddox took his fingers out of me before thrusting in again.

"From now on, no more miscommunication." He slapped my ass with one hand and fingered me with the other. "No more letting me simmer in guilt so that you don't have to own up to your part of responsibilities." His digits curled inside of me and I cried out.

"Oh, God, Maddox!" He was hitting that almost foreign, delicious spot only he had ever found in me.

"That's right baby, you like that, huh? Such a good little girl, flooding my fingers with your cum." I nodded hurriedly, thrusting back against his hand but by doing that, the armrest rubbed against my clit, making me cry out again. It felt so fucking good.

"No more sleeping anywhere else than in my bed, Sofia. You're mine and I'll be damned if I lose you over some dumb fucking argument." I could barely comprehend his words, lost in a sea of lust and desire. I needed to come, I needed to reach the pinnacle I knew only him could take me to.

"Say it, baby." He spanked my ass with force, making my ass cheeks bounce. "Say you've learned your lesson. Say you're gonna try and communicate better."

Maddox pushed on my lower back so that my clit was stuck against the sofa, the pressure rendering me speechless. My ass was most likely red by now and deliciously aching, and his fingers were still inside me. I was overstimulated but still I found it in me to nod, tears of redemption streaming down my face.

"Yes! Yes! I'm sorry, I'm sorry… I learned my lesson! I will try and communicate better! Please let me come."

"Good girl."

He went feral on me after that. His hips actually dug against my ass, where I could feel his hard cock through the fabric of his pants and he used this leverage to thrust and make my body rub faster and harder against the couch. I cried out in delight, my fist coming up to my mouth so I could bite it, afraid I'd wake my sister. A long moan escaped my lips as the rugged material of the couch was slowly bringing me to orgasm. There probably would be a wet spot on it tomorrow and I could already imagine myself looking up 'ways to get cum off your couch' on my phone.

Maddox added a third finger which made me feel so fucking full, I couldn't take it at first.

"Come on baby, spread your legs wider. If you can't take three fingers, there's no way you can take my cock tonight." That was motivation enough. We hadn't been all the way yet, mostly because of me and my apprehensions with sex. But I had been thinking of it for a week now. I wanted to experience it with Maddox, get him any way I could have him.

I widened my legs as his fingers filled me. I groaned in a mix of pain and pleasure, like only Maddox could make me feel. "Oh fuck, I'm so full, baby."

"Damn right you are. You're such a good girl." He slapped my ass and that coupled with his words, the pressure on my clit and the fullness inside me, tipped me over the edge. I muffled my screams against the cushion as the orgasm hit me full force.

Every time that man made me come felt like the best orgasm ever. Our chemistry was only getting better as time passed and I couldn't imagine a day where I wouldn't want Maddox. He represented everything I needed from life, security, kindness, generosity. He was selfless and naturally loving.

He made me feel safe, and loved but most of all, he gave me something no one else ever could: a sense of redemption

.

# 22

## LOVE

### SOFIA

Looking up at the ceiling as I laid naked in Maddox's bed with his arms around me, I couldn't help but think about how quickly my life had changed in the space of a few months.

A few months back, I'd thought I had nothing left to lose, that my life was doomed and I wouldn't ever get to experience happiness. My only goal was to make sure Valentina didn't get dealt the same hand, that she would actually have everything I had lacked growing up.

Now, though, it felt like my happiness was a possibility. Ever since Maddox came into the picture, he turned everything upside down but only in the best ways possible. He managed to get a special place in my heart, he actually came to mean so much to me in such a small amount of time, it made me feel dizzy.

But I was happy. For the first time in what felt like forever, I was truly fucking happy.

Maddox' hands were playing with my hair, and I rubbed my face against his chest, inhaling his scent. After that earth wrecking orgasm, we quietly showered together and got into bed, just enjoying each other's presence without speaking. I was just thinking we both were lost in our heads when his voice resonated.

"Penny for your thoughts, baby?" I bit my lip and wrapped an arm around him.

"I'm just thinking of how much my life has changed since you became a permanent part of it. I used to dread my future, but with you, it feels like something I should look forward to instead."

My sudden honesty seemed to have taken him aback. Especially since I wasn't an overly demonstrative person to begin with.

"I know what you mean." He kissed the top of my head. "Before you and Valentina came to live with me, I was just going through the motions. I didn't have anything to look forward to at the end of my day so I just drowned myself in work. Now that I have you two here, the house is never silent and I love it. You fill it with your presence, with warmth and… and love. It feels more like a home and less like an apartment."

My heart soared at hearing him say that. I knew what he meant. When we moved in, the house was blank and had no sign of truly being lived in. Now, some pictures of us decorated the walls, Valentina's toys were always strewn around the living room and my colorful blankets— ones I had knitted myself in one of my many hobby spurs, laid on the sofa.

The smell of spices and scented candles— I had a serious addiction to those, permeated the apartment, and it gave it an even cozier vibe. Not to mention the flowers I had taken a liking to buying each week. Roses, tulips, jasmine, sometimes dahlias when I could find them.

My mama loved flowers, and having them around always felt like having her around.

"I'm falling in love with you, too." Maddox suddenly said, making me snap my head towards him. He smiled secretively at me and I couldn't only imagine how I looked, wide eyes and mouth slightly ajar staring up at him in shock.

"Back in the living room. You said 'the last thing I want is to see the man I'm falling in love with spiral out of control'. You said you were falling in love with me. I'm telling you I am, too. Matter of fact, I'm pretty sure I'm there already."

Tears filled my eyes as I took in this strong, amazing man. The mere thought that someone could fall in love with me was foreign to my brain, so to hear the most perfect man I had ever met, the one that not only met all of my standards but exceeded them too, say that, rendered me speechless.

"I love how you love your sister. I love how you're always there for her and would sacrifice anything for her in a heartbeat." I gulped and fought the tears threatening to break free from my eyes. He had no idea how true that statement was. "I love the way you smell like flowers and sugar. I love the way your hair is so soft and shiny all the time."

"I use argan oil." Was the only dumb thing I could think of, too short for words to think of anything else.

Maddox chuckled and caressed my hair. "Well, it works wonders. I love your smile and the sound of your laugh. I love how you glare at me when I forget to take my shoes off even though we don't have carpeted floors." A watery smile made its way away on my lips as he looked at me tenderly. "I love how you never let me be in charge of seasoning the food when we cook together."

"You only use salt, it's not seasoning, just a condiment you *should* put in every meal." He laughed and I joined him as a couple of rogue tears escaped my eyes.

"I even love how you and Valentina talk shit about me when you think I don't understand." I felt my eyes widening.

"You understand us?"

"Well not really but I did download an app to try and learn Spanish. And I looked up what *gran bobo* meant. Big dummy, seriously?" He looked unimpressed but the side of his mouth was pulled up in an amused smile.

"It's affectionate!" I defended. Valentina often called him that and I guess it stuck. It really was affectionate when we used it on Maddox. He chuckled and kissed my forehead before pulling away and looking in my eyes.

"My point is, I love you, Sofia Raymond. And I love what you've made of my life since you entered it."

Tears were fully flowing down my cheeks by then and I pushed myself up to bring my lips to his. I didn't know what to say. The words '*I love you too*' were begging to be let out but something was pulling them back.

Fear.

Fear that this was too good to be true, that Maddox only loved me because he didn't know everything about me. That once he knew the truth— if I ever worked up the courage to tell him, he would be so disgusted by me he could never look me in the eye again.

So I didn't say anything and put all of myself in that kiss. Getting on my knees without breaking contact, I straddled him as one of his hands came to cup my ass. Maddox gripped my jaw with the other and pushed me slightly away so he could look at me. He tightened his hold, making me open my mouth, my tongue peeking out slightly, before he playfully licked it. Our tongues were playing around one another, and the experience was so erotic it made me moan aloud in delight. I loved tasting him, feeling his full lips against my own.

Fingers gripping his hair, I pushed away and started peppering small kisses on his jaw and neck.

"Yeah, baby. I love it when you do that." He moaned.

"I want you inside me." I moaned against his skin. I could never get enough of his scent, of his taste. "I want you so deep in me that I can feel you for days."

He moaned at that, my dirty talk seemed to have the same effect on him as his had on me. The thought was wild to me.

"Sit on my cock baby. Take as much as you can, then I'll do the rest." Him whispering against my skin made my already hard nipples even harder. They pressed against his chest like little diamonds as I gripped his stiff dick.

Since I'd been sitting against it, it was slick in a mix of my wetness and his precum. I glided my hand up and down the shaft to spread the mixture, loving the idea of my essence blending with his. Pushing myself up, I looked down to see my glistening pussy hovering over the head of his cock. I paused for a minute, just admiring the sight before slowly coming back down. I felt it nudge my entrance and Maddox threw his head back, one of his hands gripping my ass tightly as the other was fisting the sheets like it was taking all of his will not to drive into me.

That was just another thing I loved about him. He put me first. Always.

One of my hands braced against the headboard, I brought the other to his neck and gripped it tightly. From the intake of breath he had to take, it confirmed what I had previously noticed: I wasn't the only one who liked a hand around my neck occasionally.

"Look at us, baby." I had a hard time recognizing that sultry, sexy voice as mine. It was crazy how many things I discovered about myself while being with Maddox. "Look at how good I'm taking you in my pussy." I moaned against his lips as his head breached my entrance and soon I was letting myself down on him completely.

Both of us breathing harshly, his sleek forehead dropped against mine as we looked down at where our bodies were joined. I whimpered, my pussy tightening around his shaft and he groaned in response.

"Fuck baby. So perfect."

I said nothing and kissed his neck, licking and biting when I felt like it. I was doing my best to adjust to his size, but it was hard. Not only was sex never pleasurable to me before, but it had also been a while and Maddox' size was not helping. He stayed inside me without moving for another minute or two, letting me suck and bite on his neck while I adjusted.

"Maddox, you're so big." I complained even though the feeling was exhilarating.

"And yet you're taking me like such a good girl, baby."

I moaned and brought my lips to his, taking his mouth in a ravishing kiss. When finally the pain dissipated and pleasure took its place, I started pushing up on my thighs, making him slide slightly out of me, before letting myself fall back down.

We both cried out at the same time, and I did it again. Before long we were both panting, and the inside of my thighs was burning. Who knew sex could be such a workout.

"Who's fucking you, baby?"

"You are." I moaned.

"Am I yours, Sofia?"

"You are." All fucking mine, and I would die before letting anyone take him away from me.

Maddox gripped my hips and stopped my movements. "Hold on, baby. Wrap your legs around me so I can fuck this pussy like she deserves."

I didn't need to be asked twice and did as he demanded. Maddox reversed our position and toppled me over until I was lying on my back and he was above me, moving between my legs restlessly. I yelped in surprise but it quickly turned into a moan as this position gave him more space to stimulate my clit.

His thumb pushing onto it, he gripped one of my legs with his other hand and threw it over his shoulder. I had never felt that open before in my life, and the sensation was incredible. Maddox fucked me like he'd die if he stopped. He rubbed my clit with his thumb and kept on hitting that sweet spot inside of me with his cock. He fucked me until I saw stars.

"Look, baby. Look how well you're taking me." He looked positively obsessed with the image of his cock plunging in and out of my cunt, he couldn't take his eyes off it.

I couldn't either, it was too compelling, it made my heart soar and my pussy wet at the same time.

"Oh! Maddox! I'm coming, baby, yes!" As soon as the words left my mouth he rubbed my clit with fervor and at the same time, slid his pinky finger inside me. It went in with difficulty, given how filled I already was from his cock. But the sensation was incredible, especially when I already was in the midst of an orgasm. It just triggered another one even bigger.

I had to bite into a pillow to keep myself from screaming the house down. The pleasure was immeasurable, I felt myself drenching his cock and that's what triggered him as his body locked and his eyebrows scrunched. He trembled all over before not being able to keep himself up anymore and crumbled on top of me with a groan.

Tremors still wrecked both of our bodies as we laid for what felt like ages in each other's arms. The room smelled like sex, we were both drenched in sweat and cum, but somehow, it felt like nothing else existed around us.

I found myself wishing this was my first time.

I was in love with Maddox Brooks, there was no more doubt about it.

***

“What was your favorite food as a kid?” I asked while drawing circles on his chest.

The sun was already coming up, we barely got any sleep last night but it was worth it. It only reinforced that idea that Maddox and I were made for each other. The way my body sang with his, the way he felt at home when he was inside me.

This first time with him was everything I ever thought it would be.

“Chicken nuggets.” I scoffed and rolled my eyes.

“Of course it was, you're so predictable.”

He pinched my side and I yelped before laughing. “What was yours?”

“Cereals.” I bit my lip. “It drove mama crazy. She would always make these delicious Mexican dishes and here I was crying because I wanted to eat Cheerios for dinner for the fourth time that week.” A small smile grazed my lips as I thought of her and papa. “I didn’t grow out of it until I was seven or something, I was a nightmare.”

He chuckled and brought me closer to his body. “I can totally see you as brat, somehow.” It was my turn to pinch him and act like I was offended. He just laughed again and hugged me closer to his body.

“It helped that mama loved to cook, you know? She tried feeding me just about anything under the sun until I developed a new favorite food that was actually dinner appropriate.”

"What was that?"

"Lasagna." I mumbled, still not over the fact that his hot neighbor used to cook that for him. He seemed to catch onto that and laughed a little louder. I smiled, loving the sound.

"Well, you can make me lasagna any day you want, baby. I'm sure it's the best I'll ever taste. Just like you." He kissed my lips tenderly and I sighed in delight. "You seem to have been close to your mom." My smile dimmed a bit when he said that but I nodded sadly.

"Yes. She was such a strong woman. Went through a lot of shit but she would've done anything for her family. She loved flowers, you know? And she was super crafty too, a real artist."

"Yeah. I remember your treasure box, you said she'd made it. It's a beautiful piece." I nodded wordlessly as I recalled the day she gave it to me with a smile.

She knew I loved that piece and she said I should take it and give it to my daughter so that she could pass it on too. Like a legacy of some sorts.

"It's crazy how I had a totally different idea of who she was. It's almost like there were two completely different sides to Marcella Raymonds." I gulped, tensing a little bit. He was right, in a way.

We stayed in blissful silence for a few minutes before Maddox broke it.

"Sofia, I… I wanted to ask you something. It's about Valentina." I frowned and turned around so I was laying on my stomach, bracing my arms on his chest and awaiting his next words.

He looked like he didn't know how to start and for a second I thought he was going to talk about that shrink from his precinct again. I wasn't as opposed as I used to be about Vale talking to someone if she wanted to, but I really didn't want it to be what's-her-face.

Yet, what he said instead filled my heart with joy.

"It's about that daddy-daughter dance her school organized." He swallowed thickly and tucked a piece of my hair behind my ear. "Would you be mad if I asked her to go with me? I'm not trying to replace your dad or anything, I know it would be impossible, but I thought since I'm—" My lips smashing onto his seemed to shut him up. He kissed me back almost instantly making me moan softly before pulling back.

"You can ask her. You have my blessing. In fact, she was gonna ask you tonight, she spent an hour in her room trying to work up the courage to ask you. I heard her rehearse a little speech in there. She even made you a drawing because it seemed easier for her." He sighed in relief. "I don't know if she'll ask now, though, she was pretty bummed out when you didn't show." I bit my lip.

"It's okay, I got this. I have everything planned. My costumes should be here in two days." He smirked and I frowned.

"Costumes? Do I wanna know?"

He simply chuckled and kissed my lips.
"Probably not. But you will want to be there for it."

***

## MADDOX

Unlike yesterday, I was in an amazing mood when I walked into the station that morning, despite running on two hours of sleep.

Taking Sofia and I's relationship a step further was definitely a big part of why I was so happy, but I was also giddy about asking Valentina to the dance. I wanted to make it memorable for her and give her high standards so that all the little fuckers she'd go to middle and high school with would know what they were being compared to whenever they asked her out.

My mood was quickly brought down though, when Piersons caught my gaze from the other side of the room. He didn't say anything and simply stared me down before marching to his office and closing the door after him.

Something seemed off with him lately, he was fidgety and the way he insisted for us to close the case was weird.

"Coroner said results are in, grab yourself a coffee and let's hit the road." Adam's voice brought me out of my conspiracy theories on Pierson and I looked up at him.

"Already?"

"Yup. He stayed in all night. Said he had never seen anything quite like it before." I frowned.

Damn, Conan what the fuck happened to you?

***

"I have never seen anything like it!" Jerry, the new, young coroner working for the station exclaimed excitedly almost as soon as we entered his morgue.

The smell of antiseptic and death permeated the air and the cold air made me feel uncomfortable. There was also the fact that another dead body was laying on a metal table in the corner, only hidden by a white sheet.

Jerry walked to the table where Conan laid though, and pushed the same white sheet away from his face.

"Oh fuck!" Adam exclaimed and I was left staring in shock and maybe a little morbid fascination. "What the hell man? Give us a fucking warning next time!" I had to agree with my partner as I slowly brought my eyes away from the rapidly decaying body.

I could feel the coffee I'd had on the road start to churn in my stomach. I was gonna puke.

The body in front of us looked like it had been dead for months, or years, not hours. Whatever was left of Conan seemed to be decaying a little more every second. His skin had taken on a brown and blueish color, with spots that seemed to be peeling or rotting. The smell coming from it made me even more nauseous. His face was all caved in, eyes seemed to have deflated, if that was even possible and…

"Where are his teeth?" I asked, surprised.

"Oh, they fell off." Jerry answered like it was the most logical thing as he scribbled on his little notepad. "Chunks of his hair too."

"What the hell happened to this guy? You sure this is Conan Michaels?" Adam asked as he used his pen to poke the dead.

"Affirmative, sir. This is Conan Michaels. Fifteen hours after he ingested the most powerful and foreign poison I have ever encountered."

"Explain."

"Well, I stayed here all night to evaluate the samples from that water bottle, and it seemed to contain the venom of more than eleven of the most dangerous and venomous snakes in the world! " God, I wish he didn't look so excited to be telling us that. "That concoction was obviously created by a human, by the way."

"Yeah, I think we got that."

Jerry cleared his throat, clearly put off by Adam's authoritative tone.

"Well, on top of *Boomslang*— which is what caused all the bleeding by the way, *Black Mamba*— which is what caused the heart attack, and a whole bunch of other snakes' venoms which I'm sure you wouldn't know the name of even if I told you, I also found traces of other toxins. Three of the deadliest poisons in the world were inside that bottle: hemlock, mercure and *Alopa Belladon*a."

Adam and I shared a look. Whoever created that didn't just want to kill Conan, they wanted to *annihilate* him.

"It is truly fascinating! I'm sure I haven't even found everything that was inside that bottle yet, because look how fast this guy is decaying! Something's gotta be causing that, too. Whoever created that poison is a fucking genius."

I frowned, and grabbed Jerry's report from his hands. This guy sure as fuck spent too much time with the dead and it showed. He had no clue how to deal with real human beings. Alive ones.

"Whoever created that is a fucking *criminal*, Jerry, get your head out of your ass."

"Oh, come on guys! I meant it in a scientific way! They mixed the most deadliest of poisons together and made it colorless, tasteless *and* scentless so that it could be mistaken for fucking water. Guys, this is insane, I don't think you realize. If this came to be commercialized, in the black market of course, the outcome could be horrifying. The guy that did that *is* a fucking evil genius."

Adam and I shared an anguished look.

"Did you see any similarities in the modus operandi between his and the Raymonds' bodies?"

Jerry frowned. "The mayor and his wife? Nah. Nothing was even remotely similar. Their bodies didn't contain an ounce of poison or even a drug similar to what's inside this guy. Totally different things."

This case was taking a turn I was starting to hate. It seemed more and more unsolvable as we went.

After thanking Jerry and exiting this fucking morbid place, Adam and I drove back to the precinct in silence.

"This is a fucking nightmare. Piersons gave us a week to resolve this and he's acting so fucking strange, don't you think? Like he has ulterior motives for wanting us to drop the case. I think—"

"I think Piersons's right." My head snapped towards Adam as soon as he cut me off, but he stared straight ahead as we drove in silence. "Maybe this *was* just a robbery gone wrong, maybe that second guy is far gone by now."

"Are you fucking serious, right now?"

I wish I could say this didn't feel like betrayal, but it did. Adam had been my partner ever since I became a detective. I'd seen him at his worst and his best. I considered him one of my closest friends. I truly thought we were on the same line with this case.

"Listen, kid. Lemme explain before you start going off." He gave me a look and I listened, waiting to see what he had to say. "When… when we lost Abel last year, I wanted there to be a reason." I gulped and looked down on my lap.

Adam rarely spoke of his sons, especially not Abel. When he committed suicide last year, it came as a shock to all of us, not only because he was so young, but because nobody could have seen it coming.

I guess that's the thing about suicide, though. You never truly know what people are going through. They could be smiling, laughing, seemingly having fun and loving the moment, while having the darkest thoughts you could imagine.

"I didn't want to believe that my little boy," His voice broke slightly and he cleared his throat. "I didn't want to believe that my son was truly going through something and I didn't notice it. I wanted there to have been a reason, so that I could blame it instead of myself for not seeing his pain." My jaw flexed and I looked out the window. I couldn't imagine the pain he was going through. Losing a loved one was always difficult, of course, but such circumstances made it even harder.

"I was so fucking focused on searching for this thing that I drowned myself in work. There were nights where I didn't even leave the precinct. Junior had left for university, he was dodging our calls, Eva was going crazy, she felt so lonely at home and I did nothing to help her. I was so focused on my own pain I had all but forgotten about my family's. Now my son won't talk to me, we have no idea where he even is and that witch hunt also almost cost me my marriage." I had no idea about any of this.

I mean sure, I knew his oldest had left for university shortly after Abel's death and hadn't set foot in Lakestone since then. What I didn't know however, was that he didn't speak to his parents anymore. I also didn't know Eva and Adam's marriage was in such jeopardy after Abel's death.

"The reason why I'm telling you this, Maddox, is because I think you're getting too involved in that case. Sure, some things seemed sketchy but in the great scheme of things, maybe they *were* just coincidences. The most plausible route is that it was a robbery gone wrong and that the fucker who escaped is probably far away from here by now."

I could hear the truth in his words but I couldn't get Sofia and Valentina's frightened faces out of my head. Every time I considered closing this case without finding that second guy, Sofia's face from that night came to mind. The dry blood on her face, her shaking limbs, her breaking down in the shower right after. It all kept replaying in my head.

"I know you care deeply about these two girls, you're not fooling anyone." I gulped and looked elsewhere. I knew Adam suspected something about me and Sofia. He just had an eye for those things. "I think you're good for them and that they're good for you, son. But they've been through enough, and maybe it's just time to let the past rest."

I swallowed the emotions clogging up my throat. Maybe he was right.

Maybe all those things that created a case in my mind were nothing but coincidences.

Maybe it *was* time to let the past rest.

# 23

## TRUTH

### MADDOX

Six days had passed since my little conversation with Adam. I couldn't stop thinking about what he'd said. When I talked to Sofia about it, she seemed conflicted. She agreed with him, since it mostly met her own speech from the night before, but I could see something was eating at her. The deadline Piersons gave us ended tomorrow and Adam and I hadn't worked on it all week.

But I did take the files home, even though it went against protocol, to try and see if there wasn't something we had missed.

Every night after the girls went to sleep, I slipped into the living room and went over everything we had. I knew that if Sofia or Adam noticed I was doing it they'd be disappointed, but I just couldn't let go of this case until I knew I had gone through every possible resource at our disposal.

Other than that, life was good. Our routine worked amazingly, Valentina was totally used to me and Sofia being together by now, but we still did our best to hide it from the outside world. I hadn't even taken her to a real date yet, but it didn't matter, everyday living together felt like a date to me.

I noticed Valentina trying to work up the courage to ask me to her school's Daddy-daughter dance over the last few days, but something always seemed to keep her from doing so and I was glad. I wanted to be the one to ask and I wanted it to be epic, something she'd remember and something that would teach her not to settle for less from anyone in the future. I had everything ready, the only thing left to do was pick up my plan's masterpiece from Adam's and pray Sofia didn't kill me.

Speaking of whom, today was my day off and I used it wisely. I was in the process of moving all her things to my room after spending the better part of the day making space for it. I wanted her former room to be like a workshop for her, where she could paint and blast music, knit and even graffiti the walls if that's what she wanted. I'd gotten her an easel, canvas and different types of paints for her birthday, and she loved them, so I knew she'd love the idea of having a whole room dedicated to her art. It was also my way of redeeming myself for all the times I arrested her for graffitiing on public property.

After I finished moving all her clothes into my closet, I stared at both my and her side in delight. It might seem stupid but seeing our clothes together made our relationship feel even more real to me. It warmed my heart. I smiled dumbly as I went back to her room to get the last few things left: her favorite blanket and the wooden treasure box.

It sat on the now-empty dresser, the intricate designs looking elegant and artistic at the same time. As I picked it up and let my fingers follow the engravings, I found that I recognized it. Three flowers intertwined, a rose, some jasmine and what I now knew to be a dahlia. That last flower was still foreign to me until a couple months ago when Sofia brought a bouquet home and I had to ask what kind of flower it was.

Ignorant shit that I was, I always thought it was only the name of the sadly famous unsolved murder of Elizabeth Short, but it turned out it was also a type of flower. One Sofia was really fond of.

Having the box in my hands, I recognized the design as the same one Sofia was painting onto that wall the last time I arrested her right before she turned eighteen.

Turning around, my knee hit the side of an open drawer and I stumbled, the box falling out of my hands. I cursed because fuck if Sofia wouldn't kill me for breaking the one thing she had gone back to retrieve from her family's house, and immediately picked it up. Thank God it wasn't broken, and it was locked so nothing spilled out. I inspected it intently for any damage until I felt something at the back.

Frowning in curiosity, I turned it around and saw an inscription right where my fingers had been.

*Sisters. Different flowers from the same garden.*

*Jasmine Flores.*

Those were the words engraved on Sofia's box. I figured Jasmine Flores was the poet or writer behind that quote.

It made me smile, because the saying was cute and totally representative of Sofia and Valentina. They were so different yet together they created the most beautiful sight, just like flowers in a garden.

As I held the box in my hands and walked back to my room— our room now, I couldn't help but wonder what was in there. I would never betray Sofia's trust and open it, but I hoped one day she would trust me enough to show me what was in there.

I put it on her nightstand proudly before splaying the colorful blanket on the bed. It sure contrasted a lot, given that my beddings—and the rest of my furniture were mostly black, but I loved the touch of color it gave the room. It represented Sofia and the impact she had on my dark, boring life, pretty well.

Everything was perfect, all I had left to do was get ready, get Sofia and meet Adam in front of Valentina's school when it let out.

This was gonna be fun.

***

## SOFIA

"Sofia, I'm going on break!" Mary, my pain in the ass co-worker yelled right before I heard the back door slam behind her.

I groaned internally. That bitch knew we were understaffed and that rush hour would come any minute, yet she still decided to take her tenth break of the day. I couldn't stand her.

Tossing the sponge I'd been cleaning the counter with into the sink, I turned around and faced the two young customers that had just entered. Both girls looked no older than fifteen and were polar opposites style-wise. One looked like a walking, talking rainbow. All of her clothes were a different color, red shirt, purple pants, yellow sneakers. Everything was a different shade. Her lips glistened with lipgloss and she had some cute (blue) artistic liner going on. She even had pink streaks in her black hair but I highly suspected she was wearing a wig.

The other one looked like she was allergic to color, though. She had black hair too but she was dressed in total black. It wasn't a goth or alternative style exactly, she looked fancy and classy but… colorless. Her skin was a shade darker than mine and she wore a black and gold bindi on her forehead, which contrasted with the otherwise casual outfit she was wearing. Her long black hair was pulled into a high and tight ponytail. Contrary to her friend, she wasn't wearing makeup, which somehow made her look even younger.

They were both pretty short and had really slight frames. The girl in black pulled an eyebrow up, looking me up and down, making me realize I'd been staring.

I cleared my throat and apologized before making my way to them and stopping behind my counter.

"Welcome to The Coffee Bean, what can I get you girls?" I beamed, grabbing my pen and looking expectantly at them.

The blond answered first "Hey, I'll take a medium caramel iced coffee with oat milk and a dash of cinnamon, please." she smiled and I grabbed a cup, writing her order, before looking up.

"Okay, I'll just need your name, please."

"Cammie!"

"Oh, cute, what's it short for?" I expected her to say Camilla or Cameron or shit, maybe that it wasn't even short for anything, but I definitely wasn't expecting—

"Chameleon!" She beamed and I paused to look at her friend, trying to gauge if she was serious. The grump simply rolled her eyes as I scribbled the name down on the cup. Well, her parents must have a really weird sense of humor.

I grabbed another cup and looked at her friend.

"I'll take a tall black coffee, please. No sugar." When I opened my mouth to ask for a name she cut me off and said "Just write Cammie again."

What an authoritative little shit.

Rolling my eyes I did as she said and started preparing their orders. When I finally finished, I turned around and slid the two cups on the counter.

"That will be $9,78 please."

The little tyrant handed me a fifty dollar bill and said "Keep the change." Before grabbing her coffee and turning around to exit the shop.

I looked at her friend who smiled sheepishly,. "It was nice meeting you!" She thanked me and followed her friend.

What the fuck, was that how kids behaved these days? I'll be damned if I let Valentina become a spoiled little shit growing up.

Following them through the shop's window, I saw them cross the street and get into a black Mercedes with tinted windows. As soon as the doors were shut, they accelerated down the street, only leaving dust in their wake.

I shook my head. What a strange little encounter.

My shift went on quietly and when it was finally done, Maddox texted me that he was parked in front of the shop, waiting for me. I frowned because he typically would come and get me instead of simply waiting for me in his car, but I guess our honeymoon phase was coming to an end.

Sighing, I grabbed my stuff and said goodbye to Lisa and Aaron who had the later shift today, before walking out.

Sure enough, Maddox was parked down the street.

I didn't even notice it, at first. I just entered the car and said hello before grabbing my seatbelt. It wasn't until I turned towards him to give him a kiss that I saw the ridiculous costume he was wearing.

I couldn't help the shriek of laughter that came out of me.

He rolled his eyes, looking like he expected my reaction.

"Oh my God! What are you wearing?" Tears were rolling down my cheeks from seeing him dressed like that, it was just so fucking unexpected.

"I'm giving our girl high standards!" He said, pulling the car into gear and starting to drive.

"Standards in what? Clowns?"

"Laugh all you want, you little shit, you know fully well this is not a clown costume." Oh, I did. Grinning at him, I took in his green chemise and pants, the golden crown sitting on top of his head. Fuck, he even wore a cape and tried styling his hair like—

"I'm Prince Naveen of Maldonia. And you, my dear, will be relegated to the place of second-favorite-human-being today." I cackled, letting my head fall back against the seat.

Okay, I had to say, his plan was not that bad. Ridiculous? Hell yes. I would never let him live that down. I was pretty sure none of his friends or family would. But Valentina would absolutely love it.

The Princess and the Frog was her favorite movie ever and every time we watched it, she gushed about how handsome Prince Naveen was. And he was. He's definitely in my top three hottest Disney princes.

Maddox looked nothing like Naveen, but the costume made him recognizable.

"I am *so* taking a picture to send Adam."

"No need, he's meeting us there." I frowned.

"What? You asked your partner— who you know will never let you live this down, to meet us in front of Valentina's school to actually see you in action?"

"Yup. He has something I need and I didn't have time to go get it before, so he's bringing it to me." Okay, now I was intrigued.

"What is it?"

"Not telling you, it has to stay a surprise." I groaned, looking at him.

"Seriously? Come on, Maddox, tell me!"

But he didn't. I tried to guess the whole ride there, to no avail. He just wouldn't budge. When we finally made it to Valentina's school, some parents were already waiting out front but the kids weren't out yet. I also recognized Adam's car. He got out as soon as he saw us park and made his way towards us.

We got out too and people were already starting to stare at Maddox.

As soon as Adam saw him he clapped his hands and started laughing hysterically.

"Oh, man, what have you become?" He shook his head at Maddox in mock disappointment and I laughed too. Maddox simply rolled his eyes and stared at his friend.

"Do you have it or not?"

"Yup. Selena is putting it back in its box and bringing it out of the car." Maddox groaned.

"Seriously? You told Selena to come, too?!"

"You think I would miss seeing you lose any modicum of pride and respect you had accumulated over the years? Think again."

I turned around to see Detective Yakori walking toward us, a shoe box with holes in it in one hand while the other was holding her phone and clearly recording Maddox. I puffed out a laugh and he glared at me in a way that said my ass would be red tonight. I smiled eagerly, letting him know I would gladly take this punishment.

They took jabs at him, and all three of us laughed at him while he simply ignored us, flipping us off from time to time. Discreetly, so that other parents wouldn't see him. I tried peeking into Selena's box to see what that surprise was but had no luck in that department. I did have my suspicions but hoped it wasn't what I thought it was inside that box.

When finally the bell rang and kids started running out of the school's gates, I could see him tense slightly. He had absolutely no reason to be nervous, because Valentina loved him and would love how thoughtfully he had prepared all of this.

As kids went up to their parents, some stopped to stare at him, especially little girls who, no doubt, knew who he was dressed as.

When I recognized Valentina's black mane of hair, walking quietly with her eyes on the ground, hands clutching her backpack firmly, my breath hitched.

Okay, so maybe I was a little nervous myself.

"Princess Valentina of Lakestone!" Maddox exclaimed suddenly, making my sister stop and look up in surprise. When she saw who was talking and took in his costume, her eyes widened. People around us quietened and stared in curiosity.

"Would you do me the immense honor of coming with me to the Father-Daughter dance here in this castle of a school, in two weeks time?" My lips pinched with emotions and I could feel my heart beat faster in anticipation.

At first she didn't say anything, simply stared at him with wide eyes and an open mouth. For a second I was scared she'd be embarrassed or say this wasn't her age anymore. But then she started running towards Maddox, launching herself into his arms and he caught her easily, making her spin.

The sight made me feel so many things at the same time that tears were brimming in my eyes.

Valentina had her little arms around his neck and she hugged him tight. Breaking my gaze away from them, because I was seriously scared I'd start bawling if I looked again, I took in the people surrounding us.

Parents looked with small smiles on their faces, some mothers seemed to be swooning at the pretty picture they both made. Adam and Selena smiled quietly, the older man with a look of longing in his eyes.

"Yes! I'll go to the ball with you, Prince Mads!" My gaze was brought back to my sister and I felt myself grinning as I watched her pull away and grip Maddox' cheeks in each hand.

"It's Naveen." He corrected

"No, I love Prince Maddox more!" Chuckles could be heard among the parents and Maddox smiled proudly.

"Good. Actually, Ray said he liked me better than Naveen, too." Valentina's head drooped to the side as she looked at him questioningly. I, too, was intrigued. Ray was the firefly companion in The Princess and The Frog. Is that what was in that box? Fireflies?

Adam took it from Selena and brought it to Maddox's side. I got a little closer so I could have a look too.

When he opened it, at first, I couldn't really tell what was inside. It looked like a green blanky. I had one quite similar when I was a kid.

Then the *blanky* actually moved and I understood quite clearly what it was. That son of a—

"A kitten!" The giddiness in my sister's voice made it instantly impossible for me to be annoyed at Maddox. She'd been talking about kittens for weeks now, and when Maddox talked to me about adopting one I told him it was a lot of responsibilities that I wasn't sure Valentina was ready for yet.

"Oh, my God he's the cutest thing!" She shrieked again as the little white bundle of fur slowly stirred, waking up from a nap. When Valentina slowly took it out of the box, I saw it was wearing a costume. A firefly costume that looked just like Ray.

"*She's* the cutest thing, yes." Maddox corrected as Valentina brought the little creature to her chest. "What are you gonna call her?"

"Well, I like Ray. What do you think?"

"I think it's a cute name for a kitten." The white cat mewled and rubbed her head against my sister's uniform vest, clearly liking her new name.

"So that was the big surprise, huh?" I gave him an unimpressed look and he smiled sheepishly.

"Well, it was more like a way to bribe her in case she didn't dig the whole Prince Naveen thing."

"I dig it!" Valentina exclaimed before getting back to rubbing the cat's fur.

"Where did you even find the cat's costume?"

"Etsy. It's crazy the number of weirdly specific shits you can find on there." I scoffed and he chuckled.

"Hey, Valentina!" A cute little blond girl stood a couple steps ahead of us, holding the hand of an older girl— probably her older sister. "Is that your daddy?" She asked and I felt my breath hitch, eyes turning back to Valentina.

She smiled and shook her head no, "No, he's not my daddy. He's my… he's my Maddy!" The other girl simply nodded like it was the most logical explanation in the world before scampering away to a car where her mother was probably waiting.

Maddox and I shared a smile, or, well, I smiled while he full-on grinned, straight white teeth on display. His eyes were full of emotions and I rolled mine at him mockingly even though similar feelings were going through me. He would be such a girl dad.

Well, I guess he *was* a girl dad, in a way.

For some reason, I loved the thought of that.

***

**MADDOX**

Sofia had been called back at the coffee shop for an emergency. Apparently her co-worker Mary felt sick and had to go home, so she went to replace her for a few hours.

She grumbled all the way home about how she hated that bitch and, honestly, I hated her a bit too at that moment. I wanted the three of us to go out tonight, go to a restaurant, maybe play some mini-golf, or go bowling.

Instead these plans had to be pushed back to Sofia's next night off.

"Valentina, food's ready!" I heard her light footsteps echo in the hall before she finally appeared, wearing her favorite light blue pajamas, long dark hair braided and little Ray resting comfortably in her arms.

"No cat at the dinner table, young lady." I tried being stern but as soon as she looked up and gave me puppy eyes, I knew I had lost that fight.

Dammit, what was it about the Raymond sisters that made me so weak?

"But she's still new here! She's scared of being alone. I'm like her mommy and she needs to feel me around all the time, Mads! She needs to!"

Her arguments were quite valid if you asked me, but then I might be slightly biased given the fact that I considered her the cutest human being on Earth and would virtually give her anything she might want.

"Okay, but only if you put her on Sofia's chair so that you can eat properly."

"Deal!" She outstretched her little hand and I shook it, a smile on my face.

She did as I said (see who's the boss in this house, now?) and we started eating. She talked to me in giddy eagerness about the dance and it was simply the best thing ever to see her eyes sparkle so much.

"Oh! What color tie are you going to wear? Are you even going to wear one? I mean you don't have to, you can wear a bowtie, or even nothing at all! I mean not like, go naked," She giggled adorably, "You'd have to wear clothes but I mean no tie or bowtie, but I think it might be a good idea to wear one because that way we can match! The color of your bow tie should match my dress! That way people will know you're here with me and that you're my dad— Maddy!" Her nonsense rambling had me chuckling as I spooned some spinach into her plate.

Like any kids, she didn't like her greens very much, but she still ate them with a little grimace on her face, like the responsible little girl she was.

"I was thinking I'd wear a light blue tie, what do you think, Pretty Girl?"

The night went by slowly, we ate, cleaned up— she helped me because she said families should help each other when it came to chores, and then we watched some TV before it was time for her to get some sleep.

I read her a book she loved which was based off of the very famous Mexican legend of *Popocatépetl* and *Iztaccíhuatl*, as Sofia had explained. Valentina loved that book, she had us read it to her at least twice a week.

When I was done I put the book back on the shelf, turned off the overhead light and turned on the small pink one on her bedside, before coming back to sit beside her on the bed.

"Maddox?"

"Yes, Pretty Girl?"

"You're not going to leave us, right?"

There was something about how vulnerable children could be and how they could say shit that truly fucked with your heart. I had to swallow the nerves building in my throat before I could actually answer her.

"No, sweetheart. I'll stay with you for as long as you'll have me." I pushed stray strands of hair from her face and smiled down at her.

"I'll have you forever."

She smiled sadly before looking down at her bedding.

"Sometimes, I miss Mama and Papa." I sighed, nodding my head.

"Yeah, baby, I know. But you know they'll always be with you, right?"

"In my heart?"

"In your heart, but also all around you. They're watching over you from above." Her lips pulled up and she grabbed my hand in her much smaller one.

"I love you, Mads." My eyes actually stung at hearing her say that. The love I felt for that little girl was immeasurable.

"I love you too, Pretty Girl." Bending slightly over, I kissed her forehead and she simultaneously kissed my stubbled chin, since that's where her lips reached given our height differences. That was something I saw her do often with Sofia, like a little ritual. I was glad she included me too.

I smiled at her and said goodnight before leaving her door slightly ajar. I wanted to still be able to hear her if she had a nightmare about those monsters she seemed so terrified of. It had actually been a while since she had one of those, but you can never be too careful.

Once I was out of her room, I had to stop and let myself slump against the wall in the hallway. Closing my eyes in defeat I tried telling myself that Valentina was too young to really care for closure on her parents' case, that growing up with me and Sofia would be enough for her, but to no avail. My brain made up all sorts of scenarios where she grew up to resent me for never finding her parents' killers. Where she went in search of answers herself and ended up being hurt.

Fuck, I couldn't let that happen.

I still had all night to work on it. It was barely eight thirty, Sofia would be back around ten and then she'd probably be too tired to stay up late. That left me some time to comb through every last detail of that goddamn case. Tomorrow, I'll get to Piersons' office with some fucking answers.

Grabbing myself a cup of coffee, I set everything up on the coffee table. The lights were deemed inside the living room and I was sitting on the sofa, glaring at the elements in front of me.

At the center, I put a picture of Jack and Marcella Raymond I had gotten from their house on the day we went to retrieve some stuff with Sofia. They were both smiling for the cameras, Jack was sitting on a chair while his wife stood behind him with a perfectly manicured hand on his shoulder. The politician poster card. Marcella's short blond hair (she dyed it, I think) and tanned skin looked perfect, as always, and the cream high-heels she wore made her look even taller than she already was.

Staring at them, I narrowed my eyes, thinking maybe if I concentrated enough the answer would leap in front of me.

"What the hell happened to you two…" I had to cut my musings short when I started putting the pictures of our other suspects all around theirs.

Conan went in first, because even though his body was now mostly a pile of gunk— Jerry's words, not mine, I still didn't trust that son of a bitch. He had the perfect motive, he was creepy enough and we actually had proof he had a key to Raymond's house. Next to his picture, I set Harold's, wondering what these two had in common or how they could even have met. It didn't make sense, they grew up in totally different towns— Harold was from North Ravenbridge, while Conan was born and raised here in Lakestone.

It was hardly even possible these two ever crossed paths, let alone planned murders together.

I had retrieved Conan's phone information from his cell company and there were no strange numbers listed there. There weren't many numbers to begin with, to be completely honest. The only thing that threw me off a bit was that he had called Jack's number several times after his death, which didn't make sense given the fact that Jack's phone and all his personal belongings were sealed and at the station. Maybe he just wanted to hear his voice.

Weirdo.

Sighing, I set up the last two pictures right under the Raymond's. Jay Titcher and Ben Karrock, Harold's well known former accomplices and the two less likely to have anything to do with our case.

They both had alibis— Titcher moved to Maryland and was presumably at a bar the night of the murders (although nobody could testify for him), and Karrock was at his sister's wedding (and although several of his family members attested of it, he wasn't on any of the pictures, so what gave? Who the hell didn't take pictures at weddings?).

*Come on, Maddox, think, goddammit.*

There had to be something that linked one of these men to the Raymonds.

Just then, my phone rang. I was so drawn into my own thoughts that I jumped in surprise. Seeing Andrea's name on it, I picked it up and put it to my ears.

"Hey, what's up?"

My attention was still mostly on the file in front of me, the pictures, the bank and phone statements, Sofia's testimony, everything was there to help me, yet the answers still evaded me.

Andrea cleared her throat on the other side of the phone. I frowned. She sounded anguished. I immediately thought something happened with her husband, Wesley, maybe they got into a fight or, fuck maybe it was Adrianna? Maybe something happened to her?

We had barely spoken since Valentina's incident. She didn't come by, said work was busy, and she answered my calls maybe three times in the last month, when she usually was the one to call at least two times a week.

"Andie? You okay?"

"Y-yeah. I'm fine, Maddox. How are you? How is Valentina?"

I let myself fall back against the couch and sighed. "We're good. We're fine, her school is having a Daddy-daughter dance in two weeks. I officially asked her today. Sofia will probably send you the pictures given how ridiculous I looked." I chuckled but she didn't.

"Yeah, I'd love to see that."

"Okay, Andie? You're seriously starting to worry me. Is everything okay? Are you in trouble right now? Only answer yes or no." Now, that earned a slight chuckle from her.

"I'm good, Maddox. I just wanted to check on you. I know I— I've been distant lately, but I think I just needed to get my thoughts in order." I nodded even though she couldn't see me.

"I get you, sis, truly. You don't have to explain yourself to me if you need some time away from family. I know we can be overbearing sometimes." She didn't say anything and for the longest time none of us spoke. It's like we were both lost in our own thoughts.

She eventually said she had to go, though so I said goodnight. Told her to come by the apartment sometime with Adrianna, Valentina would love that. Tossing my phone on the couch next to me, I was fully intent on going back to studying this case.

But that was without counting on the little steps I heard coming from the hallway.

"Mads?"

Of course Valentina would wake up now. I cursed, ready to push all the papers and pictures back into the file when her arms suddenly encircled me, halting my movements.

“What’s wrong, pretty girl?” I put a hand on her back and she leaned against me, her head hitting my shoulder in an awkward hug.

“Ray woke me up, I think—“ She stopped suddenly and gasped.

I looked up only to see her frightened, wide eyes staring back at me like I’d done something to her. I frowned, confused.

“What's wrong?” There was an urgency in my voice that only matched the panic in her eyes. I grabbed her elbows, shaking her slightly. “Valentina, use your words, honey, what’s wrong?”

She swallowed thickly and I noticed tears were brimming in her eyes.

“Are the monsters coming back, Maddox?” Her voice was nothing but a whisper.

“What? No, baby. Of course not.”

“Then why do you have a picture of them?”

I didn't get it at first. But then it hit me. The pictures on the table. She had seen them. And she recognized her parent’s killers in them. Oh fuck, this was *huge*.

If Sofia was here, she would probably freak out. She might very well kill me if she knew I let Valentina see our suspects' pictures. But as of right now, I knew this was the only way we'd solve this case.

"Valentina? Can you show me where the monsters are?" She seemed reluctant to even look back at the pictures, "Please, pretty girl. I know you can do it."

She pursed her lips, looking so sad and scared and vulnerable, before nodding lightly.

I followed her little hand with my eyes as she picked up the picture that seemed to have triggered bad memories in her. My heart was beating fast in anticipation and eagerness to finally be able to close this case.

But when I saw what picture she held, I was rendered speechless. My whole body just stopped functioning. My blood ran ice-cold and it felt like I couldn't breath.

Every single time she had spoken of monsters, I had assumed she meant the people who killed her parents and hurt Sofia that night.

I couldn't have been more wrong.

Because those monsters she seemed so scared of? Those monsters Sofia had *chased away*?

They were none other than Jack and Marcella Raymond.

# 24

## SACRIFICE

### SOFIA

Valentina was going to love this.

I got to finish a little earlier than I was supposed to because customers were few and Aaron and Lisa said they could handle it themselves. God bless their souls.

I was fully planning on getting back home as soon as I could to spend a little bit of time with Maddox before we both called it a night — Valentina was probably already asleep. But then I saw the prettiest little dress in a new shop's window not too far from where I was parked. The boutique had only opened a week ago, but the owner came by the café a couple of times and she was adorable. Her name was Aria and she and her husband had just moved here from Seattle. She made all kinds of gowns. Evening, cocktail, wedding, you name it. She was hella talented, too.

As I passed her window a sparkling lilac princess dress grabbed my attention and I just knew this was the dress Valentina had to wear to the dance. She didn't have a favorite color— said all colors were beautiful and it was too hard to choose, but I knew she had a secret sweet spot for blue, purple and pink.

This one was perfect.

Aria had several sizes, she dressed both women and little girls and said if it didn't fit her or if she didn't like it we could come back and exchange it.

It cost me a hefty sum, for sure, but just imagining my sister's smile as I'd show it to her tomorrow morning was worth it.

I entered the apartment with a smile on my face, hoping Maddox wasn't already asleep just so I could show him my new purchase.

As soon as I locked the door behind me, though, something felt off.

The living room's lights were turned off, the whole apartment was plunged into darkness, only illuminated by the moon glow shining through the large bay windows.

I took my shoes off and put my purse and keys on the side table before turning around.

I yelped when I noticed a shadow sitting on the armchair right in front of the couch.

"Jesus Christ, Maddox! You scared the shit out of me!" I chuckled before taking off my coat.

I draped it on the back of a chair which sat next to the side table before grabbing the big bag with Valentina's gown inside and walking towards him.

"I found the prettiest dress ever! Valentina is going to love it, I can't wait to see her— what's wrong?" As soon as I saw his clenched jaw and his bloodshot eyes, I knew something was up.

I knew my first instincts were right and something happened.

"Maddox?" Blood drained from my face, my mind immediately jumping to worst case scenarios. "Where's Valentina, Maddox, is everything—"

"Sit down." He was so cold, so unlike his usual commanding or playful tone.

I frowned. What was his deal? What the fuck happened?

"Is Valentina—"

"Valentina is fine. Sit your fucking ass down."

His voice didn't leave anything up for debate so I immediately fell down on the couch, mouth slightly open in shock. My heart started beating furiously. This whole scene was how a lot of my nightmares started.

"Maddox, please. You're scaring me." Tears were gathering in my eyes. How come every fucking good day I had ended up in shit.

That man in front of me that looked like Maddox but didn't act like him chuckled darkly.

"*I*'m scaring you?" He narrowed his eyes at me and I swear my heart stopped for a second there. "That's fucking rich coming from a *killer*."

I stopped breathing.

A killer.

*Killer. Killer. Killer.*

The word echoed in my head, like the aftershock of a bomb going off. It was deafening.

Blood froze in my veins as my eyes opened wide. *No*. No, no, no.

This couldn't be happening.

Panic rising inside of me had me gasping for air. I couldn't believe this was happening. He couldn't know. Maddox couldn't know my secret. He couldn't know the one thing I swore to never speak of, the one thing I tried to push to a dark corner of my mind just so I would never have to look back at it.

A killer.

That's what I was, wasn't it?

I had killed.

That night, that lie of a night, I had killed. And I didn't mean only Harold Crawford.

And now Maddox knew it. And my world came crumbling down, again.

Chuckling weakly, I tried denying it. "I have no idea what you're —"

"Don't fucking lie to me, Sofia!" He leaped to his feet and my flight or fight instinct kicked in. I stood up too, trying to put as much space as possible between us.

“Maddox, you're scaring me! I’m taking Valentina and I’m leaving until you calm down!” I tried turning around but his words chained me to the ground.

“Valentina is not here.” Dread settled in the pit of my stomach as I slowly turned around, fingers trembling slightly.

My worst nightmare.

That’s what was happening.

“She's safe, sleeping over at my sister’s house. Away from you. And don’t you fucking think of leaving this apartment, Sofia, cops are everywhere surrounding the building. They’re just waiting for my order.”

My head was spinning, a deafening sound rang in my ears as I took in his words. Valentina wasn’t here. Cops everywhere.

No. This couldn’t be the end. This couldn’t be how everything ended, not after everything I sacrificed, after everything we’ve been through.

Stupid girl that I was. I knew letting people in was never a good idea. I knew I never should’ve accepted his help. I knew I never should have let my guards down and fucking fallen in love with him.

Now everything I had worked so hard for, everything was up in flames.

“Maddox, what have you done?” I whispered in fright.

Energy was slowly leaving my body, it felt like I could lose consciousness at any moment.

"You don't get to act that way now, Sofia! Not when you've betrayed me in the worst possible way! All this time and you were only fucking using me?"

Tears started rolling down my cheeks, I was shaking my head hysterically, I wanted to say that wasn't true, that I never used him but no words would come out of my mouth.

They were all stuck in my throat, so much it felt like I couldn't breathe.

"I trusted you! Fell in love with you and you went ahead and stabbed me in the back! How fucking could you, Sofia?!" His screams were the only thing that echoed in my brain, that and the whispers that said everything was over.

I hadn't felt guilty that night. After all, I was only doing what was best for my sister. But right then seeing Maddox's red eyes, his clenched jaw as he yelled at me and flung his arms in the air like a madman, the guilt I experienced was soul-crushing.

"I can't believe I let you around Valentina while all this time you were the killer, Sofia." He hissed the last part of his sentence with so much disappointment and rejection it made me ill. Had I been able to, I would have thrown up his words just so that they'd stop plaguing my insides and making me sick.

"Fucking dammit, Sofia, answer me!"

"My name is not fucking *Sofia*!" My shrieking voice seemed to take us both by surprise and Maddox took a step back, stunned. "It's not, it's not, *it's not*!" I couldn't stop screaming, grabbing my head as tremors wrecked my body. It was like something in me had broken, like the last thread holding my sanity together had snapped.

"I hate that fucking name, *I hate it, I hate it, I hate it*!" I cried.

But I didn't hate it. Not really.

Or at least I had gotten used to it since it had been mine for the last six years. The thing about it was that it wasn't my real name. And it represented my whole identity having been stolen, no, *snatched* away from me by force.

So yes. In a way, I resented it. I hated what it represented. I resented that it wasn't mine. That it wasn't the name mama had given me.

When a few minutes passed and my tears relented a bit, I finally gathered the courage to look up. Maddox' mouth was hanging open and he looked at me like he didn't know me.

I guess he didn't, in a way.

"Who are you?" He breathed.

I probably looked insane. Mascara running down my cheeks, hair matted to my sweaty forehead, fists balled out so tightly my nails were probably drawing blood inside my palms.

"I'm my sister's keeper." Was all I could mutter, the only words I thought could explain my actions.

None of us spoke. The sound of our erratic breaths was the only thing you could hear inside this room. Eventually, Maddox broke the silence.

"Sit down and start speaking." His tone was less cutting than earlier, but it was still nothing like its usual warmth.

Swallowing down my pride, I fell back on the sofa.

"Can you bring me my treasure box? I swear I won't be moving from here. You got me surrounded, anyway."

I hated the taste of betrayal that knowledge left on my tongue. But there was nothing I could do about it, not when I was the one to betray his trust first.

Maddox seemed to hesitate, but then he rushed towards the hallway leading to our rooms and came back a second later with my box.

He handed it to me and I grabbed it with weak hands. That night, my little wooden box weighed a ton, probably because of all the heavy secrets it contained.

Pushing down on the engraved flowers, I turned the little locket on the side and it snapped open. I gulped.

What I was about to reveal to Maddox was something I had never told anyone.

It was something I had planned on telling him one day, when I actually gathered the courage to do so without being scared of him leaving us.

Opening it up, the smell of dried jasmine hit my nostrils and I inhaled it like an addict.

It had been a while since I took a walk down memory lane.

Retrieving the small piece of paper I knew would pretty much sum up everything, I handed it to Maddox. He frowned, reading the cut-out newspaper article I had printed seven years ago.

I didn't need him to read aloud to know what was written there. I had read it so many times I knew it by heart.

*Flores family massacre: parents were found slaughtered in their house, children are missing.*

*The town of Faithview is mourning four well-loved members of its community this Monday morning. Jasmine and Antonio Flores were found dead in their home late last night. The alert was given by a neighbor who was woken up by screams coming from their house. Their two daughters, Dalia and Rosa Flores (13 and 4) are currently missing, Faithview police forces are doing their best to find them and bring justice to their parents.*

Only they didn't. Find us, I mean.

They didn't find us. Because by the time this paper was published, we already were in another country.

"What does that mean?" He looked at me incredulously as his hand still gripped the paper tightly.

"My name is Dalia Flores. I'm the daughter of Jasmine and Antonio Flores."

I could never explain the lightness I felt go through me as I said those words. Tears actually started flowing down my cheeks as they left my mouth. For eight long years, I had been incapable of muttering these words to anyone. And now that I was reclaiming them, it felt like being given back parts of my identity.

"You don't know how good it feels to say that." I whispered, closing my eyes as a sad smile made its way to my lips. I stayed that way for a minute, just bathing in the peace that came with acknowledging my true self.

Even though everything was over, even though I had failed, the simple fact that I could tell the truth and stop clutching onto that lies-filled life I was forcefully given, was heaven.

"What happened to you?" Opening my eyes and taking him in, I could see he looked more and more like the man I loved.

Like the man I had betrayed and drowned in lies.

"My mother had a… she had a really bad childhood." The words were an understatement and it hurt to speak but I figured I at least owed the truth to him after everything he did for us. For me. "Her parents were killed when she was really young and she had to go live with her uncle, Oracio."

He stared at me intently so I continued.

"Does the nickname The Mexican Oracle ring a bell?"

Maddox frowned, thinking for a bit, before nodding, "The famous Mexican crime lord? Reigned over all of Texas and several other southern states on top of the North of Mexico?" I nodded. "Yeah, I do. He was ruthless, the FBI tried tracking him down for years but it was like he always knew what they were gonna do and where they were gonna be. That's why they nicknamed him the Oracle. He saw their every move coming. He was found dead a year ago in one of his warehouses." I nodded again. All he said was very true.

"Well, Oracio was my mother's uncle. She went to live with him when she was seven." The look in his eyes told me he understood where I was getting at. Oracio was a ruthless man. He was known to dabble in all kinds of traffic. Drugs, arms… sex.

"He… he abused her, sexually. For years." I gulped, knowing very well the pain my mother had gone through. "Until eventually, she got pregnant. With me. " I pinched my lips together to keep me from crying. It was never easy acknowledging the fact that that monster was my biological father. Not after what he did to my parents. Not after what he did to us.

I couldn't look up at Maddox.

"When she found out she was pregnant, she decided she could not stay there, so she fled Mexico. She only had the clothes on her back, a few snacks and water, and a couple thousand dollars she had stolen from him. She got into the US, I don't know how but she made it to a small town in Louisiana, called Olympe." A small smile graced my lips when I thought of what happened next.

"She met my dad there, my papa. Ro— Valentina's biological dad. Not mine."

I could see how the news about Valentina and I being half-sisters surprised him. You wouldn't guess, because we both looked exactly like our mother, black hair, brown eyes, light brown skin. Just like mama.

"She was fifteen, heavily pregnant and in a country whose language she didn't speak and hardly even understood. Papa was only three years older than her, spoke Spanish fluently and when he saw her, it was love at first sight. At least for him. At first, she rejected him, because she was scared of getting hurt again. But my dad was persistent and eventually, they got together. Dad's family was heavily against their union. She was pregnant with somebody else's child, and that was a hard no for his very much catholic family."

I gulped, looking down, wrenching my hands together.

"So they ran away together. They went all the way up to Canada, where they were sure no one would find them, and started a new life there. Dad worked at a car shop, he loved cars, loved building them back from scratch." I smiled at the memory of the man that never treated me like I was anything but his, no matter what my DNA stated. "Mom worked part-time at a small flower shop in town. It wasn't much, but it paid the bills. She loved flowers." I remember our house always being full of plants, she had them all over the patio, the kitchen, the living room, even had some in our bedrooms. "When Rosa came along, I was over the moon. Getting to be a big sister was everything I ever wanted, it meant the world to me. I took it very seriously, from a young age."

"What happened then?" I bit my lip while Maddox' eyes dug into me.

Taking a deep breath, I resumed my story.

"Oracio found her. My mom." My chin was shaking so much from trying to hold tears in, and I couldn't even do it properly since a lot of it escaped and ran down my cheeks.

"He came one night, with some of his men. One minute we were all asleep after a night of playing board games, the next we were awoken by the screams of my mother. They did so many horrible things to her,

Maddox..." I cried softly, “They made my father watch while they—” I couldn’t bring myself to say it. It hurt too much reminiscing.

“They slit her throat when they were done with her, then they stabbed my father. Several times.”

I knew my words must have been familiar to him, because that's exactly what I had told him and Adam when they interrogated me the day after the murders. I knew I wouldn't be able to fake being sad over the crazy fucks that were Jack and Marcella, so I had to put some truth in my words.

“Oracio took us. Said mama owed him for running away, and we were the payment. We never saw Canada again.”

I could see this was a lot for him to take in.

It was a lot for me to say. I felt lightheaded, I just wanted to sleep.

“Did he— did he hurt you and Valentina?” I smiled sadly at his question.

“Only me. I would have died before I let him anywhere near my little rose. Plus, we had a deal.” At his frown, I felt the urge to elaborate. Shame warmed my stomach at what I was about to admit. “Our deal was simple. If I didn’t fight him, he wouldn’t touch my sister.”

I saw him being confused for a second before it dawned on him. Blood drained from his face as he stared in stunned silence for a few seconds.

“Fuck, Sofia, how old were you?”

“Thirteen.”

Internally, I cried for the little girl I had been. I cried for the fact that she didn't get to grow up and have a normal childhood. I cried over the fact that she had to learn of sacrificing herself before she ever saw someone sacrifice themselves for her.

I could see Maddox's eyes brimming with tears and it felt so foreign. Nobody ever cried for me.

Nobody but Maddox.

“How did you—“ he cleared his throat, his voice raw with emotions. "How did you find yourself here?”

“You know Oracio was in all sorts of traffic. Children were one of the things he—dealt.” I licked my lips, they felt suddenly dry. “Jack couldn’t have children. He was an old loan shark who suddenly decided he wanted to make it into politics. He chose Lakestone because it was secluded enough that nobody would know him, but still big enough to start a career. He needed a family for that, though, you know, to give the impression he was a family man. He had a wife, he only needed a child.” I rubbed my temples, my headache becoming worse.

Maddox frowned before it finally dawned on him what I meant. “He only wanted Valentina.” I nodded, tiredly.

“I had to… I had to convince him to take me with them too. I struck the same deal that I had with Oracio. Me, for my sister."

“I… I’m so sorry you had to do this.” My eyes were drooping in exhaustion but I still managed a small, tired, smile.

“I’m not. I would’ve done it a thousand times if it meant my sister got to hold onto her innocence. But that’s the problem, Maddox. She didn’t.”

I saw the exact moment he understood the meaning behind my words, because his whole demeanor changed. Fury burned in his eyes as his shoulder tensed. He looked at me intently while shaking his head no, unbelieving.

“I always made sure he was never alone with her. When I had a late shift at work, she had strict instructions to lock herself in my room and wait for me to get in through the window at night. Same thing went for when I went out to paint, or when I tried to get in trouble to spend the night at the police station. It was always better than to spend it there because then he would have free access to me before he went to sleep.” For some reason, that’s when it always hurt the most, like he was taking his day’s frustrations out on me.

“Valentina stayed locked in my room, because I didn't trust this son of a bitch, not for the life of me.” I could feel the rage gathering in my body, it awakened me when I was so close to passing out a few minutes ago.

“One day, though, two weeks before their death, he was supposed to go on a business trip. He had left that morning before we went to school and wasn’t supposed to be back until the following Monday. I took the chance to get in more hours at work. I had a plan, you know?” I smiled sadly. “I almost had enough money to get us the hell out of there. But I needed more shifts. So I stayed late. It was around eleven when I got home.”

I closed my eyes, knowing what came next was something I would never forgive myself for. The pain was suffocating but somehow getting it out of my chest was liberating.

"I knew something was wrong when I saw his car in the driveway. He always left it at the airport when he went away on business so that he could drive back in it when he came back." I pursed my lips. "I never climbed the tree in front of our house so quickly, Maddox. It was like I could feel it. It was like I knew something bad had happened." My lips were quivering as I sobbed silently.

Closing my eyes, I was brought back to that night.

*As soon as my feet hit the hardwood floors of my bedroom and I saw her lying on my bed, covers pulled up to her chin as she quivered slightly, I knew. I remembered my trembling hand clutching the blanket and gently pulling it off of her.*

*And there laid my sleeping little rose. Bright red smearing her pink pajama pants and seeping into my sheets as dry tears stained her rosy cheeks.*

*A bloody rose.*

*And I could feel my dahlia heart darkening as blackness slowly took over.*

*It felt like an out of body experience. I gathered her in my arms as she woke up and cried silently, but I could also see myself from the outside, lying down with her, little hands clutching my shirt like a lifeline.*

*I could see us slowly withering, a red rose and a black dahlia.*

*When she fell back asleep, I still held onto her like my life depended on it. My failure to protect her cost her her innocence and I would never forgive myself.*

*Tears I had managed to hold in for the longest time finally broke free. But tears seemed so inconsequential compared to the war, the annihilation that was taking over my heart. I felt destroyed inside.*

*I wanted nothing more than to shout my pain to the world. Let them know how it felt to be so completely demolished emotionally that it seemed like your whole world had stopped spinning.*

*But I couldn't.*

*I couldn't share my pain with anyone. I couldn't share my rage with anyone.*

*So I cried. I cried until the sun came up.*

And my sobs were silent but I could hear my soul screaming. It screamed for justice.

It screamed for revenge.

# 25

# DEVOTION

## MADDOX

"Maddox, are you sure you want to do this?" Adam's anguished voice came from beside me. "There's no turning back after that." I pinched my lips as I read the name plastered on the door in front of me.

*Deputy Chief Piersons* in gold lettering stared back at me.

"I know. I have to do it, Adam. It's only right."

"Fuck what is right man, I don't know in what world you're living but what you're about to do right now? There's nothing fucking right about it." He seemed annoyed with me, and it honestly saddened me, knowing I had disappointed him somehow.

Adam was a great friend but I did see him as a father figure, sometimes too. I wasn't super close to my own dad, our relationship was pleasant and nice but it really didn't give anything more than that. Adam took me in as soon as I started here, I knew his family, he often came over to watch games and we occasionally went out for drinks from time to time. Most of all, we talked. I knew I could confide in him.

So yeah, I understood why he reacted the way he did when I told him the news.

"Come on, man. Just think it through." I looked at him and shook my head. My decision was made.

Piersons' voice coming from behind us broke our staring contest.

"Detectives? To what do I owe the pleasure?" We turned around but I could still feel Adam's eyes on me.

Piersons was there, briefcase in one hand, his coat hanging from his arm, while the other hand held his coffee. He stared at us curiously, one eyebrow drawn up.

"Do you finally have answers for your case or are you turning it into the cold cases?"

I opened my mouth to speak, but my words wouldn't come out. This was no doubt one of the hardest things I'd ever had to do, but I knew it was worth it. I took a deep breath and finally said what I came here to say.

"I am handing in my two weeks notice, sir. I'm resigning."

The shock on his face was clearly visible, he and Adam shared a look, I could see my partner— or, well, ex-partner clench his jaw.

"I think it's the right thing to do after I failed at finding out what happened that night." I lied.

More like I fell in love with the killer I was tracking down and refused to turn her in.

I couldn't, in all good conscience, continue working here. I used to love my job but this case changed everything. This case made me look at the people surrounding me with a different eye. I would have never suspected Jack and Marcella Raymond to be the monsters they were, yet look at them. And the truth was, we *worked* for people like Jack Raymond.

Important people with enough money to shut anyone up had they needed to.

Chief Piersons knew Raymond personally, they golfed together, had dinner together. Maybe he knew what Jack was really like, maybe he was the same as him.

I think what happened yesterday was proof enough that you never truly knew anyone.

After Valentina told me about Jack and Marcella being the monsters she was so scared off, the monsters Sofia had always protected her from, I was livid. I don't think I'd ever felt so betrayed and angry in my life, like my world had tilted out of its axis. I instantly jumped to conclusions, thinking Sofia and I getting together was all part of her plan to get away with murder.

I was hurt, like never before.

But then she came in and told me everything and I wanted to puke. How the fuck could this have been going on right under our noses without anyone in this fucking town noticing a thing?

"This is ridiculous, Maddox!" Piersons puffed, agitated. "You cannot just give up on your career because of one unsolved case. It happens to all great cops, it might be your first but it won't be your last, trust me."

"My decision is final, sir. Here is my letter."

I handed him the paper I had spent a good chunk of the night writing, after Sofia finally fell asleep while sobbing against my shirt.

Piersons' lips pinched together and he looked like he wanted to say something else, convince me of staying, but he must've seen the sheer determination in my eyes because he chose to drop it instead.

He nodded angrily, taking the letter from my outstretched hand with a clenched jaw. "Fine. I wish you well." He sidestepped me and slammed the door to his office, leaving only me and Adam in the hallway.

I finally looked at him and he shook his head. "I just hope you know what you're doing, kid."

"I do." I gave him a small smile and a friendly tap on the shoulder before turning around.

I hurried back to my car to get back home.

After everything that happened yesterday, I was only scared of one thing; that Sofia actually didn't trust me enough and decided to flee while I was gone. As soon as she finished telling me about her parents — her real parents, I confessed I had lied about the cops surrounding the building. There was no such a thing, I didn't tell anyone, I would never do that to her without hearing her out first.

I was head over heels in love with that girl. Actually, what I felt for her went beyond that word. It knew no bound, no morals, it encompassed any rule. That's how I knew she would be my undoing. Because if there was something this morning proved, it's that I would do anything for Sofia. Or maybe I should start calling her Dalia?

Whatever name she wanted me to call her, she was mine first and foremost. My girl, my warrior, my survivor.

When I told her I would resign this morning, that I would keep her secret until the day I died, I could see she seemed uncertain. She wanted to trust me, but she was still wary and I guess I got it now that I knew more about her past.

I still barely managed to wrap my head around all the information that was thrown at me yesterday. Anger coursed through my veins every time I recalled what she had confessed to me. What those bastards had done to her and Valentina truly broke me. I cried for a good ten minutes last night after she finally fell asleep.

I cried for two little girls who had been through what no children should ever have to go through. Fuck, I hadn't shed tears since I was a kid myself, but last night, they just wouldn't stop. And I held Sofia so tight all the while, I thought she might have woken up, but she was so exhausted she slept right through it.

This morning, things were silent between us.

I hated it, I hated that she seemed scared, that she didn't know how to act around me anymore. I hated that she was so unsure about what her next move should be.

We woke up on the couch, my whole body was sore from the uncomfortable position I had fallen asleep in, and Sofia was already awake. Her head was resting on my chest and she looked at me tiredly. There was some fear in her eyes and I fucking hated that it was there.

I'd seen her in vulnerable states in the past, but never like that. She was never vulnerable and scared to the point where she looked like she wanted to flee.

Of course I tried reassuring her, telling her that I would never turn her in or do anything that might get her separated from her sister. I swore myself to secrecy and told her she needed to trust me.

I told her I would be back as soon as I could and that she had to stay home and wait for me. I made her promise not to run away from me and she did, weakly.

But I was scared her instincts would be too strong and that she'd end up leaving, anyways.

That was why I found myself speeding on the drive home and ignoring all speed limits. I parked hastily once I reached the building, not even sure I locked my car before getting out and sprinting to my apartment.

Once I came to face the front door, my heart was beating fast. I didn't know what I would find once I opened it. I just hoped she was still here so that we could talk, now that the initial shock had worn off.

Walking inside warily, I looked around. Nothing seemed out of place, but I had a bad feeling.

"Sofia?" I called and after a few seconds passed and no answers were heard, I strode down the hall and to my room, heart beating so fast I thought it would jump out of my chest. I called her name again, and just like before, no response came through.

Pushing open my bedroom's door, I froze.

A couple of dresser drawers were left open, their emptiness matching the hollow that was growing in my heart. The colorful quilt I had put on my bed yesterday was nowhere in sight, and the same went for her treasure box.

I wrenched the closet's doors open, and just like I feared, most of Sofia's clothes were missing.

I cursed, slamming it shut before running out of the room and into her old room. It was empty too, but most of her painting supplies were still there.

Swallowing the pain and betrayal that were clogging up my throat, I dejectedly walked to Valentina's bedroom. The chances of her leaving without her sister were nonexistent, so I knew she must've been in there at one time during the hour and a half I wasn't home. Then she probably went and retrieved her from school, since she was listed as a parent.

My conscience was screaming at me to call Adam and have him dispatch a team to look for them, but I couldn't do that. They had been through so much and it would only be cruel of me to set a whole search party for them that would only result in getting Sofia in trouble.

But I'd be damned if I didn't use all of my private resources to track them down and bring them home myself.

As I turned the knob to Valentina's room, though, the faint scent of flower and sugar drifted to my nose, and once I could peek inside, my eyes widened.

Sofia was sitting on the bed, her head looking down, dark hair hiding my view of her gorgeous face. On a corner of the room was a big suitcase that was undoubtedly filled with her and Valentina's stuff, since the little girl's closet was open and I could see half her clothes were missing. For a few minutes, none of us spoke, I just took her in, trying to convince myself I was not hallucinating.

“My brain screamed at me to get away while I still could.” Her voice was hoarse and weak, she probably had been crying.

My thoughts were proven right when she sniffled, her head slowly coming up to stare into my eyes. Her golden orbs were glistening and red.

I couldn't explain what it did to me, seeing her there, after thinking she was gone for good. I could never explain the relief, the love, the pride I felt at that moment, it was just insane.

“But I couldn’t do it, Maddox. You’re the best thing that’s ever happened to me— to us. And I could never put you through the pain of betraying you again. All the secrets were eating at me, and—” she hiccuped, the sobs keeping her from speaking freely. I wanted to hug her and tell her she didn’t have to say anything but my feet were glued to the ground.

“And I know you probably won't ever think of me the same, but I love you too much to run away from you. I love you too much not to trust you.”

That seemed to get me moving because the next thing I knew, I was standing in front of her and gathering her in my arms. She wrapped hers around my neck as her legs came to encircle my waist.

I seemed to have lost the ability to speak, but what I wanted to say I could show with my actions. I needed to touch her, I needed to be around her, next to her, *inside* her. I wanted her to feel me, I wanted her to see that I was here to stay, I wanted to anchor her and make her understand that I was not going to leave.

Even when I thought she was a cold killer, even when I thought she had been manipulating me all this time, I never could have turned her in. I was in love with that woman, I was a slave to her and would have done anything for her.

So I carried her to our bedroom and deposited her in the middle of the bed.

She was wearing a pair of gray sweatpants and a matching gray sweatshirt, which both ended up strewn around the bedroom floor. Once we were both naked on the bed and I laid between her thighs, I simply stared at her for the longest time. My hands caressed her face, pushing some strands away from it so I could see her better.

She too let her hands travel all over my body, she rubbed my back, intertwined her fingers through my hair and spread kisses all over my neck. For a few minutes we only did that, sharing body warmth, caresses and light kisses.

"Could you… I think I need a spanking." She whispered shyly, biting her lip and barely daring to look in my eyes. "Please. I just have all this guilt for lying to you and—" her chin was quivering as she searched for the right words. But she didn't need to.

I never thought I'd like to spank my partner during sex, I never felt the urge to and no previous partner ever requested it.

But that first night I spanked her, I had never felt something so strong. It was like we were two missing pieces of the same puzzle, like it just made sense. I loved making her ass red and watching her squirm under me. It wasn't a way for me to get my anger out, though. It was all about giving her the discipline I knew she craved. Watching her get wetter with each slap was an added bonus.

"Get in position, baby." She didn't hesitate, I pushed off her as she got on her knees and pushed her face and shoulders against the mattress. I had a perfect view of her wet pussy that way and it took all of me not to simply bury my face or my cock in there. I had to tell myself this would come later because right then she needed something else.

When the first slap came, she yelped in surprise. God, I loved that sound. I kept on spanking her ass until I heard the first sob. Her skin was red but she clearly wanted more as she kept on thrusting back against me.

"Open your legs, baby." She heeded my order and spread her thighs wider. I could see a drop of clear cum dribbling along her thigh as she did. Her pussy was glistening with arousal and I couldn't believe she loved being spanked so much.

Deciding to try something different, I aimed my hand a little lower than where I had been slapping up until then and instead smacked her wet cunt, making her cry out. She was so drenched it made a loud squelchy sound and fuck if I wasn't hard as a rock.

I slapped her pussy lips a couple more times and before I could even understand it, Sofia was coming against my hand as I looked on, stunned.

Fuck, I needed her. Not waiting for that climax to rescind, I rolled her onto her back and got back between her legs before I entered her in one go. She cried out and her hand shot out to grip my hair. She tugged at it hard but I loved the sting it brought.

"I love you, Maddox." She breathed against my lips and closed her eyes in ecstasy.

My expression matched hers because the warmth, the sentiment of belonging that came with us being joined in that way, it was all too good to be true.

“I love you too, baby." Dipping my head in the crook of her neck I inhaled her scent of flowers and sugar. “I fucking love you so much. I’m never letting you go.”

I bit her skin and she moaned louder. The sound of skin slapping skin, her hand in my hair, mine gripping her thighs, the wet sound my cock made every time it drove into her cunt… all of that coupled with the delicious way she was tightening around my shaft threw me off the edge and soon we were both coming hard.

***

“Thank you for trusting me and always giving me what I need.” She snuggled closer to me under the covers as her arms wrapped around my waist. I brought her even closer and inhaled her hair like an addict. “I love you so much.”

I guess that’s what I was. I was addicted to that tiny woman lying next to me.

“It feels so good to finally say it, Maddox. I’ve wanted to for so long but it never felt right given what I was hiding from you.” Drawing circles on her naked hip, I hugged her tighter.

“Sofia, this doesn't change a thing for me. From the moment you showed me that newspaper article, I knew you did what you had to do. I love you too, baby.”

Silence stretched as we both got lost in our thoughts. I had never been naive enough to believe that the system was totally dependable. I would have never thought that a man, especially one in a position of power, could have an equal opportunity of being brought to justice and getting what he deserved like the average citizen could. This system had been created by rich men, and so it naturally benefited them.

I knew if Sofia had spoken up, if she'd tried to go to the police or something, it would've been her word against his. Raymond would probably have sent her away and taken advantage of her absence to force himself on Valentina.

The simple thought made me so fucking mad.

"It was horrible living there." She confessed quietly, eyes lost in the distance. "They were so awful, they constantly put Valentina down. She had to be careful of how she spoke, how she dressed. She was bullied at school, but I couldn't do anything about it because that would have created a fuss and possibly risked a punishment for us. They were especially strict with her because they thought I was a lost cause, since I was older, but Valentina was just the right age that they could shape her into the perfect little daughter."

My nostrils flared because that was no way to raise a child. But I didn't say anything and simply let her unload on me. I had a feeling she needed that.

"They didn't want us to speak Spanish, I had to teach Valentina in secret, because we had always spoken Spanish at home when I was little and I wanted Valentina to experience that growing up, too. They tried so hard to steal our identities but I wouldn't let them take our heritage from us."

I admired that. I loved that about her, in fact, how much her culture meant to her.

“They punished her regularly. Even when she didn't do anything. I tried taking the brunt of it, but still, they slapped her around, they locked her in dark closets, they—“ She let out a small intake of breath. “Marcella was the worst when it came to punishments. I think she resented us for being there in the first place. She knew very well what Jack did to me, and she didn’t care as long as nobody found out. It would have stained the perfect reputation she had spent so long creating. One time, Valentina was eight, she brought her upstairs while he… While I was being–” I froze as she started crying silently.

“She made her watch for ten minutes as my sister cried and said if she didn't behave, that would be her next. Valentina ended up throwing up all over the floor.” Sofia sobbed against my chest, hiding her face in shame. “Somehow, that was the time I felt most humiliated in my life, Maddox. I hope you don't think less of me, but … if I had the chance to kill them again, I would.”

“If I’d known all of that while they were still alive, I would have killed them myself.” There were no other options for people like them. Their cruelty knew no bounds, and they didn't deserve redemption. “That’s why… that's why you freaked out when Valentina got her period, isn’t it?” I felt her nod against me.

“I think your sister knows something is up. When you went to speak to Valentina, she spoke to me in private. She asked if I had endometriosis, I said I suspected I did but never got diagnosed. She said Valentina was showing really early signs of it but that most doctors would say it was too soon to tell.” She sighed, snuggling closer to me. “Then she asked if… if something had happened to Valentina.” I froze. Fuck. That would actually explain why Andrea had been distant since that day.

“I denied everything, of course. But she said a lot of little girls with sexual traumas experienced bleeding earlier than the norm. She also said a lot of women with endometriosis suffered from sexual assault as a child.” She quietened for a beat, lost in her thoughts. “Turns out a thirteen year old’s body isn’t made to accommodate a fifty year old man’s.” I hugged her a little tighter to me when she said that, because no words could make her feel better about any of that.

No word could heal the years of abuse she had endured, the things she had heard and seen and been through. I felt so fucking useless at that moment. So fucking helpless, knowing that there was nothing I could do about it.

But hearing her talk about what my sister said just made so much sense. That day she had a panic attack, it was not because of the blood alone, it was because the whole scene must have reminded her of the night she found Valentina in her bed after that bastard hurt her.

Actually, so many things made sense all of a sudden, how I didn't even know they could speak Spanish, her not wanting Valentina anywhere near pictures of Jack and Marcella, the way she reacted when she saw Aisha, the foster mother that had taken Valentina in, months ago. Valentina had said she looked like their mother and at first I thought she meant the way she spoke or held herself. But when I saw Sofia stare at her with stunned eyes, I'd thought something was weird. Because Aisha didn’t look anything like Marcella Raymond, but I’d bet she looked a great deal like Jasmine Flores.

“I’m glad they're dead. I hope they’re rotting in hell.” I griped, hugging her small body closer to mine.

“Me too."

"How did you do it, though? I can't believe you took three people down on your own. What was Harold even doing there?" I truly was a detective at heart, because the logistics of this case didn't make sense, even if I knew the truth now.

Sofia was silent for a moment then she resumed drawing circles on my chest. "You had an accomplice, didn't you?" My mind was reeling, and my eyes grew wide at how much sense that made, "Oh my God! That's who set the house on fire, right? And-- fuck, did you have anything to do with Conan's death, too?"

She bit her lip as she looked up at me. "I did have help. And he did burn the house to erase any possible clue we had left behind. But I had nothing to do with that son of a bitch's death and neither did my accomplice, this I swear to you."

And I believed her. Conan's death was nothing like Jack and Marcella's and she truly looked shocked when I told her he was poisoned.

"What was his deal, anyways? I could have sworn he was the killer, we would have taken him in had he not died. We had very incriminating evidence against him."

"Yeah, the key, right?"

I started nodding but then I stopped, "Wait, that was you?" I frowned, looking down at her and she smirked tiredly.

"My friend. He's really good with computers, he can find dirt on anyone and when he can't, well… he fabricates it." Surprise reduced me to silence as I tried taking in everything that was being said. "Why do you think that bitch Candi Stein came to apologize so quickly and withdrew her complaint? He found out she had an affair a year ago and threatened to tell her husband… He's also got dirt on Piersons and was pressuring him to make you close the case." She confessed sheepishly. "Sorry about that."

"I knew it! That son of a bitch." I shook my head, caressing her smooth skin to calm myself. Still, there was one thing I kept asking myself, one thing I needed answers to. "Did Conan ever hurt you, Sofia?"

She gulped and hid her face against my chest again. I didn't let her though and grabbed her chin making her look up. "Did he?"

After a second, she nodded. Fuck, I was glad that bastard was dead. I should have poured more poisoned water down his throat.

"Jack loved him like a son. When I turned seventeen and he received some kind of award from the city, he wanted to celebrate and show Conan some… gratitude." I could feel bile rising up my throat. "He gave him free rein over me for a night." Her lips quivered as she looked away.

"It was so humiliating. Dehumanizing. Like I was just a disposable object one could pass around like he pleased. I hate them so, so much, Maddox. I hope they're burning in hell."

I couldn't take it anymore and pushed away from her, sitting down on the edge of the bed, breathing deeply, my feet on the ground. Elbows on my knees, I held my head between my hands as I could feel a killer headache make its way to me.

How strong did you have to be to deal with all of this and still try to live your life? That was killing me inside and I wasn't even the one who experienced it so how did *she* cope?

“But he's dead, now Maddox.” I heard Sofia shuffle behind me and her arms circled my waist as she rubbed her face against my back like a cat. “I don't want to let dead people ruin my life anymore. They’ve done it enough while they were alive.”

“What happened that night? How did you do it?"

I heard her take a big breath before she started her tale.

“First, we needed a scapegoat. My friend found Harold on the police data server when he hacked into it. He was registered as a recidivist sex offender, so we knew he wouldn't be missed. He approached Harold at a bar and convinced him to rob the mayor’s house with him while he was supposedly away on business and then split whatever they found. Harold was in. I let the backdoor open before going upstairs that night and that’s how they got in once I gave my friend the signal. I waited until Jack and Marcella were both asleep before going to their room and holding them at gunpoint so that they’d follow me downstairs.”

“Where did you find the gun?”

“It wasn’t mine.” I nodded, understanding it was her friend’s. I didn't know how I felt about her being friends with hackers who owned guns and would gladly be complicit to murder, but it would have to wait.

“Once we were downstairs, my friend restrained Harold, he tried to flee as soon as he saw the mayor and his wife were still in their house and that I had a gun. My friend didn’t let him, though.” She stopped, breathing softly against my skin.

“Go on. I want to know the rest.”

“Are you sure, Maddox? I don't think you want to hear how I killed them.”

“I do. I hope those fuckers suffered.” I turned around and grabbed her around the waist to make her straddle me. A small, unhinged smile appeared on her face as she looked away, reminiscing. Weirdly, it turned me on.

“Oh, they did. They begged for their lives like pathetic little bitches and— I had never felt as free as I did watching them lay in a pool of their own blood with their dead eyes opened wide.”

Maybe that should have made me uncomfortable, to hear how she spoke of the people she had murdered in cold blood, but it didn’t. If anything, pride was more akin to what I was feeling looking at her at that moment.

Because Sofia Raymond, *Dalia Flores*, was a survivor. She survived seeing her parents die in front of her, she survived years of abuse, she survived being stripped of her identity and still, after all of that, she not only evaded her demons, she fucking *slaughtered* them, too.

Not only that, but she survived while making sure her sister didn’t have to go through everything she did. And that just made me want to give her the world. Because she deserved it.

Bringing her closer to me, we stayed chest to chest for a while, simply breathing in sync with one another. I played with her hair as she drew pointless figures on my back with the tips of her fingers.

"What are we gonna do now, Maddox?” She muttered dazedly.

“We’re gonna get our girl and the three of us are gonna have the best fucking life. Fuck those monsters, they’re dead, and they're never coming back. Family isn't always blood, sometimes, it's the people who would give anything to see you happy. And I would. I'll do everything in my power to have you and Valentina happy, forever."

She smiled at me and pushed her head up, bringing her lips to mine.

My beautiful girl. My black dahlia.

# EPILOGUE

## MADDOX

*Five years later.*

Looking at the sparkly princess dress hanging in front of me, I was brought back in time. One of the best memories in my life was Valentina's first Daddy-Daughter dance when she was nine.

From seeing the sheer joy on her face as she discovered the lilac dress Sofia had bought her, to getting to hold her hands as she stood on my shoes, softly swaying to the rhythm of whatever song was playing then, everything about this memory was special.

I still remembered how we tried several stores before finally finding a tie which was the exact same shade as her dress. Valentina had charmed many salesladies that day with her adorable smiles and sparkling eyes. They all assumed she was my daughter and I didn't bother correcting them, because why would I? She was like a daughter to me, in every way that mattered. She may not have my blood running through her veins, but I would bleed for her all the same.

We had an amazing night, dancing, eating from the buffet and then, when she was too tired to stand anymore, just resting at our table while she told me all the gossip about her little schoolmates. I even remembered a certain Connor having peed his pants in gym class and a Jinnie having kissed some boy's cheek at recess. I also remembered being glad my little Valentina wasn't kissing boys.

Those were just details of what was one of the best nights of my life.

And as I took in the new dress in front of me, several sizes bigger than the one Valentina wore five years ago, I couldn't help the wave of emotions surging through me.

How did she grow up so fast?

"Are you seriously still here?" A voice called from behind me and I turned around, startled.

I sniffled and cleared my throat, folding my arms over my chest.

"What? Me? No. What?" Seeing the clearly unimpressed look on my beautiful wife's face, I sighed dejectedly.

"I forgot my wallet, I'm going okay?" She'd told me twenty minutes ago to get some more candles at the store because we ran out.

She planted a hand on her waist while the other was rubbing her round stomach, where my babies grew each day.

I thought I was in love with Sofia before, but it was nothing compared to what I felt for her when she was pregnant with my children. She never looked so beautiful than she did the last four months, and that was saying something given how gorgeous she was before.

When Sofia finally got diagnosed with endometriosis, we were really scared to try for children. The doctor had said women who have it can have trouble getting pregnant and I really feared the emotional charge that trying for kids would put on her. I knew she would pressure herself, thinking she wouldn't be enough if she couldn't give me children.

But she was. Lord, she was more than enough. And technically, she gave me one already.

So it came as a surprise to both of us when we received that positive pregnancy test after only two months of getting her off the pill.

Soon, two beautiful angels would come and add themselves to our already beautiful family of three.

I couldn't wait.

"Maddox." Sofia breathed softly. "It's okay to be a little sad, baby." She entered our room, bigger and brighter than the one we had back at the apartment, and wrapped her arms around me. "I'm sad too, you know. I can't believe she's growing up so fast."

Tears shone in her eyes and I knew she would blame them on the pregnancy if Valentina ever caught us. I smiled sadly and tucked a strand of hair behind her ear.

"Sometimes I still hear her little voice asking if we can watch The Princess and The Frog for the fourth time that week." I chuckled and it earned me a watery smile from Sofia. "I can't believe five years ago, we were getting her ready for her daddy-daughter dance and now she's in her room, with her friends, putting on makeup for her *quinceñera*."

Life worked in mysterious ways, and somehow, five years ago, two girls were put under my care and everything changed for me. For us.

"Yeah."

Sofia put her head against my chest and for a few seconds, we stayed that way, simply staring at the beautiful pastel blue gown Sofia,

Valentina and her friends had chosen a month or so ago for her big day.

"Dada, have you seen my curling iron– What's wrong?" We both turned around and watched as a teenage Valentina stood in the doorway of our room.

She had curlers on her head, her makeup was halfway done and she wore a long white robe with her pajamas underneath since she didn't want to risk staining her dress with makeup. A worried frown marred her beautiful face as she took us in. I looked like my dog had just died and Sofia was definitely crying.

As soon as we saw her, my wife detached herself from me, pushing away with all her force and wiping under her eyes. "What? Me? No. What?"

I pinched my lips to keep from laughing.

"It's the pregnancy hormones. I'll go see if the guys need help in the backyard."

Just like that, she disappeared from sight, running out of the room. Valentina didn't look like she believed her, and once Sofia left, she looked back at me with an eyebrow drawn up.

"Seriously? Don't tell me she's emotional about my *quince* again?" Letting go of the door frame, she entered and plopped down on our bed.

I puffed out a laugh and joined her, still looking at the dress and the heels sitting under it, on the floor. The same heels I'd have to put on Valentina's feet tonight as they replaced her flats.

For the longest time, neither of us spoke. She didn't want us to notice, because she thought we were too busy for her now that we had two other babies on the way, but I could tell she was nervous.

Not only about turning fifteen, she was nervous about our family getting bigger too. She acted really similarly when we moved away from Lakestone to Hollowside, Canada, four years ago. As much as she liked to pretend it didn't, change terrified her. It was normal, given her past, I just wished she would talk to us more about it.

Her therapist said Valentina had a tendency to keep everything bottled because she knew we had a lot on our minds and didn't want to add to it. It's been that way since she was a child, really. Again, given how she grew up, it made total sense. She only had Sofia back then and given everything she sacrificed for her, Valentina didn't want to add more weight to her shoulders.

But I was there now. And I was ready to take on the world for these girls.

"It's normal, you know. Sometimes I feel like we didn't get to enjoy your childhood enough. You grew up too fast." I looked at the pictures decorating our walls and standing on the dresser and all I could see was her.

Her tenth birthday, our first trip to Mexico together, the first time I took them skiing (that time was a mess and Sofia ended up breaking her ankle). There even was a picture of the two of us the night of the daddy-daughter dance five years ago.

"It's okay. Soon the twins will be there and you'll get to enjoy their childhood. You won't need me anymore." She bumped my shoulder with hers jokingly and I frowned.

I knew she thought there was a part of truth in her words. In her head, we would love them more than her solely because they had our DNA. It was bullshit.

“Don’t say that, Pretty Girl.” She looked away and I instantly knew it was because she didn’t want me to see her tears. It always made her emotional to hear me call her that.

I knew her like the back of my hand.

“Hey, come here.” Slinging my arm around her shoulders, I brought her to my chest.

Light sniffling could be heard in the room and for a second I just couldn’t speak, emotions clogging my throat.

“I hope you don’t seriously believe the twins will replace you, Little Rose.” She shrugged. “Valentina, look at me.” After a few seconds she did and seeing her cry made me feel miserable, as always.

“You know I love you, right?” She gulped and nodded wordlessly. “That will never change. We might not be blood, but you and I, we’re family, Pretty Girl. You’re the family I chose, and, in my heart, you will always be my first daughter, you hear me? Nobody can replace you.”

She didn’t say anything and simply pushed her face against my chest, sobbing. I wrapped my arm around her and rubbed her back like she’s always loved. My own tears were threatening to fall but I wouldn’t let them. This was a day of celebration. Our daughter turned fifteen.

"I-I thought about what we talked about over Christmas." She whispered against my shirt and I looked down immediately.

"You did?"

She nodded. "I want you and Sofia to adopt me. I want to officially be a Brooks."

The watery smile she gave me made my heart stop and I engulfed her in a bear hug, holding her tight.

This idea had been coursing through my head for three years, ever since Sofia and I got married. When we decided to tell Valentina about it last Christmas, two weeks ago, she looked really touched, but also lost. She was unsure of what taking my name would mean for her, she didn't want things to get more confusing and the lines between sisterhood and motherhood to get even more blurry when it came to her and Sofia.

A part of me thought she was also scared of what it would mean once the babies would be here. I think telling her that she was mine no matter what helped her make a decision.

"You and Sofia have been the only parents I've ever known and you were the best I could have asked for." She squeezed my hand once I let her go. "Plus, I'll be the best older sister ever. Those kids will be lucky to have me." I grinned, about to agree with her, when a voice came from the hallway right outside my and Sofia's room.

"Mrs. Brooks, are you crying?"

"Oh my God, shut up, Nikki! You just blew my cover!" Came my wife's hissing voice.

"She was totally eavesdropping." Valentina rolled her eyes, wiping at the tears lingering on her cheeks. Well, it was a good thing her makeup was only halfway done when she came in here because she would totally need to redo it.

As she looked back at me with a small smile, she didn't look like she minded though.

***

**SOFIA**

Our backyard was beautifully decorated, thanks to the team of friends and family that had gathered here to help us earlier. It was everything I dreamed of when I was fifteen and everything my little rose wanted.

Flowers adorned the tables, fake candles were lit and strewn a bit everywhere in the yard and lights hung on the trees and against the house, making it seem like a million fireflies were illuminating us. The tables were draped in blue, white and gold, the scent of delicious food invading our nostrils as Georgianna and Adam's wife, Eva, worked the buffet.

Their son and his fiancée were also here. Him and Adam had worked out their differences a couple years ago, though it hadn't been easy.

Ray lounged lazily on a chair as kids ran around and tried to caress her. Against my own will, I'd gotten attached to that damn cat. Valentina loved her, she even made a little tiara that matched her own for the animal.

All evening, I had watched with a smile on my face as my sister had fun with her girlfriends, as she danced with them and laughed her heart out to whatever funny thing her best friend Nikki was saying. That girl was a firecracker and she and Valentina were like two sides of one coin, totally different, but essential to each other. They met on her first day in Hollowside's school and had been inseparable ever since.

When it was time for the changing of the shoes and she sat down as Maddox, taking on the role of a father, swapped her ballet flats for high-heel shoes, I couldn’t keep my tears from falling. Damn pregnancy hormones.

Next to me, Andrea rubbed my shoulder softly with a small smile on her face. Maddox' family flew in from Lakestone a couple days ago to help us prep for everything. They were amazing people.

It had taken us some time but eventually, Andrea and I talked and flattened things out. I hadn’t admitted to anything, but I had a feeling she knew anyway.

When Maddox and Valentina started waltzing to a slow song, I watched in nostalgia. The two most important people in my life and the love they had for each other never ceased to fill me with joy. I put my hand on my stomach, knowing in five months there would be two new additions to our little family.

But when Valentina pushed away from Maddox with a smile and he let her, making his way to me, I frowned, not understanding why they had cut the traditional father-daughter dance so short.

“What’s wrong?” I asked my husband as soon as he was close enough.

“Nothing. She’s waiting for you.”

He took my hand and brought me back to the dance floor as our friends and family watched, a smile on their faces. I followed, dumbstruck, but I didn’t understand what was going on.

Hollowside was nothing like Lakestone. I loved it here. We had friends, some actually so close they were practically family. The latin community was strong here too, which was always a bonus because it meant Valentina got to grow around people who looked and spoke like us, who shared similar cultures.

Maddox’ Spanish was getting better, although it was not perfect. I still vividly remembered our first night in Mexico when he absolutely wanted to show off his skills by ordering for us at the restaurant. Only he said he wanted *polla* instead of *pollo* and the waiter thought he was being propositioned. That never failed to make me laugh.

Soon after we left Lakestone, four years ago, he started his own private investigation and security company. It worked well and specialized in missing person cases. Ever since the role he played in solving the *Ravenbridge 5* case, five years ago, Maddox had made it his mission to help as many families find their loved ones.

He never said it but I knew the fact that Valentina and I had been unsolved missing person cases also weighed in how much effort he put into his work. If someone had found us, maybe we wouldn't have gone through so many horrific events.

Maddox loved this new job and I loved seeing him happy, so it worked for us both.

Once we reached Valentina in the middle of the makeshift dance floor, he put my hand in hers and kissed both our foreheads before joining his friends in a corner of the yard.

"What's the meaning of this, mami?" I asked with a smile as my sister started swinging from side to side, dancing with me. I joined her.

She was gorgeous. No doubt the most beautiful flower in the garden. Her dress looked like it had been designed specifically for her, her long dark hair cascaded around her shoulders and her makeup was done to perfection. On her neck hung a small pendant, a golden snake with emerald eyes which she never took off. It was a gift from someone who had become quite important to us during these last few years, although we didn't see her often.

My eyes went back to her which shone with unshed tears.

"You've been both my mother and father for almost ten years, Dada. You deserved a bit of that dance as much as Mads."

I was already weak from reminiscing so many good memories and seeing her dance with Maddox. Plus, their little chat in our bedroom earlier definitely already had me crying so when she said those words, I couldn't keep my tears from falling anymore.

"You…" her voice broke slightly with emotions. "You've been so many things for me, Dalia. You were a mother, a father, a sister, a friend, a protector… you gave me everything you never got and I don't think I've ever even thanked you for it."

She sniffled, burying her head against my neck, just like she used to do when she was younger. She was slightly taller than me now. What a beautiful young woman she was becoming.

"Hell, look at that." She pushed away from me slightly and gestured to the decor surrounding us with her head. "You gave me the quince you never had, you made sure all my dreams came true. You gave me a family who loves me and whom I love with all my heart. I'll never thank you enough."

"You never have to thank me, Rosa." I cupped her cheek. "I did what I had to do. You're my favorite person in the whole world. And not just because you're my sister." I chuckled through a sob and she joined me, recognizing the words she had told me five years ago. "I'd go to hell and back for you, mami. Never forget that."

She smiled, and put her hands on my round stomach. Soon, she would understand what it felt like to be the older sister. To love your sibling so much you would do anything for them.

"We're different flowers from the same garden, baby."

# BONUS CHAPTER

## *On the day of Jack and Marcella's funeral (chapter 12)*

### SOFIA

*Jack Raymond, beloved husband, father and mayor.*

*Marcela Raymond, beloved wife and mother.*

The words mocked me as I stared them down. They pissed me off because nobody suspected a single thing those fuckers were capable of. No one knew what truly was going on inside our house of horror. To them, our family lived a dream life, while in reality, a nightmare was more akin to our everyday routine.

"We'll wait for you in the car. Find me if you need anything, okay?" Maddox's voice got me out of my thoughts and I simply nodded as he grabbed my sister's hand and started walking to his car. Valentina looked back at me and I sent her a small, knowing smile.

This was the last stop before we could finally start the life we've always wanted. The life we deserved.

I ended up being glad she had assisted to the funeral. I knew seeing the monsters who took so much from us finally being put into the ground would bring her closure, make her understand there was no way they were ever coming back.

I was alone. The guests were all on their way to the reception. Maddox was a few meters away, in the parking lot where I knew he could only see my back, but other than that no one was here to see me.

I couldn't help the chuckle that poured out my mouth and before I could do anything about it, I was laughing hysterically, my shoulders moving up and down. I laughed for what felt like ages, so much my belly hurt, so much I couldn't even stand straight and actually fell on my knees in front of their graves. The wet soil was staining my skin, but I didn't care.

I was free.

I was free of those monsters, free of their punishments, free of their violence.

I did it. I protected my sister and I avenged my family. Monsters didn't scare me anymore, because I found out even *they* weren't immortal, they bled just like you and me, and the sounds they made as they died slowly and painfully was music to my ears.

I remembered that night. Walking into their room, waking them up.

I remembered the look of fright on Jack Raymond's face as he saw the gun in my hand, pointed right at him.

He shouldn't have worried, though. I wasn't about to waste a bullet on him. I'd much rather gut him from the inside out.

*"You whore." He'd spat when I had him on his knees in the living room, my knife shining in the moonlight.*

*His glare was as dark as his soul.*

*"I'm no whore." I whispered, close enough to his face that my breath was probably the last warm thing he'd felt before dying. "But I'm about to make you my bitch."*

Coming back to the present, I saw his name stare back at me on the tombstone and smirked.

“They wanted me to pray for you,” I said suddenly as unshed angry tears replaced my laughter, “well, here’s what I got to say. Fuck you two. Fuck you two to hell and back for what you did to us. I hope you never get salvation, I hope you’re rotting in the pits of hell as I’m speaking right now.” I actually spit on the dirt on Jack’s grave. “Fuck you for what you did to me. Fuck you for what you did to my sister. I hope you’re suffering as much as you made me suffer all these years.”

Silent tears made their way down my cheeks, which truly made me feel like I was losing my mind. Going from hysterical laughter to angry tears in a few minutes. But it didn’t matter, since I was free. I just needed to get it all out before going back to living life the way I always dreamed to.

“I win, motherfuckers.”

“You won, indeed.” The voice coming from behind me made me freeze.

My heart seemed to jump in my throat. Fuck.

I didn’t dare turn around but the person— the woman who spoke, didn’t need me to. She walked until she stood a couple of feet in front of me, next to Marcella’s grave, her back to me. All I could see was her long curly black hair and that she was dressed in all black.

Quite similar to me, actually, only she wore a hat, gloves and glasses that made it hard to see who she was.

"I have to say, I'm glad you got to him first. I would've done more damage but… you deserved it more."

"I'm sorry?" My eyes narrowed as I felt anguish starting to invade my body.

She turned towards me only slightly and smiled, her eyes invisible through the thick black sunglasses. I could see she had brown skin, though, maybe a shade darker than mine. She also had a red and gold bindi on her forehead, which matched the blood red lipstick on her lips. She looked slightly older than me, but not by much.

"Don't worry, your secret is safe with me, little flower."

My blood froze in my veins. Little flower. That sounded way too similar to what mama called me. I straightened my spine, ready to pounce if I needed to.

"Who the fuck are you?"

The strange woman chuckled at that, but I didn't find it funny in the least. Whoever she was, she knew things I didn't want her to know. Things I didn't want anyone to know.

"You got her fire. You look just like her too." She smirked as she looked at me wistfully.

"What?"

"Your mother. Jasmine."

I could feel my eyes widening as I stared back, speechless. I was still on the ground while she was standing, but somehow I couldn't make my limbs function enough to get on my feet.

"You- you knew my mother?"

She looked at the ground and sighed. "She was the first person I ever considered a sister."

Who the fuck was that woman?

"Why didn't I ever hear of you before?" I could feel my eyes narrowing in suspicion. Mama had never spoken of any *sister*.

"Because I'm from a part of her life Jasmine never wanted to think about again. I was just a child when I met her, really. She was pregnant with you at the time and had just arrived in the US. Does the name Olympe ring any bell? That's where I'm from." I gulped, unbelieving.

That woman knew mama.

"We… We were raised in the same home. The Singing Serpent home for girls, in Olympe, before she fled."

"Why did she flee?"

A long pause.

"It was not a place to raise a child. And Jasmine always wanted the best for you, *Dalia*."

"Yeah. I know." I breathed, still in shock.

I didn't bother asking how she knew my name. That woman seemed to know a lot of things.

"I looked for her, you know. Once I was old enough, I spent years looking for her. The night I finally did find her was the same night that son of a bitch Oracio did, too. He got there before me and by the time I did, it was too late. Jasmine was dead and he had taken you and Rosa."

She kept staring at the tombstones in silence.

"It took me years but I eventually got to him."

"You… you were the one to kill him last year, not that rival cartel?"

I had heard that son of a bitch had died a year ago. There weren't many details in the article but he was found in one of his warehouses, twelve of his men were killed too, and the media speculated it was one of the rival cartels. I was stunned to know it wasn't, after all.

"Of course I did. That cunt pleaded and cried like a little bitch for his life, but in the end I left him bleeding out like the pig he was." Fire blazed in her eyes as she spoke of him, "I looked for you for months, Dalia. When I finally found you I saw I didn't really have to do anything. You had taken matters into your own hands. And your mother would've been so proud."

She looked at me with pride in her eyes and somehow, for one second, it felt like mama was staring back at me. It was strange but I still wasn't sure I liked that woman.

"Although… there is one loose end in that plan of yours." When she saw my confused face, she added, "Conan. He suspects you, doesn't he?"

I gulped and nodded, avoiding her eyes. That fucker loved Jack so much, I knew he was wary of me. The glares he'd sent me at the funeral were one big clue.

“Don’t worry, little flower. I’ll take care of him.”

“What do you– why would you do that?” I didn’t know that woman and although she seemed to know a great deal about me, I didn’t understand why she would help me in any way.

“Consider me your witchy godmother.” She smirked. “I owe it to your ma’.”

I stared at her, somehow more confused than ever. That woman was… an enigma.

“You’ve been strong. You don’t need to anymore, though. Start taking care of yourself, you deserve it, Dalia.” She nodded and turned to leave without another word towards the woods on our right.

“Wait!” I called, getting on my feet. “ You didn’t tell me your name?”

With a smirk she turned to look at me.

“My enemies call me Medusa. You, however, can call me Aveni.”

# THE END

# ABOUT THE AUTHOR

Macy T. Riosa is a young author with a deep love for caramel iced coffees and kitten videos. As most authors, she's also an avid reader, especially when it comes to romance and the occasional fantasy or thriller. Being in her twenties, she's really attached to anonymity as it's what gives her the confidence to write without the fear of being judged or recognized.

She's been writing since her youngest age and loves to twist words so that readers can understand them one way when they're meant in another.

Her books are meant to mess with your head, but only in the best ways.

## ACKNOWLEDGEMENTS

First and foremost, I wanted to thank you for giving my book a chance and reading Sofia's story. I hope you enjoyed the ride and that you didn't guess a thing until the very end.

Thanks to my amazing beta readers: Kayla and Priyanka, may God bless your souls, I am so glad we found each other, this book wouldn't have been the same without you my loves. Nissrine, Sahra, Muna and Meena, your support gave me the courage to continue on the days I wanted to quit and I'll be forever grateful for that. Claudia and Salma, you helped me a lot especially on those rocky first chapters. I'm really grateful for you and your kind words of encouragement.

Thank you to Meena, my graphic designer who made this beautiful cover as well as those of all my upcoming books! Can't wait for the world to see your work.

Thanks to Marzy for helping me and answering all of my annoying questions about the publishing process, I hope I wasn't too much of a pain!

Thanks to the amazing reader community of instagram and to all of you who have stood by me and helped promote my book! A special thank you to all of you who signed up for an ARC of RRBD, you don't know how much it meant to me. I love you all.

F, thank you for being my best friend since elementary school and being the only person I can be myself around.

To my aunt, M, who always believed in me and who's a reader at heart. It did it for both of us, auntie.

Also, thank you mama, I didn't become a judge like you wanted but at least I write good smut!

Lastly, I wouldn’t have written this book if it wasn't for my sisters. Lord knows I want to unalive you sometimes but in the end, you're the best thing in my life and I love you. No friend is worth a sister and I'm glad to have you with me.

# WHAT'S NEXT?

Playing the PART—Available on KU and in paperback!

Freezing Bonds That Tie our Hearts — Coming in 2023

Medusa Standalone (title TBA) — Release date TBA 2023

Follow me on social media for more!

*Instagram:* @author.mtriosa

*Tiktok:* @mtriosa.author

*Facebook readers group:* Macy's Minxes

Printed in Great Britain
by Amazon